THE
FOREVER
MAN

To
Todd

PIERRE OUELLETTE

THE FOREVER MAN

A NEAR-FUTURE THRILLER

JORVIK
P R E S S

ISBN: 978-1-7331007-6-2

Library of Congress
Control Number: 2022943854

Cover design and formatting: Keith Carlson

Second edition

Jorvik Press

5331 S Macadam Ave., Ste 258/424,
Portland OR 97239

JorvikPress.com

Pierre Ouellette lives in the Portland Metro Area and is the author of seven previously published novels that span a diversity of subjects and settings. He served for two decades as the creative partner in an advertising and public relations agency focused on science and technology. Prior to that he was a professional guitarist and played in numerous pop bands and jazz ensembles, including Paul Revere and the Raiders, Jim Pepper and David Friesen.

ALSO BY PIERRE OUELLETTE

A Shot Away

Haight St.

Bakersfield

The Deus Machine

The Third Pandemic

WRITING AS PIERRE DAVIS

A Breed Apart

Origin Unknown

I have no plans to die.

Rupert Murdoch
as quoted in The Wall Street Journal, December 10, 1997

Consume my heart away; sick with desire
And fastened to a dying animal
It knows not what it is; and gather me
Into the artifice of eternity.

William Butler Yeats
Sailing to Byzantium

Prologue

WYOMING PLAIN

At one hundred twenty-seven years, Thomas Zed is forever cold, as the capillaries in his skin continually scream for the blood his frail heart cannot provide. The walls of the ventricles are severely thickened, and the various chambers hopelessly compromised. The arteries that feed the cardiac muscles are fat with collagen and calcium, so they no longer stretch and recoil with enough vigor to power a strong pulse.

Zed moves forward on wobbly legs, with small careful steps that measure the safety of the ground beneath him. His bones have ossified to brittle relics, leached of minerals and ready to snap during the slightest fall. The shovel that he drags with his right hand skews his gait and leaves a tiny furrow in the ground as he moves forward. Through eyes with bloated lenses and constricted pupils, he searches the grass ahead for the right spot. Even in the glorious blaze of prairie light all is dim, and he must search carefully. Then he sees it. A single stone, an aberration in the local geology, a rock too large for the earth around it.

Zed grasps the shovel handle with swollen, arthritic joints and winces at the pain they radiate. He could have asked for help, could have avoided the ordeal ahead. The security people are young, strong and resilient. They would have perspired freely as they dug with strong backs and thick shoulders. But when they reached the target of the dig, they would be repulsed by what they saw, and he would be obligated to explain, which was simply not possible. He must suffer the pain of his labor, no matter what the physical cost.

He gingerly puts his weight on the shovel and feels the steel tip punch into the ground through the dry thatch. He removes his foot, pries the dirt loose from the earth's grip, and throws it to the side. The volume of his excavation is pitifully small, and the magnitude of the task becomes sadly clear. He has only half the muscle tissue of his youth, and it will be severely stressed as it runs a large deficit in oxygenated blood. Nevertheless, he must go on. He raises the shovel and bites the cold ground once again. Already, he can feel pain where the back of the blade presses the sole of his shoe.

As Zed digs, his heart heaves and does its best to meet the cruel demands of the muscles in his limbs and back. His pulse soars to ninety beats per minute, and its rhythmic components begin to collide with each other in a silent scream. The orderly pattern of one hundred twenty-seven years is being pushed out to the frontiers that define the border with chaos. Still, he digs.

Zed can feel himself on the precipice of physical catastrophe, but he must go on. He dips the blade in for one last gouge of earth and thrusts down feebly. Then his shovel hits something solid, and he knows instantly what it is. He drops to his knees in exhaustion and relief. His heart pulls back from the boundary line of disaster. Then he stops and looks at the small swell of earth piled up against the enormous weight of the prairie sky.

Zed feels a small measure of relief as he claws at the loose earth and parts it with wrinkled hands. He feels the rough surface of rotting canvas and knows he has found it. He goes back to the shovel and gingerly widens his excavation, and the canvas is revealed to be a small, lumpy bundle tied with several turns of twine. Throwing down the shovel, he fishes a small penknife from his pocket and cuts the twine. Next, he makes a small incision at the base of the bundle, and feels the decaying material yield easily to the touch of the blade. Impatiently, he inserts his fingers so he can rip the bundle open in a single motion. He tears at the incision, and a thin cloud of dust rises as the fabric disintegrates, followed by a strange and musty smell. The skeleton of a small infant looks up at him, with arms held tight to the rib cage and the hands open with palms out, as though defending against a coming blow. The jaw is open and the toothless mouth seems caught in mid-scream.

Zed's face collapses into a grim facsimile of a smile, his cheekbones scarcely concealed beneath the desiccated flesh with its distorted matrix of wrinkles. "There you are," he says in a hoarse whisper. "It'll just take a minute. That's all. Just a minute."

He reaches down and grasps the midpoint of one of the femur bones and gently begins to twist. "You're giving a most magnificent gift. I promise to use it wisely. I promise," Zed whispers as he works the bone loose from the hip socket and knee joint. He winces slightly at the cracking of the dry cartilage, but pushes on. Then the bone comes free, and he rises to his feet. It is colored a dirty ivory mixed with a faint yellow, but to Zed's ancient eyes the yellow is only a vague mustard gray. He reaches in his overcoat, pulls out a plastic bag and carefully inserts the femur. Then he turns once more to the skeleton.

"Good-bye, now."

He picks up the shovel and begins to close the grave. Its tiny occupant looks up at him with hollow sockets and seems to give a mute howl as the dirt rains down. Zed avoids looking at the infant directly and gazes into the distance, where a far-off squall line paints a band of dark purple just above the horizon to the south. Tiny fingers of lightning flick out and silently stab the earth. The immense distance eats their thunder.

Arjun Khan comes off the fender of the utility vehicle and grinds out a cigarette butt beneath his heel. He walks to the top of the road cut, where can see the old man back on the shovel, but filling instead digging. He must have found the source material.

Arjun methodically checks the defensive posture of the men, the vehicles. There's little chance of trouble out here, but his action has become automatic, a habit ingrained from years of service. He turns back and sees Zed moving toward him in that slow wobbly gait that sorely tests his patience. Khan is an engineer by training and admires precision and symmetry. The old man has lost both and is rapidly descending into physical anarchy.

Khan calls out to the men, who rise like russet ghosts from the prairie grass and drift back toward the line of three vehicles, all painted in camouflage tones that match the soiled beige and gold of the ground and the grass.

Zed negotiates a small incline down to the gravel road, using the shovel to maintain his balance. Khan approaches him and takes the shovel, which he gives to one of the men to stow.

"We're done," Zed announces in a raspy whisper. "Let's go."

Khan goes around and opens the passenger door of the middle vehicle, whose classic utility style is augmented by military trappings. Bulletproof windows. Armor plating. Emergency ventilation system. After Zed carefully plants his foot on the running board, Khan helps him up into the interior. The old man lets out an involuntary grunt of pain as he exerts himself.

Khan returns to the driver's side and motions the lead vehicle to move out as he climbs in. The old man's mouth is open and his unblinking eyes stare out the windshield. Khan turns to the embedded microphone and orders the other vehicles to start. He looks at the map display and calculates their transit time.

"Slowly," the old man murmurs. "We must go slowly."

"Of course," Khan replies. Zed is paranoid about accidents, among other things. Even a minor one would plunge him into untold agony or even death. In spite of therapeutic effort, he is now an utter prisoner of his physical decline. While watching him, Khan has come to realize how the periphery of one's personal world shrinks in the final years, during the final age of aging. Khan himself is nearing seventy and finds his observations depressing. He's fastidious about his health, except for the cigarettes, which will probably be his undoing. Maybe that's a good thing. Maybe he will have no final age to struggle through.

"We were out here a little longer than I expected, but we should be back before dark," Khan tells Zed. After nightfall, the roads become perilous, and Khan's job is to minimize all risk to the old man.

"That's good." The old man nods. "Turn the heater up."

Khan punches a button to activate a propane-fired auxiliary heater that will elevate the vehicle's interior temperature until the engine-driven heater warms up. The old man likes the temperature in the high seventies, which Khan finds oppressive, but he has no say in the matter.

They lapse into silence and hear only the gravel chewing at the big tires as they head west, where the Gallatin Mountains reach out to grab the afternoon. Ten miles roll by.

"There were four men out here today," Zed says abruptly. "They need a change of scenery. I think it's time you rotated them out of service. For a vacation."

Khan nods. "Yes. For a vacation." He understands. Absolute security requires absolute silence, the kind found six feet under.

By the time they reach the airstrip, the sun has dipped behind the thunderheads looming over the mountains to the west. Two men with slung combat weapons have come out to the gate, where coils of barbed wire wrap around a hinged wooden frame. The transponders in the vehicles have already identified them to the guard post, and the encrypted identification signals have passed through the finest of algorithms on the fastest of machines. Still, you can never be too careful. The lead vehicle stops, the sniffer scans are completed, and one of the men trudges back toward Khan and Zed. A neural-trained camera mounted on an armored vehicle tracks his motion.

The approaching man wears mirrored sunglasses that present twin microcosms of the prairie's cold brilliance. "Afternoon," he says and scans Khan. Then he moves to the third vehicle. Zed is exempt. Nobody scans Zed. No RF device is allowed anywhere near him. Besides, he doesn't sport the lobe.

The man completes the check and signals to open the gate. The vehicles head toward the small jet at the far edge of the runway. Khan notes the additional guards and vehicles around the plane. The rule of law is a hollow, desiccated shell out here. No sheriffs cruise the county roads. No state patrolmen monitor the highways. The rural West is once again the West of the old American cowboy movies; however, the armament has vastly improved.

Zed sinks into the thick padding and looks out the plane's window at the parched hills as the turbofans whine to life. He reaches into his overcoat, pulls out the plastic bag containing the tiny femur, removes it, and holds it in a slightly palsied grip with a hand densely speckled with liver spots. Without the bone, this entire undertaking would be completely in vain.

From down the aisle, Khan watches as Zed rotates the bone with his thumb and forefinger. Everything depends upon it.

LANE

—

1.

SPORTIN' THE LOBE

PORTLAND, OREGON

"How much more if I suck you?"

The girl leans forward across the booth, her breasts shoving at her tank top and her cleavage a bottomless canyon. Her smoky blue eyes peek out from a cluttered maze of makeup. Twin waves of blond hair flop down to obscure her vision and her bony arms are chemically tanned, probably through a biogene spray. Her forefingers tap the shellacked plywood tabletop with vicious ebony fingernails.

"You know, I'm really a pretty sensitive guy," Lane answers. "And that makes me feel bad."

The girl pulls her breasts back across the table and slumps in her seat. "Yeah, sure."

Lane doesn't know her name, and she'd lie if he asked. Anonymity is rule number one out on the street, and this shabby little bar is definitely an extension of the street.

"Tell you what," Lane counters. "I'll buy you a pipe before we go do the deal. How's that?"

She brightens a little and sits up straight. "I like that."

Lane slides out and gets to his feet. The musical blast of the junk crew hits him full on, and he imagines getting a pipe for himself and drifting around inside their percussive crosscurrents. But he's on the job, even now. Too bad. The crew is good. They're called Olds, because all their instruments were extracted from a wrecked 1979 Oldsmobile. Hubcaps, radiator, air filter, water hoses, and so on. No lyrics, no amps. Just riffing and chanting.

Lane smiles as he heads for the bar. The department thinks he's crazy to groove on the junk scene, but then again, the department thinks he's crazy in general, just like all the other contract cops. But he also knows that their opinions are secondhand at best. Those at the top of the police department never come out here anymore. They stay in the Trade Ring on the other side of the river and calculate the budgetary savings from hiring people like Lane, with no retirement benefits to choke the city's operating costs. Sure, there are still a few regular cops, but they stick to the West Side and the occasional high-rise homicide or white-collar business fraud.

Portland's Middle East is basically a contract gig, which is to say that the East Side of the city has mostly slipped out of civil control. It happened in stages. First, they lost the Far East, the big urban sprawl east of the 205 freeway – which the gangs now run as a toll road. Then the blight and anarchy slowly seeped west until it reached the Willamette River in the middle of town.

Enter the Bird, who now runs everything for fifteen miles out, starting at the river. Lane is reminded of this when he gets to the bar. "Gimme a draft beer and pipe of yellow dream," he orders the bartender, a corpselike figure with razor eyes and bony knuckles. He turns to check on the girl. She sits staring at her nails and swaying her shoulders to the junk crew. He can't afford to have her back out now. He's spent two weeks setting this thing up.

"Twelve crows," demands the bartender.

Lane turns back around as the bartender shoves the beer and flat pipe with its nickel-sized bowl across the bar at him. Lane fishes in his pocket and pulls out a roll of bills. Each is the size of a dollar and printed on banknote stock, but where the presidents usually reside is a picture of a crow, its beak breaking out of the traditional oval. The Bird is vain, and the crow is in his image, a sign of his economic sovereignty over a vast hunk of the city. The Bird is also a very bad man, but that isn't the problem. Lane is here because the Bird's monetary power is making bigger ripples than are politically tolerable over in the Trade Ring.

"You take card bucks?" Lane asked, out of idle curiosity.

You could see the fear expand the circumference of the man's eyeballs. "You fuckin' crazy, man?"

Lane raises his hand in a conciliatory gesture. "Just askin'. Twelve crows. You got it." He pushes the bills across the bar, and grabs the pipe and the beer. The punk would clearly take a bullet in the groin before he took Lane's bank card, a fact central to Lane's presence here. The Bird collected all the bank cards from every wage earner on his turf, including the temps, a relatively prosperous minority. The legitimate banks in the Trade Ring and the Chip Mill had always issued debit cards. No more dirty bills or clunky coins. You just shoved data around in abstract ledgers. Eventually, they stopped accepting cash altogether. All the country's money now had an audit trail behind it, a blockchain of incriminating thread that embroidered the pattern of your lifestyle for inspection by various regulatory agencies.

Of course, the banks and the government had not anticipated the Bird, an economic genius in the rough. Every payday, his people marched the wage earners to the bank booths, where they deposited the contents of their debit cards into a maze of accounts maintained by the Bird's bean counters. In exchange, they were given crow money, negotiable everywhere inside the Bird's turf. The Bird held the equivalent of hard currency, while his flock dealt in the soft coin of the immediate realm. The local merchants exchanged crow money through the Bank of Bird to obtain legitimate funds for outside purchases. The Bird took a simple transaction fee for every bill exchanged.

You didn't have to be an economist to understand that the Bird and his peers in other cities were now a force of considerable weight in the local business system. But they were equally difficult to bring to justice. By now, there were several ugly cases to prove the point. One was in St. Louis, where a police operation to arrest a local boss resulted in a full-scale urban battle that killed twenty-seven police officers and forty civilians – all with no arrests.

Here in Portland, the Middle East holds maybe a third of the urban population. And in the long hours of the night, the Middle East leaks into the rest of the city. Weapons pop and sirens wail. Everyone who can afford it now resides in one of numerous secured compounds surrounded by razor wire, armed guards, dog patrols, motion sensors and neural-driven video surveillance.

To present the political illusion of positive action, the police have adopted a strategy of hit-and-run harassment. If they can't shut the Bird down, they can at least keep him off balance. That's where Lane comes in.

The solo crazies writhe like vertical snakes to the call of the junk crew as Lane crosses the floor with the beer and the pipe. In the booth, the girl bobs her head in synchrony with the elusive 7/4 meter, and her palms catch the accents as they descend on the table. Truth is, she looks pretty damned good. Skin smooth and taut, hair thick and shiny. She is in the peak of bloom and determined to grab what she can before the petals close forever.

Lane sighs inwardly as he sits down. Beyond the immediate call of the girl's flesh, he knows another force is at work: the raw, unfettered attraction of her youth itself. At forty-six, he can see that quality clearly, more than he could in his own youth, when everyone's age was a given, not a treasure.

She pulls a lighter out of her purse as he pushes the pipe across. The ocher color of the hashish in the bowl tells him it is probably from one of the new Mongolian sources. Lane takes a sip of his beer and watches the girl apply the lighter to the pipe, a lighter designed for this operation. As she pushes a button on the top, a horizontal jet of flame ignites the drug while she sucks greedily to get the best hit. Her bosom swells to maximum circumference as she puts the pipe down and holds the smoke in the laboratory of her lungs, where the gases quickly dissolve into her bloodstream and are pumped posthaste into her brain. When she exhales, he sees her sinuous arms unfold into a smooth plane as the tension dissipates before the onslaught of the psychoactive molecules.

She stares at him dreamily through a crooked smile. "You're cute. Did you know that?"

In fact, Lane no longer knows that, but this is hardly a time for self-exploration. "So what you gonna do with the card bucks?" he asks.

She focused into the far distance over his shoulder. "I got plans. Yeah,

I got plans."

"What kind of plans?"

He can see her arms begin to knot up again. He's pushed a little too far.

"Just plans. That's all."

He knows her plans, of course. Get behind a gate. Get some nice clothes. Get some fine food and fast drugs. Get plugged into the Feed. It's always the same. But it won't happen. She'll blow the money and be back blowing the trade in no time at all.

As he watches her, he feels himself locked in a nasty little cycle. She's a victim of circumstance, a microscopic effect driven by a macroscopic cause. He should feel her pain but doesn't. His years on the street have built up a powerful immune response to this kind of thing, a protective barrier against personal devastation. Yet he hates his vacant heart, his lack of compassion. The only way out is to focus on the job, on the mission.

"Shall we go?" he asks gently.

She looks at him suspiciously. "Let's see the card."

He scans the windowless room, a professional precaution. The junk crew blasts on and the crazies gyrate in their singular spaces. The other booths are mostly empty. At the tables in the back, the Oldies play cards. Looks okay, so he gets out his wallet, keeping it below the tabletop as he pulls out the card and shows the girl. The holographic logo sucks in the dim light and flings it out in a strange braided pattern. She seems satisfied.

"Okay, let's go."

He takes a last sip of beer and watches her rise. Her hips and thighs move gracefully against the tight restraint of fabric worn to the point of gloss. He feels a distant longing, but finds it easy to squelch. Far too easy.

They walk out onto Foster, where the inverted heat of early fall fills the street. The trolley rumbles past on its way to the river, and scooters dart around it like small fish around a whale. The heat carries the smell of the rice carts and the green stink of cooked cabbage. The Bad Boys are clustered on the corners, feeding off the strength of the pack, but they don't bother Lane. The Bird is the law here, and the Bird says the Bad Boys will not hinder commerce. They merely posture and drink the fuel of fear they get from the frightened stares of the Oldies.

When they reach the end of the block, they turn onto a side street, where dilapidated bungalows dwell under the skimpy shade of defoliated trees.

"Sabrina! Darlin'! Don't leave now! Don't leave me 'lone! What you say, bitch?"

The voice comes from behind them, an affected whine laced with amphetamines. The girl beside Lane winces. Lane turns to look and sees one of the Bad Boys broken out of the pack and starting their way, skinny hands jammed deeply in the pockets of his car coat. Has to be her pimp. Lane doesn't like it, but stays cool. Most likely, the punk thinks Lane is a john and is reminding his whore that she'd better settle up with him later. He plays the part, shrinking in fear and quickening his pace. He checks a half block later, and the Bad Boy is merged back into the pack.

"So, it's Sabrina, is it?"

"Yeah, it's Sabrina."

"You know, there was a movie called that one time. They even made it twice."

"Oh yeah?" The girl seems mildly interested, but not enough to look at him. No matter. He's just filling in the spaces until the job is done.

They walk past an old Plymouth minivan. Curtains line the windows, and a woodstove chimney pokes through the roof. It's a curber, pockmarked with rust and settled permanently on flat tires. They populate the curbs for miles in any direction, neighborhoods within neighborhoods, too numerous to tow, too critical as housing to be destroyed. The majority of them are fat, beefy vehicles that carry nomenclatures from an age gone by: Suburban, Explorer, Tahoe, Pathfinder.

Icons of a great economic delusion, when the media regarded the "oil crisis" as a bad dream that had long since passed. In reality, the world began to terminally drain the global oil drum shortly thereafter, when it was discovered that the planet's "known reserves" had been relentlessly inflated for various political and economic reasons. Suddenly, the rate of petroleum consumption surged past that of production, and prices began a rapid upward spiral, triggering a calamitous series of economic events that eventually spawned the vast population of curbers now lining the world's streets.

They walk a few more blocks past weed-choked yards and dying houses. Big sheets of weathered plywood cover picture windows. Porches rot and sag. Garbage and rusting appliances fill front yards. Makeshift woodstove chimneys poke though dilapidated roofs. Lane takes it all in with a wry grin. The real estate people over here still speak of the "imminent housing recovery."

"You want to go over the plan once more?" Lane asks.

"Nope." The girl is still sailing on yellow dream but she has her wits about her. It's a good combination. She'll go through the routine without arousing too much suspicion.

Lane and Sabrina round the corner back onto Foster and come to a deserted storefront with soaped windows. "This is it," Sabrina announces. The door is unlocked, and they walk into an open space with a warped wooden floor populated with the posts and ropes of a queuing system, which is now empty. At the end of the maze, a steel-lined doorway leads down a short hall bathed in feeble white light from the overheads. As they duck under the ropes to shortcut through the maze, Lane hears a mechanical thumping coming from the floor above and smells the pungent solvents and inks of a printing plant.

He's hit it. He's found the bank, where debit card balances turn into crow money. More important, he's found the mint where the money is printed.

Now they can see the length of the hall, which is guarded by the arch of a metal detector with a security camera mounted on top. In the space beyond, a man sits at an old metal desk, a slender man in a cheap suit and Ivy League tie. He gives them a sour stare as they advance down the confines of the hall. The pale yellow walls are smeared with a cloud of grime at child level and a jungle of graffiti above, a spontaneous documentation of boredom in the extreme.

As they near the metal detector, Lane can see that the clerk is flanked by two men who slouch arrogantly in metal folding chairs. They wear the car coats and wool slacks of the Bad Boys, with the coat collars turned up and fronts left open with the big wooden buttons hanging limp. One wears lensless glasses with black plastic frames that are highly compressed along the horizontal, giving him an Asian cast.

They ignore the girl and focus on Lane, and he knows what they see. They are looking at a middle-aged man of six feet who is in better shape than a middle-aged man should be, a handsome man whose thick brown hair is salted with just a hint of gray, a man whose bright eyes devour the detail around him and convert it into a physical calculus of self-protection.

He puts them on edge, but he doesn't care. He'll do the deal, present his card, get his crow money, and get out. He already has what he needs: the physical location of the Bird's bank, the central terminal in his financial operations. Back downtown, they'll use the data to set up a surgical strike to take out the operation. A sudden storm of men, machines, and weapons will race through the facility and lay waste to the computers, the microwave links, the presses, and the networks.

"One at a time!" the clerk shouts in a voice of castrated authority. "Girl first."

Sabrina advances through the metal detector and places her card in a slot on a raised spot on the desktop. The Bad Boy with the glasses continues to watch Lane while his partner eyes the girl. Lane looks back down the doorless hall, which is only two people wide. He has to admit it makes for good security, minimizing the strength of any frontal assault on the banking room.

The debit card Sabrina inserts has a ten-dollar balance, her compensation after a 50 percent cut to the Bird. When the card is fully inserted, the display activates and a floating image shudders into view a foot above the desk. A duplicate logo appears and does its serpentine fold in three dimensions as the clerk watches. The card is legit. Then a column of figures materializes, with a blinking line at the bottom showing the card's balance.

"Five bucks," the clerk announces. His voice is picked up by an invisible microphone, and the figures change on the screen to show a zero balance. At the same time, the logo image unknots, and a whirring sound comes from inside the desk. In a trough at the front, five bills in crow money spit out into a curved trough.

Sabrina turns away and starts out. "Say, how much pussy does five bucks buy?" the clerk asks with a leering grin. "Can you tell me that, sweetheart? I don't get out much anymore."

The two Bad Boys respond with minor grunts that approximate a chuckle, and the clerk belches out a disgusting giggle. Sabrina ignores it, walks past Lane and on down the hall. She's done. She's gone.

"Okay, big boy," the clerk says to Lane. "Whaddya got?"

Lane already has his card out as he shuffles through the metal detector. The Bad Boy with the glasses comes out of his slouch and straightens in his chair. His hands stay in his coat pockets, one of which undoubtedly holds a cocked pistol of medium caliber. Lane senses trouble, but can't pin it down. He puts the card in the slot and watches the display come up with its contorted logo dance.

"Seventy-five bucks," the clerk announces. "Big guy, big money." He looks up at Lane as the trough spits out the cash. "Big guy. Right?"

Rather than acknowledge the humor of this little clerical martinet and prolong the exchange, Lane simply puts on a faint grin and reaches for the money. Then it all goes wrong.

"Hey, buddy," the Bad Boy with glasses says as he comes to his feet. "Where's your lobe? How come you're ain't sportin' the lobe?"

Lane's heart jumps, a quick pre-atrial contraction. He knows immediately what's happened. He's forgotten to put on his cover lobe after removing his real one. The cover lobe was issued by the department and recovered at the end of the assignment. It was, of course, a vast work of data fiction. A square centimeter of false information polished to high gloss, installed in a fashionable setting of platinum and worn as an earring. Birth records, school records, medical records, résumés, taxes, finances, felonies, genome profile. It was all there.

But somehow Lane had forgotten, and his naked earlobe was screaming trouble to the Bad Boy. But no time to worry. He gauges the distance between himself and his adversary. Too far. And now the other one is coming to his feet. He has to stall until the position is right. His best move is to go on the offensive.

"You didn't scan the girl. How come you gotta scan me?"

The clerk smiles and settles back like someone anticipating a critically acclaimed piece of entertainment. "Seen the girl around," he smugly explains. "Never seen you around."

"Doesn't mean I haven't been around," Lane shoots back. "Just means you haven't seen me."

"Don't think so," the clerk replies. "Think I've seen just about everybody." He turns to the Bad Boy with the glasses, who stands several feet to Lane's right. "Wouldn't you say so, boys?"

"Yeah, I'd say so," Mr. Glasses offers. He shoots Lane a nasty smile and moves forward. "I think we better have a little talk about this, friend. And I think we'll start with you putting your hands behind your head."

Because of the metal detector, they've assumed Lane isn't armed. As he crosses his hands behind his neck, his thumb and forefinger reach down his shirt collar and close on a slender plastic cylinder holding a single charge of pressurized pepper spray.

Lane glances to his left and sees the second Bad Boy on his feet, hand jammed in his gun pocket but not moving. It'll be close but he can do it. If he doesn't, he's a dead man. The police don't recover bodies anymore. They just cancel your contract and put the balance due back into the operating budget.

Mr. Glasses comes forward to check Lane's pockets. As he moves into range, Lane draws the pepper spray out of his shirt and brings it front and center. Mr. Glasses raises a hand toward his head for protection, but it's too late. Lane squeezes hard on the tube and the burning mist rockets out, bursts through the empty glasses frames, and saturates both of the Bad Boy's corneas. As he howls in pain, Lane lets go of the tube, steps forward and reaches into the man's coat pocket for the gun he knows is there.

By now, the second man has come to his senses and drawn a pistol. Lane feels the gun handle in the pocket of Mr. Glasses and pulls the weapon free. At the same time, Mr. Glasses lurches in agony, cups his eyes, and spins to face the second man.

"Shoot him!" the clerk screams at the second man.

Reflexively, the armed man obeys in a panic and fires three shots from a medium-caliber automatic. The bullets rip through Mr. Glasses's torso, leaving foaming tunnels of wasted tissue through the lungs, heart, and liver. One bullet lodges in the spine, but two others exit out the back just as Lane starts to bring his gun up. The bullets smack his multilayered vest hard enough to knock him back a few inches, but not enough to stop him from taking aim before he loses the temporary cover of dead man.

As Mr. Glasses remains pitched forward, Lane fires two shots that punch through the second man's sternum within an inch of each other. One vaporizes the aortic arch and terminates all circulation, and the second man falls backward and collapses.

By now, the terrified clerk has run to a steel door with no handle, and is pounding on it as he drops to his knees. "Get me out! Get me out! Please, God! Get me out!"

Lane makes a cynical note that the little asshole has suddenly got religion now that the goons are gone. He leaps over the body of Mr. Glasses, runs down the short hall and out into the open space with the queue ropes.

"He's out there! Get him! Kill him!" the clerk screams.

Lane has a major problem: In a second or two, armed men will be running down the short hall and will catch him in the open room, without cover. The path to the exit is blocked by dozens of rows of ropes and posts.

He has only one option. He sprints down one of the rows, and hurdles the rope at the rear just as he hears a shot fired and feels the shock wave of a bullet tickle the air near his head. He makes an airborne leap and folds into a ball as he crashes through the soaped window. A shell of exploding glass cuts the hot air and forms a brief copper mist against the setting sun. On the sidewalk, he rolls once, scrambles to his feet, and sees a trolley nearly upon him. He sprints across its path and then runs along the far side until he matches its speed, grabs a railing by the rear door, and pitches himself aboard. As he takes a seat by an Oldie, he looks back to see three Bad Boys clambering out the vacant window and looking up and down the street. He discreetly tucks his pistol away in the belt of his jeans. Before the last round of budgets, he had a cell phone with a direct connection to police dispatch. No more. He can't deliver the location of the press until he gets back across the river.

"You're pretty old to be a Bad Boy."

The Oldie is a sweet woman in her seventies, with pink cheeks, a mischievous smile, and lively blue eyes. She issues her judgment without malice, and seems highly amused by what has just transpired.

"You're right," he replies. "Maybe it's time to try something else."

"Well, I suppose you could," the woman speculates, "but there really isn't much else, is there?"

"No, there's not." Lane slumps in his seat and suddenly feels a stabbing pain in his forearm where he collided with the pavement. He tries to ignore it and think about the upside of what he's done. By now, the Bird has been notified, as he lounges in his downtown high-rise and barks orders to his minions on this side of the river. They will try to move the bank before they're hit by the cops, but there's too much gear and not enough time.

Lane looks up at the promo cards that line the trolley walls. Most are for the Temp Malls, the big halls that broker transactions between temporary workers and the companies that hire them. Their ads deliver feverish pitches about bigger bucks, shorter hours and better conditions, when in fact they all contract with the same pool of companies.

Lane closes his eyes. The thought of the Temp Malls, with their long lines and empty promises, makes him even wearier than he already is. Even by the standards of a contract cop, this has been a bad day. There have been fewer than half a dozen times in his career when he's wound up in a jam like this and resorted to extreme violence. And in all the others, the precipitating circumstances were beyond his personal control. But this time, the whole ugly episode came down to one simple fact.

He forgot his cover lobe.

Jesus, that was like forgetting your wallet. Was he losing it? It was a terrible mistake that might've got him killed, and there was nobody else to blame. Damn, he'd always had a pretty good memory and an excellent eye for detail, but now he had to wonder. If a major item like this had slipped through the cracks, what else had oozed out?

Maybe he was just getting old.

These days, that in itself was terribly wrong. The national safety net was now completely unraveled and the populace left in free fall. No social security, no pensions, no Medicare, no Medicaid, no welfare. A world where both nuclear and extended families had dissolved into a transient goo left no one to look after Grandpa and Grandma.

Lane glances over at the Oldie next to him. The woman senses his gaze, turns his way, and smiles. Lane has to wonder if the smile is genuine or a learned device to solicit compassion, her only defense against the predations of strangers. At the same time, he notices the bulge on her neck. Some kind of tumor, maybe like his mother's, a lymphoma or some such thing. She'll wind up at one of the Palliative Centers. He remembers passing one a few weeks ago, with its windowless front and discreet signage. Some wag with an airbrush had scrawled "the last pal you'll ever need" on the wall beside the entrance.

For the first time, Lane imagines himself sitting where the woman sits. It frightens him. More than the Bird, more than the Bad Boys. He turns away from the woman and looks ahead, where the sun is setting and little wisps of cirrus stretch across the fading light.

2.

STREET PARTY

"Know what they call that?" The desk sergeant at the Justice Center says as he points at Lane's forearm, which is now grotesquely swollen and radiating a low but persistent pulse of pain. "Hematoma. My uncle had one. A real asshole. Tried to smack my aunt, but he missed and hit the wall instead. Served him right."

"Wonderful," Lane says. "Makes me feel a whole lot better."

"You know, you better have that looked at," advises the sergeant.

"Yeah, I'll do that." Lane wonders if the sergeant has any great ideas about who might pay for all this. Contract cops don't have any benefits, and a trip to the emergency room is going to tear his financial guts out. What a nice reward for pinning down the Bird, he thinks. Especially since everybody at the briefing seemed so pleased with his work. In fact, the Chief himself popped his head in and gave Lane a nod.

A second sergeant comes up to the desk just as Lane is turning to leave. "Hey, Anslow, you'll never guessed what happened," he says with a self-righteous smirk.

"I'm not in the mood for guessing right now," Lane says wearily.

"Well then, let me be the first to inform you that your genius brother is an overnight guest in our accommodations upstairs."

"Jesus," Lane mutters. "So what happened?"

"According to the arresting officer, there was some kind of philosophical disagreement among several gentlemen in a downtown drinking establishment, your brother being one of them."

"Okay," Lane says crossly. "I got the idea." As he heads toward the elevator to the jail upstairs, his arm broadcasts continuous assaults of discomfort.

When the deputy opens the cell door, Johnny springs to his feet as if free of mass and gravity, as if he were athletically exempt from all the wearisome physical laws that govern everyone else. Lane looks on sadly. He knows the source of the spring in his brother's legs.

"Hey, bro," Johnny says with a sheepish grin that obviously wants to explode into a smile full of radiant teeth.

Lane's relieved that Johnny doesn't appear to be hurt. Johnny. The brilliant one, the gifted one, with an intellect that sprints all the way to the end of an idea while others are still coming out the gate. But in the end, the liabilities inside Johnny's brain outweigh the assets. John Anslow is two years younger than Lane but appears several years older. A thin gray fog has settled over his blond hair. His eyes have retained their manic beam but are slowly receding into some unknowable distance. A cracked web now spreads beneath them.

Lane no longer argues with his brother about his affliction, the collection of behavioral symptoms that indicate bipolar disorder. He no longer pleads with Johnny about taking the drugs that can easily compress his emotional excesses into a tolerable range. Johnny's defense for not medicating is devastatingly simple. "It's like hell when I'm down," he once told Lane, "and it's like heaven when I'm up, and everything in the middle is just one big, unbearable bore."

Johnny crosses the cell, and as his arms open to embrace his brother, Lane feels the terrible vulnerability and boundless affection that will bind them forever. It has endured all the exuberant highs and crushing lows, the hysterical joys and darkest rages, the spontaneous generosity and unchecked paranoia. Lane knows that a scared little boy struggles to keep afloat at the eye of this emotional storm that never ends. And it's this helpless child that he loves, the one that will never grow up, because the very nature of his brain won't allow it.

"Thanks, man," Johnny says softly as they wrap their arms about each other. "Thanks for checkin'."

"So what happened?" Lane asks as they part, his forearm shouting pain from the pressure of the embrace.

"Hey, you know," Johnny says with a mirthful smile. "I'm in the bar at Jake's. And pretty soon, there's a little pushing here, a little shoving there, and next thing you know I'm trying to explain it all to this police officer, who fails completely to understand the subtle dynamics of the situation."

"I see."

"I talked to my attorney," Johnny continues, "and he's going to get it downgraded from assault to disorderly conduct. He's arranging bail right now, so I'm almost out of here. Good thing. I got a hot date tonight."

Johnny sports a cashmere sweater and perfectly pleated slacks. Despite his affliction, he glides deftly high above the ruins of the national economy. The Medplex provides him with a generous stream of compensation for his research. He holds twin doctorates in computer science and molecular biology. Did it all in just three years. Then a trough set in. Tattered clothes, stinking mattresses, rented rooms. Eventually, he pulled out of that and began a spectacular professional ascent. But there's been trouble on the way up. Regardless of the subject, Johnny's convictions verge on absolute as he flies ever skyward. But the world hasn't always conformed to his glorious arc.

"Jesus!" Johnny exclaims, noticing Lane's injured limb. "What did you do to your arm?"

"Line of duty," Lane says stoically.

"You've got a hematoma. A bad one. You busted a blood vessel in there somewhere, and it's leaking fluid. You'd better get it drained."

"Yeah. I figured as much. What I haven't figured is how to pay for it."

"No problem. I got it."

"What do you mean you got it?"

"Just hang on a couple of minutes downstairs. As soon as I'm out of here, we'll go over to the ER at Health United. We'll pay cash off my lobe."

"Cash off your lobe, huh?"

"Absolutely. Simple as that."

Lane looks away. It isn't simple at all. Nothing with his brother was simple. Some time back, Johnny had soared out of his latest cerebral catapult toward a maniacal heaven of his own making. All while gazing down benignly on those less fortunate, Lane included.

It seems ironic that this fragile creature would finally assume the role of benefactor and caretaker. After all the years, all the scrapes, all the jams, all the interventions by Lane.

Lane stows his feelings. "Don't think so."

Johnny's entire face falls under the sudden tug of emotional gravity. His grand moment, gone. "Why not?" he asks.

"I can handle it myself." It was mostly a lie. He'd built up a meager financial buffer between himself and the street, but this incident would pretty much wipe it out.

Johnny brightens as his endorphins surge. "Well, the least you can do is let me buy you a drink. Hey, why don't we meet up at Headwaters tonight? Before I meet Rachel for dinner."

So now it was Rachel, whoever she was. It was a safe bet that she was attractive, smart and competent. During his ascending phases, Johnny had always reeled in the good ones. His unbounded confidence and unshakable conviction carried the day. It took a while for them to understand the reality behind the fetching persona. Over the years, Lane had learned to gauge their intelligence by how quickly they cracked the code. Johnny's moods and personality were a moving target, both going up and coming down.

Lane shrugs. "Yeah, sure. Why not?"

He's too tired to say no.

Oak paneling, green carpets, crystal chandeliers, starched white waiters. All wrapped in Class 10 security. Headwaters is out of Lane's financial grasp, but not Johnny's. They sit in the bar, both nursing a glass of Glenfiddich.

"We're getting' old, bro," Johnny observes as he rotates his glass around some imaginary axis. The surface of the liquid dips and rises in perfect symmetry. His brother's grasp of the mathematical, spatial and mechanical still amazes Lane.

"No foolin'," he replies.

"Know why? Because our genes are getting old and telling us to die. It doesn't take much. Ever hear of Werner's syndrome?"

"Don't think so."

"If you've got it, you enter old age at twenty and you're dead by fifty."

"Bad deal."

"Really bad deal. A single gene codes for Werner's syndrome and it doesn't work like most genes, which make various things happen inside your cells, like muscles twitching and neurons firing. Instead it goes off and works on other genes and tells them how to make you die. Think about it. One gene out of thirty thousand and it can bring down the whole house if it's defective."

"So how does it work?"

Johnny breaks into a sly smile. "Good question. Very good question."

Lane doesn't take the bait. It will lead to a scientific exposition that features his brother's genius. He changes the subject.

"My contract with the cops is coming up for renewal. Cross your fingers for me, okay?"

Johnny raises his hand. "Not an issue."

"Oh yeah?"

Johnny leans forward. "Here's the deal. I'm leaving for New York tomorrow. I'll return in a couple of days. And then you're set for good, believe me."

Lane senses the growing tension as his brother tries to keep a lid on himself, tries to keep from spewing out a jumble of gloriously agitated verbiage. Johnny wants to retain his dignity in front of Lane, to keep his malady in check so it doesn't burden his brother, whom he both admires and loves.

"What do you mean, I'm set?"

"You'll never have to work another day in your life."

"Come on now…"

"Hi, John. Sorry I'm late."

Lane looks up to a woman in her thirties with short dark hair and intense green eyes. She wears a loose silk blouse and trim skirt over an obviously athletic frame. It has to be Rachel. Attractive, smart, competent. No surprise.

Johnny stands, Lane follows. "Hey, Rachel. No problem. This is my bro, Lane."

She lightly shakes his hand with a palm both dry and cool. "Pleased to meet you."

"Likewise." They sit. Johnny flags the waitress. Rachel orders before Johnny can ask her what she wants. Competent.

"Lane's in the security business," Johnny volunteers. "He has his own consulting firm."

Yeah, sure. In his two-room apartment on the fringe of the Null Zone next to the Trade Ring. Johnny doesn't want her to know he has a brother who's a bottom-dweller.

"The security business," Rachel repeats. "Well, I'm sure business is quite good."

Lane shrugs. "I can't complain. And what business are you in?"

"Politics. I work for Harlan Green."

Her green eyes scan him intently to gauge his reaction. Nobody's neutral about Harlan Green, but Lane plays it cool. "Oh yeah? So how are things in the Street Party?"

"Never better."

"I'm sure you're right." Actually, he was certain she was right. Five years ago, Green was a salesman in a discount store in Phoenix. Today he sat atop a political party growing faster than a mushroom in the warm drizzle of the rain forest. It was already seeping into both houses of Congress, and a shot at the presidency was almost certain. At first, the DC Beltway pundits wrote Harlan Green off as a joke, a populist caricature. The Street Party? I mean, come on. But the ridicule soon faded into serious concern, which rapidly descended into paranoia.

In the seats of power, they did what they could to squelch him. The Feed all but ignored him. The Meternet filtered him out. But in every major city, Green drew large crowds, telling them what they already knew. Their houses were gone, jobs evaporated, safety net riddled with a million holes, with their streets verging on anarchy. He consolidated the collective rage and blew it back at them with amazing force. Such was his genius.

Lane would love to engage Rachel in discussion about the dark side of the Street Party, the side he frequently encountered on his excursions into the Middle East. In every city, the party had quietly formed alliances with local gang leaders like the Bird, and was transforming them into a militia of sorts. Ultimately, it was quid pro quo, because Green had survived two assassination attempts and needed security.

But tonight, this minion of Green's has a date with his brother, so Lane opts for civility. "And what do you do for Mr. Green?"

"I'm his chief of staff."

She was turning out to be more than competent. She was becoming a force to be reckoned with. "In most places, that means you're the one that actually runs the thing," Lane observes.

"That might be true, but the Street Party is not like most outfits," she replies. "Our mission is public, not private."

Spoken like a true politician, Lane thinks. Did she get that from Green or was she equally gifted? This isn't the time to find out. He puts down his glass and stands. "You guys are probably getting hungry, and I've definitely got some things to do."

Johnny stands to acknowledge Lane's departure. "Hey, bro, I'll talk to you when I get back from New York."

"All right then." Lane turns to Rachel. "Nice meeting you."

The guttural hum of tires assaulting pavement leaks out from the underside of the Morrison Bridge as Lane strolls beneath it on the walkway bordering the Willamette River. The hematoma in his arm pulses pain and radiates trouble. He'd better get it fixed before it turns into a full-blown medical catastrophe.

A lone seagull perches on the old cement railing and looks at him disdainfully, its feathers a soft, radiant white. So what was this raving from Johnny about New York and never having to work again? Not good. But right now the least of his troubles.

Lane stops and looks out over the river, blown into a shiver by the late evening breeze. He shrugs in resignation and heads for the emergency room, where he will undergo both physical and financial surgery of the most unpleasant sort.

3.

THE GOMPERTZ CURVE

Mount Tabor. A volcanic cinder cone, an artifact of the earth's rage gone cold. A dome of forest rising 600 feet above the surface of the surrounding city, it formed a compressed oval occupying 120 square blocks under a canopy of dark green fir. Once covered with walking trails, picnic sites, open reservoirs, and even a small amphitheater carved from the ancient residue, but then the fiscal crisis hit and never ended. The crushing debt load brought the city to its knees. Ever saleable asset went on the block, including city parks. Private interests from around the globe swooped in and acquired the finest of them, including Mount Tabor. Razor-wire fences sprouted on its periphery, with a clear field of fire in all directions. Watch posts hid on its slopes, and access was limited to a single bombproof checkpoint. Multistory buildings thrust out at key points on the mountain's slopes, structures of unknown purpose, the target of endless speculation.

Johnny knew this but stifled all reflection as he approached Mount Tabor in the armored SUV. He fixated on his contribution, his genius, the scope of his accomplishment relative to his two peers, who would share equally in a new company with assets beyond valuation. He considered how to approach Arjun Khan, the gatekeeper of the nascent enterprise.

His work spoke for itself. He had modeled the entire journey of the human genome on its way from the womb to fully realized adulthood, a span of about twenty years. He could take the genome of any infant and watch it evolve from newborn to young adult. He knew when certain sequences shut down, when others activated. He fully synthesized the role of the so-called epigenetic factors, which dictated which genes were expressed at what time. Johnny knew it all; he had extracted the organizing principles. Equally important, he knew how to encode it into a set of computer algorithms.

His research contract with the Institute for the Study of Genetic Disorders up at the Medplex had provided the platform for his work. The research there focused heavily on gene-driven maladies that express themselves in childhood. How do you find which genes cause a specific disease? How do you reveal the host of regulating elements that accompany them? And once you've found it all, how do you do the repair work? A staggeringly complicated challenge. Needless to say, Johnny's work was essential. But there were other fundamental issues. How do you package the replacement genes for introduction into the patient? How do you transport them to the nuclei of the affected cells? His two peers had taken on these challenges with Institute research contracts similar to his own, and with equal success.

But to Dr. John Anslow, their work is a sideshow, a set of procedural issues, all dependent on his sweeping achievement, the Rosetta stone that linked human growth and genetics. You could now put all a person's genes in a computer and slide the dial of time backward and forward at will. You could see what went right, what went wrong. You could see when and how. You could see what to fix and what to leave alone.

It was worth more than a third. He was sure of it. He had pondered the matter deeply. But would Arjun think he was grandstanding? The plane to New York was scheduled to leave late this afternoon, and he was just now digging in his heels. As an engineer, Arjun was probably as brilliant as Johnny was a scientist. A native of India, he was charged with converting all of their research into a workable technology, one that could be replicated and operated by those less gifted.

The driver turns onto Sixtieth, and Johnny peers up into the trees lining the western slope of Mount Tabor. A complex web of global corporations deliberately obscures its ownership. Its management operates in permanent shadow, answerable only to what the spin people call an "investment group." Arjun is as high up the food chain as anyone has ever seen, but Johnny doubts that he's even close to being in charge.

Especially when you considered the Other Application.

That's what he and his two peers call it. Only they and Arjun and

Crampton at the Institute know its full extent. It resides in a squat building high up the slopes of Mount Tabor, with heavily restricted and com-
partmentalized access. All the other buildings on the dead volcano are
dedicated to its care and feeding. Computer complexes, chemistry labs,
robotics facilities. All march to the anonymous tune of the Other Application. All except the fortified residence that occupies the summit.

The driver approaches the access point on Salmon Street, with its
barbed wire, blast barrier, concrete bunkers and steel gate. The neighborhood on the far side has been replaced by a small military facility,
which houses security people and their gear.

A small knot of demonstrators stands across the street. Street Party
people. They work in shifts. They wave provocative signs, hand-lettered
and homespun. "Tell Us the Truth About Tabor." "Give Our Park Back!"
"Bring Down the Tabor Pigs!" "It's Time for the Next Eruption." They
shake their fists, thrust their placards and yell at the SUV.

If only they knew, Johnny thinks. A guard with a slung combat weapon scans his lobe and the driver's. They are quickly cleared. Johnny has
priority access. The gate opens and they start up. A reservoir passes below them, a flat-bottomed basin of concrete now devoid of water. Two
helicopters nestle within it, secure from observation.

They wind through a pair of switchbacks until they reach a windowless cement structure with a single entrance and a small parking lot
leading to a loading dock. The building burrows back into the hillside
and the shadows of the overhead firs obscure its surface. No signage
identifies it – or anything else up here. Johnny exits and the driver de-
parts. Vehicles are forbidden to loiter here. Multiple cameras track him
as he reaches the entrance and a big steel door swings open of its own
volition.

Johnny enters the environs of the Other Application. To his left, a
corridor done in monolithic cement stretches for a hundred feet. A river
of pipe and electrical conduit flows along the high ceiling, and the inner
wall is punctuated by a series of doors. A number, stenciled in sans serif,
gives each room its only identity. Each is configured to hold a single
patient, along with a maze of tubing, wiring, transducers, monitoring
instruments, drug dispensers and cameras.

They were volunteers, Johnny always has to remind himself. They gave informed consent. They knew the risks. They glimpsed the rewards. It was all done properly.

Or so he was told.

"Dr. Anslow. Nice to see you."

Arjun Khan has come out of his office to Johnny's right. Close to seventy, he is slightly stooped and anonymously dressed in dark gray slacks, loafers and a blue oxford shirt. "Let's use the conference room. Would you like something to drink?"

Johnny declines and they head down a short hall to the right. "Are you looking forward to New York?" Arjun asks.

"That all depends."

Khan nods his head thoughtfully as they enter the conference room and sit. "I understand."

"Look, Arjun, you of all people have to understand my position. You've watched the whole thing go together. My work is the platform, the bedrock. It all rests on my work."

Arjun nods. "Yes, you can most certainly make that case. But you have to understand your timing is something less than impeccable. The deal has been all prepared and reviewed. Your trip is really just a ceremony to sign the final documents and then have a little fun on the town."

"I know that, and I'm sorry. But I've given it a lot of thought. I've given it more than a lot of thought. Parity among the contributors simply isn't fair. At least half the contributor equity should go to me. It's only right."

"So what's this all about, John? Power? The investors retain the controlling interest, and that's not going to change. Is it about money? Well, you'll have more money than you ever imagined." Arjun leans forward. "Be reasonable. We've kept this thing in a state of absolute secrecy to control the timing. We have to move quickly to stay on schedule and roll it out in the proper manner."

"It's not about power, it's not about money. It's about who did what to make this happen. The deal has to be changed. I'm not signing unless it's changed. I'm not even getting on the plane until I have a guarantee."

Arjun sighs and rises. "I see. Wait here, please."

He leaves and Johnny gets up and starts to nervously circle the conference table. With each orbit, his agitation rises. He should have asked for even more. Maybe he should have demanded two thirds. Or a seat on the board of directors. He should even be chairman.

Arjun returns. He seems relaxed and potentially agreeable. "Come with me."

They cross the hall and Arjun unlocks a door to a long hallway. At the far end is an open elevator. Johnny visually orients himself. They are moving deeper into the hillside. When they reach the elevator, Arjun presses a single unmarked button. They step in and the elevator moves slowly upward. Very slowly.

On the way up, Johnny does spatial calculations and realizes where they're going. The giant residence on the mountaintop, a place billed as a corporate retreat. But which corporation? Somehow, it has something to do with the investors, but precisely what seems lost in a fog of disinformation.

The doors open, and a security guard in a black blazer scans both their lobes. They move down a hall and into an enormous living room with a view toward downtown. Persian rugs cover a floor of bamboo. Custom furniture merges into a perfect assemblage to accommodate the space. An eclectic range of paintings adorns the walls, each work masterful.

But it all fades before the figure sitting on the couch.

It's him. Johnny knows instantly. It's all about him.

He verges on impossibly old, with a white, hairless skull, paper skin, and eyes nearly extinguished.

"John, I'd like you to meet the director," Arjun says as the old man extends his boney hand without rising.

Johnny gently grasps the cool, dry flesh, nearly devoid of muscle. "Nice to meet you." The director? Who the hell is he? What's his name? Where did he come from?

"And it's nice to meet you, Dr. Anslow. I've been a fan of your work for a very long time." His voice is a dry whisper. His lungs no longer expel sufficient air to maintain normal speech.

"Thank you. And I assume that means you understand its significance." Johnny should be careful about what he says. But the manic
bulge inside him swells relentlessly as he takes a seat next to the old man.

Thomas Zed nods. "Absolutely. And I'm afraid I must apologize. We
should have made proper allowances for your achievements right from
the start, and obviously we didn't. So I'm going to ask you to enter into
a gentleman's agreement with me. If you make that flight this afternoon,
I'll contact New York and make sure the deal is modified to give you half
of the contributors' equity. It'll be done by morning and ready to sign.
Agreed?"

Johnny hesitates only for an appropriate moment. "Agreed."

Johnny now understands why the elevator moves at such a feeble
crawl as he and Arjun descend back toward the building below. The old
man can't tolerate anything faster.

"He's beaten the Gompertz curve, hasn't he?" Johnny refers to a
mathematical function that defines the extreme limits of human life.

"As a matter of fact, he has," Arjun replies, but says no more.

From Arjun's answer, Johnny knows that the director is at least one
hundred twenty-five years old.

The ultimate test for the Other Application.

Two pairs of Bad Boys come down the hall from opposite directions,
hands shoved in the pockets of their car coats.

Lane stands in front of his apartment door. So much for building
security.

The Bad Boys stop a few steps away, out of swinging range. One of
them nods at Lane's door. "It's open. Go on in."

"And why would I want to do that?" Lane asks.

"The Bird wants to see you."

Lane stares at the man. If they're going to kill or main him, better
to do it inside than out here. Still, he stands no chance against four of
them. He'll just have to play it by ear. He twists the handle. Sure enough,
the lock mechanism has been defeated.

He opens his door to see the Bird sitting in the easy chair watching the Feed. The man wears a meticulously tailored suit cut in the Shanghai style with the narrow lapels. A perfect knot cinches a silk tie around a starched white shirt collar.

The Bird turns toward Lane's entrance and smiles. "Mr. Anslow. It's high time we met. I've been watching your work for some time. You're good. Very good."

Lane sits down on his couch opposite the Bird. His face is a racial composite that defies any particular ethnicity. Dark brown hair, yellowish eyes, coffee skin. You saw that everywhere now.

"Thanks," Lane replies flatly.

"Like this latest thing, with the bank and the mint. How long did it take you to put that together?"

"Couple of weeks."

Bird shakes his head in mock disbelief. "Amazing. Simply amazing."

Lane sags. The Bird wouldn't be so sanguine about this if the bank and the mint were really in jeopardy. He'd made some kind of deal inside city hall.

"You know, I hate to see someone with your talent going to waste with this contract cop bullshit. You need to be thinking about your future, about doing your best work, the work you'll be remembered for."

"And what kind of work might that be?" Lane asks.

"I run a business," the Bird says. "It used to be a small business. Back then, things were simple. But now it's a much bigger business, and things have gotten complicated. Really complicated. So I need smart people, senior people to make it run right. People I can trust, people with a sense of integrity." The Bird paused. "I guess you could say I need people like you."

"I guess you could," Lane has to be careful. If he disrespects the Bird in front of his men, this whole civilized façade will come to an abrupt and violent end.

"I think you're somewhat undervalued in your present position. Besides, they're probably about ready to cut you out of the deck. Permanently."

"Oh yeah? You know something I don't?"

"Nope. I think we both know the same thing."

"And what's that?"

"You're getting old."

Lane's insides choke. It isn't the reply he expected. It's the truth. He looks away from the Bird and out the window.

The Bird takes up the slack. "So you must be pushing fifty, right? You need to forget about this street shit and assume some kind of executive position. Problem is, with the city, all those jobs got gobbled up a long time ago. So where does that leave you? No gig, pension, no nothing. Street people."

"Maybe so," Lane replies. It's the best he can do.

The Bird rises. He's in his early forties and his legs power him effortlessly out of the chair. "You think on it, okay? Just think on it. That's all I ask."

He motions his men toward the door, and just like that, they're gone.

Lane doesn't get up. He doesn't reclaim his easy chair. He settles back and closes his eyes.

The damage has been done.

Dr. John Anslow doesn't like being put on hold. He's reminded of this as he rolls his suitcase out of the World Flight building at Hillsboro Airport. He listens to his phone's earpiece for some kind of apologetic response but hears only a light sprinkle of static. The others are already on the small jet, whose twin engines moan in repose. He's waited as long as he can.

One of the ground crew accepts his bag as he climbs the stairs to the interior and takes a seat up front by the door. His two peers sit aft, reading. None of them share any personal bond, so travel is a muted affair.

The woman in New York finally comes back on the line. "Dr. Anslow, I'm sorry. I've checked with the lead attorney. We don't seem to have any communication regarding a change in the documents."

"You're sure about that? You're absolutely sure?"

"Yes, I am. I'm sorry. Do you want to check back later?"

Johnny breaks the connection. He clenches his fists in his lap. He's been screwed. Or maybe worse.

He manages to downshift emotional gears and methodically reviews his communication with New York. He'd decided he wanted to review the modified legal documents during the flight. Not wanting any surprises during tomorrow's meeting, he phoned the law firm and asked that the documents be emailed. They never showed up. He phoned back. They stalled. He just now phoned again and finally got the truth, probably by mistake.

He looks back at his peers, lost in their technical journals. Just the two of them. And nine empty seats of handcrafted leather.

He bolts up out of his seat and whirls to the flight attendant, who sits by the cabin door. "I want off. Right now."

"But sir…"

"Tell 'em up front I'm getting off. Right now. Do it."

The woman looks stricken and grabs the intercom. The two scientists look up at the commotion but keep their distance. Dr. John Anslow's emotional issues were well known.

Johnny cranks the cabin door open as the attendant jabbers with the crew in the cockpit. Daylight and fresh air stream in. Johnny sits on edge of the cabin floor, pushes off and leaps to the tarmac. He briskly walks away without looking back.

The sniper perches on a branch sprouting from a lanky fir tree and plants her weapon across a second branch at chest height. It gives her a clean line of sight across the expressway below to the end of the runway, about 250 yards distant. A thick line of alders shields her position from the passing traffic.

She adjusts her gear, an M24 bolt-action rifle joined to a 10-power telescopic sight. She uses a laser range finder to calculate the distance. A fairly simple shot, especially with a light breeze. Her watch reads slightly after four p.m., and she understands that the departure time for this private flight is variable. She moves the scope off the runway and downfield to the designated aviation center. The plane sits motionless on the tarmac. She comes up off the rifle, reaches into her fanny pack, and retrieves a can of high-energy drink. It's still slightly cold and goes down nicely. She deserves it. Tree work is never easy.

She checks her watch again, 4:20 p.m. There's been some kind of delay. She again trains her scope on the aviation center. Good. The plane is moving. It's on the taxiway and rolling toward her end of runway. She readies her gear for a shot at the tire under the right wing.

Johnny stands alone in the parking lot of the aviation center, which now appears closed for the day.

Even in high-end private aviation, business isn't what it once was. He watches the jet in the distance as it turns onto the main runway and rotates for takeoff.

The plane will never reach New York. It seems so very clear to him. The key players possessing the key knowledge to the key science: All on the same flight. All suddenly gone. And if the plane crashes, who's left who knows? Only the old man and Arjun Khan and Crampton, the director at the Institute. That's why the corporate paperwork was never modified on Johnny's behalf. There was no need. There would be no company.

But what if he's wrong? What if the deal goes ahead just as the old man outlined? He'll look like a grandstanding fool, a slave to the great tidal forces that tear at the core of his soul.

He stands in a puddle of agony and doubt. Just like so many times before. Then he hears the plane's engines rise to a howl.

The aircraft's right tire spins madly as the jet surges past V1, the velocity of no return. All the while, pressurized nitrogen blows out of the rubber sidewall where the sniper's bullet has already entered. A wave forms in the tread, a violent ripple that feeds off the friction of its contact with the runway. The temperature soars. The tire explodes. Fragments fly up and back into the right engine.

The pilots feel the blast and the lurch as the engine fails. Too late. The jet surges ahead at over 160 miles per hour, far too fast to stop. It pulls violently to the right from the drag of the failed wheel. It leaves the runway and sleds across the dry grass toward a curve in an expressway filled with traffic.

An articulated bus rounds the curve, two buses joined into one by a flexible centerpiece. It carries maintenance people from the Chip Mill, those who man the mops, the scrubbers, the buffers, the leaf blowers. It's just after quitting time. The bus is packed.

Inside, a chorus of screams goes up from those with window seats facing the airport. Passengers crammed into the aisle bend to see what's causing the commotion. They're dead before they can even get a glimpse.

The plane collides with the bus just to the front of center. Its speed upon impact is over 100 miles per hour. Twenty-six thousand pounds of aviation fuel instantly ignite.

Johnny has an unobstructed view of the fireball from his vantage point in the parking lot. It rises from over a half mile away. The distance throws the dirty orange boil into abstraction. It prompts him to focus on a more immediate catastrophe. They want him dead. If not now, as soon as possible.

Maybe Lane can help. Just like always. He reaches for his cellphone and stops. Maybe Lane can't help. Maybe it's bigger than the both of them.

He turns from catastrophe and trots toward his car. He needs to act quickly, preemptively; before they figure out he's still alive. The germ of a plan presents itself to him. If he can pull it off, he'll expose the entire operation and gain sanctuary. If he fails, he's as good as dead.

4.

LUCKY DAY

Lane looks at his naked reflection in the smoke-tinted bedroom window thirty-two floors up in the Trade Ring. For someone well past forty, he's holding his own. He glances back at the king-sized bed, where a nude woman slumbers entwined in the silk sheets. She's rich, kinky, and has a thing for cops.

He considers his expertly bandaged arm. Very nice work. Very spendy work. It pretty much cleaned him out, just like he thought it would. His paramour had picked right up on the dressing, and had to hear the whole story in great detail. She particularly liked the young hooker and violent Bad Boys. The part Lane liked most was that the pain was now gone.

He quietly slips on his clothes and heads for the door. No need to wake her up. The truth is, he doesn't really have anything to say to her.

On his way out, he spots the note. It droops down from an antique vase that secures it to a marble tabletop. "For Your Arm." A vertical arrow points up to an envelope leaning against the vessel's elegant, glazed curve. Lane opens it. A neat row of hundred-dollar bills stares out at him. She knew. She knew he didn't have insurance. She knew he couldn't afford it. She knew by the scuffs on his shoes. She knew by the coarse weave of his shirts. She knew by the cheap watch, the bargain ties, the outmoded handheld.

He closes the envelope slowly and deliberately and places it back where he found it. His sexuality might be negotiable. The rest of him is still private property.

As he leaves, he takes one last look at the urban vista out the big picture windows.

At the very least, he'll miss the view.

· · ·

An insistent drizzle falls from the bottom of an overcast sky as Lane walks down the transit mall through the long string of buses that collect workers off the sidewalks. The wet air beats down the blue diesel exhaust and mutes the growls of the idling engines.

He stops and buys a coffee at a little shop on the corner and drinks it standing at the counter. His visit from the Bird represents a serious complication. The Bird's job offer cuts both ways. From now on, if he goes into the Middle East representing the city, and the Bad Boys catch him, he's dead on the spot.

A depressing development. He suddenly feels extremely weary. Time to go home. He catches a streetcar and slumps into his seat as it rolls through downtown to his apartment, which faces the entrance to Multnomah Stadium.

Lane stares out his living room window at the dying day. The pavement and sidewalk glow with a wet sheen. He lights a cigarette, inhales and blows out a blue cloud. The only sound is the distant grumpy murmur of the city grinding through its daily gears.

He looks up from the street to a backlit HDX billboard pitching vacation getaways. A small boat, a skiff, sits beached on the white sand of a tropical lagoon. Its shipped oars point skyward to the bluest of blues.

And then it comes.

Miller Bay.

It's the same boat, he's sure of it, the same design. Only the colors are different. And the great span of years.

He closes his eyes and sees the skiff rocking in the water, tied to a piling hopelessly encrusted with barnacles. It couldn't have been much more than six feet in length. Squared at both ends, its outer hull was a robin's egg blue, with the inside done in white. Bright orange life jackets peeked out from under the backseat, still wet from the last outing. They emitted little clouds of steam in the early summer sun. You had to wear life jackets. No exceptions. If mom caught you without them, you couldn't use the boat for the rest of the trip, and she had an excellent view of the water, so you were almost always in plain sight.

She watched from the porch of their summer cabin built from aging logs, with a granite fireplace and old rugs of Native American origin hung as tapestries on the interior walls. It looked out over Miller Bay, which was only a couple of hundred yards across, with a long sand spit that kept out the big waters of Puget Sound. The skyline of downtown Seattle rose over the far shore like a distant dream.

Lane steered the skiff toward the graveled shore below the overgrown lawn in front of the cabin. At twelve years old, he did all the rowing and navigating. At ten years old, Johnny was simply along for the ride. When they reached the shore, Lane moored the boat to the gnarled root of an upended tree stump, the legacy of some ancient winter storm. They crossed the narrow beach and climbed the stairs to the yard below the cabin. And that's when he saw it, on the open water of the Sound, just outside the bay. A yacht. Its gleaming white hull, forty meters long, floating broadside to the sun.

"Johnny," Lane said quietly as he tried to damp his excitement.

"Yeah?" Johnny replied as he stared at a dragonfly hovering nearby.

"I said this was going to be our lucky day, didn't I?"

"Yeah, that's what you said, all right."

"And you didn't believe me, did you?"

"Not really."

"Well then, look where I'm lookin', then tell me what you believe."

Johnny swiveled his gaze toward the water and his eyes sprang open. "Oh my god!" He turned to Lane. "What are we gonna do?"

"What do you think we're gonna do?" Lane asked smugly.

"We're gonna check it out?"

"Yeah, we're gonna check it out."

They scampered down the stairs to the boat and grabbed their life jackets. "You want to bad-mouth our lucky day anymore?" Lane asked. He buckled a sodden strap around his waist. "Well, do you?"

"Nope," Johnny answered sheepishly as he poked his arm into his jacket's shoulder piece.

"Good." Lane untied the mooring while Johnny finished securing himself. He coiled in the rope, pushed them off and took to the oars. As the shore receded, he pointed them toward the sand spit on the far side of the bay. Once there, they would make their way through its twisted mass of driftwood to the far side where the yacht sat at anchor.

"How we gonna do it?" Johnny asked when they approached a narrow strip of virgin sand that marked their landing spot.

"You'll see," Lane replied enigmatically.

"What if they spot us?" Johnny asked as they beached the skiff and started to thread their way through the driftwood.

"I dunno. They'll probably take us prisoner."

"You're kidding, right?"

Lane shrugged. "Who knows?" He couldn't help but savor Johnny's obvious alarm.

Just a hint of the yacht's superstructure came and went over the top of the driftwood tangle.

"Do you think it has a pool table inside?" Johnny inquired.

"Of course it does." Lane was the final authority on all such matters.

They abruptly came out onto the beach and beheld the great vessel, which was moored about twenty-five meters out into the Sound. In their young minds, it took on the dimensions of a battleship. Near the bow, Lane could make out its name inscribed in bold, block letters:

THE ETERNAL HEART.

They lingered a while in awed silence and detected no motion aboard the ship. Eventually, the novelty of it dissipated into the late afternoon. Lane rose, brushed the sand off his legs and turned to Johnny. "Show's over. Let's go."

A lucky day, for sure. Maybe the luckiest ever.

Lane turns away from the billboard with its little skiff resting in the white sand. As he does so, Miller Bay recedes into the distant past.

He has the sound down on the Feed, but it visually screams about some kind of airplane crash. The Feed loves disasters. He's not interested, especially this evening. He turns it off and fixes himself a whiskey and soda.

5.

PRINCE VEGAS

NORTHEASTERN OREGON – DESERT COUNTRY

"You really didn't need to come along," Arjun tells Zed. "I can handle it."

"Handle it, huh?" Zed spits back, "If things were being handled, we wouldn't even be here." The old man looks out into the night through one of the van's armored windows. The dim outline of a flat, arid plain rolls by as they travel east. Road signs creep up, then vanish in brief flashes of green and white.

"Let me get this straight." Zed says. "First, he got off the plane. Second, he slipped in up on Tabor. Third, he left with proof positive. Correct?"

"Correct."

"So how in the hell did he get past the gate and into the lab?"

"A procedural error. Before we arranged the crash, he had a Type-A security clearance on his access card. We had no idea he'd survived, and he managed to get in and out with the van before we canceled it."

Zed scans the road ahead. Black, empty, devoid of headlights. Nobody takes casual nighttime trips out here. The law ends at sundown. "So now what?"

"We know he stopped for gas about twenty miles back. We intercepted his lobe scan and confirmed the license number on the van. It's definitely the same vehicle. Anyway, we're closing in. The next town is La Grande, and we already have assets on the ground there."

"We'll see about that."

"Yes, we will."

Frank Turner hunches over the wheel of his old Ford pickup and stares out at the spray of his headlights on the freeway ahead. He pushes his face even further toward the windshield, as if it will somehow improve the view. It's just too damn dim to go any faster. He simply can't see well enough. Too bad. When he was young, he once tracked a rabbit by moonlight.

Frank checks the speedometer. Fifty-five. Pitiful. But it's the best he can do. Damn! He shouldn't have fallen asleep at his daughter's place back in Hermiston. When he woke up, they'd gone to bed, so he just took off.

Oh well, he'd phone her in the morning. A preemptive call, so he could defuse some of her scolding. He wasn't a little kid. He just wished she could understand that. But how could she? Like all farmers, he has a fatalistic streak that rapidly sorts the impossible from the possible and moves on.

He pulls his face back from the windshield to check the speedometer once again. Hell. The damned dash lights are out. He fiddles with the rheostat that controls them. They flicker on, then off again. Goddamn. Thought it was fixed. He'll have to take the old rig back up to his son-in-law tomorrow and see what they can do.

Far ahead, Arjun spots twin pinpoints of red light on the black horizon. They quickly disappear. He doesn't bother asking Zed if he saw them. The old man's night vision is largely a thing of the past. Maybe, if they're lucky, it's Anslow and the van.

Prince Vegas. It's the only logical destination given Anslow's direction of travel. If he can make it, he'll seek asylum and probably get it. Because the Principality of Las Vegas is no longer officially part of the United States. It operates as a U.S. protectorate administered by an international entertainment cartel, which shares the profits with a cash-starved U.S. government. A place of princes and their princesses, but not from the lumpen backwaters of the United States. The Vegas customer base is worldwide now, with Americans in the minority. As they roll along, Arjun visualizes the enormous complexes, the exotic architecture, the maze of brilliant distractions, each more astounding than the last.

The two red taillights suddenly appear up ahead again.

Arjun presses the mic button and speaks to a second vehicle that's following them. "We've got a vehicle about a hundred yards in front of us. Stand by." By the time he finishes, the red lights disappear.

"Damn!" Frank mutters. This time, he's lost the headlights as well as the dash lights. He reaches down to jiggle the exposed wiring. The headlights come back on.

Just in time to expose the deer. A big buck, fifty feet dead ahead.

No time to brake. He yanks the wheel to the right. His left fender collides with the deer's left haunch. A sickening thud sends his old truck onto the shoulder and off into the desert beyond.

It happens so fast, Arjun has to wonder if it's real. Up ahead, the vehicle's lights come back on just as it collides with what looks like a deer. It sails off the road and down a short embankment, which launches it into a violent series of rolls. Its headlight beams rotate rapidly across the grass, sky, dirt and sagebrush. It finally comes to a stop in a cloud of dust.

Frank Turner hangs upside down in his seat belt. Hot oil, gasoline, and coolant mix together like smelling salts and yank him back to his senses. In a terrible moment of fright, he tries to remember what got him here, the world inverted and lit only by the beams cast at crazy angles onto the dry grass and dirt. His head is mashed up against the ceiling of the truck, and he feels the warm, wet flow from a huge laceration on his scalp. His left arm is numb and his broken right clavicle shoots out a gusher of pain. He tries to move his right hand to unbuckle the seat belt, but it's wedged in between pieces of wreckage. When he attempts to move his legs, he finds his knees jammed into the collapsed dashboard. All the while, the electronic warning beep for an open door pulses through the darkness. In the engine compartment, something rips loose and bangs down onto the hood.

The last thing he remembers is dozing off at his daughter's, sitting in the big old recliner with his shoes off.

The warning beeper stops and the only sound is the bubbling of the various fluids. The truck is upside down, with the hood tilted down into the dirt and undercarriage raised toward the sky. The repeated rolling has severed the fuel line, and gasoline now begins to bleed into the cab.

Then Frank hears the rush of rubber on pavement. As it grows closer, his fear turns to humiliation. Whoever it is will stop and find him in this awful predicament, hanging helpless in his overturned vehicle and will ask him what happened, and he will have no answer. None at all.

He can turn his head just far enough to make out an inverted image of the highway. Any further, and his cervical vertebrae register a sharp pain. Headlights come into view and the night is filled with the snap of small rocks as a pair of big vans rolls to a stop up on the shoulder. A door opens and the bouncing beam of a flashlight approaches. In the moonlight, he can make out the faint figure of a man behind the light.

And even through the shock of his injuries and befuddlement, something strikes him as odd. The man should be yelling toward the flipped vehicle, asking if anyone is in there, if anyone is hurt. Instead, the man advances in silence, his boots pushing little poofs of moonlit dust.

By the time the man reaches the wreck, Frank's humiliation has turned to fear. This is not right. The dark outline of a muscular figure descends to a squat about a yard away from the truck. The beam of a flashlight probes the cab and settles briefly on Frank's face.

"You see a white utility van out here tonight?" The voice of Zed's security man is hard and pitiless.

Frank stares at the figure. Nobody's ever pushed him around. Nobody's going to start, now. His dignity is all he's got left. He remains silent and motionless.

The figure thrusts the light out at arm's length, so it's closer to Frank. "I know you can talk. I saw your eyes move. Let's make a deal. You answer me, and I'll get you out of there."

Franks looks away from the light.

The figure sniffs the air. "Hey, you smell anything funny? I sure do. Smells like gasoline around here."

Frank tries desperately to move, to gain some semblance of control. But he's hopelessly wedged.

"You look a little squirmy to me. Maybe you're trying to tell me something, huh?"

The figure backs off a few feet, takes out a cigarette, and lights it. "Saw a man burn up once. Only it wasn't like this. It wasn't an accident. You don't die right away, you know. He just screamed and screamed."

Frank can't help himself. "I didn't see nothin'!" he blurts out. "I don't remember nothin'!"

"Now, that's better," the figure says. "That's much better."

Then he flicks the cigarette into the cab, where it sails past Frank's face, lands on the ceiling, and comes to a stop by the shattered dome light.

"Let me go," Frank pleads in a weak voice.

The security man is halfway up the embankment when the truck explodes. No screams come from the burning wreck. The explosion itself must have got him. The contractor recalls a similar incident in Yemen, during the third incursion.

He continues his climb and reaches the shoulder of the highway, where Arjun Khan stares at the blaze. "Was it him?" Arjun asks.

"Negative."

"So why did you torch the vehicle?"

"Seemed like a nice night for a cookout. Know what I mean?

"The driver was still inside?"

"Yes, I do believe he was."

Arjun chooses not to pursue it. The man's clearly a psychopath. You saw that a lot with these contract military types. "Get back to your post," he orders.

The contractor moves off to the rear van, while Arjun turns to the lead vehicle. He opens the door, where Zed sits in the semidarkness.

"That wasn't him," Arjun says.

Zed seems not to notice. "I'm cold. It's the start of fall. It's beginning to get chilly at night."

Arjun winces inside. The old man is drifting, his focus temporarily gone. It's happening more often now. "I'm sorry about that. Is there anything we can do to make you a little more comfortable?"

"Take me out by the fire."

"What?"

"You heard me. I want to go out by the fire. So I can warm up."

"I'm not sure if that's advisable. We haven't secured the area. And there's always the danger of a secondary explosion."

"I don't want to argue. I want to warm up. Let's go."

The light from the flames dances in faded peach over Zed's wrinkled skin. The old man gets up very slowly and comes to the door, where Arjun helps him to the ground.

"My coat, please. And my hat."

Arjun reaches in, removes the overcoat and the hat from a hook and helps Zed struggle into them. The motion strains Zed's connective tissue to the point of pain. He hands Zed his cane and helps him down the embankment, one cautious step at a time.

When they reach the truck, it still burns vigorously, with bright flames billowing out the broken windows, an angry furnace stoked by gasoline, oil, upholstery and human flesh. About ten yards away, Arjun's nose takes in the stink of the smoldering corpse. It repels him, and he looks to Zed, hoping for a similar reaction so they can leave. Zed smiles and puts out his hands to catch the warmth of the blaze.

"It's wonderful," mutters Zed. "There's nothing quite as nice as a big fire on a cold night. Don't you think so?"

"I suppose."

"I mean, you can have furnaces, you can have heaters. But they just aren't the same."

Arjun looks at Zed's face. Only the eyes seem alive, small wet pockets that glisten in the firelight.

"Have you ever been camping, Arjun?"

"Yes, once or twice."

Their conversation is interrupted by a dull thud and the outline of motion inside the truck, followed by an extra rush of flames. For a horrible moment, Arjun thinks the man is still alive inside. Then he realizes that the seat belt has burned through and the body has fallen onto the ceiling of the cab. A flaming arm flops out the window and ignites little tufts of dry grass.

Zed stares at the sizzling arm and continues. "I went camping once. When I was a young boy. My father and I took the trolley to the edge of town. We had a blanket, some bread and a bottle of whiskey. We walked up into the hills and built a fire when it got dark. My father drank the whiskey and passed out." Zed pauses and wheezes out a laugh. "As soon he as he was out cold, I took the blanket away from him and sat by the fire until it went out. It was warm. It was wonderful." He sighs. "Oh well, I guess nothing lasts forever, does it?"

"I wouldn't know, Mr. Zed."

The little wet eyes flash bright with fire. "Nor does anyone else. At least, not yet."

And in the center of his head, as he basks in the warmth of the ghastly fire, Zed feels a strange little clock spring forth, a clock that only tocks and never ticks. A clock whose tocks were launched so long ago, at the time of his birth, in the twilight of the nineteenth century. He tries to keep count, to see how far back the tocks will take him, but the lateness of the hour and pleasant blanket of radiant heat make it difficult to concentrate.

As best he can tell, they stop when he is about fifteen.

The crisp morning air of San Francisco Bay invigorates a young Thomas Zed as he walks down Market Street and watches the first light of dawn paint the big buildings. His hands are stuffed in his pockets and he feels the twin wads of dollar bills. He's a smart lad, they say, the men on the waterfront that let him gamble with them far into the night. Got a way with numbers. Never forgets a card. Several have silently backed him, and he splits his winnings with them. The boy's a moneymaker, and they protect their investment from sore losers and drunks.

At Third, he looks up at the Hearst Building as he turns south off Market. Someday, he will have a building like that. Others dream it, but he can feel it, and the power of that feeling propels his youthful legs down the deserted sidewalk. A wagon comes up from behind, the clop of horses' hooves bouncing off the buildings. As it passes, he sees its teamster stare stonily down the street, with a slack grip on the reins. The back is open, so he jumps aboard for a few blocks before hopping off and heading into the tenements, the ramshackle buildings built mostly of wood and rising four or five stories.

When he reaches home, he climbs the stairs to the fourth story, walks down the dingy hall and unlocks the door to the single room he shares with his father. The old man dozes in an alcoholic stupor on the bed. He is fully clothed and sprawled on his back. His Adam's apple bobs from the beneath the stubble on his scrawny neck and mirrors his snoring.

Zed sits on the cot that has served as his bed for as long as he can remember. The old man is out of work again, fired from his livery-stable job. Each time he's fired, the intervals between the new jobs grow longer and longer. Zed would have left long ago, but the old man loves him in a crippled sort of way. The only time he raises his voice is when he finds that Zed has been skipping school. Then he raves about how bright the boy's mother was, and how she never had the chance to finish school, and about how tragic her death was, and the horrible episode out there on the prairie, and…

Zed gets up and goes to the room's only window, nearly opaque with grime. He's home later than usual, so he'll probably skip school today. No problem. He can miss a week and make it up in a day if he has to, although his teachers won't admit it. He looks out at the thin morning light and back into the semidarkness of the room. It stinks of cheap booze, stale tobacco, sweaty clothes and mite-laden dust. He wants out.

It's too late to grab any sleep. Soon, the old man will awaken, hack violently, and take his shrinking bladder down the hall to relieve himself. Then he will return and flop back down on the bed. Zed decides to walk back up to Market Street, buy a roll and some coffee and watch the city come alive. He will sit on a stool and look north across the trolley tracks to the big buildings, the great strongholds of the rich and powerful. To him, their march up the hill is transcendental in nature, a journey to a mystical plateau of monetary privilege. Munching on his roll, he will consider the first steps of this journey, the acquisition of enough capital to get him underway.

He crosses the room, takes one last look at the pathetic figure on the bed, and slips out the door.

He will never see the old man again. Because when he reaches the sidewalk, the ground beneath him buckles in a jolt of boundless violence.

Instinctively, he sprints out into the middle of the street, into a narrow zone of safety between the buildings on each side. The force of the quake tries to knock him off his feet and nearly succeeds as it begins to buckle the pavement around him.

Dry wood snaps and splinters. Bricks crash to the ground. Metal ducts screech and rip. A dog howls in terror.

Then quiet. And dust. A great cloud of devastation sent heavenward into a cruelly neutral sky.

As the dust clears, Zed sees that his tenement has collapsed into a jagged heap of riven lumber. Four stories are now one. The same is true all up and down the block. He scans the street for survivors. At the end of the block, a man in striped pajamas kneels quietly, as if in prayer. Nearby, a woman in a nightgown walks delicately around the debris, her long, curly hair falling over her shoulders. She carries an empty birdcage, its bottom missing.

The fires ignite almost immediately. Shorted wires, overturned stoves, flammable chemicals all join to start a conflagration that will eventually burn out the entire heart of the city. The whole block begins to belch great sheets of flame and smoke, and his own tenement is no exception.

From beneath the burning wood, the screaming starts.

The heat tries to clutch his skin and broil it as he runs down the block toward Third, where some of the structures are brick and have yet to catch fire. Ahead, a great geyser of water shoots from a ruptured main.

Zed turns on Third and jogs back up toward Market. After a few blocks, the blazing monster is behind him, and the streets have become strangely calm.

With the immediate danger past, he slows to a walk. On the far side of the street, a few people huddle around a man hopelessly pinned in the debris of a collapsed building. He screams that the fire is coming, that the fire will burn him alive, that someone should shoot him before he suffers.

A block later, he hears a single shot from a revolver.

He continues on and decides to cross Market Street, the perennial border between wealth and poverty. Today, no one will scorn him for his dirty clothes or greasy hair. Today, no beet-faced cop will shoo him back where he belongs.

On Polk Street, he comes upon a saloon, its windows broken and its door open. Inside, half a dozen men are at the bar, with big, foaming schooners of beer.

"Come on in, lad," yells a beefy man with red hair sprouting from beneath a bowler. "Have one on the house!"

Zed does a cautionary scan up and down the street and then enters. As he steps up to the bar and plants his foot on the brass rail, the red-head puts a big arm over his shoulders.

"You lookin' for work, boy?" the man asks with maniacal grin.

"Depends," Zed says as a beer is pushed his way.

"Depends on what?" the redhead asks, taking mock offense.

"Depends on what it is."

"It's the opportunity of a lifetime, that's what it is," the redhead declares. "It's a chance to get into the jewelry business. It's a chance to get rich. So what else do you need to know?"

"What if we get caught?"

The redhead pulls back from Zed, looks at him in amazement, and then looks at the other men. They all explode in laughter.

"And just who do you think might be catchin' us on this fine morning? Your mother, maybe?"

"I don't have a mother," Zed answers as he takes a sip of beer.

"Well, to tell the truth, sonny, neither do I. But I do know an opportunity when I see one." He puts his arm around Zed again and steers him toward the door. "So let's take a little walk."

A few blocks later, they approach a large jewelry store. The displays are in chaos from the shaking, but the windows are intact.

"You see, on a day like today, nobody's going to know whether a little broken glass is God's work or man's," the redhead instructs. He picks up a fallen gargoyle off the sidewalk and hefts its mass of pitted stone.

"Perfect." He throws it through the glass door, which shatters inward onto the carpeted floor.

"Maybe I better keep guard," Zed volunteers. "I don't know what's valuable. I'd pick up the wrong stuff."

"Good thinkin', boy," the redhead says. "You see any kind of a uniform, you yell. I'll go shoppin' for both of us." He ducks in through the doorframe and reappears in the front window, pawing through the display.

As the redhead continues to rummage inside, Zed backs off a respectful distance and sits on the curb opposite the store. The sun goes red with wood smoke and a cat slinks across the deserted street. A few minutes later, he sees the soldiers. Seven of them with rifles slung, coming down Polk, right toward him.

Without hesitation, he rises and walks down the block to meet them.

The one in the lead has the chevrons of a sergeant on his sleeve and a nasty face with a broken nose. Before the man can speak, Zed takes the initiative.

"Sir," he says respectfully. "I saw a man break into that store down there." He points down the street to the jewelry store. "I think he's still inside."

"How long ago?" the sergeant asks.

"Just a few minutes ago. He wanted me to help him."

"Good thing you didn't," the sergeant says. "Now get the hell out of here."

"Yes, sir." Zed moves away as the soldiers ready their rifles and approach the store. He conceals himself behind a pile of rubble and watches.

Two of the soldiers enter the store. A moment later, they march the redhead out at gunpoint. He is gesticulating wildly.

"Didn't you see him?" the redhead asks desperately. "A punk kid. I caught him breakin' in here and went to see what the damage was. Don't tell me you didn't see him!"

The sergeant ignores the man's pleas and gives an order to two of the soldiers. They raise their rifles and each chamber a round, while the redhead bolts and runs in naked panic. Before he can get ten yards, the soldiers have shouldered their weapons and fired into the fleeing man's back. He lunges forward, skids along the pavement on his belly, tries to rise and then flops down.

All seven soldiers walk up to the body. One turns it over with a shove of his boot. Apparently, they are satisfied. Without a word, they follow the sergeant's lead down the street, where they round the corner and head south toward Market.

Zed rises cautiously, walks into the street, and looks in both directions. No one is visible. He runs past the jewelry store to the corner and looks down the hill. The soldiers are already rounding another corner and heading away from him. He turns and looks at the dead looter in the intersection, where a pool of blood is forming around the torso. Boring.

He trots over to the jewelry store, ducks through the shattered glass in the front door, and spots a shopping bag tipped over on the floor near a display case. Inside it, he finds a gleaming jumble of jewelry all knotted into wild blossoms of gold and silver encrusted with diamonds and other stones beyond his knowledge. He grabs the bag and exits. Later, there'll be plenty of time to inventory the haul. Right now, the important thing is to minimize his exposure.

He walks swiftly to his hiding place, where the façade of a five-story building has collapsed onto the street. After a careful inspection of tumbled masonry, he uses a splintered stick of wood to dig a tunnel to stash the jewelry. Right now, it's far too risky to keep it on his person. In a funny kind of way the redhead proved to be a good teacher after all. He'll come back after dark and move it to a safer location. Before he stashes the bag, he looks inside once more. Now he has the capital he needs to prime the pump. He stuffs the bag into the tunnel and carefully covers it.

When he's through, he walks past the dead looter once more and looks down the hill. The trolley tracks glow like pink silver in the smoky air.

The obnoxious buzz of his old cellphone drags Lane out of a deep sleep. He answers on the third ring.

"Lane, it's Johnny. I got a problem. A really big problem."

Lane blinks himself fully awake. Whatever it is, it's bad. His brother's voice is dipped in fear and coated with pain.

"Don't tell me you're in jail again."

"It's not that simple. Not this time."

"Where are you?"

"I'm in a motel in La Grande."

"La Grande? I thought you were going to New York. How in the hell did you wind up in La Grande?"

"Oh shit, they're here! I'll call you back."

"What do you mean? Who's there?"

The connection is gone. The call is dead.

"Where did he put the van?" Arjun asks as he climbs out of his vehicle and into the motel parking lot in La Grande.

"It's around back in the alley," the security man says. "The engine's still warm."

"So what happened?" Arjun asks as they stride briskly toward the rear of the building.

"We got a hit when he charged a room on his lobe. We must have just missed him. If he had any time at all, he would've taken off in the vehicle."

"Organize a search. Right away." Arjun knows it's most likely futile. This is wide-open country, and any real search effort is going to attract way too much attention.

They reach the alley, sandwiched between the back of the two-story motel and a tall fence that masks some kind of milling operation. It fills the dim space with the mindless industrial murmur of machines that never sleep.

A parked van hugs the fence halfway down the darkened alley. The security man produces a flashlight, and Arjun asks him to hand it over. "Stay here."

He scans the van's license plate as he swings open the rear doors. Sure enough, it matches the one stolen up on Tabor. His nostrils are already filled with a singular stink that he knows all too well. He points the flashlight beam into the back to confirm its source. Yes, one of the test subjects, obviously dead. As his light glides over the slumped form, Arjun thinks of how horrific it would appear if it ever got on the Feed. Public knowledge would be disastrous.

He climbs back out into the alley. "Post some people at either end," he tells the security man. "Nobody gets any closer until the recovery crew shows up."

Arjun's phone rings. It's the team leader. "It looks like we've lost Anslow for now, but I think we found his cell."

"Where?"

"On the shoulder of a road on the west end of town. It's been stomped on to defeat the GPS, and the memory card's missing."

"It has a videocam, right?"

"Right."

Arjun's head begins to throb. Without the memory card, they can't trace any calls, at least not easily. Worse, the missing card may contain video from the back of the van.

He returns to the parking lot and climbs into Zed's armored vehicle. Exhausted, he slumps in the driver's seat and looks over at the old man. Sound asleep. Head thrown back, mouth wide open, jaw flexing in a spastic quiver.

Arjun sighs and thinks of what he just saw in the back of the van. He visualizes the image recorded on high-definition video revealing every nauseating detail. Then he imagines the possible destinations for such a video, and all the damage that might be inflicted.

They can't let it happen. They're too close. They've come too far.

6.

A DECENT LIFE

Lane barrels through the blackness in the unmarked police sedan past a blur of blacktop and desert juniper.

To get the car, he pulled in every favor owed him by the night shift downtown. Still, he'll have to replace the gas, which will cost him a month's pay at standard contract rates. But money's not the issue. Johnny's the issue. What the hell is going on? He resists the urge to speculate. He has nothing to go on except the naked fear in his brother's voice.

The headlights catch a man frantically waving from the shoulder of the road. Behind him, a pregnant woman lies on the ground in front of a pickup partially tipped in the ditch. Lane feels for the shotgun propped beside him on the passenger seat. His peripheral vision catches the man pulling out a pistol as he roars by. He sees the muzzle flash in the side mirror. Fortunately, the round goes wide and the car is spared.

He drives on. The miles whiz by and he climbs into some shallow hills. The halo of dawn spreads across the eastern sky. The sparse lights of La Grande play out in the valley below as he descends.

He sees the motel from the freeway. There may be more than one, but not likely. He takes the exit. Empty parking lots, darkened buildings, damaged signage. Lane knows it probably looks much the same even at high noon. The motel sits next to a mill of some kind that grinds on through the wee hours. The only game in town.

Lane pulls into the parking lot, which holds a half dozen junkers. He strides directly to the office and taps the bell on the desk. After several minutes, an annoyed young woman appears, her hair still creased by sleep. "Yeah?"

Lane pulls out his contractor's badge. "Portland Police. I need to see your registry."

"Oh yeah? How come?"

"I'm looking for a guest named Anslow. Dr. John Anslow. He would have checked in sometime last night."

"I'll have to look on the computer."

"Yeah, I guess you will."

The girl ignores him and clicks some keys. She stares vacantly at the results on her display. "No Anslow."

"Anyone with a Portland address?"

"No. No one from Portland."

"No Anslow, no Portland. You're sure?"

"Yes, I'm sure," the girl replies, with mounting exasperation.

Lane pulls out a photo of Johnny that he brought along for precisely this reason. "He might have used a different name. Here's a picture. You recognize him?"

The girl squints at the picture through puffy eyes. "Nope."

Lane looks out the window at the decaying business strip. "Where's your police department located?"

"It closed."

"Then who has jurisdiction here?"

"The county sheriff. But they don't open until nine. No night shift."

"So what if somebody wanted to rob you right now?"

The girl comes up with a sawed-off shotgun from behind the desk. "I'd blow their fucking brains out."

Outside, Lane circles the building. A gravel drive stretches along the back. No vehicles, only a black cat padding over the crushed rock. He returns to his car and leans back in the seat, exhausted. He suspects that the girl is lying, but he has next to no leverage way out here. Besides, whatever happened, he seriously doubts that Johnny is anywhere near.

He closes his eyes against the mounting morning light. There's no use sticking around. The sheriff's office won't be any help. With the highways and countryside slipping into virtual anarchy, a missing person report verges on the ridiculous. The best move right now is to grab a little sleep in the car and head back to Portland.

Lane starts at a thump on the hood. A cat, the black one from the rear of the motel. It stares at him through the windshield with eyes of predacious yellow.

He ignores it and closes his eyes for a moment. When he opens them, the cat is gone.

He takes note of the news about the plane crash for the first time when he stops for coffee at a dilapidated roadside joint where he's the only customer. The Feed belts it out over a display behind the counter. A business jet went down on takeoff from Hillsboro Airport, just west of Portland. The plane was bound for New York when it skidded into a packed bus at about 4:00 p.m. yesterday. Everybody involved was incinerated.

Rescue workers mill around the charred frame of the bus and the plane's blackened tail section. Yellow tape restrains frantic loved ones. Smoke and steam still rise skyward. No one can see the hole in the right tire, which is now a mass of rubberized goo. No one will find the lead slug, which has completely melted.

Lane stands up at the counter. Johnny's plane. It had to be. So why wasn't he on it? Why did he call from out here in the desert?

"You need somethin'?" the waitress asks from where she leans on some shelving.

"Yes, I do," Lane says. "I need to get going."

Outside, he stands in the empty parking lot, where a hot breeze eddies about him. The woman, Rachel, Johnny's date. He'll start with her and work backwards. Heinz, was it Heinz? He's not sure. Then he remembers she works for Harlan Green and the Street Party.

"Street headquarters," a perky little voice informs him after he connects "How may I direct your call?"

"Rachel Heinz."

"And can I say who's calling?"

"Anslow. Lane Anslow."

Lane paces as he waits. Up the highway, a vigorous herd of wind turbines spins in the morning heat.

"Rachel speaking."

Lane matches the voice with the face. He has the right person. "It's Lane, Johnny's brother. Have you heard about the plane crash out in Hillsboro?"

"Don't tell me that was him. His trip to New York?"

"Hard to say. Very hard to say."

"You mean they haven't informed you yet?"

"I mean I need to talk to you. In person. I can be there in a couple of hours."

"Well, we have a pretty full schedule but, yeah, of course."

"See you then."

Lane disconnects. He looks out at the stunted hills of wrinkled brown and the huge sky.

Johnny, you've really gone and done it this time.

The man on the roof with the RPG launcher spoils the illusion, but just for a moment. He quickly ducks out of sight, and visual calm descends. The Street Party's national headquarters still maintains respectability, with clipped hedges, new storm windows, walls of sandblasted brick.

Lane manages a wry smile. You could almost forget that it sat deep within the urban confines of Birdland and operated as a protectorate. As a cop, he knew the security was heavy, yet discreet. All the houses in the surrounding neighborhood were occupied by Bird operatives. They mowed lawns and painted porches, weapons within easy reach.

Lane remembers when the building was still a high school, albeit a deteriorating one. That was back when there was still a school district over here. It shut down when the graduation rate sank below 25 percent. No longer worth it. Now the curriculum is defined exclusively by the street and the Feed.

He stops at the double doors and wonders how many cameras are tracking him. At least one is probably a neural model that picks your face out of a crowd a billion strong.

"Good afternoon," a woman's voice says over an invisible speaker.

"How can we help you?"

"I'm Lane Anslow, and I'm here to see Rachel Heinz. I believe she's expecting me."

"One moment."

A solenoid clicks. The doors swing open. He ascends a short flight of steps, where a cheerful young woman meets him. "Mr. Anslow, do you happen to have a Street Card?"

"I'm afraid not." Lane knows the drill. Everyone formally associated with the party carries one of the digitized cards. It's your ticket of admission here.

"No problem. Would you mind if we did a lobe scan?"

"Go ahead."

The woman runs a handheld device over the lobe on Lane's ear. Several armed individuals hover in the wings awaiting the outcome. The woman looks at the device's display and smiles. "Very good. Rachel is tied up for a bit. Mr. Green is giving an address in the auditorium. She asked if you'd like to attend. She'll be free as soon as it's over."

"Sure. Why not?"

Lane follows the woman down a hall to a large auditorium, once given to basketball games and pep rallies. No longer.

"And so friends, I ask you. What stands between you and a good life, a decent life, a secure life? Only one thing. And that one thing is you, friends. Just you. Nothing else, really. Now, unless each of you stands and marches in the same direction, you will not be heard. You must make that promise to yourself that you will stand, that you will be counted, and that you will be heard!

"Yes, there will be sacrifice. Yes, there will be suffering. But God knows, there's already been plenty of suffering, hasn't there? You've seen your lives slip between your fingers. You've seen your children's lives slip between your fingers. Remember the America your parents lived in? And your grandparents? Remember the new cars? The private homes? The free schools? Well, I'm here to tell you: You must not forget. Because that is your heritage. That is your right.

"But now look. Look around you. Who's worked for a year straight? Let me see the hands. I count maybe a half dozen. That's some depressing arithmetic, friends. It just doesn't add up."

Lane Anslow listens to the thunderous tones of Harlan Green shake the sound system and spill across the auditorium. From behind a bulletproof podium, he sways to the rhythm of his own oratory. The crowd roars when Harlan hits a high point, then sinks back to load the next batch of vitriol.

Lane checks out Green's personal security people, the palace guard. They wear identical green blazers and slacks and black ties, an egalitarian mix of racial types. All gaze benignly yet alertly at the crowd, which seems oblivious to their presence. Many in the folding chairs are overweight, with big bellies thrusting out of cheap blouses and T-shirts. But many others appear leaner, smarter, with a kind of shabby dignity about them. And their numbers are growing rapidly. Lane is sure Green understands that these people are the unprocessed fuel of incipient revolution.

As the speech rambles along, Lane decides that the most troubling thing about Green is that he's right about so many things, even if his attitude seems to come out of hell itself. It's the first time he's had any direct exposure to the man. The Feed keeps him out on the far fringe, not because he's a demagogue, but because he can't be bought, can't be molded, can't be shaped. At least, not yet. Clearly, the man is playing a high-stakes game of political poker, seeing just how far he can get before he has to stop and negotiate. And to date, he's gotten farther than anyone thought possible and done it faster than anyone expected. A platform in the middle of the floor bristles with cameras and media gear, and a swarm of camera operators cruises the isles and prowls the stage, where Green's staff sits in the same type of folding chairs as the audience.

"Now, what did all those people in Washington say they'd do to make things better for you? I'll tell you. They said all you needed was a little training, right? Just a little trip back to the classroom to retool you for a new life. Yes, that's right, they were going to train you for the new jobs in the new world economy."

"Now, if they're so damned smart, why don't you have one of those new jobs? I'll tell you why. Because they're not so damned smart. That's why. And maybe it's time you stopped listening to them, and listened to someone who's making a little sense!"

The crowd leaps to its feet in undiluted adoration. "Harlan! Harlan! Harlan!"

He stands with arms over his head, fists clenched and thumbs up. The man has such a reasonable appearance, like one of those doctor-type dads on the ancient TV dramas, the kind of man firmly centered, who radiates an aura of unshakable conviction.

"And I know that there are those who say I am extreme in my message. That I am extreme in what I represent. That I have hidden agendas. That I will take you to the streets. But I ask you, have you heard anything extreme here today? I don't have to speak to you about the things that are extreme. You live in the extreme.

"At one time in this great country, the gate was open, ladies and gentleman. Then, bit by bit, it started to swing shut. And today, I tell you, the gate is closed."

He waits a perfect beat, then pounces. "And just what do think we should do about that?"

They rise as one and explode into the chant.

"Tear down the gate! Tear down the gate! Tear down the gate!"

Green pivots and abruptly exits stage left. The crowd chants on, and just when they start to lose momentum, Rachel Heinz takes to the podium and thanks them all for their dedication and devotion. Lane has to smile. Her timing and delivery are masterful, the perfect punctuation to Green's prolonged rant.

The audience files out, the bile temporarily drained. Volunteers pack up the folding chairs and stack them on carts. The floor is half cleared when Rachel comes out from the side of the stage and greets him.

"Lane, how are you doing?"

"Could be better."

Her eyes dart to the volunteers and back to Lane. "Let's go to my office." They walk in silence down the hall past open doors to classrooms that still look like classrooms. Kid-sized desks, blackboards, video screens. Each is fronted by a portrait of Harlan Green. He appears firm yet kind, practical yet visionary.

Rachel notes his interest. "We're starting to offer basic schooling to the children of party members," she tells him.

"Do they learn how to genuflect when they meet Mr. Green?" Lane asks.

Rachel smiles wryly. "Don't think so. For one thing, he's not around much anymore. We now have field offices in twenty-seven cities."

They pass through a glass enclosure into what were once the administrative offices. Lane points to the open door of a spacious office. "Let me guess: Harlan gets the principal's office."

"You got it," Rachel admits as they move down a door and enter her somewhat smaller office. "And here's where the vice principal lives." She shuts the door as Lane sits down in front of her desk. "I watched the Feed for follow-up on the crash," she says. "There wasn't anything about the victims' names."

"Doesn't matter."

"You mean that wasn't his flight?"

"Oh yeah, it was his flight all right."

Her face hardens. "So what are you getting at?"

"He wasn't on it."

"How do you know?"

"I talked to him by phone several hours after the plane went down."

"And what did he tell you?"

"Very little. That's the problem."

"Now wait a minute. I don't know your brother like you do, but he seldom had very little to say. You think he's in some kind of jam?"

"It wouldn't be the first time."

She sags a little. "I'm sure you're right."

"As far as I know, you were the last person to see him. Anything you can tell me might help track him down."

She crosses her arms on the desktop and leans forward. "I'll only do that if you're a little more forthcoming about what's going on here."

Lane considers his options. None are good. "He called me in the middle of last night from a motel out on the desert to the east. Scared to death. All he had time to say was that he was in a real pickle. So I took off and went out there. Drove all night. When I arrived, they said he'd never checked in."

"And you let it go at that?"

Lane feels a touch of irritation. "Yeah, I let it go at that. Now let's keep on sharing. Let's talk about the night before last, your date. Did he go home with you?"

"Well, fuck you very much. What's that got to do with any of this?"

"I won't know until you tell me."

Rachel sighs. "Yeah, he went home with me."

"Okay, now look," Lane says. "I don't care what you did. All I care about is what you said."

"He was higher than a kite. You just couldn't keep him down."

"Did he snort any synth?"

"No synth. He didn't need it. He kept on talking about how New York would change everything, but he wouldn't say why or how. He came across like a dam holding back a reservoir."

"Anything else?"

"That's about it. So where does that leave us?"

Lane stands up. "Simple. I keep looking until I find him."

"And we'll continue to share, right?"

"Right," Lane says as they walk to the door.

Rachel stops and looks down reflectively. "You know, there's one thing he said, right before he went to sleep. It seemed kind of weird, but he was on such a roll, so I let it go."

"Yeah? And what was that?"

"He said he was going to live forever."

7.

MISTAKES ARE MADE

Arjun Khan barely feels the quiet descent of the elevator as it moves through the hillside toward the building below, the Other Application. Zed sits next to him on a fold-down seat and rests his forearms on his walker. The old man hates the walker and all that it implies about physical decline. In truth, he should be grateful he can walk at all.

Arjun closes his eyes. The bright fluorescent lighting bothers him. It holds the potential to deliver a nasty headache. Ah yes, the headaches. A legacy of times gone by, times best forgotten.

He was rising along his professional arc back then, a promising arc in India's pharmaceutical industry, which was heading toward the top of the global heap. He was an engineer by training, an extraordinary one. He straddled the interface between science and manufacturing, between concept and product. He could visualize how the output of the labs became a saleable item. He saw through the miles of wiring, piping, coiling, computers and robotics and understood how they would converge to form a process optimized in terms of cost, quality, and efficiency.

He lived for his job. No wife, no children. Just a high-rise condo in an upscale section of Mumbai. Domesticity would come later, if at all. Then, at age thirty-one, he left the shelter of a mega-corporation and joined a biotech start-up as one of the principals. The project was risky, the payoff huge: a cure for rheumatoid arthritis, a malady afflicting hundreds of millions worldwide.

At first, it went well. They labored far into the night. They grabbed catered food on the fly. They applauded themselves on a regular basis. Then it went badly. One failure after another in clinical trials. Still, they sensed a positive outcome. They just had to hold on a little longer. But they had burned through their cash at a suicidal rate and lacked the funding to continue.

Then, one night at an elegant bar in an exclusive restaurant, he met a man who suggested a solution. The man was well dressed, articulate and highly sympathetic to the young entrepreneur's dilemma. In the weeks that followed, the full nature of his proposition rolled out in palatable chunks. Arjun would be hired as a consultant to design a pharmaceutical plant, a relatively simple one. His compensation for doing so verged on incredible. He would earn enough to fully resuscitate his company and significantly enhance his equity position.

All he had to do was design a state-of-the-art facility dedicated to the processing and refinement of raw opium. At first, Arjun was assured that the substance was part of India's enormous volume of legally grown and licensed opium. He was shown numerous documents to that effect, and took them on faith. His genius lay in engineering, not law or business or politics.

The police detectives showed little professional courtesy when they appeared at the offices of his start-up firm. They simply barged in, put Arjun in handcuffs and led him out, with no explanation or apologies to the staff or the principals. A common criminal. His humiliation verged on unbearable as they transported him to jail.

In time, charges were filed, attorneys retained and the full extent of his transgressions played out in a series of pretrial hearings. The government painted him as a key player in a conspiracy to illegally process and distribute opium siphoned from licensed crops. A key player. A man deserving the maximum allowable penalties. A man destined to experience excruciating headaches.

Then, deus ex machina. Several new attorneys joined the team. Somehow, certain legal barriers dissolved. Bail was arranged. He walked out into a glorious flood of light and a warm breeze.

The next day, his attorneys visited him at his condo and gave him the long-term legal prognosis. The government's case was essentially airtight. He would eventually be convicted and sent to prison. He would spend many years pacing cement floors in plastic sandals. He felt a headache coming on, a bad one. The attorneys sat in silence. The whisper of the air-conditioning filled his living room. The skyline of the city played out through tinted windows.

The lead attorney breached the awkward stillness. It seemed other options could be explored. Arrangements could be made that would guarantee Arjun's freedom. The final decision, of course, was up to him.

Rain pelted the fuselage of the small jet and spattered the window by Arjun's seat. Mumbai International Airport was lost in the glare of the floodlight as the plane lifted off and headed west over the Arabian Sea. The ruin of advanced age consumed the face of the man sitting opposite him.

In the course of their flight to Dubai, he would learn that the man was over one hundred years old and named Thomas Zed.

The elevator sighs to a stop at the end of its descent to the Other Application. Arjun watches as Zed grasps the handles of his walker and struggles off his seat. The doors open to a wheelchair. Zed totters toward it. Arjun walks around and steadies the wheelchair as Zed painfully deposits himself. He knows better than to offer assistance to the old man, who cherishes these brief bouts of physical independence.

"I want to stop at Bay Three," Zed announces as Arjun pushes him down the long corridor.

"That bay's not currently occupied," Arjun replies.

"I'm quite aware of that."

Zed sits alone in his wheelchair inside Bay 3. He stares at the empty bed, with its myriad adjustments. The monitors and their cabling stand lifeless in the background.

Autumn.

He still has vivid memories of her arrival, deep in the night. The navigation lights on the helicopter, the rush of the gurney over the cement floor, her exposed hand flexing on top of the blankets. He should have stayed by her side then, but he didn't. He should have fixed his gaze upon her sedated face, but he couldn't. In time, he would come to regret these actions, especially when his love became fully realized. He should have shown his loyalty, his commitment, right from the start. But back then, all he had was purpose and intent. The rest would come later.

To this day, he still hadn't told her the story, the precipitating incident that launched this entire episode. Perhaps she wouldn't understand. Few would. Most would see him only as a megalomaniac, and they would be at least partially right.

It happened so long ago, in the former half of the last century. On a day when a heavy snow fell outside and clung to the treetops in Central Park. New York City was frozen, both literally and financially. Sixteen months ago, the market had crashed. Black Friday they called it, the genesis of a chill that now penetrated to the very bone of the nation. His empire had dissolved; his liquidity had vanished. Mines, mills, factories lay idle. Debt had supplied the leverage to create Zed's holdings, and now debt had brought him low.

He stared in sorrow out the window at the cruel gray sky. He could no longer afford this lavish apartment, this opulent lifestyle. His wife had smiled bravely when he told her, but it belied a disappointment that would inevitably turn to bitterness. Her friends would call less often. The lunch invitations would dwindle. Their social calendar would dissolve into solitude. Shades of schadenfreude would color every aspect of their lives. He knew that she would quietly endure, and he loved her for that, but he also knew that she would become a cistern full of quiet rage. It would seep into every aspect of their marriage. Their son, so young and unaffected, would be steeped in it as the years passed.

He examined their misfortune from every angle before reaching a conclusion. He had to leave. His only path to redemption demanded that he travel unencumbered.

He intuitively understood that times of economic calamity eventually terminated in war. And the bigger the calamity, the bigger the war, and this current depression was a truly colossal calamity. It would take him far away, beyond the reach of his creditors, to murky places where the coming conflict would generate business opportunities truly global in scale.

And it was better to go now, while he could still provide his family with a buffer to heal. He had a modest reserve of cash that his creditors hadn't uncovered, and it would allow them to survive in modest comfort until he returned. He had no idea how long that might be, but it would most certainly come to pass. In the meantime, he would periodically let them know that he was out there, diligently working his way home.

He walked out of the living room and down the hall to the bedroom, where his wife lay sleeping. She faced away from him, and he could see through her nightgown, so soft and silken, the slight rise of her shoulder with each breath. He got as far as the bed, then turned away.

He didn't even consider visiting the next room, where his son slumbered in the white bassinet. The pain of it would take him to the brink, to a point where his resolve might falter.

Before he left, he carefully packed bundles of cash into a box that he left in plain sight on the kitchen counter. He wrote a note saying that he loved them both, and would be in touch, but nothing more. What else was there to say?

Zed grasps the rails on his wheelchair and idly rocks back and forth on the polished cement floor of Bay 3. One of the medical devices issues an anonymous beep, a call to no one in particular. He ignores it. The past beckons again and he quietly follows.

The Second World War raged on and on, startling in its scope and intensity, magnificent in its profitability. Zed traveled ceaselessly, in cargo holds of freighters, in cabins of DC-3s, in smoke-filled railcars, in armored vehicles. He crafted networks of common interest, webs of mutual advantage, and grand assemblages of monetary leverage. His operations grew in size, in wealth, in political power. Their scale and potential consumed him utterly. His notes back to his family became less frequent and more abbreviated. Eventually, he automated the process so that a monthly sum was sent to them without his intervention. They became an artifact, a relic from an era he would just as soon forget, a time of personal defeat and failure.

But while the past can be buried, the truth cannot be forgotten, and it nipped away at him. He had forsaken his wife and son. The possibility of redemption had come and gone. Markets could be manipulated, governments swayed and banks brought to heel, but a breached family yields to no one.

He had defaulted on the only contract that really mattered.

In Bay 3, Zed looks over to a cabinet beside the empty bed, a utilitarian work of metal and plastic. A glass vase sits on top, cut from crystal of the finest quality. It once held flowers: prize roses, exotic orchids, Casablanca lilies, peonies. Symbols of life. Celebrators of death.

Nobody invited the ravens to his wife's funeral, just as no one had invited him. They came of their own volition. Natural history blew them in, an inexorable surge of events propelled them forward. Just like him. He stood back from the graveside gathering and listened to their cawing. They were the only attendees he recognized, with one exception.

He saw just enough of himself in his son to be sure. The pale eyes, the prominent jaw, the slight widow's peak, even at twenty-five. A young woman stood at his side and grasped his arm. The warm air of spring settled snugly about them as they stared at the casket draped with flowers. Prize roses, exotic orchids, Casablanca lilies, peonies.

His son suddenly looked up, looked right at him. His heart gave a solitary thump. Did the boy know? Zed quickly broke off eye contact, and when he looked up, his son was once again staring at the casket.

The ravens chose that moment to depart. Big black wings beating through a sky of cloudless blue.

Zed scans the darkened screens of the monitoring equipment. They once danced with the imagery and numeric symbols of life in progress. Pulses, beats, pressures, electrical waves. Now they stand like silent scriveners, waiting to once again take note and bear witness. Just as they had in that hospital room over sixty years ago, when his only child lay dying.

He had entered the room only after hesitating out in the hall to gather his composure. The bleak light of late winter imposed itself from outside, and the instruments around the bed displayed all the signs of imminent decline brought on by lymphoma. Weak pulse, vacillating blood pressure, falling oxygenation. Seventy years of life circling for a final stand. His son lay motionless with his head propped on the pillow, his cheeks sunken and his color gone.

Zed pulled up a chair and sat down. His son did nothing to acknowledge his presence. His only offspring stared out into a space known only to those on the final precipice. Zed took a deep breath and moved into his son's field of vision.

"I'm sorry," he said. "I wasn't there for you. It was a terrible mistake, the biggest of my life."

His son stared back at him blankly. Not a hint of motion in the pale blue eyes, their common legacy. No response anywhere on the dying face.

Zed looked away and out into the grim winter. No resolution, no forgiveness, no reconciliation. His son's final silence would fester within him always, an open sore prone to spontaneous eruption.

"Is it cold?" Zed asks Arjun as he wheels himself out of Bay 3 and back into the corridor. "It seems cold to me."

"Yes, it might be a little chilly," Arjun agrees. "I'll check on it." They kept the temperature down here at almost 80 degrees to accommodate the old man. Any higher and you would break a sweat just by walking. But Zed's comfort comes first. Always.

Arjun grasps the handles of the wheelchair and they start down the corridor at a brisk pace. "I think you may be humoring me," Zed observes. "But we'll deal with that later. Now let's review the facts."

Arjun reviews the possible repercussions of Anslow's escape. The scientist's cellphone turned out to be a cheap bootleg from Borneo. All the data from calls and video resided exclusively on the memory card, which was missing and presumably with Anslow. Zed's generosity with the current administration had bought them deep access with the National Security Agency and others of its ilk, so it might be possible to trace any calls, but it would definitely take time. And that still left the possibility that video shot inside the van was on the card.

"Just remember Yogi Berra," Zed says.

Arjun stares down at the old man's bald skull as he wheels him along. A brown spray of age spots covers the pallid dome. "Who's Yogi Berra?"

"It's not over until it's over," Zed responds, with no further explanation.

They reach an unmarked door at the far end, beyond all the numbered bays. They knew from the outset that this additional space would be necessary. It holds a fully equipped examining room that doubles as a morgue, with the most advanced autopsy tools and diagnostic instruments. Arjun does a lobe scan to let them in, and they face three portable tables, with the body lying face up on the center one.

The operatory fixtures pour a merciless light down upon the subject. No detail hides in shadow. The subject is young. The subject is old. Take your pick. The jaw strong and firm. The neck wrinkled and withered. The nose not yet bulbous. The eyes reduced to lifeless pits. The forehead clean and smooth. The earlobes swollen and hairy. The arms thick and muscled. The hands knotted with arthritis. The calves strong. The thighs withered. The haunches firm. The belly a puddle of white flab. All topped by a mouth open in an expression of bottomless horror.

The subject holds no shock for Zed and Arjun. The 101-year-old male was one of the first. They're intimately acquainted with his bizarre farrago of biological triumph and tragedy. They know that CT and MRI imaging shows even more chaos inside him. The robust heart, the wheezing lungs. The vigorous liver, the shriveled colon.

"Have we determined when he died?" Zed asks.

"It was in the early morning, somewhere out on the road in the van with Anslow."

"Are you going to cremate him?"

"Not yet. First, we want to fully understand the nature of his death."

"Yes, of course. Well, no matter what, he gave himself for a good cause."

"Yes, he did," Arjun says. A good cause! What did that come from? Madness? Genius? It was hard to tell. And getting harder all the time.

8.

NATIONAL PANCAKE WAREHOUSE

"Nice piece," the security guard says as he examines Lane's pistol, one of the new 10 mm weapons with an auto-correcting laser system.

"Goes with the job," Lane mumbles. They stand at the screening gate for Store Land, a commercial zone on the old highway just east of Hillsboro, the county seat. The lobe scan informed the security people that he was cleared to carry it, but routine procedure demands a check of any weapon that comes through the gate.

The guard hands the pistol back to Lane, who tucks it in his shoulder holster and walks toward the big building directly ahead. A large, electrified sign on the roof explains the enterprise below: national pancake warehouse. Even at mid-afternoon, people are streaming toward the entrance, seeking a nutritional bargain that lets them fuel up on fats, sugar and carbohydrates at minimum cost. Most have the soft yet inflated look of the chronically overweight. A few carry the extraordinary bulk of the hopelessly obese.

Lane enters through the sliding glass doors and waits patiently in the ticket line. The interior is a big, industrial cavern lit by a grid of fluorescent lights installed in the metal framework overhead. They pour their cold illumination onto a cement floor covered with a multitude of folding tables and chairs. Off to the right are the big gas-fired griddles and the prep tables where batter is mixed, bacon arranged, butter whipped, and syrup bottles refilled. In front of the griddles is a long counter built from folding tables, where the patrons file by with plastic trays and paper plates to pick up their fare.

Lane avoids this orgy of cholesterol and goes to the end of the line, where he pours himself a cup of coffee from a ten-gallon container. He surveys the sea of tables and spots Bellows sits at the far end, right where he said he would be, underneath the giant screen for the Feed. As Lane weaves through the tables, people look up at him suspiciously before diving back into their heaping plates. He shouldn't be here. He's too hard, too lean. He can only mean trouble.

Bellows doesn't bother to rise as Lane approaches. He nods and takes a sip of his coffee. Not a good start. Bellows is the number two guy in the Washington County coroner's department. The plane disaster has him on edge. The department has gone from maybe a half dozen bodies a month to more than one hundred all at once. All burned beyond recognition by a hellish blaze of jet fuel.

"Sorry," Bellows says, without any formalities. "I can't tell you anything about your brother."

"I didn't think you could," Lane says.

"So what do you want to know, Mr. Anslow? As you might suspect, I'm a busy man."

"I want to know if you'll ever know anything about my brother."

Bellows sighs. "You got me there. You got me good. It's a real mess, I'll tell you that. Our lab can't handle it, that's for sure. Sooner or later, we'll send everything off to the state. Maybe we'll get something back, maybe we won't. It's not like it used to be."

"I'm sure it's not," Lane says. "Anyway, thanks for your time. Keep in touch, all right?"

Bellows stands and lightens a little. "Sure. And I'm sorry about your brother, okay?"

"Okay." Lanes watches Bellows walk off through the crowded tables. He and Bellows are informally connected as members of the law enforcement fraternity. He'd asked for a favor and got one. Sort of.

Bellows was bought and paid for. Lane is sure of it. The DNA would never come back from the state. The fate of his brother's body would remain permanently unresolved. Sorry, Mr. Anslow; it's the best we can do.

Lane gets up and heads out through the seductive smell of grilled bacon. The meeting was a success. He'd sent a signal that he thought his brother was dead. Just in case someone was watching.

The interior of Johnny's lab is stereotypical, at least from Lane's point of view. Counters full of chemistry, cubicles full of computers, hulking machines dedicated to purposes unknown.

The place is empty and quiet. Just the drone of the cooling fans in their endless thermodynamic battle against the march of the electrons. Lane finds Johnny's cubicle at the end of the row, a double-wide model befitting the leader of the pack. Arcane papers and notes litter his desk, full of graphs, math symbols and chemical equations of the sort that have mystified Lane ever since high school. The spot reserved for Johnny's laptop sits empty. End of story. Peoples' lives reside on their laptops, and without it, Lane has little to go on.

He sits in Johnny's chair and looks up to the burlap-like surface of the cubicle wall. A blue pushpin secures a photo to its surface, a snapshot of him and Johnny with the water, the firs and the wooden pilings encrusted with barnacles that mark the annual extent of the tide.

Miller Bay.

They were in their late teens then, and their swimming trunks hung loosely from their spare frames. An idle summer afternoon stretched out before them.

"Let's check out Old Man Simmons's boat." Johnny sprang up off the porch steps as he said it, powered by an effortless muscularity.

"We've still got work to do," Lane protested. A rotary power mower sat idle down on the wild grass. Little waves of heat still rose off its finned cylinder head. "We've got to finish the lawn."

"We can do that later." Johnny started to pace between Lane and the end of the porch. His head kept thrusting forward in an avian fashion, as if to an invisible rhythm. He'd been doing more of this kind of thing lately, and it bothered Lane. The more he paced, the more he thrust, the more determined he became. "Let's have some fun, man. This is it. You know that, don't you? We're not coming back. It's gonna be gone."

Lane did know that, and it pained him. Someone would buy the place for sure. Some couple would think it was the pinnacle of rustic charm, and that would be the end of it. And his dad kept dropping the price, just to make sure.

"Okay, but let's be quick," Lane said. They walked across the partially mown lawn to a buffer of tall grass that marked the edge of the Simmons property.

They followed a narrow path that cut through to the far side, and stopped to take in the house, a Cape Cod bungalow with white siding and powder-blue trim. Simmons was ex-Navy and ran a tight ship. His grizzled flattop looked just like its nautical namesake. He seldom spoke and never smiled. A permanent scowl creased his mouth, and his pale eyes assessed you with merciless calm whenever you encountered him. But on this day, Simmons was absent. Only the brown oil spot in the empty driveway remained.

"Okay, let's go," Johnny said, and they moved quickly across the lawn and down some stairs to a wooden boathouse. Halfway down its side was a door, and on this particular day it was secured with a big padlock.

Lane felt a flood of relief. Johnny's ill-advised expedition was now over. Old man Simmons's boat dwelled safely out of reach.

And what a boat it was. A classic speedboat, sporting a fifteen-foot white hull of plywood reinforced with fiberglass. The mahogany topside held fore and aft seating spaces, with a big curved windshield and a car-size steering wheel. When Simmons took the boat out, you could hear the snarl of the big engine all over the bay. It threw off a mighty wake, with twin ridges of foaming white cutting a big, violent V into the water astern.

But today, the craft floated in silent repose inside the boathouse. And the padlock barred their entry to admire it. "It's all locked up," Lane observed. "Let's go."

"Don't think so," Johnny said, and started for the door. A large paper clip extended from his thumb and forefinger. Big trouble. Lane knew it instantly. Johnny was a mechanical wizard. Machines became nearly transparent in his presence. In no time at all, the lock was sprung, the door was open, and Johnny was inside.

"Come on, chickenshit," he called out to Lane. "Check it out."

After a cautionary glance up at the house and driveway, Lane stepped into the structure's dim recesses. The craft floated pointing toward the shore, and Johnny was already in the stern, reaching out over the motor. Lane heard sliding wood as the front doors opened to a great blast of marine light. "Now, that's a little better, isn't it?" Johnny said.

And indeed it was. The polished varnish on the mahogany topside caught the gleam of summer sky and dazzled Lane's young eyes.

Johnny climbed forward, plunked himself down in the driver's seat, and looked up at Lane with a febrile smile.

"So let's take her out."

"What?"

"I said, let's take her out."

"Are you fucking crazy?"

"Don't think so, bro." Johnny leaned over to examine the little panel on the dash where the ignition key went.

"I'm outta here," Lane declared.

"Okay then, you're outta here." Johnny had already pulled a few wires down from under the panel.

"You're on your own, dickhead. You're very seriously on your own," Lane said, and spun and stalked out the door. He made his way to the stairs leading up to the yard.

Just then, he heard the monstrous engine fire up.

The boat came into view, with Johnny standing at the wheel. He maneuvered the craft over to the dock's edge, where he looked up at Lane with supreme confidence and conviction.

"Just a quick spin. That's all. Then we can say we did it." He paused. "Or maybe you just want to remember how you sweated over the lawn mower, like a good little boy."

It wasn't the taunt that tore at Lane. It wasn't the transparent manipulation. It was the thought of abandoning his brother in this moment of supreme recklessness. He simply couldn't do it. From the dock, he stepped down into the rear compartment and worked his way up to the passenger seat.

Johnny said nothing. The engine murmured in a low hum and burble as he rotated the boat toward the center of the bay. He stood with one hand on the rim of the windshield and the other on the wheel, and looked straight ahead. His head once again fell into that birdlike thrust to a rhythm of some unknown internal origin.

Soon they were entering the bay's mouth, where the water turned from green to blue and the waves went from modest ripples to the whitecaps of the open waters of Puget Sound.

"Hang on," Johnny commanded from where he stood. He took his hand off the windshield and shoved the throttle all the way forward. The motor spun up to an angry howl.

Lane felt the surge as the bow lifted and the acceleration shoved him back into the seat. The waterline disappeared and only sky remained.

"Yes!" Johnny shouted as he held the windshield's rim to steady himself.

The boat picked up speed at an alarming rate. The bow settled back down to reveal the choppy water, all blue and gray and white with waves.

Bam! The hull smacked a wave crest and shuddered as it sailed high in the water.

"Yes!" Johnny screamed. The wind tossed his hair back.

Bam! The hull smacked another wave crest. Spray flew. Lane felt the mist on his face.

"Yes!" Johnny screamed. He made no attempt to ease the throttle back. The motor roared like a cornered beast.

Bam! The hull smacked yet another crest. This time, they nearly went airborne. Lane knew he had to act. Sooner or later, they were going to lose it. He shot his hand out to pull the throttle lever back.

Johnny caught Lane's move out of the corner of his eye. "No!" he yelled and reached down to stop Lane's hand.

At that moment, he took his eyes off their forward motion and unintentionally pulled the wheel to the left.

Bam! The hull caught the white cap just as the boat veered to the port side.

Lane instinctively held on to the lip of the topside to secure himself against the violent twisting and rocking. The boat nearly flipped and came down hard. Lane reached out, grabbed the throttle lever and pulled it all the way back. The engine descended to a low growl and the craft quickly lost headway.

But Johnny was gone. Only the empty seat and gently oscillating steering wheel remained.

Lane looked up and fought panic as he took his bearings. The boat pointed toward the shore north of the sand spit. He turned and scanned the water to his left rear, toward the mouth of the bay.

And there he was. Just a dot on the rolling waves, a pitifully small dot in an ocean of trouble. "Stay right there! I'm coming!" Lane screamed. He crossed to the driver's side, spun the wheel to port, and thought about the cold as he closed the distance. The stunning, numbing, paralyzing cold of the waters of Puget Sound. Johnny might already be slipping into shock.

At ten yards out, he saw that his brother's jaw was already shuddering as he trod water. "Are you okay?" he yelled. Johnny only nodded. A bad sign.

Lane had to be careful. He had no experience controlling the boat, and he'd lose precious time if he overshot. He lined the boat up to intercept Johnny on the starboard side and pulled the throttle all the way back. He desperately scanned the craft's interior. No ropes, no life jackets, nothing of any use.

Johnny was coming up fast. He had to act. In a moment of blind inspiration, he leaned over the edge and locked his left leg into the spoke and column of the steering wheel. His arms reached the water just as Johnny came sliding slowly along the side of the hull. He plunged his hands into the freezing water, shot them under Johnny's armpits, and clasped them together on his brother's chest.

"I'm cold," Johnny declared softly. "Jesus, I'm cold."

"I know you're cold," Lane said. "But you gotta help me. I'm going to twist you around, and you have to reach up and grab the side. You got that?"

"I'm cold," Johnny repeated. "I'm really cold."

"Yeah, if you don't do what I just told you, you're also going to be dead. Here we go." Lane twisted his torso as far as he could without losing his foot lock through the steering wheel. "Do it."

His nose was just inches from the back of Johnny's head. His brother's arms remained limp in his grasp. "Do it!"

Johnny's right arm came up, grabbed the topside, and held fast.

From that point on, it was a clumsy struggle, but a manageable one. The boat tipped to port under their combined weight, but that made Johnny's crawl to safety somewhat easier. Once he tumbled into the interior, they both sank into mute exhaustion.

The big outboard engine burbled along merrily at idle, as if nothing had happened.

Lane blew up halfway back to the boathouse. "What the fuck did you do that for? What the fuck were you thinking? You didn't know shit about this boat, and you took off like a fucking maniac! What the hell were you thinking? Are you crazy? What's going on with you?"

The answer would play out over the years to come. The euphoric highs, the paralyzing lows. But not today. Johnny's eyes gleamed and he went into that avian thrust with his head.

"I'm fine. I'm even finer than fine."

They reached the boathouse with Lane at the wheel. They both surveyed the Simmons house and driveway up above, but it looked clear. Lane sighed. It was their first break since this whole horrible business started. He gingerly maneuvered in through the open doors, which Johnny closed while Lane secured the boat to the mooring cleats. They climbed out into the semidarkness broken only by the softly lapping water. Lane led the way outside onto the dock, and Johnny stopped to secure the padlock. "Just like new," he said, as if that somehow fixed everything. Lane refrained from comment. They started down the dock.

They were a couple of paces from the end when Old Man Simmons stepped out from behind the back of the boathouse.

They froze in terror. Simmons wore his perennial Hawaiian shirt, with a pattern resembling burning embers fanned by a breeze from the depths of hell. His burly arms hung in a cloud of gray hair and his pale eyes bore down on them with no trace of compassion, empathy, or pity. He let the silence nearly suffocate them before he spoke in a snarly rasp.

"You're gonna do exactly what I tell you."

Exactly what ripped three weeks out of their late adolescence. Under the sun of late summer, they chipped, scraped, sanded, and painted the boathouse and then put on a new roof, one shingle at a time. Their parents thought it was a paying job, but of course it was nothing of the sort. They served as a de facto work crew on a penal site that was also the scene of the crime.

They seldom spoke during the exercise. Hours would pass without a word. Johnny threw himself into the work. His brush glided back and forth with an incessant rhythm. His head would begin to bob in time with the brush strokes.

Lane consoled himself with an internal justice. His rescue of Johnny absolved him of any guilt. Had he not gone along, his brother would most likely have drowned. Sometimes, he paused and looked over at the beachfront next door, the site of their cabin. It had just been sold, to someone from a software start-up that had just gone public, someone looking for a little timeless charm.

The pilings of the old dock marched out, one pair at a time, into the chilly waters. A white encrustation of barnacles marked the high-water point on their circumference.

The planking they once supported had vanished entirely.

In Johnny's lab, Lane scans the rest of the cubicle wall. No other artifacts of humanity. No kids, dogs, girlfriends, wives, uncles, or buddies. Only charts, diagrams, spreadsheet printouts, and presentation graphics. One of the graphics catches his eye, the only comprehensible document of the bunch. It's the first slide of a progress report of some kind, and it addresses the Institute for the Study of Genetic Disorders. It includes six bullet points that delve into technical arcana. Lane moves closer and checks the date in the slide's bottom right corner. It's only a few weeks old. It appears that the Institute holds Johnny's current research contract, and that he's giving them an update.

Lane had never paid much attention to the organizations that Johnny worked with. They came and went, and after a while he'd lost track. Bio this and bio that. Lots of gens and more than a few zymes. But, obviously, this one deserves a closer look.

He looks at the photo again, at the beach and sky. Both boys seem so happy. Could he ever be that happy again? He removes the picture, puts it in his pocket, and leaves.

"I had a hit today on one of your plane victims."

"Really? Which one?"

"Anslow. John Anslow."

"And who was asking?"

"His brother, Lane Anslow. He's a contract cop. I couldn't just blow him off."

"I understand. So tell me this: Have you managed to identify Dr. Anslow's remains?"

"It's a real mess out here, Mr. Khan. I doubt that we'll ever identify Dr. Anslow."

"That's too bad. I'm sure you're doing your professional best."

"Yes, we are."

"And I'm sure you will continue to do your professional best."

"Absolutely. You can count on it."

"Well, good-bye then." Arjun hangs up. So now they may have a competitor in their search for Dr. John Anslow. But the incident seems a minor nuisance compared to what he sees on the CT scan up on the big display on his office wall. The cancer has metastasized. He's not a radiologist, but his powers of professional observation are extremely keen, built up over many years in the medical industry. The originating tumor is plainly visible in the left lung, and now new growths have popped up in the opposite lung, the colon, and various lymph nodes.

Arjun is Hindu, if anything at all. The tumors could be construed as the forces of the god Yama, who prepares to command them in a final assault. He gets up from his desk and looks down the long corridor at the numbered doors of the subject bays.

Yama, the lord of death, will soon pay a deadly and unexpected visit to this place.

. . .

Harlan Green is an asshole. Harlan Green is a job.

Rachel Heinz idly speculates on the relationship between these two facts as she sprawls on the couch in her apartment and cycles through the Feed looking for political news, however slanted, corrupted, or misdirected it may be. Like most political professionals, she is once and always a political junkie as well. She watches politicians from local council members to the president of the United States with the same practiced eye. She compulsively analyzes their words, delivery, gestures, messaging, and subtext. She always spots the flaws and the fixes, regardless of ideology.

In some ways, the Street Party is an ideal home for Rachel because she grew up very close to the street. Her adolescence featured a long-gone dad and alcoholic mother. But while other disadvantaged girls turned to sex as a weapon, she saw a much larger battlefield. Politics was power writ large, and she intuitively understood this. She stayed in school, she worked on campaigns, she studied the issues, and she came to understand the intricate web of relationships that formed the essence of the political milieu. But she kept her personal ambitions to herself: First, a seat on the city council, then state rep, then the U.S. Congress. Then, who knew what?

But before college, the incident intervened. She knew she needed a degree, but had no financial aid. With student loans already a relic of the distant past, she worked long hours while pursuing a degree in political science. If she excelled, maybe she had a shot at a grant and an advanced degree. But employment was hard to come by for a young woman with no social leverage, and she had to take whatever she could get. She wound up working nights as a "model," where she performed for men of means who peeped in at her through a small glass window. Then, one night, the police showed up. Someone hadn't paid off someone, and the place was going down, and Rachel's dreams of higher office along with it. She served no time, but it didn't matter. The conviction was there, waiting for any inquisitive future journalists to dig up and fling out over the Feed.

She finished school and decided to stay in the game, even if she had to play from the sidelines. She started as an intern on the mayor's staff and quickly ascended. Then along came Harlan and the Street Party. She recognized his potential long before others did. Working with him gave her a shot at the national stage. She quickly signed on.

While Harlan's politics didn't quite synchronize with hers, they were close enough. And she resonated with his personal ascendancy from the lower strata of American life. Still, she was immune to his charisma, and he seemed to value her distance. A sycophantic chief of staff was a liability.

The early days were the good days, but now they were long gone. As Harlan gradually consolidated his power, he had canonized himself. He became a higher court, a court of no appeal. He was astute enough to conceal this monstrous conceit from his followers, but in private, the symptoms were all too apparent. History had witnessed them countless times in others of his disposition. Angry outbursts, paranoia, insufferable vanity, and capricious cruelty.

She sighs and shifts her weight on the couch. A window pops up on top of the Feed and interrupts her rumination. It's from the security camera down in the lobby.

"Johnny! What are you doing here?"

"I look pretty good for someone who's dead, don't you think?"

In fact, he looks pretty awful. "What happened to you?"

"Hard to say. Why don't you buzz me up and we'll talk about it?"

When she lets him in, he looks like he's just climbed out of the plane wreck. Dirty clothes, stringy hair, smudged face and hands.

"Wow," she exclaims. "You want to get cleaned up?"

"Later," he says as he plops down into an easy chair. "Right now, a deal has to be made."

"A deal? What kind of deal?"

He reaches into his shirt, produces the card from his discarded handheld, and hands it to her. "Take a look at this. It'll be the first clip to come up."

She picks up her phone off the end table, inserts the card, and starts the video. It shows a thing, an awful monstrosity pulsating in the back of what appears to be a van. Half young, half fantastically old. The only motion seems to be some kind of respiration, with yellow bubbles forming around the nose and mouth.

"Oh Jesus! What is this?"

"Let me have the card back and we can talk."

"This is sick, really sick," she says as she hands the card back.

"And it's only the opening act. You know, I don't follow politics too closely, but I do know a bit about your boss. It seems that he's made Mount Tabor a symbol of sorts, a place where big corporations do evil things behind closed doors. And you know what? Turns out he's right. What a lucky guy!"

"That creature on the video came from Mount Tabor?"

"I've played all the cards I'm going to without talking to Mr. Green himself. The deal is simple. I'll trade Mount Tabor for personal protection of the highest order."

"I don't know. I'll have to see what I can do. By the way, your brother's looking for you. He's really worried. You need to let him know you're okay."

"He doesn't need to know anything about this, at least, not for now. I can handle this by myself. Keep Lane out of it. Completely. If he gets wind of it, the deal's off."

Rachel shrugs. "Your call." He reminds her of a surfer who's cleared the crest of a big wave and started the long ride down.

9.

THE GIG IS UP

At police headquarters, Lane hunches over a computer in a vacant office, one of many such vacancies brought on by ever-shrinking budgets. The buzz of random conversation floats in from outside as he types, points and clicks. Whoever's behind Johnny's disappearance might be onto him already. He's Johnny's only family, the only interested party, and a cop to boot. But they can't trace him to this particular machine, which is more or less public property. Besides, it gives him a free ride to the higher access levels of the Meternet.

It takes him no time at all to run down the Institute for the Study of Genetic Disorders. It has an impeccable provenance and credentials, along with nicely crafted text that explains its mission and goals. Since the majority of the mutation-triggered diseases strike in childhood and claim their victims at a tragically early age, the Institute's mission is to put a stop to this, once and for all. It funds and coordinates a variety of research efforts in the search for a comprehensive cure. The site lists the executive staff, which is led by a CEO named Linda Crampton. Her photo shows a mature but attractive woman with a slightly showy hairstyle and clever eyes.

Lane leans back. So much for the management, what about the funding? Where's the money? No mention. Then he sees a link that leads to press releases, and he follows it. He finds no money but he does find Johnny. A release from eighteen months ago announces Johnny's latest research contract, with its emphasis on the computerized simulation of genetic action in human development. Beyond that, it makes little sense. Lane suspects the PR people had little idea what they were talking about and blew several paragraphs of thick smoke.

He moves on and finds no more on his brother. But he uncovers two other releases in the same time frame that announce major research contracts. One is to a principal investigator named Dr. Martin Griffen, and the other to a Dr. Juan Ortiz. Both specialize in areas too esoteric to make any sense within the confines of a press release.

Griffen and Ortiz. Two more big players in the science sweepstakes sponsored by the Institute. What if they were part of the big deal, the trip to New York? Lane grabs his cell and punches in Bellows at the Washington County coroner.

"Yes, Mr. Anslow," Bellows says with transparent impatience.

"I'm sorry to bother you again, but I should have asked about my brother's associates, Griffen and Ortiz. They're both friends of the family. Have you managed an ID on either of them?"

"No, we have not. And as I told you about your brother, it's unlikely that we ever will. Is there anything else?"

"No, that'll do it. Thanks."

Lane pockets his phone and smiles. Bellows just gave away the store without even knowing it.

"Lane, they told me I'd find you in here." Lieutenant Siefert comes in and plops down in a chair on the other side of the desk. "What are you working on?"

"I'm not sure. I'll let you know when I know. How's that?"

"That's great." Siefert scratches the scruffy brown fringe wrapped around his bald head. "But there's something else we gotta talk about. As of now, you're off the active contractors' list. No more gigs."

"And why's that?" Lane doesn't want to feel sick, but he does.

"You know why. You're too old. We've already bent the rules for you, and if we bend them any further, they're gonna break."

"Okay then, just tell me one thing. Did you think this up all by yourself, or did somebody whisper in your ear?"

Siefert manages a sad smile. "I know you'd like to think it's some kind of plot, but it's not. Sorry. It's quite simple. You're too damn old to be running around the Middle East mixing it up with Bad Boys half your age. End of story."

"Yeah, end of story."

"You've done good work. We can do letters of commendation. You can get a consulting gig."

"Sure."

Siefert gets up and heads for the door. "Keep in touch, okay?"

Lane doesn't bother answering.

Lane doesn't go home. It feels better to be immersed in the hustle of the city. He drifts down to a little joint on the river and orders a straight whiskey. In one of the booths, a young woman beams and giggles at her clueless boyfriend. In another, a fat guy lays waste to a cheeseburger. He washes it down with beer straight from the pitcher.

Lane sits at the bar, where the Feed drones on about oil prices topping a thousand dollars a barrel. He pulls out his cell and checks his bank account. He has enough for maybe six weeks. Then, the street.

Or the Bird. Undoubtedly, the Bird would pay well. Lane might even be able to get behind a gate somewhere.

He takes a gulp of whiskey and feels its buttery burn on the way down. All he'd have to do to earn his keep was whatever the Bird told him. Impossible.

Time for a distraction. He pulls out his cell and connects with Rachel Heinz at the Street Party.

"How are you, Mr. Anslow?" She comes across cool and confident, like she's won the race before it's even run. He has to admire that.

"About the same. I'm just following up on our agreement to share. Anything new?"

"Nothing new."

He catches it. In the shape of the words. The micro-changes in pitch. The slight shift in accent. She's an excellent liar. He has to admire that, also. Still, this isn't the time for a confrontation. "You'll keep in touch, right?"

"I most certainly will."

"Later, then."

"Later."

He disconnects and takes another gulp of whiskey. He'd bet everything that she was covering up.

Unfortunately, his everything was now next to nothing.

Rachel puts down her phone and leans back. Outside her office, the clerical buzz drones on relentlessly. She breathes deeply and lets it wash over her as she struggles to absorb her feelings.

She doesn't regret deceiving Lane. After all, she'd already promised Johnny that she'd keep Lane in the dark and she meant to honor that commitment. It had left her no choice but to lie. That wasn't the cause of the queasy feeling in her stomach. The cause was Lane himself. He had a kind of moral certainty about him, but not in the smug, righteous way you'd expect from a cop. Instead, it sprung from an almost complete absence of guile. It seemed ironic that someone like him would have this quality. It also made him more attractive than she wanted to think about.

She stares at her hands, those of a woman in her later thirties. A slight freckling of the flesh, a modest yet growing presence of veins and tendons. Once there had been boyfriends, relationships, suitors; but they had thinned over the years and now had vanished completely. She feels no sorrow over their absence, no regret. She's transmuted the output of her libido into fuel for her job, and it's paying off handsomely. She's an integral part of an organization that's poised to assume the national stage.

Still, she can feel the subtle yet insistent tug of the man, like an undertow at the beach that washes the sand from between your toes, but leaves you upright and still anchored to the shore.

She smiles to herself now that she's confronted the fact of the matter. It's definitely manageable. At least, for now.

The South War Front they call it. A tight cluster of high-rises situated on ten blocks along the west bank of the Willamette River, Portland's principal waterway. Great shells of tinted glass and treated steel thrusting a dozen or more stories above the pavement. Once a bold adventure in upscale urban residency, it was a concentrated haven of upper midrange prosperity, with concrete caverns housing Hummers, Escalades and BMWs.

It was the South Waterfront back then, several decades ago, in the time before the trouble. But then came the ballistic assault from Ross Island, a thickly wooded stretch of land about a mile long in mid-river. The island's west shore sat only 200 yards across the river channel from the front row of luxury residences.

The first barrage came in the wee hours of a moonless summer night. Stones the size of grapefruits crashed at murderous velocity though windows on the sides of the buildings nearest the water. They lodged in walls, mirrors, side servers, couches, and floors of the finest natural woods. They shredded Persian carpets, cratered granite countertops, and atomized glass coffee tables. They launched a fog of crystalline shrapnel that penetrated deep into the psyches of those within.

In the morning, the police combed the island's dense forestation and found nothing, until a forensics team noticed bands of stripped bark on two adjacent trees ten feet up their trunks. About fifteen feet back, more banding was found on the trunk of a third tree.

A slingshot. A winch-powered slingshot. The details didn't matter. Only the damage.

The residents across the river found no consolation in this discovery as they contacted their insurance adjusters. The police responded with nightly boat patrols. Their focused beams raked the tree-studded shore and revealed nothing of interest.

The media speculated at length on the attackers' identity. An unaffiliated gang. A rogue splinter of the Street Party. A lone madman with advanced engineering skills. An enormous extortion plot.

The months rolled by. The beams relentlessly scanned the shore, draining the city's public safety budget. The media lost interest. The patrols wound down.

Then it happened again. With increased elevation, range, volume, and accuracy. The original fusillade had reached only the fourth floor of the affected structures. This one went up a full dozen and shattered nearly two thirds of the windows in each of the half dozen buildings.

Come morning, police found tree marks suggesting three separate weapons of even larger scale than before.

Boat patrols now circumnavigated the entire island on a continuous basis to deny the attackers a beachhead. Residents who were renting moved out. Those who owned saw their investments in mortal jeopardy and screamed for more action.

And they soon got it. A nighttime patrol vessel cruising the east channel took a nasty hit in the stern that extinguished the engine and left the boat dead in the water. A second rock screamed a few feet over the occupants' heads and splashed a few off the port side.

The patrol boats were obviously defenseless against shore fire coming from the mainland east side. The true gravity of the situation quickly sank in. An operation to occupy the river's east shoreline was out of the question. The city had neither the money nor the manpower.

Then the police union weighed in. Their members were being subjected to unreasonable danger on a long-term basis. They would no longer patrol.

The attackers waited a week and then took out the remaining windows in a spectacular display of marksmanship. Insurance coverage collapsed due to exclusions for civil disorders. Vacancies rose far above sustainable levels and the buildings quickly went bankrupt. By the following summer, they were all but deserted, creating an economic malady that rapidly infected the remaining buildings.

The South War Front was born, and a new class of residents arrived, those paying rock-bottom rents out of minimum wages.

And on this night along the War Front, Rachel Heinz and Harlan Green sit in the back of an armored SUV parked on the far side of the streetcar tracks. She looks up at the sparsely populated matrix of lit windows in the nearest building. Johnny's most likely taken refuge up there, in one of the vacated units on the upper floors facing the river. One with a shattered glass front open to the elements, with mildewed carpeting and warped wooden floors.

But right now he's directly across the street in a shabby bar right off the streetcar line, their designated meeting place. The bar's front door opens and someone nods at them.

"Okay, he's in there," Rachel says. "Shall we go?"

"This better be good," Green intones as he reaches for the door handle. "I'm up way past my bedtime." An inside joke. In fact, he sleeps only a few hours each night.

"You checked out his credentials?" Green asks as they pass beneath a pallid neon sign that names the bar.

"I did. Dr. John Anslow's exactly who he says he is." She omits the fact that they had a romantic history.

Inside, postindustrial décor dominates. Buffed cement floors. A concrete slab for the bar. Minimal indirect lighting. Maybe a dozen tables of chrome and clear plastic. All pointing back to a time closer to the zenith of the empire.

Rachel scans the occupants. Nine men and two women randomly seated, nursing drinks. How many were Harlan's security people? The Street Party org chart adheres to a pattern of ancient origin. All the staff report to Green through her – except the palace guard, which reports directly to Harlan.

She spots several pairs of dead pitiless eyes and has a pretty good idea who's who. They come to Harlan through the Bird, an individual she'd just as soon forget. Populism has always had its dark side, like Huey Long's state troopers, and you just had to accept that it came with territory.

She spots Johnny, sitting alone in the rear, idly watching their arrival. He doesn't bother to stand when they sit down, an omission that undoubtedly rankles Green, although he doesn't show it.

"So, Mr. Anslow, maybe you can explain to me what I'm doing here at this hour."

"Rachel's told you what I've got on video, right?" Johnny asks Harlan.

Green nods silently.

"I don't follow politics much," Johnny declares. "But I do know that you have a thing against Mount Tabor. It seems to be kind of a big deal with you."

Like celebrities of all stripes, Harlan Green seems scaled down when encountered close up. He appears about Johnny's age, a man of medium height with blue eyes and short-cropped, sandy hair. He could easily be a checkout clerk, your car mechanic or insurance agent. Just a guy trying to get by.

Until he speaks, that is. No matter what he says, there is an overtone of utter certitude, a sense of absolute purpose.

"There was a time, Mr. Anslow, when Mount Tabor was a city park. Unfortunately, that's a time long gone. It's become a place of fortified wealth and power, owned by an anonymous multinational corporation. It looks out over the ruins of what were once good neighborhoods, neighborhoods now infected with periodic gunfire after dark."

Green leans in closer. "So, Mr. Anslow, you shouldn't be surprised if you see some of our people picketing the place. It's become a metaphor for everything that's gone wrong in this country."

Johnny glances at Rachel and settles back on Green. "I need to talk to you privately. Just you."

"And why is that?"

"It's confidential. You'll understand when I tell you."

Rachel fights the urge to lash out. What the fuck is he doing? Harlan wouldn't even be here except for her.

Green looks at Rachel, then Johnny. "Five minutes, Mr. Anslow. You've got five minutes. And they'd better be very productive." He turns to Rachel. "Would that be all right with you, Rachel?"

As if she had any choice. "Five minutes," she reiterates as she caps her rage and stands to leave.

"Thank you," Green says. As if he actually meant it.

Rachel leaves the water faucet on in the ladies' restroom as she stares into the mirror. She'd heard that running water had a calming effect. Something about positive ions. Good. Right now she felt anything but positive.

It wasn't always this way. Early on, Harlan constantly sought her counsel and trusted her judgment. But now he's disappearing into the mist of some Olympian peak of his own making. She can no longer trust him. The Street Party can no longer trust him. Already, she's had a number of circumspect discussions with others in the organization about this issue. And they've sent signals of concern, heavily coded, of course.

She senses something's wrong the moment she leaves the ladies' room and turns the corner back into the bar. Sure enough, Johnny's no longer at the table with Green, who casually sips a glass of beer.

Maybe he's in the restroom, she hopes. Maybe not. She strides over to their table and sits across from Green. "Where'd he go?"

"He left."

"What do you mean, he left?"

"I didn't buy his story, so he got pissed and lit out. The guy's obviously a flake."

"Did he show you the video?"

Green puts on a patronizing smile. "Anybody with a bucket of plastic goo and a little makeup could've made that." He chuckles. "He's your perfect mad scientist. Right out of central casting."

"And so what was his story, the one that didn't wash?"

Green stands to leave with an irritated look. "It doesn't even bear repeating. Let's go. We've burned enough time on this already."

Rachel moves to protest but checks herself. It won't do any good. It's all wrong. She can feel it. Her suspicion is confirmed on the way out. All but two of the security people have already left, a glaring breach in normal protocol. Where did they go?

The alarm signal burrows mercilessly into the center of Lane's somnolent brain, right through the residual alcoholic stupor. When he'd gotten home, he'd finished what he started in the bar downtown. Why not? He had all the next day to sleep it off. And the day after that, and so on, until all his funds were exhausted.

He rolls over and squints at the security screen on his alarm clock. Rachel Heinz. What the hell? He checks the time. 1:30 p.m. He puts her on audio. "Yeah?"

"I'm downstairs."

"Obviously."

"We need to share, just like you said."

"I'm not in a generous mood right now."

"It doesn't matter."

"Call me in the morning, okay? But not too early."

"I saw Johnny today."

Lane sits straight up. "Where?"

"Right now, we're being digitized for posterity, don't you think?"

"Yeah." She's right. His building's security system is recording this entire transaction. "I'll card you on up."

By the time he lets her in, he's risen to a slow simmer. "You knew when I called you, didn't you? Why didn't you tell me?"

She remains perfectly composed. He has to admire that. No bullying allowed. "Why don't you ask me to sit down?" she says. "And while you're at it, why don't you ask me if I'd like something to drink?"

He exhales deeply. "Right. Have a seat. What would you like?"

"Nothing right now. Maybe later."

"Okay, now what about my brother? How come you put me off?"

"Because he insisted that I don't tell you. Just like you're insisting that I do tell you. So which master am I supposed to serve?"

He looks away from her and out over the years gone by. "Easy. The one that still has all his wheels on the tracks."

"Okay then. He showed up at my place last night, a real mess. He wanted to cut a deal with Harlan, a sort of quid pro quo."

"And who got what?"

"He said he knew what was going on over on Mount Tabor. He showed me a video. It was hideous. A badly deformed thing that might have been human, but you couldn't be sure. In exchange, he wanted the Street Party to give him protection on a permanent basis."

"Protection from whom?"

"He wouldn't say. He wanted to deal directly with Harlan. He stayed at my place long enough to get cleaned up a little and left. I set up a meeting, but it didn't come off like I thought it would. The two of them cut me out of the deck. Completely. I left the table for a few minutes, and when I got back, Johnny was already gone. Harlan claimed he stormed out because Harlan didn't believe his story, but I don't think that's what happened. I think they cut a deal, and Harlan had him leave with some of our security people."

"So Harlan didn't tell you what the deal was?"

She sighs. "You know, there was a time when I trusted him. Biggest mistake of my professional life."

"And now?"

"And now you and I suddenly have a lot of overlapping interests. I want to know what the deal was that Harlan covered up. And you want to know what kind of jam Johnny is in and how you can help him. In either case, we need to find out what's going on up on Mount Tabor."

"And when you do find out, what happens to Harlan Green?" Lane asks.

She lapses into a moment of icy silence. "I'm going to assume that you never asked any such thing."

"So be it. Now let's try and line all this stuff up and see what we've got."

"He showed up at my place with the horrible video and said he knew the truth about Mount Tabor and wanted to make a deal. Then he and Harlan pulled the disappearing act. I think Johnny told him something pretty extraordinary."

"What makes you say that?"

"Harlan's slick and calculating. His disappearing-scientist story was way too clumsy. He had to improvise on the fly. So anyway, where does that leave us?"

"On one side, we have the video and Mount Tabor," Lane replies. "On the other, we have Johnny's research and the Institute for the Study of Genetic Disorders. What we don't have is the connection between them."

"And how do we go about getting that, Mr. Policeman?"

"Money."

"Money?"

"Are you in a position to dig around in the Street Party coffers and free up some funds?"

"I suppose so. What for?"

"I'm currently unemployed. I need you to keep me afloat until we get to the bottom of this."

"I think we can handle that. I mean, really, much does a cop make?"

For the first time, Lane manages a grin.

"Not much."

Johnny can visualize the intricate structure of the molecules. They're extracted from the hemlock plant and delivered in a dosage of about 100 milligrams, just enough to disable his neuromuscular junctions without killing him.

It wasn't supposed to be like this. It wasn't what Green had promised; it wasn't sanctuary. It was imprisonment, confinement of the most hideous kind. It had started with some kind of intramuscular injection as soon they had him in the vehicle outside the bar. Then a drive through the night, followed by the hemlock.

So now he lies here on his back in the dark, completely paralyzed. Only the sullen hiss of respirator breaks the silence as it forces air down the tube in his throat and into his utterly passive lungs. And that's the genius of it. He's incapacitated in the most profound manner possible, hovering a single degree above death. Only the respirator keeps him alive. No restraints or guards required.

A grand parade of paranoiac scenarios strut their stuff before his prostrate form. A power failure triggers asphyxiation and he dies eyes wide open. A warped medical team performs a vivisection and he can't even scream. A rodent chews on his motionless extremities and he can only endure.

So why were they keeping him alive? Like a fool, Johnny had told Green all about Mount Tabor, about the stunning breakthroughs. He now realizes that he lost all his bargaining capacity in the process.

The throw of a switch. A shower of fluorescence. Twin tubes of fuzzy illumination hanging from the ceiling. His eyes won't focus. Only his ears hold a hard edge.

"Don't bother to get up," a deep male voice says with ironic pleasantry. "I just thought I'd check in and see how you're doing."

The owner of the voice avoids Johnny's cone of vision.

"Ah yes. I dare say you've looked better."

The voice comes from his right and not far off. Johnny strains to identify it, but fails. A stranger.

"Say, what's this?"

A switch flips. The respirator stops. A terrible silence sets in.

From deep within Johnny's limbic recesses, alarms begin to scream. Respiration has ceased. Asphyxiation has begun. The screams beget echoes, and the echoes spawn yet more echoes.

The respirator comes back on. "Whoops. I never was very good with gadgets."

Johnny can feel a cool mist of sweat crawl across his face.

The lights go out. A door shuts. A lock clicks. Then a second lock.

"Now, tell me again why we're doing this," the Bird demands as he comes down the hall of the safe house near Street Party headquarters. "Why not a little duct tape and some plastic handcuffs? This is a real pain in the ass."

"He's a very clever fellow," Green answers. "I don't want to take any chances."

"So why did you grab him?"

"He posed a problem, and I need some time to figure out a solution." Green fails to mention that part of the problem is that Dr. Anslow might share what he knows with people like the Bird in an effort to negotiate his release. The hemlock treatment eliminates this possibility.

The Bird shrugs in resignation. "Well, the sooner he's gone, the better. Good night."

"Good night." Green watches the Bird walk out the door. The man is a real annoyance, but a necessary one. Not permanently, however. Because time may now be on Green's side in ways he'd never even considered.

10.

WARHEAD

He doesn't just bury the past. He cremates it. The memories, the re-countings, the recollections never have a chance to fester and molder. They become ashes, anonymous dust. Like they never had any form or substance at all.

Rachel marvels repeatedly at Green's ability to pull this trick out of his political hat, only this time the trick is on her. They sit opposite each other at the meeting table in his office, where the morning sun casts brilliant stripes of light through the blinds. They discuss his upcoming schedule, just as if they'd never been to the South War Front or seen Johnny's horrific video or listened to his proposition.

"So what's up?" he asks cheerfully.

"Tomorrow, you're back on the road. You have the rally out at the Expo Center this afternoon, and then we have you in transit the next day, then in Cincinnati, then Cleveland."

"Cleveland? Aren't we going to do something with the Healing Group while I'm there?"

"Yes, we are. You're out in a Zero Zone for a couple of hours before you go to the stadium. We'll do it right in front of their offices."

"Good. We need to do more of this kind of thing. I need to start building a credibility base when it comes to foreign policy and international relations."

Rachel nods. The Healing Group is the Chinese equivalent of the old U.S. Peace Corps. They work in areas of the United States and Europe where all employment outside the service sector has fallen to zero and stayed there. The so-called Zero Zones, where a lucky few wait on tables and everyone else wallows somewhere below subsistence level.

"And what do we have after that?"

Rachel consults her laptop. "We have maybe a half dozen other events under development, but not completely firmed up yet."

"Good. I want you to send me the dates. We may have to plan around them. If everything works out, I just might take a little time off."

Rachel goes to full alert. Green has never taken any time off, never.

Green offers an amused smile. He's a master at reading people, and she's no exception. "You look a little shocked."

"I don't ever remember you doing anything like this."

"And that's exactly why it's a good idea," Green says as he heads out the door.

She pushes back from her laptop. He's giving himself room to move. He's formulating some kind of contingency plan.

Whatever Johnny told him in the bar last night has put an invisible set of gears in motion. But what are they grinding toward?

"So this is it. Right?" asks Lieutenant James Siefert as he types a password into the computer in an isolated cubicle within the Portland Police Headquarters. He's clearly not happy with the deal.

"This is it," Lane promises.

"We're even."

"We're even," Lane assures him.

"After this, you're on your own."

Lane nods to Lieutenant James Siefert of the Portland Police Department. "I'm on my own."

Siefert gets up and looks at his watch as Lane slides into the chair. "You have ten minutes," he tells Lane. "And remember, you can only leave with what's in your head. No notes. No storage devices. If you try, you're dead meat from here to DC."

"Got it."

"See you then."

Lane looks at the screen, which displays the portal for the National Security Database, or NSD. No one hides from the NSD. If you're not in here, you're either dead or well on the way.

Lane already knows where he wants to go. There's no use trying from the Mount Tabor end. He doesn't have names or a company. The Institute for the Study of Genetic Disorders is a different matter. The board members and top layer of management are all publicly available and he'd memorized their names before coming here. So now it's time to get personal. Where do these people live? How do they relate to one another?

Five minutes later, he has a commonality: Pinecrest, a gated community south of the city, with a Class 10 security rating. Lane uses the remaining five minutes to snoop around to some of the other major biotech players up at the Medplex. Sure enough, Pinecrest keeps popping up.

He leans back. All these people see one another at the same grocery store, the same cocktail parties, the same golf course and pool. Such is the insular nature of living behind a gate. It's a dangerous pain in the ass to leave and go anywhere else during your free time.

"Time's up. Get what you need?" Lane turns. Siefert. Right on schedule.

Lane nods. "Got it."

Thomas Zed sits at the counter in the bathroom of his private quarters, his stomach ablaze with indigestion. He shakes a bottle filled with a prescribed fluid and takes three teaspoons. In the mirror he beholds a shrunken figure with a buzzard neck and eroded head poking out of a silk bathrobe. His face records the history of a series of losing battles against extreme old age, the skin etched with tiny trenches, foxholes and craters.

Some years back, the most critical battle had come to a disastrous end. The third clone, the last one, was stillborn, just like the others. An entire warehouse of nearly priceless replacement parts gone forever.

At first, the clone solution had seemed so promising. Young, healthy organs with no rejection problems. He was pushing one hundred ten when the technology first became feasible, and he wasted no time. All three clones were implanted in the same time frame, one in the United

States, one in Europe, and one in South America. The surrogate mothers who lent their wombs to the effort were generously compensated and agreed to surrender the babies at birth.

The gamble was clear. The organs would not be usable until the clones reached their middle teens, and by then, Zed would be pushing the limits of human survival. But for a man in his position, it was relatively cheap insurance.

But time wasn't the only gamble. There was another scientific question that was almost completely overlooked during the original furor over the human potential of cloning.

The general principle of cloning seemed simple enough. You first conditioned a cell from the donor so that its replication cycle was synchronized with a receiving embryo, from which you removed the existing genes. You then inserted the donor's genes, and let the embryo begin the billions of divisions that would turn it into an exact physical copy of the donor. A parasitic ride on the genetic expressway to fully formed life.

But in practice, it wasn't quite that simple. One basic assumption was that the DNA strand one starts with in the embryo remains precisely the same through every division on the way to producing a fully formed infant. Given this assumption, the donor genes held a perfect, unadulterated chromosomal blueprint for reconstructing the donor. But it turned out that the blueprint was only half the story and didn't include the construction process. It seemed that you also had to consider all the molecular factors that turned the genes on and off, factors that had a complex yet unique blueprint that changed over time. If you didn't get it right, the resulting clone was a biological catastrophe. It seldom survived the gestation period and was riddled with defects and disease even if it did. And so it was with the three clones of Thomas Zed.

Zed reaches in a drawer, pulls out another plastic bottle and shakes out a single pill. Human growth hormone, hGH, recently cast in a new form that allows it to be taken orally.

As he swallows the pill, he contemplates the curative powers of this natural compound that is pumped out of the pituitary gland in minute amounts with such great influence over the body's growth and maturity. Also known as somatotropin, hGH stimulates growth in children, causing their cells to divide on the journey to adulthood. From deep in the brain, the pituitary squeezes out minute spurts of hGH during the first few hours of sleep, when the child dreams of lizards in meadows or ships setting sail on meringue seas. It moves with great chemical stealth through the circulatory system and vanishes after just a few minutes. But it leaves a trail of other tell-tale compounds in its wake, evidence of the march toward full physical realization.

Then, at maturity, the pituitary throttles back. Its anterior lobe slowly diminishes the output of hGH as the years roll by. Denied the fuel of youth, the body slowly succumbs. Muscles wither, bones ossify, tissue regeneration slows, and excess weight piles on.

Naturally, there was great speculation about what would happen if hGH levels could be elevated in the aging. Would it be the magic bullet? The great hormonal elixir? For twenty years, its molecular structure remained hidden from view but finally yielded to persistent research. Even then, it could be extracted only from pituitaries of recently deceased humans and only in extremely small quantities. The juice of life, squeezed from the newly dead. A biochemical transmogrification of the first order. The tiny amounts available were used exclusively to treat victims of natural growth disorders.

Still, the speculation over the magic bullet persisted. Another ten years passed before hGH could be produced through recombinant DNA technology, and that's when the situation suddenly changed. Now there was more than enough hGH to go around. While the bullet was something less than magic, hGH produced definite physical reversals in aging subjects. Demand soared while the medical community held its ground, restricting use to people with clinically defined growth deficiencies.

But the barrier to supply became increasingly porous, and hGH began to leak through to those with means and international mobility. An ideal situation for the likes of Thomas Zed, who financed an entire clinic devoted to none other than himself. A carefully synthesized cocktail was created specifically for his personal use, a hormonal brew of potent force. At its core was 0.2 milligrams of genetically engineered hGH, a low-enough dose to avoid side effects such as high blood pressure and carpal tunnel. Thrown in for good measure were various quantities of pregnenolone, thyroid, testosterone, and progesterone. After six months, significant amounts of fat evaporated from his belly, and additional muscle mass thickened his arms and legs. His cholesterol dropped and his cardiovascular stamina soared.

Now, as he stands before the mirror and swallows the pill, it seems like a little beacon of vitality descending into his belly, although Zed knows that's just his imagination. hGH has bought him time, but not eternity. Recently, it was discovered that other chemical systems within his body had exposed the fraudulent behavior induced by the hGH. The arrow of time was now finding ways to pierce his pharmaceutical armor, to thaw the frozen clock and set it in motion once more.

His legs are tiring, but he fights the feeling and rests his palms on the countertop. The nurse will come to check on him soon, and he doesn't want to be seen slumped, exhausted, in bed at such an early hour.

The pigs. The pigs should have done it, but he'd lost that battle, too.

Through cloning and various other techniques, pigs were developed with major organs specifically tailored for human transplant: hearts, kidneys, lungs, livers. The core organs that drive the system of life. Young, fresh and serviceable.

And in Zed's case, desperately needed. He already had a borrowed heart. And a borrowed kidney. But he'd lived so long that these organs were rapidly aging of their own accord, and he needed fresh ones.

Much work had been done to optimize serviceability of the pig's organs in the human host and to minimize the problem of rejection. In fact, each recipient could now have their very own pig, customized for the specific quirks of their physical profile. Several of these porcine organ farms were reserved for Zed, who stood by cautiously as others underwent the transplants for the first time. And once again, catastrophe intervened. The prions struck.

Prions are more a shape than a thing: a series of molecular wrinkles and twists that produce a devastating pattern of destruction. They lurk in the biological labyrinths beneath the world of parasites, bacteria, rickettsia and viruses. A prion is a preacher of chemical perversion, teaching normal proteins how to reinvent themselves by folding in an aberrant manner. The new converts then spread the word to their neighbors, until entire cells are gradually glutted with a twisted new order.

Under the right conditions, prions are capable of forming spontaneously and, given the right sequence of ingestion, they can silently march up the food chain. Which is exactly what they did. Only this time, the chain was pork.

There was no practical way to determine which pigs carried the bad chemical seed. So in the case of the neo-pigs, the organ recipient risked contracting a disease that caused physical debilitation and madness, followed by death. This was not a chance that Zed was willing to take. The pigs were shipped off and slaughtered, their meat sold in the more desperate pockets of the third world, where the populace was willing to face a gamble with disease as opposed to the sure thing of starvation.

Zed pulls his wheelchair back from the bathroom counter and pushes himself into the master bedroom, the only bedroom. He has exhausted all the known biological options.

Very soon, it will be time to try something else.

The streetcar halts at the Pearly Gates. The doors hiss open and the security people trudge in and start scanning the lobe of every passenger, Lane and Rachel included. The gate marks the entrance to the Pearl District, a Class 9 security area, which stretches for another dozen blocks down Tenth Avenue. The residents here value civility, cherish safety and aspire to keep the high life at cruising altitude. Thus the gate lives up to its moniker, and functions as a portal into a heaven of sorts.

The doors slide shut and the streetcar moves on. Lane and Rachel have this particular car to themselves in mid-afternoon. Given their suspicions about Green, Johnny and Mount Tabor, it seems best for them to confine their meetings to public places.

"I've got about as far as I'm going to get from the outside," Lane tells Rachel. "The next step is going to be a little on the spendy side."

"What step?"

"You've heard of Pinecrest?"

"Of course. It's probably the most exclusive gate between here and San Francisco. Mostly biotech and pharmaceutical people. We haven't made it a political target because it's too far out of town. They use an air hop to commute."

"Well, then so will I."

"How so?"

"Turns out that most of the upper echelon of the Institute for the Study of Genetic Disorders dwells out there, including the CEO. I'll need to get inside and start to pal around. It's the only way we're going find out how the Institute is related to Mount Tabor. If I play it straight and go to the Institute as a cop and Johnny's brother, I'd trigger all kinds of alarms. I need to take the long way around."

"And just how might you do that?" Rachel asks.

"I need a new identity, which can be easily arranged. But that takes money. Then I buy a house in there and make some new friends."

"Which also takes money," Rachel observes.

"Yes, it will. And that's precisely why it'll work."

"Let me see what I can do," Rachel says. "The Street Party has certain contingency funds that are off the books."

"I'm shocked," Lane quips.

"As well you should be."

Through her window on the streetcar, Rachel watches Lane exit and start down Eighteenth Avenue into the afternoon shadows. He walks briskly, sharply aware of his surroundings, something he must have picked up through years on the street. She likes the way he moves. It has a power and purpose you don't often see. She's sure that the women in Pinecrest will be drawn to him and, for a brief instant, she envies them. The force of it launches her into an unbidden fantasy: She's there with him behind the gate. They bid good-bye to the ugly world outside and settle into a very comfortable life full of quiet, beautiful moments.

The streetcar starts up and yanks her back to reality. She's left feeling a little guilty about her indulgence. Her whole ideological thrust is toward a society where the gates are gone, and quiet, beautiful moments are accessible to everyone. She looks back down Eighteenth as it slides from view, but he's already dropped from sight. She breathes deeply. Politics isn't the central issue here. It's Lane.

She reels her heart in and gets out her laptop. There's much to be done.

. . .

After a quick scan for Bad Boys, Lane hops off a trolley in the Middle East and walks into the deepening shadows of twilight. In the scrawny trees, the birds sing their last sad song, and scruffy children dart in and out between the rusted vehicles. Fall pushes hard against the oncoming night and wood smoke drifts on the breeze.

In spite of the poverty, the desperation, the violence, the pain, the place carries a heavy charge that repolarizes him in some primitive, ineffable way. He knows what those behind the gates can never know, that predictability is a slow, comfortable poison which eventually smothers you to death.

He ducks off the street where a set of cement stairs descend to the basement floor of an old walk-up apartment building. At the bottom of the stairs, a metal-lined door painted a dull shade of rust awaits him, with a minicam mounted above the old spotlight. He stands before the camera and waves silently.

"I think I see the Man," comes a voice from a hidden speaker. "But I could be fooled now, couldn't I?"

"Yes, you could," Lane answers the coded query. "But not by me."

With a hydraulic hiss, the door swings open and Lane steps into an anteroom with a security scanner. Passing through, he enters the apartment proper. To his left is a neatly maintained kitchen, where a middle-aged woman of mixed race is wiping off the countertop. To the right is a large, open room with a mass of electronics and machinery mounted along both walls. The maze of indicator lights and small displays is broken only by a large Ultrares video screen where an ancient sci-fi movie called *The Magnetic Monster* plays on in silence.

"I hear you're a cop without a contract."

The voice comes from Warhead, who occupies a heavily motorized wheelchair now rotating to face Lane. The rotation reveals a quadruple amputee, a stump of humanity with long hair parted in the middle and a dark brown bristle of beard. His mouth is obscured by a framework that holds a hashish pipe, but his eyes are bright and hard.

"You heard right," Lane admits. "No more contract. So what else do you hear?"

Warhead ignores the question. On the roof of this building a small dish points up to a satellite in geosynchronous orbit, and a big fiber cable snakes into the basement. Some say Warhead owns the satellite. Word on the street is that he's punched through to the Outernet, although he emphatically denies this.

"You wanna puff?" Warhead offers.

"Don't smoke much anymore."

"Suit yourself." Warhead mutters something in what sounds like an exotic foreign language and the wheelchair moves to a mechanical stall at the far end of the electronics racks. When the chair stops, mechanical grippers poke out, take the pipe, empty it, and refill it with ground hash-ish from a chrome hopper. A spring-mounted rubber ball comes down, tamps the load, and then the pipe is passed to Warhead's waiting lips as flame is applied from a butane orifice and he puffs away.

"Good stuff," he declares as he exhales twin blue clouds through his nose. "Wanna know how I got trimmed to my current dimensions?"

"Sure. Who wouldn't?"

"Air crash. Dump of a plane. An old 737 with its guts ripped out for dope. I was ridin' shotgun and we lost it comin' in at night. Plane like that has a high airspeed when you're landing. Couple of hundred miles an hour. Last thing I knew we were sailing past the last runway light, and the airspeed still said one twenty-five. Landing lights picked up the trees and that was it. Woke up in a hospital in Bogotá with everything clipped clean off."

Warhead gives Lane a mischievous grin. "But not my pecker. Still got my pecker."

Lane smiles. He's heard Warhead tell dozens of different stories about how he parted ways with his limbs. One time, he was the victim of a hideous radiation accident in a covert nuclear lab outside Kabul. Another time, he was tortured by the agents of some tin-pot African dictator. In still another, he was the hapless recipient of a genetic misfire, and fell from the maternal bomb bay as a wingless missile plunging earthward at a ruinous velocity. In any case, the story always ended with the retention of his pecker, phallic redemption to offset his physical calamities.

"After that, they wanted me in porno," Warhead informs Lane. "Really bad."

"So why didn't you go for it?"

"I thought about it, that's for sure. I had the wood. But most important, I had the focus."

"The focus?"

"Yeah, your normal male performer has five appendages, if you count his dick. Me, I got only one. Terrific focus. And all kinds of new camera angles."

"You would've been good, but it's a tough business," Lane says. "You're probably better off doing what you're doing."

"And speaking of that, what can I do for you?"

"I need an ID package."

"Cash up front. And not Bird shit."

"Absolutely. But it's got to be the very best."

"Costs more."

"Not an issue. It has to survive a Class Ten stress test."

Warhead breaks into a broad grin. "Hey, hey. Now we're talkin'. So if it's for around here, it's gotta be Pinecrest. Right?"

Lane shrugs. "Can't say."

Warhead shrugs back. "Then I never asked."

PINECREST

—

11.

CONCOLOR

The scent of fresh leather. The relaxed feel of soft cotton. The welcome quiet. The careful presentation of subtle colors.

Even after several days of affluence, Lane still wallows in the experience as he leaves the highway and heads west toward the main gate into Pinecrest. The legion of microprocessors inside his car constantly strives toward perfect motion, while the big engine yearns to explode into runaway acceleration. He has his window down, and the wind flutters the fabric of his open shirt and silk sports coat. As he guides the wheel, his big Rolex watch catches the afternoon sun with an arrogant sparkle. He idly fingers the lobe on his ear, mounted in a platinum setting adorned with microcarving. Somehow, the lobe feels fat, swollen with prosperity, just like Rachel Heinz said it would back in Portland.

Allen Durbin, that's who he is. The lobe chronicles his pseudo-life in great detail. The schooling in Europe, the construction projects in Asia, the electronics consortium in India, the three ex-wives. And now, at last, he has achieved the rarified status of investor: one who simply tends his fiscal fields and watches the seedlings of cash poke through the soil and head toward the sky.

All of which makes him a perfect candidate for Pinecrest. When he met with the compound's representative on the phone, she politely requested a Class 10 lobe scan to extract the basics and he courteously agreed, holding the phone's scanner up to his ear. An hour later, she was back in touch, and quite enthusiastic about the possibilities of having Mr. Durbin take up residence. There were several homes available that might suit his needs.

The gate into Pinecrest is a massive structure of reinforced concrete with a cosmetic stucco glaze and a tunnel in the middle where the street passes through. On its roof are crenellations, slots for small weapons that give it a medieval cast.

When Lane arrives at the gate and stops, the security people smile politely and ask how they can help. His car tells them most of what they need to know. After naming the representative he is meeting, he is scanned and his appointment checked. Once inside, the road curves several times through a park-like setting. He enters a village with small buildings set tastefully into the luxuriant vegetation. Above the village, rolling green hills of oak, pine, and fir rise to a soft curtain of fog that hangs limply over their crests, all topped by a clear, blue sky. By design, no houses or roads are visible.

Lane parks and steps out into the clean air swept in off the Coast Range. At the realty office he meets the representative, a perky young woman named Nicole Harris, who apparently has never had a bad day in her life.

"Mr. Durbin," she says to Lane as she puts her fingers over the back of his hand, "I'm so pleased to meet you. Is this your first visit to the Portland area?"

"No. But before, it's always been on business."

"Well, this time, I hope we can get you to stay a little longer," she says with just the right hint of humor and the thinnest glaze of sexual in-nuendo. "Now, before we go out and look at houses, let me spend a few minutes on the community itself."

"Of course," Lane responds as they cross the office to a conference room with a wall-mounted plasma display that she activates with a laser pointer. On the screen, a three-dimensional model of Pinecrest rotates against a black background. As she emphasizes certain facts, the view zooms in, all with no loss of detail. Sixteen square miles of secured liv-ing, with an average of .75 acres per house. All medical, professional and food services available on-site. An eighteen-hole golf course, a scenic pond, bike paths and jogging trails. The security perimeter includes a buffer zone replete with enhanced dogs, electronic sensors and twenty-four-hour surveillance. The normal complement of security personnel includes eighty people, fifty on duty and thirty in reserve at an on-site barracks. Plus there's a secondary reserve of more than two hundred at a central barracks in West Linn. With the exception of the gate, all security measures are cosmetically concealed from the casual viewer, and are carefully designed to harmonize with the community's environmental integrity.

When they leave the office, Lane follows Nicole's car up a winding two-lane road into the foothills. Occasionally, they pass a small address number on a cement post marking a gated driveway that disappears into the trees.

A mile later, they pull into one such driveway and arrive at a large, two-story house with a turnaround in front. Although new, the house reflects a popular style from the 1930s, an eclectic marriage of art deco and art moderne. Many of its smooth cement corners and edges have been softened into graceful curves. The railing on the upper deck uses fat metal tubing, and one surface near the entrance gleams with a matrix of blocked glass. On each side of the front door, two fluted columns are inset in the cement and topped by sunrise patterns.

"What if I want it furnished?" Lane asks as Nicole unlocks the front door with her card.

"Then you're in luck." Nicole smiles. "This place was chosen as a demonstration site by an interior design firm. I'm sure something could be negotiated, if you want."

As they make their way through six thousand square feet of oak, teak, silk, marble, leather, chrome, gold plate and submicron silicon, Lane thinks of all the other residents nestled in similar opulence. What do they do every day in a community like this?

Nicole is not shocked when he says he wants to take possession right away. She's obviously used to dealing with people cut free from normal economic restraints. She does one more lobe scan, interacts with her laptop, and the house is his.

After she leaves, he goes upstairs to the master bedroom and walks out onto the south-facing deck, with the afternoon light casting a golden glow onto the low-slung forest. He leans against the railing and looks at the fields and vineyards rolling into the distance. To the south, the cerulean sky glows with sun and promise.

He looks down at his hands curled around the tubular railing, which is painted aquamarine in the modernist style. The light plays craftily across the tendons and the veins, and a thin matting of hair sweeps toward the outer side of his palms. Under the brown, freckled hide, the hands are infused with considerable power, and he tightens his grip slightly on the warm metal, just to make sure it hasn't fled.

Just to make sure it hasn't gone south without him.

Because in truth, he longs for the comfort of some mythical lower latitude, always brighter than the present circumstance, always warmer. Yet always receding. An impossible journey.

He turns and walks back into the house, shutting the sliding door behind him. Air-conditioning whispers from the venting system. He pauses by a stairway to a lower level of bedrooms and recreation areas. The whispering air shifts from white to pink and seems to carry the pale and distant sounds of children squabbling. A boy and a girl, he would guess. Children he never had. He walks on to the kitchen, where his once possible wife would be. She leans against the big array of tile counter and writes something in a calendar or journal. Her slim hand guides the pen across the page with a grace and articulation that is beyond him. Her flaxen hair is pulled back and held by a turtle-shell barrette, where it bursts into showers of ringlets.

A soft beep cuts through the silence, and Lane turns to a small color monitor on the wall. The security camera has detected a car pulling into the turnaround out front. Its neural circuitry detects the driver getting out and zooms the figure to full frame. A woman, stylishly dressed in loose cottons, with blond hair brushed back to accentuate the streaks of shading.

"Hello. You must be Allen," the woman chirps as Lane opens the door. She looks at him with a curious combination of naked appraisal and congeniality. Well-kept middle age flows over her even features.

"That's right," Lane answers as he steps out onto the porch.

"I was just talking to Nicole and she told me about you. It's so nice to see a new face here, and I wanted to welcome you. I'm Virginia Bradford.

We live down the road a bit."

"Well, it's good to meet you," Lane replies as he gently shakes her cool hand. "Would you like to come in?" He feels self-conscious in his new role. Social niceties have never come easily.

"Oh no," Virginia replies as she reaches out to pat his wrist. "I just wanted to invite you to a party we're having tonight. Mostly people from the community. It's a great way to get acquainted. You will come, won't you?"

Lane smiles. Her intonation makes it sound like the party would be a catastrophe if he chose not to attend. "I'd be delighted."

"Oh, good! You can take the shuttle. Just say it's for the Bradfords. We're starting with drinks about seven."

"Got it."

The light is fading as the driverless shuttle cruises into the turnaround and stops at Lane's front steps. He appraises the vehicle's design and notes the compromise between luxury and utility as the door slides open for him. Inside, a hidden speaker bids him welcome in a calm female voice and then requests a lobe scan from a handheld device in the wooden console.

As the shuttle moves down the driveway it confirms his destination, and Lane settles back to take in his new neighborhood. He quickly discovers that the vehicle handles itself with amazing efficiency, rivaling the best of human drivers. A logo on one side of the dashboard confirms that it is Malaysian in origin. By the time they pull onto the main road, he has nearly forgotten that a machine is in control and settles back to watch the Feed. One hundred fifty channels. Each completely different, all entirely the same.

The vehicle ascends a gentle hillside that holds the residential part of Pinecrest. Ironically, no pines are visible. They've been replaced with elaborate landscaping cleverly designed to be tended robotically. Terraces of exotic trees, shrubs, and plants mask most of the residences, revealing only a hint of roof or the watchful glow of a security light.

Lane turns off the Feed and takes a moment to review his mission, as jointly defined with Rachel. They know that Johnny has some kind of ominous connection to Mount Tabor and that he's been a prime contractor with the Institute for the Study of Genetic Disorders. Lane has discovered Pinecrest is a popular residence for the Institute's upper management. As he put it all together, Lane was poised to start probing their connection to Mount Tabor.

Lane looks up and realizes the shuttle is stopping in front the Bradfords' huge house, a Neo-French mansion with a vaulted porch and windows on the main floor. The car's video system powers down as the door slides open. A hidden speaker announces, "You have arrived at the home of Kenneth and Virginia Bradford. Have a pleasant stay."

Inside, the party buzz hits Lane as he spots Virginia Bradford standing in a strategic position to greet her guests. A shiny black dress clings to her trim body, terminating at just the right spot to highlight a nicely tanned cleavage. She is sipping a drink and speaking to a woman with diamond earrings of sufficient mass to actually stretch her earlobes.

"Allen!" Virginia rushes over and gives him an alcohol-inspired hug while kissing him on the cheek. "I'm so glad you made it!" She hooks his arm and pulls him forward into a spacious living room filled with clusters of people squeezing off party chatter at each other. "Before you get a step farther, I want you to meet my husband, Tom." Her breast is planted solidly against the back of his elbow as they make their way through the crowd.

Tom turns out to be a man of medium height and age, athletically trim with a graceful motion to his hands as he animates a point of conversation to a flat-bellied woman in a miniskirt and sleeveless top. "Tom, look who's here! Our latest arrival! This is my husband, Dr. Kenneth Bradford. Tom, this is Allen Durbin."

"Glad to meet you, Allen," Dr. Bradford says. "And this is Ashley." He nods to the miniskirted woman, who has the prerequisite bulge in her deltoids, along with several hundred dollars' worth of highlighting in her bubble of blond hair.

"Pleased to meet you both," Lane says as he shakes hands. Virginia has already wandered back to her greeting post.

"So what brings you to Pinecrest?" Tom Bradford asks.

Lane notes a strong hint of forced articulation in the man's voice, a good sign that he has already had more than enough to drink. "Always wanted to have a place in the Portland area," Lane replies. "And the timing seemed right. So here I am."

"What sort of thing do you do?" Ashley asks in a voice that indicates she couldn't care less.

"I'm an investor," Lane replies, hoping his cover holds.

"Ah! Stoking the entrepreneurial fires!" Bradford exclaims. "Good for you. I mean, somebody's got to do it. Right?"

"And what about yourself, doctor? Have you specialized?" Lane asks.

Ashley belts out a guffaw that nearly spills her white wine. Bradford breaks into a deep, rolling chuckle. "As a matter of fact, I have, Allen. I'm a plastic surgeon."

"And business is good, I take it?"

"In my particular part of the field, it's very good indeed."

"And what part is that?"

"Well, you see, I've limited my practice to the external genitalia."

"The external genitalia?" Lane asks, somewhat perplexed.

"He means pretty pussies. And penises, too." Ashley chimes in before Bradford can answer.

"It was really a business decision," the doctor offers in a slightly drunken slur. "If you look at the market for standard cosmetic surgery – faces, breasts, butts, that kind of thing – it's pretty damn crowded. I decided to try something a little further afield, so to speak. Turned out to be a good move."

"It did?"

"You see, we live in an age with a new sexual aesthetic. Flat stomachs, perfect breasts, taut buttocks, et cetera. And not only in youth but well into middle age. I mean, what woman wouldn't want a well-formed set of labia, symmetrical in every way? Or if you're a man, what about the glans on the penis shaped to perfection?"

"I'd never thought about it, really."

"Well, you'd be surprised how many have." Bradford waves his hand out over the crowded living room. "I'd say about half the house here has been through my office at one time or other."

"And does that include you?" Lane asks Ashley.

"I'll never tell," Ashley says with a sly look.

The doctor smiles wryly. "Maybe your facial lips won't, but your others will."

Bradford and Ashley burst into laughter while Lane smiles politely. "If you'll excuse me, I think it's time to get a drink."

Lane sees the bar set up on the patio, through a set of French doors, and heads in that direction. Along the way, he takes an inventory of the people in the conversational clusters. White teeth, trim bellies, firm jawlines and thick hair abound. But he senses something else: an undercurrent of malaise that he can't identify.

He doesn't figure it out until he reaches the bar and carefully watches the group closest to him. One of the women gives it away. Her strawberry blond hair is cut short and lightly curled in a way that accentuates a tanned face with strong cheeks and full lips. The chin curves down to a smooth neck with a weighty gold necklace. The whites of the eyes are perfectly clear, and make a great backdrop for the large blue-green irises. But her hands don't match. One clutches the stem of a martini glass, and Lane sees the ropy veins and rigid tendons, a mild bulge of the knuckles, and the ghostly remnants of liver spots over her tan skin. The woman's face is forty and her hands are sixty.

With a scotch on the rocks in hand, he circulates back through the room, looking for more evidence to back his observation. He finds it everywhere. More than half of these people are pushing seventy or more chronologically, but physically holding the line at somewhere in their forties. He can only guess at the maze of hormones, plastic surgery, exercise regimens, and organ replacements that keep them running in place while the clock ticks on.

"Allen!" Virginia closes in on him, and this time he takes a closer look. The flesh about her cheeks and mouth has the vague, lizard-like stretch of plastic surgery. He can't help but search for tell-tale scars but finds none. She grabs his arm and leads him toward a dissolving cluster, where one of the occupants is wandering off toward the bar. "I think maybe you and I ought to have lunch tomorrow," she purrs.

"Down in the village?" Lane asks as he feels the pressure of her bosom against his arm.

"Actually," Virginia says, "I was thinking more about your place."

"I see," Lane says, with as little commitment as possible.

Fortunately, they reach the cluster before she can respond, and she introduces him to a man of powerful build and big hands and a willowy woman with black hair and pale skin.

"Arnie, Beth, this is Allen Durbin. He's new here."

"Mr. Durbin," Arnie says, along with a handshake that's surprisingly mild. As Virginia peels off back into the crowd, Arnie turns back to a conversation in progress with Beth, leaving Lane time to observe. This time, it's the ears. The man's ears have a florid, puffy look of age about them, even though his face appears to be about forty.

"A lung job? You're sure about that?" Arnie asks Beth.

"Well, that's what I heard," Beth says. "She was having a real problem with oxygenation. Down in the seventy percent range, something like that. It was beginning to affect all the tissues, so she really didn't have a lot of choice."

"So what was she when they did it? Forty/seventy? Thirty/sixty-five?"

"I think she must have been more around forty-five/eighty. So you can see her problem."

"Forty-five/eighty? No kidding?"

"That's what I heard. It would've been a terrible waste to lose it all because of her lungs."

For a moment, Lane is puzzled. Then he gets it. The numbers are physical age first, followed by chronological age. In Pinecrest, the formula is obviously a familiar part of casual conversation. And the bigger the spread between the two numbers, the better.

"So where do you suppose they did it, Moscow?" Arnie asks Beth.

"That'd be my guess. They're supposed to have some new technology, something that gets around the pig problem and keeps the prions out. It's very hush-hush."

"Have you seen her since they did it?" he asks.

"No, but Gwynn has. Saw her across the room at lunch. In Kuala Lumpur. At the towers."

"Well, Gwynn's not doing so bad herself, is she?"

"Absolutely," Beth agreed. "I'd guess somewhere around thirty-five/seventy."

"Fantastic."

"She got lucky. Her bone mass was on the way down, but they recalcified her before it got too bad. Did it in New York, at that clinic up in the Bronx. You know the one I mean?"

It occurs to Lane that the basics of this conversation are being repeated all over this room in cluster after cluster. The manic obsession of people facing the same demon and warding it off with the same set of bio-amulets and techno-charms. He slips away from Arnie and Beth and drifts to the periphery of this crumbling buttress against the relentless onslaught of aging.

Lane leaves the babble of the party behind him. It takes only a few moments to locate Dr. Bradford's home office, with its big desk of chrome and glass and view of the hills. The wall to the left is the standard professional trophy collection: an undergraduate degree from Cornell, a medical degree from UCLA, numerous certificates of surgical achievement, and honors from several professional societies. Below these are various news clippings and hard copy extracted from the subnets along with pictures of the good doctor with several major film stars – most likely, grateful patients at one time or other. Is he connected to the Institute? Lane spots his computer, but thinks the better of it. Too much exposure. He turns and heads back down the hall.

He is halfway back to the bar when he spots her. It's Linda Crampton, head of the Institute, a good match for her photo on their website. She stands in a conversational cluster, wineglass in hand. A silvery dress features her handsomely engineered bosom. Probably a forty-two/sixty-one. He's already getting the hang of it.

Her cluster stands next to a large stone fireplace, a cavern framed in massive blocks of granite and filled with the blue-and-orange flame of gas-powered logs. It gives him an excuse to loiter in their vicinity, so he crosses and stares down at the flames, as if somehow warming himself. It doesn't take long. The group soon dissolves in a round of smiles and polite nods, and Crampton walks by him. She sports expertly colored hair folded in loose curls and diamond earrings of a tasteful caliber. Her dress originates from one of the upscale houses in Shanghai, probably Shi Li. Lane's downtown lover from the high-rise, the one with the cop fetish, has sensitized him to such distinctions.

He preps himself to intercept but doesn't need to. Crampton fixes on him as she walks by. "Hello," she purrs. The voice pours out as if from a slinking cat who's unexpectedly crossed paths with a fat mouse. One look at her eyes and he knows why. The whites have a faint bluish cast. Concolor, the magic hormonal compound that blows midlife female embers back into an open blaze. Concolor was the scientific designation for the cougar family and this was the Cougar Pill.

Lane replies with a warm hello. Even knowing the circumstances, he can't help but feel a little flattered. Such is the male ego.

"I don't believe we've met," she says. Lane recalls her clever eyes from the Web photo. In reality, they appear even more so, like two hard diamond bits.

"Just moved in," Lane replies. "I'm Allen." He extends his hand and feels her warm, dry palm. "Allen Durbin."

"Allen, so nice to meet you." She lets her grasp linger before letting go. "And welcome. I'm Linda Crampton."

"Nice to meet you, Ms. Crampton."

"Is your wife here?" she probes.

"Actually, there are several Mrs. Durbins. But I'm afraid they're all past tense."

She reacts with a sultry smile. Whoever did her lips did a good job. "Oh well," she shrugs. "It's always better to live in the present. That's what all the spiritual types say."

"Yes, it is," Lane agrees. "And what about you?"

She assumes a look of faux regret. "I hate to admit it, but I'm one of those people who's married to their job."

"And what kind of job are we talking about?"

"I'm the executive director of the Institute for the Study of Genetic Disorders."

"Wow," Lane says. "That may be a little more than I can digest in a single sitting."

"It does take a while," she says sympathetically. Her eyes stray across the room to a young man of maybe thirty, who fidgets nervously by the bar. Her date, Lane surmises. She comes back to Lane. "Would you like to know more?"

"Yes, I think I would."

"Why don't you come by the Institute tomorrow? We're over in the Medplex. You can take the air hop at eleven. I have a little time in my schedule late morning. I'll show you around and we can have lunch brought in. Sound good?"

"Sounds great."

"Good. See you there." She glides off toward the anxious cougar bait and Lane turns back to the artificial fire. It almost seems warm.

12.

THE REAL THING

Lane looks down on Pinecrest with a mix of fascination and horror. He hasn't flown since he was a boy, and never in a helicopter. The aircraft is of advanced design, the latest from the Chinese – whisper quiet and turbulence-free via compensatory artificial intelligence. He simply floats up and away in a soft leather seat while staring out the window on the side of the fuselage. Pinecrest recedes, the hillside houses, the upscale shopping village, the park with the ten-acre pond, the support buildings, and the cleared security strip on the outer periphery. No one else notices. The other passengers watch the Feed on their personal displays.

The air hop settles on a landing platform atop the Medplex's administration building in the hills above downtown Portland. It does so with the gentleness of an exhausted party balloon coming to rest. As Lane exits, a young man flags him down. This is James, Ms. Crampton's personal assistant. He appears smooth, muscular, fashionable and slightly dense.

He greets Lane with a practiced smile and silken delivery. "Is this your first time inside the Medplex?" he asks Lane.

"Yes, it is," Lane replies. He's been here as Lane Anslow, but never as Allen Durbin. The accounting practices of deception require constant attention to detail.

"If we had more time, we could go on a little tour, but we're running kind of tight," James says as they enter the elevator and descend to street level.

"Some other time," Lane responds. He's already had about enough of James. They board an electric shuttle, taking them up the hill to the Institute. James throws out a few more conversational trinkets and finally takes the hint and shuts up.

The Institute's lobby forms a canyon that ascends through all three floors to the building's roof. Filtered light spills through giant windows onto flooring of tiled stone. A giant Persian carpet sprawls over the waiting area with its couches of beige leather. A series of large pictures runs across the far wall. They depict doctors and children, scientists and children, mothers and children, and so on. Lane gets the idea. The Institute is supposed to be humanitarian in the extreme. After the requisite lobe scan by security, they take the elevator to the third story and emerge into a smaller lobby.

James leaves Lane with the receptionist, who assures him that Ms. Crampton will be out momentarily. Lane takes stock of the tasteful furnishings, original art and framed awards of excellence for this and that. Above the receptionist, a flat screen silently runs a video that surveys the Institute and its noble deeds. The Institute is generously funded, which means that it's capable of momentous research, which means it will produce miraculous cures. But for whom? The video presentation doesn't discuss the Institute's location in the Medplex or why it's secured by uniformed skinheads shouldering automatic weapons.

"Allen, how are you?" Linda Crampton comes across the lobby with her arms extended for a hug of socially acceptable length. A tailored business jacket and skirt have replaced the party gown of the previous evening. Heels of moderate height extend from shoes of some exotic animal hide, probably from one of the new hybrids coming out of Korea.

Lane rises and reciprocates the hug, which lasts precisely one beat longer than the conventional prescription. "Let's take a look around," Linda suggests, "and then I'll have a little lunch brought in."

As they move to the elevator, she gestures down a long hall interrupted at regular intervals by doors framed in glass enclosures. "This is all administrative and IT up here. Nothing too exciting. The real work is downstairs on the other two floors."

"Well, I hope you enjoyed yourself last night," she says in the privacy of the descending elevator.

"As matter of fact, I did." What's she referring to? The party? The pleasure of her company? Hard to tell.

"I'm sorry," she apologizes. "It seems like all we talked about was me. You got something less than equal time. We'll make up for that at lunch."

"There's really not much to say," Lane says. "I lead a pretty quiet life. The most exciting part is totaling up the dividend columns in my financial statements."

Crampton smiles in amusement. "Let's not be so modest. I'm sure there's a bit more to you than that."

The elevator door opens to a more Spartan lobby, with a security desk barring the way down the hall. "Good morning, Len," Crampton says cheerfully to the officer behind the desk.

The officer manages a slight smile. "Good morning, ma'am." Lane gets the idea. She's a benevolent dictator, an ideal blend of power and sexuality.

After another lobe scan, they start down the hall. "This floor holds all the labs and clinical facilities. We're currently working on dozens of disorders."

Each lab is fronted by floor-to-ceiling glass, and Lane looks in on spaces ordered pretty much like Johnny's. Long counters, each with a jungle of glasswork, liquids and tubing. Men and women in white lab coats spin, shake, stir and annotate. Numerous computers digest the results.

"Are you making any progress?" Lane asks. A simple yet profound query.

Crampton gives him a sideways glance of heightened interest. "It depends on which disease you're talking about. In some cases, we've increased survival rates and alleviated symptoms. In others, we're still trying to define the targets to attack. A lot of these afflictions involve a complex interaction of multiple genes, sometimes hundreds."

"Nothing's ever simple, is it?"

"Not in this business."

They double back up the hall and take the elevator to the floor below. "We're coming to the treatment facility," she explains on the way down. "It's really what we're all about. This is where patients reside when they're with us."

"You mean they're not here all the time?" Lane asks as they walk out into a lobby with a more comfortable, homelike décor. Instead of a security officer, a female receptionist sits behind a small counter.

"A lot of genetic disorders are progressive and gradual. Patients come here for treatment episodes and testing, and then they return to whatever lives they may have. A lot of patients are children, still under the care of their families." She looks over to the receptionist. "Hi, Denise. Could you tell us where we can find a vacant suite?"

"Number twelve is open," Denise answers with an accommodating smile, and they head down the hall. Closed blinds over glassed-in walls conceal the interiors of the intervening rooms. "We always respect the patients' privacy," Crampton assures Lane. "Only family and staff are admitted."

They reach the open suite, which appears much like an upscale hospital room. A standard array of medical instrumentation hovers around an adjustable bed. Several visitors' chairs sit nearby, with a tiled shower and lavatory in the background.

"Most of what we do here is limited to intravenous infusions of various substances, so we don't need anything very fancy. If surgical transplants are required, they're done down the hill at the hospital. Once a treatment is administered, we do a lot of observation and testing. The results are processed in the labs upstairs."

She backs out of the room. "Well, in a nutshell, that's about it. Ready for a little lunch?"

"Sure."

Executive Director Crampton occupies the power office in the power corner of the building, the one that looks out over the city below and the mountain beyond. She and Lane eat their catered lunches at a hardwood meeting table. Lane ordered a Waldorf salad and savors the crunch of the walnuts and apples.

"So, Mr. Durbin, why don't you tell me a little about yourself?" Crampton suggests. "Other than what's pretty obvious."

"And what's that?"

A slightly lascivious smile crosses her lips. "You're a very attractive man. You've aged quite well. But I'm sure you've heard that before."

Goddamn it. He can't help but feel the rise in his libido. In truth, he's flattered to be thrown into the same arena with her boy toys twenty years younger. Still, he plays it cool and changes the subject. "I wish I had a tale like yours to tell, but I don't. I'm just another guy who roams the world looking for things that can be bought low and sold high – without much time in between."

"I see. What kind of things?"

"The usual stuff. Like a regional airline. Or a mining operation. Or a canning factory. Not very exciting, I'm afraid."

"But profitable," she adds.

"You always hope so. You'd better win more than you lose. Speaking of businesses, I'm curious about how yours works."

"You know, Allen, I don't think of it as a business. It's an institution dedicated to eradicating a certain class of diseases," she says with an air of nobility.

"I'm sure you're right, but bottom line, everything is a business. Money comes in, money goes out. You keep some, you spend some. That's the way it works."

"What we have here is a process," she explains. "We start with the science and research. We convert that into treatments, which we test and verify. Finally, we arrange to have private entities distribute them to the medical industry at large."

"Do you do the basic science here?"

"No, we contract for that by funding various research projects. Part of our skill set is to identify the most promising science, and make sure it's adequately funded until it pays off."

Lane smiles. "I bet you don't go down the street to the bank for the money."

"The Institute itself is funded by numerous foundations from all over the world. I can't go into names but, if I could, I'm sure you'd recognize some of them."

"And I suppose they never expect a penny in return."

"Under certain circumstances, they may realize some gain," she says diplomatically. "When a treatment is perfected, we license it to various pharmaceutical companies. The revenue from licenses is funneled back into more research. Basically, that's how it works."

"Well then, I consider myself enlightened," Lane concludes. He looks out the window at the view and spots an unexpected opportunity. The forest-green dome of Mount Tabor rises over the cityscape. "You've got a great view from here," he muses.

Crampton turns and shares his line of sight. "I never get tired of it," she declares.

"I'm still learning the geography around here." Lane points toward the miniature mountain. "What's that big green hill over there across the river?"

She doesn't miss a beat. "It's called Mount Tabor."

"Is it a park?"

"No, it's in private hands."

"Who owns it?"

She shrugs and smiles. "I have no idea. I'm way too busy up here to pay much attention to what's going on over there." She looks at her watch. "As a matter of fact, I have my next meeting in about ten minutes."

Lane does some desperate deliberation. He needs more time with her. He reaches over the table and puts his hand on top of hers. "Linda, this is all extremely interesting, and I'd really like to hear more. I know you're very busy, but is there any chance we could have dinner tonight?"

She instantly perks up. He can almost feel the Concolor fuel the flame that drives the hormonal boilers. She makes no effort to pull her hand out from under his. "I'll have to check," she says with studied nonchalance. "Can I text you?"

"Sure." He removes his hand and stands. "There's an air hop back at one-thirty, right?"

"You can just make it if you leave right now. I'll call James."

"Not necessary. With all due respect to James, I think I can handle it."

Her eyes smolder in expectation. The diamond-tipped bits drill right through him. "I'm sure you can."

. . .

The air hangs still and warm over the pond, the water nearly gone to glass. Lane walks along the cinder path around these ten aquatic acres at the bottom of the hillside in Pinecrest. He sees the first signs of fall, an odd leaf fallen here and there in pale yellow or pink. It feels better to be out on foot in the seasonal cusp than back in the house that's not really his. He should be strategizing his dinner tonight with Linda Crampton, but the thought of sleeping with her might ruin this most pleasant afternoon.

He reaches a small bench just off the path and sits, stretching to rest his arms on its back edge. To the right, a thick stand of cattails pushes up against the shore. Their phallic flower heads sprout slender antennae that taper up toward the cumulus drift overhead. Insects weave their way among the plants in busy fits. He looks out over the water and catches the sun's reflection, a blazing disk turned liquid by the pond's surface. Sun, water, plants, insects. They gradually merge and transport him back to the most pleasant of times.

Miller Bay. He and Johnny. Lolling in the cabin, rowing on the water, digging in the sand. The good days, the best days of all.

Lane looks up. There she is. Out of nowhere, it seems. She squats at the pond's shoreline, pointing a camera at a pair of Canada geese. A lean, angular face with a strong nose and full mouth. Straight hair of a luxuriant brown that stops just short of her shoulders. Lean arms fully exposed by a sleeveless blouse. Muscular legs stretched taut under snug jeans. In a community full of desperately engineered youth, she's clearly the real thing, somewhere in her twenties.

She senses his attention and looks over, revealing a set of deep blue eyes. "Sorry. I didn't mean to disturb you."

"Not a problem."

"I come here a lot, looking for the birds," she explains.

"A hobby?"

She walks over and sits on a large stone nearby. Rather than answer immediately, she gazes at the grass, which is rapidly turning to straw as fall approaches. Beneath the stunning edifice, Lane senses a strange melancholy. "I'm sorry. I didn't mean to pry," he says.

She looks up at him with a faint smile. "It's all right. I'm not really a bird-watcher. I'm just tracking this one pair as they journey through the seasons. For no good reason, really."

"I don't think it says anywhere that we have to have a reason for everything we do."

"I suppose not. I've never thought about it. There's a lot of things I've never thought about."

A jogger interrupts their discourse as he trots by. Trim and gray, pacing himself against the relentless pursuit of the Reaper. His labored footsteps fade off down the path.

She stands and slings the camera strap over her shoulder. Lane has some acquaintance with camera models. This one is expensive in the extreme, one of the Ultradef models from Singapore that capture something disturbingly close to visual reality.

"Well, I've got my shot, and I'm on my way," she says. "Nice meeting you."

Lane stands to acknowledge her departure. "I'm sorry, I should have introduced myself. I'm Allen Durbin. I just moved in."

"Nice to meet you. I'm Autumn. Autumn West."

"I don't know who did your work, but they're extremely good." Linda Crampton takes another sip of her white wine, one of many. Her skimpy dress and prominent cleavage indicate that she's armed for an erotic skirmish. The Pond House restaurant's subdued lighting falls kindly across her sculpted features.

Lane ponders her remark, then it dawns on him. Of course. She thinks he's like the rest, a monument to artificial preservation. "Thank you," he responds with muted sincerity.

She presses on. "So let's have the numbers."

He hovers on the edge of blowing it. He has to assume she means his age ratio. That's what it always seems to come down to around here. "Well, since you ask, it's forty-five/sixty-nine."

"Amazing."

She takes another sip, and Lane realizes they are done with dinner and now simply getting drunk. Pretty soon, he won't have the cerebral facilities left to get the job done. "Hey, life is short," he declares. "You better get what you can while you can, right?"

"Right." Linda turns and looks out a window to the reflection of the full moon on the pond, and the residential lights climbing the hillside. The wine is rapidly contracting her attention span.

"I mean, look at that plane crash out in Hillsboro," says Lane. "Three guys in the prime of life on a luxury jet and boom, it's all over, just like that." He pauses as if in recall. "They were scientists, I think. Something to do with biotech. Did you know any of them?"

Her eyes turn from liquid back to diamonds and level on him. He's made a big mistake. She didn't get to be the executive director of the Institute without a highly developed cerebral cortex. He knows exactly what's happening on the far side of those drill bits. She's replaying her entire series of encounters with him. She is zooming in on his questions at lunch about Mount Tabor and linking it to his current interest in the crash and its victims, who all were contracted with the Institute.

"I'm so sorry, Allen, but I'm feeling a little out of sorts," she says. "I think we're going to have to call it a night. Do you mind?"

"Not at all. Is there something I can do?" He's screwed up badly. She's already reaching for her purse.

"No."

"I'll stay and take care of the bill, okay?"

"Thank you." She extends her hand and he takes it. Stiff, formal, and cool. She makes no mention of further dates.

He watches her walk out and wonders about the full extent of the damage.

13.

THE NEOLITES

The Neolites line the sides of the street in their thousands, and Harlan Green ignites a rolling chant as he travels past them, like the crest of a wave moving through an excitable human medium.

"Kill the machines! Kill the machines! Kill the machines!"

Rachel Heinz stands next to Green and holds on to the front wall of the horse-drawn wagon. For this particular event, mechanized transport was completely out of the question. "I wonder how they all got here," Rachel says to Green. "Do you suppose they walked?"

"Doesn't matter," Green replies as he waves and smiles. "All that counts is that they're here."

The Neolites have a relatively benign history as political activists, although their recent alliance with the Street Party has generated a certain amount of alarm. In their infancy, they were called the Neo-Luddites, after the rampaging factory workers out to destroy the automated looms as the industrial era ate into traditional life in Britain. As the ranks of the Neo-Luddites grew in the new millennium, the name became contracted to Neolites. Their focus was not mechanical machinery, but electronic circuitry, the great engine of the Information Age. For this reason, they tended to cluster in places like Portland with its Chip Mill, as well as Silicon Valley, Tokyo, and Shanghai.

And now the faithful of this angry flock raise their wooden staffs in salute to Green as he rolls by. They seem evenly split between men and women, and both sexes wear simple robes of earthen color that end at the knees. Long, unkempt hair is the norm, along with worn leather sandals and a complete absence of jewelry. Every hundred yards or so, a leader stands atop a wooden crate (no plastic), with a tapered cone rolled into a primitive megaphone. The leaders are directing the pacing and phrasing of the chant, with their wooden staffs cutting the air like rocking metronomes.

The wagon eventually rolls to a stop at the south security gate to Mount Tabor, where the private forces have retreated from sight. Up the side of the mountain, a column of armored vehicles sits just off the road in a distant display of force. The Neolites have spilled out into the street and blocked traffic. Someone hands Green a microphone, and he raises his hand to silence the crowd. Their chanting comes to an abrupt halt.

Green launches his speech by pointing up the slope. "We gather here at the foot of this mountain, once a sacred symbol of how nature and man could work in harmony for the common good. But those days are past, my good friends. Now if you look up these slopes, you see the machinery of destruction and decay everywhere. This place, once so public, is now home to a private abomination. Those who dwell here refuse to share its secrets, because those secrets stain this place with great shame."

The angry shout of an auto horn interrupts him. By its second burst, Harlan can see the problem. Up the packed street, some fool in an SUV on his way to Mount Tabor is trying to assert his right of way and wedge through the crowd.

By the third beep, the Neolites have had enough. They set upon the vehicle with their staffs.

"Kill the machine!"

Metal crumples. Glass shatters. The security alarm shrieks. The driver panics and accelerates. Robed figures fly through the air, over the hood, and under the wheels. The panicked crowd opens just wide enough to provide a clear view of the vehicle as it comes to a stop.

Dead quiet. The throng of Neolites stands motionless. The victims sprawl in shock on the pavement. The car rests at a diagonal angle across the center line.

Then the victims start to scream. Broken bones, torn cartilage, and severed nerves come alive and sing stridently into the late morning air.

Green turns to one of his security people in the back of the wagon. "Get us out of here. We can't be part of this." He and Rachel are quickly handed down to the street and hustled off toward a side street, where several vehicles wait.

With Green gone, the recovering crowd looks for new leadership. One of their robed supervisors mounts his wooden box with his megaphone.

He slowly levels an accusatory arm at the SUV and screams into the megaphone.

"Kill the machine! Kill the machine! Kill the machine!"

In a great and angry roar, the robed legions lunge forward and begin to smash wildly at the car once again. The noise is horrific as the staffs rain down on every square inch of the car's surface, smashing all the glass and sending tiny chunks spraying everywhere. The burglar alarm's voice system activates and starts to bellow: "Warning! You have approached a secure vehicle! You have relinquished your right to litigation over countermeasures! Warning!"

As the alarm continues its ridiculous and hollow threat, the staffs fly with unrelenting fury. Some break and splinter, and others come forward to replace them. The vehicle's occupants remain trapped inside, suffering the terror of the damned.

Six hundred feet above, Thomas Zed and Arjun Khan watch the mayhem play out in vivid detail on a set of large screens fed by video cameras mounted on the south gate.

"We could intervene," Khan suggests. "We might be able to save them."

"Absolutely not. The driver was an arrogant fool to take on a crowd like that."

"This is the largest disturbance yet," Khan observes. "I don't like it. They keep getting worse. Sooner or later, they'll try to get in."

"Maybe not." Zed offers no further explanation. He sinks back in his padded chair to sooth his aching back. No matter what, something always aches.

On the monitors, the pair can see the crowd losing focus on the battered vehicle and turning to fresh targets. They run wild through nearby shops and offices, ripping out all forms of electronics and mechanicals.

Cash registers, terminals, laptops, palmtops, monitors, coffeemakers, blenders, fans, stereos, televisions, disc players. They are dashed against the pavement and piled up in great heaps on the walkways.

Zed watches until the Neolites' fury is spent and their leaders herd them off. He and Khan are the sole viewers of this event. It will never be seen on the Feed. Appropriate filters are in place to prevent politically aberrant material from getting through. Celebrity perversions, serial murders and the like are all fair game, but any material that reflects poorly on the public interest is stringently managed.

But Zed knows that the filters will eventually fail, that all the countermeasures will fail. The government will fall and Green will win.

Not a problem. A new government means new opportunities. It's simply a matter of negotiation. A century of personal experience of the symbiosis of politics and business has verified this conjecture. However, there is now a more pressing issue.

"How close are we?" he asks Khan.

"Very close. Any day now."

"Good."

"The Feed will redact the whole thing," Rachel informs Harlan as they ride back toward Street Party headquarters. "The Neolite story is going to be dead on arrival. Too bad."

"Yeah, too bad," Harlan says absently. In fact, the incident has served precisely the purpose that Harlan intended. Very soon, he will make contact with the people up on Mount Tabor, with the old man that Johnny called "the Director." And when he does so, he wants to negotiate from a position of strength. The Neolite incident did Mount Tabor no real harm; but served as a dramatic demonstration of Harlan's expanding political power. If the old man is as astute as Harlan suspects, he's already taken this into account.

He turns to Rachel. "Don't worry. In the end, we're going to win."

Rachel nods in confirmation. Yes, they were going to win, but win what?

A gray carpet of stratus occludes the late afternoon sun, and a chill creeps through the fall air. A soft breeze wafts across the pond, blowing the scent of fermented plant life over Lane as he walks along the cinder path. He wears only a cotton shirt, and the wind raises goosebumps on his forearms.

He considers heading home but spots her up ahead. Autumn West. She sits on the bench, camera in lap, gazing out over the ripples that wrinkle the water's cloudy green surface. A sweatshirt and sweatpants flow loosely over her. She doesn't seem to notice as he sits on the bench's other end. The breeze threads gently through her unbound hair.

"Are you waiting for your feathered friends?" he asks.

She manages a small smile and slowly turns her head toward his. "They won't be coming today," she declares.

"You're sure about that?"

She turns back toward the water. "I'm sure."

"How do you know?"

"I'm not sure I could tell you. I knew the moment I arrived."

"Is it the wind? The color of the water?"

"It really doesn't matter. What counts is that they're not coming."

"Are you disappointed?"

"Not anymore. I guess you could say that I live beyond reach of expectations."

"That's a good place to be – at least I think it is."

"And just what are you waiting for, Mr. Durbin?"

"You mean right now?"

"I mean anytime."

"I'm not sure how to answer that."

"Most of us spend most of our lives waiting for something. The last thing we wait for is to die. After that, we're though fidgeting in line. No more treading water. It must be a good feeling, don't you think?"

"I would imagine so. But that's all I can do: imagine."

"Then I guess that'll have to get you by, at least for now."

The thud of running shoes interrupts their conversation. Two pairs coming up the path from behind. She shows no interest and stays focused on the water. The runners appear from behind a curtain of reeds and cattails.

It's Linda Crampton and a young male companion. Her drill-bit eyes go first to Autumn and then to Lane. She becomes a muted mask as they hurry down the path.

Lane sighs. By sitting here with a beautiful woman less than half Crampton's age, he's managed to overlay her previous suspicions with a scalding layer of narcissistic animosity. His stay in Pinecrest may be coming to an abrupt end.

Autumn turns to him once again. "Something wrong?"

"Not really," Lane lies. "It's just getting a little chilly. I should have worn a sweatshirt or something."

"Maybe you need a hot cup of tea."

"You could be right." Maybe he can salvage the remains of the day with this very attractive and strangely oblique girl.

She stands and shoulders her camera. "I live close by."

"I'm glad to hear it."

Linda Crampton steps out of the shower and towels down her pampered skin. Her hair will have to wait. She dons a bathrobe of blue silk with the ghostly imprint of a solitary rose on the back. The boy toy is already in bed and looking at her expectantly as she strides through the bedroom and down the hall without comment. Too bad. He'll just have to pout until she takes care of business.

In her home office, she drums her fingers on her desktop while the secure video link to Mount Tabor is established. Arjun Khan comes up on the screen. "Yes, Linda. What can we do for you?"

Crampton bristles inside. Khan always says "we" to remind her that he is the sole representative of Thomas Zed. "I think we might have a security issue."

"And how's that?"

"A man moved in here a few days ago named Allen Durbin. He was curious about the Institute, so I gave him a tour, the usual stuff. He started asking questions, way too many questions. Then, at dinner, he wanted know about the crash."

"Now, you weren't trying to seduce him, were you?"

"It doesn't matter what I was trying to do. He wanted to know if I knew any of the people on the plane."

"And what did you tell him?"

"Absolutely nothing. But that's not the end of it: When I went running today, I saw him talking with Autumn."

Arjun pauses to absorb. "I see." He absently strokes his chin. "If you took him to the Institute, it means that you have video and a lobe scan on him."

"I do, and I'm sending them to you right now."

"Let me take a look, and then talk this over with Mr. Zed. I'll get back to you. Don't have any more contact with him unless you have to. We need to play it safe until we know more."

"And how long is that going to take?"

"Not long. I'll be in touch."

Arjun disappears from the display. Crampton curls her fists into anxious balls. Originally, six of them had full knowledge of the project and now three of them were dead, by design. That left only Zed, Khan, and herself.

And maybe that was one too many.

The windows in Zed's office turn semi-opaque as Arjun brings up the security video from the Institute. The old man shifts in his chair, seeking the comfort that never comes, as he faces the screen. His mind drifts back over the evolution of surveillance imagery in his lifetime. Drawings in pen and ink, fuzzy monochromatic photos, color telephoto shots, low-res security cams, and now this. The video of the lobby is almost brutal in its clarity, a hyper-realistic representation of an alternate reality. The Feed won't use it. The Feed peddles the stuff of dreams.

"Here he comes now," Arjun narrates.

A trim man in his late forties stops at the security post at the Institute for the Study of Genetic Disorders for a lobe scan. The resulting data comes up on a display next to the video.

"He scans as Allen Durbin, and someone's done a good job with his personal stats and history. It all cross-checks, even through Homeland."

"Keep looking," Zed advises. "We've got to be sure. Especially with the Green thing coming up."

He curses his luck. Earlier, it looked like the whole Dr. Anslow business was nearing resolution. They'd received an encrypted communication from Harlan Green. Apparently, he was holding Anslow in what he called "protective custody." After the scientist had related details of the activities on Mount Tabor, Green suggested that he and Arjun and Zed meet to discuss, which was a good sign. If he'd wanted to use it as political ammunition, he would have screamed it out over the media. But he didn't. It seemed that under his populist veneer, Harlan Green was a man who could be reasoned with, maybe on a grand scale.

But now there was the brother, the cop, who might be something more than just a street tough. If Allen Durbin and Lane Anslow were one and the same, they had a major breach to deal with.

Zed feels a sudden wrenching in his chest. His heart twists and tumbles and spins in a bottomless dive. He grabs the edge of his desk for support and holds on desperately. His implanted monitor is already screaming a wireless warning to the medical staff. They will be here in seconds. He tries to breathe calmly and regularly, as if his heart will heed the example of his lungs and get back to business as usual. But the erratic tugging, thumping, and tumbling rolls on, with no relief.

He hears the welcome stampede of footsteps and the roll of rubber wheels. Powerful arms lift him gently onto a gurney, and electric scissors cut away his shirt and sweater. Electrodes and sensors descend onto his chest. In the circle of faces, he sees his physician and several nurses.

"Don't worry," his doctor assures him. "We've got it under control. You're going to be just fine."

Sure he is. Just fine. Bullshit. He's dying. Again.

14.

ROAD TO RIO

Autumn's house catches Lane off guard. It's no more than a cottage, with weathered wooden shakes for both siding and roof, and a simple wooden porch two steps up from the turnaround. A small barrier of sand, rocks, and plants separates the structure from the forest beyond, and bougainvillea hang from two big pots on the porch. Autumn hasn't bothered to lock the door, and they walk right in.

Lane finds himself in an open space with kitchen, dining room and living room all visible. Cedar planking lines the walls and he can smell its dry perfume as he follows her. Several paintings hang in the living room, lit by spots in the naked rafters. One is clearly classical, the others modern. Coarsely woven rugs spill across the pine floors at energetic angles, and the furniture is of simple design and earthen tone.

"I think I'll call you Mr. Durbin. It has a nicer ring to it than Allen. Do you mind?" she asks as she heats water for tea.

"Not at all," he answers. "How long have you lived here?"

"Longer than I care to remember," she says, watching the teapot as if it resided somewhere out near infinity.

Lane doesn't pursue it. He still doesn't have a fix on her and proceeds carefully. His attention returns to the paintings. A large one dominates the far wall. Something about the colors, the geometric sprawl.

"That painting," he says. "The big one. I'd swear I've seen it before."

"You probably have. Online and in print somewhere. It's a Diebenkorn."

His high-rise lover with the cop fetish had several coffee-table books he'd thumb through while she watched the Feed. One was a survey of modern art, and that's where he saw it. "You're right. I saw it in a book."

"It's one of the Ocean Park series. You can see a little Matisse in it, but then he goes somewhere else entirely."

Something under the picture's surface seems to be shouting at Lane, taunting him. "It's a landscape, isn't it?"

"You got it," she replies. "Diebenkorn lived in Santa Monica and worked with the light and oceanfront he found there. His painting kind of hovers between abstraction and reality."

"So you obviously like that kind of thing," Lane adds.

She puts tea bags into a pair of cups. "There was a book a long time ago that had a crazy Indian who thought he could walk into a painting and actually be there. I don't think he was crazy at all. Sometimes I walk into that picture and stay there for the longest of times. When I'm there, it seems like there's not really any time at all."

She pours hot water over the tea bags. Outside, the sun breaks through the clouds and spills through the windows. As sometimes happens in early fall, it brings instant warmth. "Good. Now we can sit outside."

She picks up the tray and they head out through a set of French doors to the backyard. A round table and chairs sit on a wooden deck a step above the ground. Beyond is a rock-lined garden where flower beds alternate with gravel walkways.

As Lane follows her, he tries to get a bearing on her physical presence. The soft slap of the sandals on the planking cuts an aural trail through the chirping and buzzing of the forest. She moves with a fluid grace that seems to transcend space and time.

"There we are," she says as they sit down. "Sugar or cream?"

"No, thanks." Lane steals a private snapshot of her as she concentrates on pouring his tea. She wears a bandana with a blue flower print that pulls her hair back, with just a light application of makeup. He rapidly explores the contours of her face, neck, and ears, looking for something he can't find.

"How did you get interested in art?" he asks.

"It started when I was a child. On trips to the city, my mother would take me to the museum. I always loved it."

"You lived out in the country?"

"In a small town in Nebraska."

She leans forward, shifting her weight off the chair back and onto her elbows, which rest on the table. A simple motion tracing a graceful curve through the low heat of the afternoon.

"And what about you, Mr. Durbin? Where did you grow up?"

"Miller Bay," he answers from off in the twilight. What was he saying? How did he get here?

"And where's that?"

"Oh, it's up in Washington," he replies as his normal sensibility returns. "Actually, we lived in Seattle, but that's a long time ago."

"It can't be that long. You're not that old. What are you? Mid-forties?"

"Yeah. Mid-forties. Which is pretty young around here."

He watches her for a reaction, but she remains supremely detached. What's she doing here? She's far too young, she has no peers.

"I suppose so," she answers.

"I think I heard that someone could hang on until about a hundred and twenty. Do you think any of us will make it that far?"

She sips her tea. "Possibly. We'll just have to wait and see, won't we?"

Lane shrugs. "Somehow, I don't think my clock is wound tight enough to get me anywhere near that."

"Would you like to live that long if you could?"

"It all depends on health. I'd rather die in battle than retreat, if that's what you mean."

"Do you have any children?"

"No. No kids." He thinks of the empty house, the interior all cool and dim.

"Do you have unfinished business of some kind?"

"Yes."

"And what happens when it's finished? What then?"

"I haven't thought that far ahead." And with good reason. These days, only the wealthy have plans and dreams that extend beyond next week.

The alchemy of history has transmuted the golden years into lead.

Autumn puts down her tea. "Pace yourself, Mr. Durbin. You've got a long way to go. There's really no hurry." She pushes back her chair and stands. "I'm afraid you're going to have to excuse me now. I always take a walk this time of day."

"Alone?"

"Alone. Can I call you a shuttle?"

"No, I'll take care of it," Lane says as he rises. "Could we continue this conversation another time?"

"Not this one," she says. "But maybe another." She holds out her hand. "Good-bye now."

As Lane takes her hand, it feels almost unnaturally cool. "Thanks. I'll show myself out. Have a nice walk."

Lane can feel her presence fade as he walks back through the house to the front door. He stops and looks back through the screen door, which lets him see all the way through the French doors into the garden and out into the woods.

He continues to watch for several minutes, standing in the resurgent warmth and buzz of insects. She's gone. He can almost hear the hoarse whisper of the dry grass as it gives way beneath her sandals. A carnal moment flashes its beacon and he desperately wants to follow, to stalk her though the forest and then fall with her to the soft earth.

The beacon fades. Lane is left with the porch, the warm afternoon, and the insects. He steps forward and tries the screen. Still open.

Once inside, he moves slowly and carefully, and has the odd sensation that he's actually floating a hair above the floor. He walks through the house and garden and checks the path to the woods. Nothing but chirps, buzzes and floating seedlings. She's really gone.

He goes inside and roams through the place with a practiced eye, finding next to nothing. No computer. No personal effects or paperwork. No mementos of times gone by. No messages or outgoing numbers on the phone system. It's as if Autumn West doesn't really live here, yet obviously she does, with dishes in the sink, unmade bedding, and clothes in the hamper. He's never seen anything quite like it.

Only one item floats above this sea of anonymity. A framed picture on her nightstand, a color photograph of dubious quality. She smiles at the lens, just a few years younger than now. She wears a thick coat and wool cap, and the background reveals a series of storefronts in the classic style of small-town America.

Lane sets cell camera at max resolution and captures a picture of the picture. He wants to know more – but not as much as he wants to find his brother. Autumn West is a detour Lane simply can't afford to take.

He goes out the door to the porch, where he scans the landscaping and finds a decent spot. He pulls a video nanobug from his pocket and pushes it into a convenient stone crevice.

He promises himself that she'll remain a diversion, an entertainment, a distraction. Nothing more.

A little squadron of spent leaves flutters by the kitchen window, twisting in the morning sun. Lane tracks their path as he waits for the coffee-maker to finish. The device is super-automated, with several "gourmet" settings that are lost on him. A polite beep signals him to pour a cup, and he sits at the kitchen table with its roughly polished hardwood top. Upscale rental furniture sprawls out around him, all cleaving to some consistent sensibility in the mind of some interior designer, the ghost of good taste.

The silence and cruel façade envelop him as he sips. The pseudo-home of Allen Durbin, the pseudo-home of Lane's family that never was nor ever will be. He shakes it off and connects his laptop to his cell. He's sure it can be plucked out of the home's wireless cloud and delivered afar, but he's willing to risk it. While the connection initializes, he plays with the pieces in his head. Johnny, Ms. Crampton, the Institute, Mount Tabor, the plane crash. They slither about like drops of oil on hot metal, skittering, colliding, bouncing, but they never settle into coherency.

He lets the puzzle go and retreats to something more entertaining: Autumn West. He brings up the picture he took of the photo in her bed-room, the solitary artifact of her past. He does a modest zoom and pans to the left of her face. A sidewalk lined with one-story businesses stretches down the main street of a thousand towns across the Midwest. She said she was from rural Nebraska and the picture seems to confirm it.

He pans a little more to the left, almost into the foreground, and comes across the front of an old movie theater from the golden age of cinema. Vertical green neon descends to spell "Avalon." Underneath it, an elevated wedge of marquee juts out over the sidewalk. Hand-placed capital letters in lurid red spell out the title of this week's feature, some movie Lane's never heard of.

He opens another window and does a Meternet search of Diebenkorn paintings. A few pages later, he lands on the one that hangs on her wall. One more page and he receives an estimate of its value: twenty-five million dollars.

He goes back to the painting and stares at it. Twenty-five million dollars. It's one thing to live in Pinecrest and quite another to be here in your mid-twenties with a major museum piece hanging on your cottage wall.

An alert issues from the laptop's audio transducer. The neural circuits in the video bug at Autumn's are busy bearing witness to something they judge to be significant. A window opens on his display, and he sees her walking down the path. She's dressed in a stylish pantsuit, not the kind of thing you wear to watch birds or hike to the store. The bug's micromotors pan the lens to the street, where an air hop shuttle pulls up.

She's going downtown. But where? He looks over at the stupendously valuable painting and then back to her boarding the shuttle to the air hop terminal.

He folds the laptop shut and resolves to follow, at least for now.

An air hop shuttle drops Lane at the terminal, which sits on flat terrain on the far side of the pond. Two choppers rest on the tarmac in front of a two-story building with a front of tinted glass. Covered walkways extend out to the periphery of the aircraft, with their drooping rotors at rest. The upper story offers a mezzanine view of the lobby below and the tarmac beyond, and Lane has stationed himself here.

Each craft has a separate exit with a display mounted above. The left exit announces a boarding time in one minute, and to confirm it a soft whine floats in as the aircraft's engine fires up. The other exit's display is dark, and its machine idle.

From up on the mezzanine, Lane can see where Autumn sits in the lobby along with several other passengers. She gazes serenely at the scene outside. A perfect body at perfect rest. A woman's voice announces the flight to downtown will now board, and the display confirms it.

The passengers rise to board, all except Autumn. The exit door slides open and passengers file through the lobe field and down the walkway. All except Autumn.

A few minutes later, the air hop lifts and rotates in the direction of the Trade Ring. Autumn sits alone in the lobby.

Lane watches the aircraft disappear into the distance and looks down at her solitary state of repose. What now? He checks his watch. How much time does he want to put into this highly speculative venture?

Once again, the soft whine of an engine. The exit display to the right lights up with a single declaration: charter only. Autumn rises. The woman's voice comes back on and announces the destination: "Mount Tabor charter now boarding."

Autumn walks slowly, almost hesitantly, through the lobe scan and down the walkway.

Lane feels a surge of interest. He's uncovered another connection between Pinecrest and Mount Tabor, a completely unexpected one. The terminal has a business center with several complimentary office cubicles. He grabs one for privacy and opens his laptop. He considers trying to trace the ownership of the Diebenkorn but decides it's hopeless. The inner workings of the art world have long since disappeared from public view, for both political and security reasons.

That leaves him with Autumn's bedside photo. He opens it and stares. It has a certain quality found only in pictures from the pre-digital age, a product of chemicals, dyes and paper, not photons striking pixels.

He focuses on the movie marquee in the background. He pans and zooms and reads the title of the movie spelled out in big, block letters: Road to Rio. He opens a second window and does a search of movies based on the title, and there it is, release date and all. He does some simple arithmetic to derive her age. He subtracts the current year from the release year, and adds twenty-five years to approximate her age in the photo.

Autumn is at least one hundred years old.

Astounding. He's seen her up close. She's not a product of preservation technology, like most of her neighbors. What's going on? He needs another data point to corroborate his calculation and returns to the detail in the picture. The storefronts stretching down the sidewalk all have display windows, and each contains a faint reflection of the street at curbside. Several of these reflections contain the images of parked cars. He cuts out one and puts in its own window, where he runs a series of image-enhancement filters. And there it is, a Chevrolet pickup truck with a rounded hood and a grill of four parallel chrome bars. He does an image search and comes up with the year it was made, which is consistent with his calculations.

He repeats the process for several other display windows. All the vehicles fall into the same age range. He's looking at a little town, probably in Nebraska, as it appeared over seventy-five years ago.

He doesn't want to believe it. He wants her to be twenty-five. For real. Maybe someone pasted her into the scene. But if so, they did a terrific job matching the lighting, especially with an old film-generated photograph.

Lane leans back from the laptop and turns to stare out at the empty tarmac. Fantastic as it seems, it would help explain Autumn's detached, dreamy air, with the touch of melancholy, like an aging immigrant clinging to the Old World. Maybe she doesn't really live here, at least in her mind. Maybe she lives not only in another place, but another time.

Autumn gazes out at the fractured grid of the city below from her window in the air hop. Except for the vague rush of the rotors, the cabin is deserted, the seats empty. She knows the route by heart. They are about ten minutes south of the landing pad at Mount Tabor, where Mr. Arjun Khan will greet her, and they will drive up the hill to the sprawling residence at the top. Arjun will explain to her that Mr. Zed is once again in imminent danger of dying. His heart, it's always something about his heart.

She can't deny him her presence. He's given her the most unique epilog imaginable, even though the ultimate truth of it seems lost on him. He attended her resurrection and it only seems right that Autumn should attend his death, whenever that might be. There was a time when his demise might have caused her sorrow, but that time is past. Because back then, she adored him, Thomas Zed, her savior, provider, benefactor, and a worker of miracles.

He never seemed old to her, and why would he? After all, she herself was one hundred and one years of age. She can still picture the joy radiating through all his creases and wrinkles when he first looked down on her intubated and supine form. It calmed her and gave her a course to follow through the days of confusion that followed.

Where am I?

You're not in the hospital anymore. You're at a specialized facility. We pulled you back from the brink. You're doing very well, even better than we expected.

But why? I was ready to go. What's left for me?

Let me show you.

Zed brought the mirror up to her flawless face.

15.

THE MUSTARD SKY

The Bird, thought Arjun. It has to be the Bird. The dark hair, so carefully sculpted. The skin of copper. The leather overcoat. The silk tie knotted in perfect symmetry.

Of course. Who else would Harlan Green charge with security for a meeting of this magnitude?

Arjun Khan and the Bird stand by the stairwell on the fifth level of a ten-story parking structure where the Trade Ring fronts the river. The cool air of late night pervades the space. All is monochrome like the concrete, save for the Bird, who turns to Arjun and says, "Your people swept the place, my people swept the place. Have we got a deal?" he asks.

"Not quite," Arjun replies. "We still need a personal cam scan on both parties. It's all set up. All they have to do is walk through."

The Bird looks down the row of deserted parking stalls to where the scanner is set up, with its portal of gray plastic. "Okay, but first I want it tested."

"Agreed," Arjun says. No one on Arjun's side wants a record of this particular encounter. The same is probably true on the Bird's side, but you can never be too cautious. He reaches into his pocket and pulls out a little case containing a nanocam. "I think this will do."

He hands the case to the Bird, who opens it and looks at a capsule only a few millimeters in diameter. "It's active?" he asks.

"It's active."

The Bird closes the case and walks out into the parking structure. His footsteps bounce in a hard echo off the walls and floor. He passes through the scanner. The alarm promptly sounds. He hits a switch and it stops. He hits another switch and an arming light comes on once more.

"Okay, we're done," the Bird declares as he walks back. He elevates his arm to raise his coat sleeve and check his watch, a Ming from Chen Ho. "Ten minutes."

"Ten minutes," Arjun confirms.

The two men enter the stairwell. Arjun walks up, the Bird down.

Arjun opens the metal door to the parking structure's roof, where the chopper rests on the helipad. The craft is dark, the engine silent, the pilot absent. Arjun scans the skyline as he walks to the machine. No buildings have an easy line of sight. No telephoto lenses are likely to be peering their way.

Thomas Zed's face is illuminated by the soft glow of the chopper's computer display as Arjun opens the door. "We're ready."

"All right, then. Let's get this done."

Green watches in fascination as Zed totters through the security scanner. The old man seems like a grotesque caricature of advanced aging. When they arranged the meeting, he had no way of knowing whether or not Zed had undergone any treatment. Apparently not. It's all the ancient figure can do to join him at the railing on the edge of the parking structure.

"Good evening, Mr. Green," Zed says in a reed-thin voice. "I hope you're taking good care of Dr. Anslow. He's a bit misguided, but really quite a decent fellow."

"I'm sure he is," Green agrees. "And also quite brilliant. I could hardly believe what he told me."

Zed smiles shrewdly. "It does seem astounding, doesn't it?"

"I have to say I'm a little disappointed, though. I thought that you yourself would be proof of concept, and obviously that's not the case."

Zed's eyes narrow and nearly disappear in the massive wrinkling. "Look at me closely, Mr. Green. Very closely."

"I've already done that. I never forget a face. An essential tool of my trade."

"Good. Because the next time you see this face and hear this voice, you'll have your proof."

"And how long might that be?"

"Soon. Very soon. So as it turns out, our meeting is well timed. But enough about me. Let's talk about you, and where you're going. I have to congratulate you on a brilliant career. You've come a long way in a remarkably short time."

The pair stares out over the river to the East Side of the city. Random bits of light dot the darkness. The bright ribbons of streetlights that once formed a dazzling grid are gone, victims of declining budgets.

"I've come only as far as history will let me," Green replies. "The times make the man, not vice versa. If it wasn't me, it would be someone else."

"Ah, but it's not someone else. It's you. That's why I'm here."

"Should I be flattered?"

Zed smiles. "Your life is a matter of public record. Mine is precisely the opposite. You see, I've never been a prime mover like you. I've always been a facilitator, a mediator, a consolidator. And to be quite honest, I've profited handsomely in this role. But that misses the point."

"The point being?"

"The world needs both of us. We're both indisputably the best at what we do. You supply the social vision. I supply the economic means to realize it. You might say we're complementary sides of the same coin. But most important, we need to stay in our respective roles on a more or less permanent basis. The world owes us that, and the world will benefit greatly from it."

Green nods. "So where do we go from here?"

"For now, I think you should retain Dr. Anslow as collateral. Once I've demonstrated that the process works and you can derive benefit from it, we'll talk about other arrangements. As a public figure, you're a special case. We'll need to moderate the treatment so you don't suddenly appear dramatically different. From then on, it will be a matter of periodic applications."

"And what about yourself?"

"Anonymity has its benefits. There's no reason that I can't be a young man again."

"Congratulations."

"And the same to you, Mr. Green."

"I'm still having a hard time with this," Rachel admits as she and Lane step off the MAX train at the Goose Hollow station. "I mean, you've traced this Autumn West to Mount Tabor. Wonderful, but the twenty-something centenarian part is pretty wobbly. Are you sure that the picture by her bed wasn't doctored? Or maybe she's just the best work ever out of some big-time rejuve shop."

"Don't think so," Lane says. "I think she's something else."

"What else?"

"That's what we're here to find out."

They enter the Goose Hollow Inn through the rear door. It's early, so the booths and chairs in the back are empty. A woman in her middle sixties is pouring a glass of beer for a bearded patron who hunches over an open book. Wynn Pearson expertly dumps the excess head, tops off the pour and wheels the beer around to the bar, where the patron grasps it without ever looking up. As she plunges the patron's smart card into the machine, she whisks back a stray strand of gray hair that escapes her ponytail.

"Lane!" Her blue eyes brighten. "How you been?"

"Same as always. Cutting class."

"You could afford it," she says. "You had the brains."

"Why didn't you tell me that back then?" Lane asks. "I might have buckled down. Might have become a professor."

"'Fraid not," she says with a slightly naughty grin. "You were way too hunky for anything like that. Besides, I don't think biology was exactly your favorite subject – except for the reproductive process." She looks over to Rachel with appraising yet kind eyes. "So who's your friend?"

"This is Rachel. Rachel, Wynn Pearson."

"Watch him," Wynn twinkles at Rachel. "He's definitely cute, but he's a lot of trouble."

Lane can still remember Wynn in his sophomore biology class at Lincoln, steering their young minds through cell chemistry, taxonomy and basic genetics. She was a great teacher. They all loved her. "I can still see you with the scalpel and the frog. You were magnificent. Why aren't you still doing it?"

"I think we've had that conversation, big guy."

After the public schools collapsed, her only real option was to take a private teaching job, but she wouldn't even consider it. As she told Lane more than once: "Goddamned if I'm going to show rich kids how to get even richer."

"Well, guess what?" Lane says. "I'm ready to repent. I want to go back to class. And this time, I promise I'll pay attention."

"Aha, Lane the scholar," she quips. "Truth is, you were always a bit of scholar, especially for such a cute kid. You were curious, and you read all the time – at least when you weren't raising hell. So what to do you want to know?"

"How long can people live?"

"Easy one," she says playfully. "Exactly as long as they're supposed to."

"Let's suppose for a moment that we don't believe in predestination. Then how long?"

The place is empty except for Lane and the patron immersed in the book, so she leans back against the counter and folds her arms. "The maximum human life span is generally agreed to be about one hundred twenty years – with no time off for good behavior."

"And how often does that happen?"

"I can't give you an exact number, but it's probably only one in several hundred million people. It's rare enough that the international media gloms on to those who make it and hauls them out on a slow news day. Besides, from a biological standpoint it doesn't really matter. In the end, we're all slaves to the Gompertz curve."

"What's that, Ms. Pearson?" Rachel asks.

"It's the rate at which we age. Let me put it this way. Remember when you were a kid?" she asks Lane. "Maybe ten or so?"

"Yeah, vaguely."

"Except for accidents, do you remember anyone in your class at school dying?"

"I don't think so."

"It's the healthiest time of our lives. We're past childhood diseases, and the bad grown-up stuff has yet to hit us."

"So when does the curve get thrown at us?"

"Now think back to your high school class. Remember anyone dying?"

Lane can still see the faces. Two girls and a boy. Cancer, or leukemia, something like that. "Yes, I can. Three people."

"That's the curve starting up. Now think back over the last ten years to people about your age that you know. Anybody expire of natural causes?"

"More than I want to think about."

"The curve shifting into a higher gear. Let's go back and start with that class of ten-year-olds, all alive and kicking. Each year, the odds go up that one or more of them will expire during that year. Very small at first, maybe one in a few thousand. But by the time they reach high school, it's maybe one in a few hundred. Still pretty small, but big enough that you see it working. But by the time they hit your age, it's down to one in say fifty. Get the idea?"

"Unfortunately, yes."

"Well, by the time you hit one hundred twenty, the odds are essentially one in one. As you age, more and more people in your age group die each year of natural causes. If you plot it all out, it's a curve, called the Gompertz curve, after the guy that figured it out."

"Lucky fellow."

"Let's go back to where you started. You asked how long people live. I'm a little disappointed in you, Lane. There's a much more fascinating question that's hardly ever considered, and that's why do people age at all?"

"If we didn't get old and die, we'd overrun the planet, which we've almost done anyway."

"That's a problem, but it really doesn't answer the question."

"Then what does?"

"If you put aside spiritual beliefs, evolution requires only two things of you. The first is to survive until you're old enough to reproduce. The second is to pass your genes on through the so-called germ line, which extends all the way back to the origins of life itself. Now, as it turns out, nature is very finicky about the germ line, and much less so about you personally."

"So what's that got to do with getting old?"

"Every organism, yourself included, has a limited amount of energy at its disposal to do things. Nature assures that you'll have a big energy budget to spend on keeping your eggs or sperm in good shape to maintain the germ line, and something less on the upkeep for the rest of your cells. As it turns out, this second part of the budget is just enough to make sure that you live until you reproduce and take care of what popped out for a while."

"And then you start to go to hell."

"Pretty much. In the past, natural selection let us last until about thirty, then pulled the plug. By that time, we were past our peak and got sick, murdered, eaten, or all three. The bodily upkeep budget no longer mattered. So now we have the answer: All your cells have repair mechanisms, but by the time your salad days are over, they can no longer keep up with the damage. You get old. You die."

"So what if you could repair the damage faster than it accumulates? Could you prevent someone from aging?"

"Great in theory but almost impossible in practice. Your cells are the product of millions of years of evolution. They don't answer to you. They answer only to life itself."

Lane thinks of Autumn, of the stunning contrast between her youthful beauty and her apparent age. Maybe it has nothing to do with prevention. "Okay, so what if a person was already old and you wanted to wind the clock back to when they were young. What then?"

Wynn smiles patiently. "Boy, you drive a hard bargain, don't you?"

"So what would you do?" Lane persists.

"Simple. I'd put everything back in original working order. I'd repair all the genetic damage to each cell."

"And how would you do that?"

"Through some kind of extraordinarily advanced genetic therapy. To pull it off, you'd have to raise an entire army of very specialized artificial viruses."

"Viruses?"

"Yes, viruses. You see, nature has already provided us with a highly evolved vehicle to deliver genetic material into the cell nucleus, where the genome resides. It's called a retrovirus."

"So why does the virus have to be artificial?" Lane asks.

"Many reasons," Lynn answers. "For one thing, the immune system usually destroys real viruses before they can reach all their destination cells. What you need is a little protein vessel that's of no real interest to the immune system. Now there's all kinds of such devices."

"You think they'd do the job?"

"Not really."

"Why not?"

"There's a very old song with a line that goes, 'Got to make it real, compared to what?' You have to have some way to define exactly the extent of the damage that's accumulated over the years. A tricky business, at best. The human genome has about three billion base pairs. So which ones are still good, and which ones have gone bad and mutated? And you also have to analyze when and how the genes are expressed. Then you have figure out how to imprint them onto the proper locations with the genome."

"But if you could do all that, could you wind the clock back to that golden age?" Lane asks. "When the genes in all your cells were in an optimum state of repair?"

Wynn smiles. "Lane, you're still quite the clever boy. Now, you get back to me when you've figured out how to do that."

"Well, hello Mr. Durbin," Warhead says as Lane enters into his chaotic jumble of technology run amok. "Are you having fun with your new self? Getting a little more pussy than usual?"

"Not really. You got a minute?"

The maze of indicator lights and small displays is broken only by a large Ultrares screen that shows a woman in coveralls binding a some-what younger woman with bungee cords to the crumpled chrome bumper of a wrecked highway rig in a junkyard somewhere in the urban wasteland.

"A minute, huh?" Warhead says. That's my minimum billable increment."

"I'll take it. And maybe a few more, if you can help."

"So what's your problem?"

"There's a woman named Autumn West. She was born about a hundred years ago in a small town somewhere in Nebraska. I need the location and the date of birth."

Warhead spews an incomprehensible stream of phonemes into the microphone mounted on his headset. His wheelchair twists toward the array of consoles and displays, which are rapidly shifting their visual content. He rattles out yet another verbal stream, which spins him back toward Lane.

"This might take a minute. I told you about how I got to be a stub, right?"

"You mean the dope and the plane crash?" Lane hopes he has the right version.

"Yeah. Well, they put me on trial for drug smuggling. Didn't work. All the evidence went up in the fireball at the crash site. Everything except me. I wound up in a tree, like a big piece of trimmed meat. After all that, they just gave up and sent me home."

Something beeped and Warhead rotated back to his gear and smiled. "Well, what do you know about that? Autumn Denise West. Born in Elkton, Nebraska, population seven hundred and fifty-three. Died in the same place one hundred and one years later. Too bad about her twin."

"Her twin?"

"April Clarisse West. Died two years after they were born. Some kind of staph infection."

"That's all?"

"That's all, and given the time span, I think that's a lot."

Warhead softens a little. "Next time, I'll tell you about the rehab place where they dumped me after I got home. But right now, I'll just give you a little hint: Horny nurses come in pairs."

"I need to fly to Nebraska. With you or without you. As soon as possible." Lane tells Rachel on his cell as he strides through the parking lot.

"You're serious?" she asks.

"I'm serious."

"You're assuming that I can get us there."

"I have no doubt you can get us there. That's why you do what you do."

"We'll see about that."

Autumn West sits at Zed's side in Bay 1, where he lies in a maze of tubes, wires, and sensors. He reaches out for her hand, and she takes it. His skin feels cool and parched.

"We can't really know if this is the beginning or the end," he whispers, as the sedation starts to set in. "But we'll soon find out. Wait for me. Please wait for me."

"I'll wait," she assures him.

From across the room, Zed can hear the sound of an antique clock that he specially requested. It holds an elegant assemblage of springs, gears, cams, levers and artful inscriptions. As he retreats to the border of somnolence, the ticks of the clock fade away and only the tocks remain, little subtractive pulses that reverse the cruel vector of time. The pulses become integers, and the integers become years, and the years become burning posts impaled in a featureless desert full of yellow sky.

And there his father kneels, beside the heaped stones marking the little grave. He turns toward Zed's febrile gaze. Diphtheria, son. It took your brother down. Your only brother, your twin, your perfect twin. It got your mother, too. I left before she died, you know. Tears fill his eyes. I had to. It would've killed you and me, too, and we were all that was left.

The yellow overhead turns mustard. The posts lose their flame. They glow and smolder, sending blue smoke into a dying sky.

Autumn finds it odd to see Zed in such a vulnerable and helpless state. His eyelids twitch and his head oscillates. She still wonders how he can be so tender with her yet so callous to others. At first, she took all his attention at face value. After all, she was confused and vulnerable, and he fabricated a credible foundation to ground her. In the process, he provided only a highly simplified description of how they had peeled seventy-five years off her. Instead he focused on the need for a careful and controlled recovery. "We must handle you like a beautiful yet fragile work of art," he told her. "You need to be gradually reintroduced to the outside world."

They often dined together and he regaled her with stories of his adventures abroad. He cautioned her about potential pitfalls. If the media discovered her secret, they would hound her incessantly. She would become a freak, naked and exposed to the predation of lenses and microphones. She heeded his warnings and was content to remain within the confines of Mount Tabor, at least for now. Her strange revival had left her in a state of emotional shock, hardly ready to face the world at large.

It didn't take long for her sexuality to return. She felt it most strongly when she strolled through the lavish gardens that surrounded the residence. It felt like her erotic core had never really died but only lingered in a deep slumber. And with this reignited lust came a surge of passion for Thomas Zed and all the power, charisma and mystery that attended him. It was accompanied by a persistent regret over the difference in their physical age, which would prevent her from consummating a union. He'd already explained that she was a rare and special case not applicable to humanity at large. For this reason, she assumed that what had worked for her would never be available to him.

She was wrong, of course.

16.

DEAD RINGER

"I need to feel good about what we're doing," Rachel says as they start across the tarmac outside the flight services building at Portland International Airport. "And I'm not quite there yet. So let's go through it one more time."

"Can't say I blame you," Lane sympathizes. "I'm sure this is a lot of trouble."

Up ahead, an exotic yet beautiful plane awaits, a Piaggio 180. Twin canards project from the sides of its sleek nose, and its turboprop engines face backward off each wing.

"It's more trouble than you can possibly imagine," Rachel says. "So let's have it."

"After I found out that Autumn West had an identical twin, I went back to Wynn Pearson," Lane explains. "I wondered if you could somehow leverage the infant twin's genes to capture that perfect moment when you physically peaked as a young adult. She said no, because the baby hasn't developed into an adult yet and a lot will change along the way. I think Johnny figured a way around the problem, a way to wind an infant's genetic clock forward to that golden moment. Are you with me so far?"

"So far."

"Autumn West's dead little sister was a perfect genetic copy of her. With Johnny's help, they could predict exactly how she would turn out as a young adult. Then, up at Mount Tabor, they had some way to correct the mistakes in her old body, and truly rejuvenate her."

"So you're sure about this?" Rachel asks with a trace of skepticism.

"If I'm right, we're going to find a grave at the local cemetery in Elkton, Nebraska, for an April Clarisse West. And when we dig it up, we're going to find it either empty or tampered with. Why? Because they took the genes and ran."

They've reached the foldout stairs leading up to the cabin right behind the cockpit. For the first time, Lane notices that the plane appears unattended. He stops at the foot of the stairs.

"Where's the crew?"

"You're looking at it," she said.

Twenty minutes later, Lane watches Mount Hood slide by off the starboard side. Rachel arms the autopilot and settles back. "So how do we pull this thing off when get there?" she asks.

"We need to have a talk with the doctor who signed her death certificate. Somehow, I don't think her papers are exactly in order. Think about it. She's over a hundred years old. She's outlived her entire family and all her friends. She's alone in the world. No one's going to make much of a fuss about the disposition of her body. So the doctor pronounces her dead slightly in advance of the real thing. And the undertaker plays along. In the meantime, they swoop down, grab her, and transport her to Mount Tabor before she actually expires. And then they start to work their magic."

"But who's they? Who's directing all this?"

"I don't know yet, but it's a pretty good bet that they're both very old and very wealthy. It's also a pretty good bet that Autumn is some kind of prototype. I can't believe that they would spend that much time and money on someone of such modest origins."

"Maybe she's not alone," Rachel suggests. "Maybe they've done it with others. There have to be numerous cases where a person lived to a ripe old age and also had an identical twin that died in childhood."

"You might be right. And if all this is being done on Mount Tabor, your boss hit the political jackpot. Poor people tolerate a lot of things, but they won't sit by and die quietly while the rich live on forever."

Rachel lapses into a reflective silence. The harsh whisper of the displaced stratosphere spills through the cabin. "He may have hit the jackpot, all right," she finally says. "But I don't think he plans on sharing the winnings. Johnny must have told Harlan exactly what was going on up on Mount Tabor, and he decided to keep it to himself." She slams her fist into her palm. "Damn! I should've seen it coming. He's going to make a deal with the devil, and why not? He came to me the other day and said he was going to be taking a little time off. Bullshit. He's never taken time off. He's setting the stage for something."

"Like coming back as a college boy?"

Rachel shakes her head. "Never happen."

"Why not?"

"He never went to college."

Lane shrugs. "Too bad." He slumps in his seat, closes his eyes, and promptly nods off.

Rachel does her periodic scan of the avionics, then looks over at Lane's slumbering profile and smiles. He has this remarkable composure about him. Is it sadness and resignation that lets him surrender to the moment like this? She hopes not. She resists an impulse to reach out and gently touch the back of his hand.

Lane awakens to the prairie landscape coming up from below. Thin lines crease the fields, defining roads that run straight north or south. They form a land of countless rectangles and squares. Numerous earthen circles crowd within these shapes, their patterns etched by the sweep of giant irrigation arms.

They dip to the right and Elkton appears. The main street runs about a quarter mile and terminates in a couple of grain elevators and railroad tracks. Houses spill off for a few blocks on both sides, and then the fields take over.

The airport's single runway comes and goes from view as they line up to land. "So how do you propose we go about this?" Rachel asks. "I mean, this is your area of expertise, right?"

"Right. First thing we do is buy ourselves a ride into town. Then we see if we can pick up the paper trail. Elkton is the county seat, so that helps. We go there first and check out death certificates. Next we track down the doctor who signed them. Then we have a chat with the local funeral home. Finally, we make a little trip out to the cemetery, which can't be far from town."

Their plane touches down and goes to full brakes and reverse to avoid shooting off the far end of the short runway. They turn left onto a short taxiway and stop in front of an old hangar with a small office in one corner. An elderly man in jeans and a plaid wool jacket opens the door.

"And that would be our ride," Lane announces.

"So you guys are attorneys, right?" Mr. Larson, the airport custodian, asks. He drives down the main street of Elkton at glacial speed in the old pickup.

"I suppose you could say that," Lane answers.

"I figured as much when you said you wanted to go to the courthouse. Especially after you came in a plane like that. A Piaggio 180. Never seen one for real. You're lucky. It used up every damn foot of the runway."

"You're right," Rachel agreed. "We're very lucky."

"If you're hungry," Mr. Larson informs them, "there's only one place left to eat, and it's not always open."

Looking out the window, Lane can see why. Aging single-story build-ings line both sides of the wide street, some brick, some concrete. Fad-ed and fallen signage prevails, along with many boarded-up windows. Weeds grow through the sidewalks like tiny tree lines of ragged green and yellow. Only three vehicles are visible, all gas powered, all hobbled by the sky-high price of even the lowest-grade petrol. The solitary pe-destrian is an elderly woman pulling a child's wagon full of used bottles.

"Folks don't come to town much anymore unless they really have to," Larson explains. "Costs too much. You don't have to drive, but you do have to eat."

They pass the theater Lane saw in Rachel's photo. Its deserted box of-fice stands a timeless watch on the sidewalk. The marquee still juts out, and a single letter, a red P, remains in the lower left corner. Lane tries to visualize giggling young girls and fidgeting boys streaming out into summer evenings long gone. He fails.

"Is that the courthouse?" Rachel points to a stolid three-story structure of cut stone surrounded by elms. Grecian columns stand in bas relief on the upper two floors. Its small parking lot is deserted.

"This is it," Larson declares as pulls up in front. "Want me to wait?"

"Only if you're not going to block traffic," Lane quips.

Larson takes it straight, or at least he seems to. "Don't think that'll be a problem." As well it shouldn't, given his compensation.

No scanning portal awaits them inside the Perrin County Courthouse. None is necessary. There is very little at risk.

"I'm off to the ladies' room," Rachel announces as they reach the main hallway. "It's kind of a nice day here in the heartland. I'll meet you back outside on the steps."

"See you, then." Lane heads down the hall and turns in the first door he comes to.

A woman in her fifties sits behind a counter, a person of librarian cast, with a print dress, cardigan sweater, and glasses suspended from a cord around her plump neck. "Yes?"

"Hi, could you direct me to the records department?"

"You're there," the woman responds, as if it should be obvious. Behind her, a couple of women of similar demeanor and appearance sit at aging computers.

"I'd like a copy of a death certificate," Lane continues. "It's for an Autumn West. She was a long-time resident here."

The woman shoves a little notepad across the counter. "I'll need her full name and the date of death."

"I know the year, but not the day or month," Lane says as he gets out a pen.

"Well then, I guess that'll have to do," the woman says with mild irritation. She puts on her glasses and reads the note when Lane is finished. She looks up at him. "There's a ten-dollar records-acquisition fee and a five-dollar duplication fee."

"No problem," Lane says and produces the money.

The woman takes it. "Do you need a receipt?"

Lane declines and the woman puts the money in a metal cash box, which she has to unlock with a little key in a drawer under the counter. "Wait here," she commands and shuffles off into an adjoining room filled with file cabinets.

Lane goes to the door and looks up and down the deserted hallway. He wonders how often they try court cases here, or do anything at all. He'd bet big money that the county's population had been in steady decline for the last forty years. Someday soon, the irrigation arms will cease to rotate, and the prairie will reclaim what was taken from it.

Eventually, the woman returns with a single piece of paper produced by a vintage copy machine. "Anything else?" she asks. Her tone indicates that it would be a definite imposition.

"Don't think so. Thanks," Lane says, as she leaves the counter without comment and returns to her desk.

Lane joins Rachel out the front steps and reads the gist of the document to her: Autumn West allegedly expired at six in the morning at Perrin County Community Hospital, Elkton, Nebraska. Dr. Wesley Fenner signed the death certificate, listing the cause as respiratory failure from pneumonia. "It happened right when the shift changed," Lane observes. "Very convenient."

They return to Mr. Larson's truck. "You still got a hospital around here?" Lane asks.

"Just barely," he tells him. "It's three blocks. As a matter of fact, everything around here is just three blocks." He manages a hybrid exhalation somewhere between a wheeze and a laugh.

"What about the cemetery?" Rachel asks.

"Oh, that's a little farther out. You gotta go three blocks down to the tracks and then take a right for a half mile or so. It's just past the Farber place."

"Let's try the hospital first."

Perrin County Community Hospital sprawls in brick over a flat expanse fronted by a withered lawn. Its single story hugs the prairie horizon. This time, a receptionist greets them warmly. Much of the corn originating in the fields beyond has found various avenues into her body in the form of fat cells, a condition quite common in these parts.

"Hello, can I help you?" she asks.

"Hi, we're looking for a Dr. Wesley Fenner. Does he practice here?"

"Oh." The receptionist appears slightly stricken. "Dr. Fenner did practice here, but he passed away last year."

"I'm sorry," Lane contributes. "I didn't know. What happened?"

"It was so sad. He was still in his fifties. He died just down the street. A train hit his car."

"Wow," Lane says sympathetically. "Did they ever figure out how it happened?"

"Not really. The train's engineer saw him stopped right in the middle of the tracks. All the warning lights were on and the barriers were down. It was too late to stop the locomotive. He was killed instantly. At least, that's what I heard."

"Well, thanks for your help," Rachel offers. "We'll remember him in our prayers."

"That's very nice of you," the receptionist says as they leave.

"So what are we going to do with that little piece of information?" Rachel asks Lane has they head for the truck.

"Nothing. We're not here to resurrect a homicide investigation. We're here to get to the truth about Autumn West."

Where Skyview Cemetery ends, great fields start to stretch all the way to the horizon, interrupted only by little islands of trees or barns. The cemetery's layout divides the ground into sixteen squares with intervening pathways. Twelve are full. Four await additional souls not yet departed.

"We'll call you in a couple of hours," Lane says to Larson through the rolled-down window on the truck.

"You got it," he replies, and heads his pickup back toward the grain elevators and town.

The chirp of birds and the distant hum of his tires are all that remain under the enormous sky. Lane peers from the shoulder into the cemetery's interior, where the intersecting paths are just wide enough for service vehicles. A utility shed sits under the shelter of a few trees at the far end. When they reach it, they find the door ajar, and Lane peeks inside. Gardening tools line the walls, and a tractor mower squats in the center of the gravel floor. He sees no sign of a map describing the plots. "Okay, let's hit it."

Lane treads slowly through the short dry grass. A few headstones poke up, but flat markers of bronze or granite identify most graves. He scans names and dates. At first, the spent lives waft up at him, but he tamps them down to stay focused. One section over, Rachel scans markers.

Insects fizz and snap. Birds chatter. Great vessels of cumulus drift by and cast shadows that stir the air slightly. Now and then, the hum of distant car tires invades the expanse of solitude. A train thunders by.

Ninety minutes into the search, Rachel makes the discovery. "I've got it," she yells.

Lane comes over to see the two adjacent bronze markers. Sure enough, the names and dates of the West twins agree with what they know. He squats down to examine the carpet of surrounding grass. It spreads uniformly over the ground and gives no hint of the time of burial or excavation.

He stands up and notes their position. The graves are on the section's right side, two rows back in. "Okay, let's call Mr. Larson, and get out of here."

"But how are we going to know about the twin?" Rachel asks.

"I don't think it's advisable for us to stand in broad daylight in view of the road and dig up a baby's grave. That comes later."

"Sorry. I'm not much of a criminal or a fugitive."

Lane smiles. "You're worse. You're in politics."

The Greer-Parsons Funeral Home occupies a modest lot three blocks off the main street. A large, solitary elm casts shade on the front lawn and the porch. Lane and Rachel stand under its shelter and ring the bell while Larson waits curbside in the truck.

A man in his forties answers the door with the practiced smile common to the trade. "Hello. Come in."

They stand in a small reception area that leads to a chapel with the usual trimmings. "My name's James Burton," he says. "How can I help you?"

"We're just following up on an old friend of the family," Rachel explains. "You handled her funeral."

"What's her name?"

"Autumn West."

"I'll have to check the records. You see, we just took over here last year, so I'm not familiar with all the names."

"We'd appreciate it," Lane says.

"Come and have a seat in my office. It should just take a minute."

Burton leads them to a neat office with a laptop on the desk. He sits and types. "Ah, yes," he says, gazing at the screen. "Autumn West. My goodness! She was over a hundred. You don't see that very often." He looks up at Lane and Rachel. "What would you like to know?"

"We'd like to know how she was interred and where the cemetery is," Lane says.

"She was cremated and the cremains were buried at the local cemetery. It's called Skyview. You can't miss it. Just go to the end of town and take a right by the tracks. It's about a half mile down the road."

"Thanks for your help," Lane says as he gets up. "So you just took over here. Would it be impolite to ask how business is?"

"Not at all. It's quite good. The average age around here is now over fifty, which bodes very well for this kind of business."

"What's the previous owner up to these days?"

"Mr. Greer no longer lives here. He came into some family money, so he wanted out. Can't say as I blame him. He's living in Italy now, somewhere on the coast."

"Ah yes, it must be nice," Lane says. Also quite perilous, he imagines.

Lane's thumb runs idly over the switch on the flashlight, which sits in his lap. He bought it at the hardware store down the street from the Imperial Café, where he now sits in a booth with Rachel after finishing a tuna melt sandwich. Outside, the shadows advance against the setting sun.

"So how did they do it?" Rachel asks.

Lane does a precautionary scan to make sure their waitress isn't around. If she'd gone home and left them to lock up, he wouldn't be surprised. They've seen no one else since arriving.

"My best guess is that it started with Dr. Fenner giving the elderly and ailing Autumn something to make her damn near dead. Very shallow breathing, no detectable pulse. Then he waited until it was time for the nurses to change shift. This guaranteed him enough time to disconnect the monitoring stuff. By the time the next nurse shows up, Fenner's declared her dead. The funeral guy knows the timing and is there in just a few minutes to pick up the body. They take Autumn to the funeral parlor and he revives her, but keeps her sedated. Next, the people from Mount Tabor show up, and off she goes along with a sample from her buried twin. The funeral guy puts some wood ashes in an urn and the burial goes on as scheduled, which earns him enough loot to move to Italy – or so he hopes. That's it."

"Can you imagine what it must have been like for Autumn when she woke up with maybe seventy years peeled off?"

"No, I cannot." Lane looks out into the dimness. One streetlight flickers, the rest are dead. "You ready to take a little moonlight hike?"

Lane plays the flashlight beam over the interior of the utility shed at Skyview Cemetery. The place smells of baked motor oil and spilled solvents. He spots a shovel on the back wall and removes it. A moth flutters through the beam as he goes back out to Rachel.

He extinguishes the light. A thick tree line separates the burial ground from the one adjoining farm, but they can't take any chances. "Okay, let's get it done," he says softly. Out here, there's no ambient noise to mask the sound of conversation.

At the grave site, he briefly shines the light on the bronze marker. April Clarisse West. God rest her soul. He turns off the light, picks up the shovel, and begins to dig. He suddenly becomes aware of just how protracted a process it might be. His soft hands run the risk of bad blistering. He stops and gives the light to Rachel. "Would you go back and see if you can find a pair of gloves?"

She nods and takes the light and leaves. He stabs the point of the shovel into the thick mat of hard, dry grass. It yields only slightly. Not good. He repeats the action, with the same result. Finally, after several attempts, he pierces the mat and reaches the underlying soil just as Rachel returns.

He puts on the gloves. "Let's hope we get lucky," he says, and brings his foot down hard on the shoulder of the shovel blade. It slides easily into the soil below, which seems to be loosely consolidated. He leverages the handle to pry the dirt free. It comes up easily.

"It's not filled in solidly," he tells Rachel, "which means somebody's been here before us."

Overhead, the stars spin slowly and mindlessly about the celestial pole as Lane resumes his shoveling. A train roars by across the highway. The ground shudders slightly. Bats swoop and dart over the fields beyond. The air cools to a mild chill.

He hits the casket just three feet down. A little more exploratory digging outlines its shape. He clears just enough space to expose the lid, which is loosely attached. More evidence of tampering.

"Okay, bring the light over," he instructs Rachel. With the beam centered, he removes the lid.

The mummified remains of a two-year-old child stare up at them and into the firmament. All except for the bones of the right arm below the elbow.

"I guess they got what they wanted," Lane says softly. "God bless you, April Clarisse West. May you rest in peace."

Lane picks up the model of a Boeing 707 off Larson's cluttered desk in the hangar office. Outside, the turbines on their plane churn the night air. The time of reckoning has come.

"What kind of plane did you say we have out there?" he asks Larson.

"Piaggio 180. Only one I've ever seen," Larson replies.

"But you've seen other big planes land here, haven't you?"

"Nope. Can't say that I have." Fear floods Larson's face. He's a rotten liar.

Lane puts down the model and leans across the desk close in to the old man. "I don't think your memory's serving you correctly. I think that some time back a plane about the size of ours came in here. And I bet they took off in the night, just like us, after they loaded a big box. And they most likely told you to shut up about it. Permanently."

"Don't know nothing about that," Larson mutters, staring at the floor.

Lane reaches out and pats Larson's cheek, causing him to wince. "Good man. That's the right answer. You stick with that."

"Okay."

Lane picks up the model again. "And if anybody asks about us, you do exactly the same thing for us that you're doing for them. Say nothing." He snaps the wings off. The fuselage falls onto the desk. "Does that make sense to you? I hope it does."

"Yeah, that makes sense."

Outside, Lane reviews the other possible sources of leakage as he heads to the plane on the taxiway. The court clerk, the hospital receptionist, the funeral guy. None knew as much as Larson, who just took a highly paranoid vow of silence. With luck, he and Rachel are okay.

He hops aboard and the engines rise in pitch as he shuts and seals the door behind him. The plane surges forward, and Rachel points them into the upper reaches.

17.

TIME OUT

Harlan Green puts on a display of casual indifference, a façade within a pose within a pretense. In fact, he's stunned by what he sees inside Bay 1, where Thomas Zed lies. My God! The man already looks decades younger than when they met.

At the end of that meeting, Green had demanded proof, and here it is. And it changes everything. He plows through the intricate structure of relationships he's constructed, but it's all too complex to deal with at this moment of overwhelming truth.

"The clock's a nice touch," Green says casually, nodding at an antique grandfather clock near Zed's bedside, with its exquisitely engraved face and dangling chimes. "Does it run backward?"

"No, but it should," Arjun tells him.

"So how does it work?" Green asks. "What's actually making him younger?"

Arjun looks up at the multiple levels of equipment and tubing overhead. If their facility had human operators, the procedure would be less technically complex by an order of magnitude, but then their security would be hopelessly compromised. They had no choice but to achieve total automation.

"Basically, he's being genetically reset," Arjun explains. "The system will launch successive waves of artificial viruses that migrate to various groups of cells, where they methodically manipulate the existing DNA in the nuclei and make the required changes. Each virus carries only enough genetic material to trigger the process and initiate a cascade of activity that carries out the actual replacement work."

"You mean a virus can do other things besides make you sick?" Green asks.

"Absolutely. Like computer code, the trigger material in the virus consists of both a program and data. The program directs the copying, swapping and rearrangements of the nucleotide sequences. The data portion of the trigger describes the precise nature of the changes at the key locations where Zed's nucleotide sequence has drifted away from its ideal state. Another set of viruses carries the code to make the enzymes that lay down the epigenetic factors, like methylation patterns."

"And what's this ideal state?"

"You reach it in young adulthood, when the developmental processes are complete. After that, you start to fall into disrepair."

"I know the feeling," Green admits.

"We all do," Arjun adds. "During the procedure, the brain and the nervous system are among the most difficult targets, and their transformation is as challenging as repairing an automobile while it's still in motion on the road. The immune system is also problematic. It has no intention of standing idle while a massive invasion takes place and, if permitted, it would react so violently as to destroy the body while trying to defend it."

"So how do you hold it in check?"

"The procedure carefully controls both the timing and sequence of the cellular repair work. It relies on feedback from the body, data gathered continuously as the procedure moves forward. Blood chemistry, body temperature, cardiac rhythms, brain waves, blood oxygenation and a dozen other factors are considered by the computational algorithms running on the supercomputers in our control center. This information drives real-time decisions, which automatically adjust the metering of the virus flow and the delivery of immune-suppressants. The margin between life and death constantly expands and contracts during the process but is kept scrupulously within specified limits. When the process is complete, the optimized genome will occupy the nucleus of nearly every cell in his body."

"Amazing," Green mumbles.

"Yes, it is," Arjun agrees. "You're a fortunate man, Mr. Green. Very few are called, and even fewer are chosen. The original process required you to have an identical twin that had expired while still young. The sibling's genes provided a reference point to initiate the procedure. But now we're on the verge of extending the process to virtually anyone. No twin required."

"You mean someone like me?"

"I mean exactly you. But first, we have a few technical details to resolve. And the only person who can do that is Dr. Anslow. We're going to need him back on the job – at least for now."

Arjun can see Green racing through countless internal calculations and coming up short of a simple solution. Arjun knows that Green is holding Anslow at some secure location, probably arranged by the Bird. As soon as Harlan hands Green over, he loses his principal bargaining chip.

"At this highest level of play, it ultimately comes down to trust, Mr. Green," Arjun interjects. "You hold enormous political capital and expertise that we can't hope to duplicate. We, on the other hand, hold considerable economic and technical power. The only way to merge them is to cooperate fully. Don't you agree?"

Green pauses. "All right, you can have Dr. Anslow, but on one condition. If we're to move ahead, I need full disclosure about the inner circle of participants. How many people are involved, and who are they?"

"The answer is quite simple, Mr. Green. Just you and I and Mr. Zed." Arjun omits Crampton from the list. To Green, she's an unknown quantity, a potential complication. "And we assume that you'll want to be directly involved in determining any future membership."

"Absolutely."

The pair leaves Zed, who lies completely still, engulfed in tubes and sensors. A heavy layer of sedation masks the great molecular migrations within him.

"When are you coming home, Daddy?"

His son. The little boy's face barely clears the bedside. The troubled blue eyes wound him deeply. How can he tell the boy what will happen to him? How can he explain that the boy will grow up, grow old, and die without a father to guide him? He tries to reach out and touch the small cheek, but the restraining straps prevent it.

"It's too late," Zed explains. "I'm so sorry. It's too late."

He closes his eyes in exhaustion beyond measure.

A movement on the video monitor in Bay 1 catches Arjun's attention. Zed's head has turned to the side. His left arm pushes against the straps, and his hand reaches out to the side of the bed. Unusual. Arjun checks all the monitor data, and sees nothing out of range. By the time he looks back, Zed is once again at rest.

Autumn has an unobstructed view of the tomato plant from where she sits on her deck in Pinecrest. It bears seven tomatoes, some fat and red, others clouded with yellow, and a few still a perfect green. A small lattice supports the burden they place on the snaking vine that binds them to the soil below.

Much of her last two decades now lies in shadow; but further back, the tomatoes remain as vivid as those hanging here.

She was picking the final crop of summer the day her husband died in 1965. She was on the last vine when she heard him call from inside. His voice gave no hint of alarm. By the time she got to the living room, he was face down on the carpet, his life already gone.

She never married again, never dated. In a town so small, the prospects were few and just not worth the effort. She simply let herself drift with the tide of time as it swept across the endless prairie. Her circle of friends, never large, gradually died off. She watched the neighbors' children grow up and leave. She attended the funerals of their parents. She saw the town slowly wither. She faded into the far recesses of its collective memory.

Each season, the tomatoes filled the vines and awaited their harvest while marking the milestones of her advancing age. While still strong, she tended a row of plants that spanned half the width of the garden. Later, as she declined physically, the crop became a single vine in a big planter on the back porch. Still later, it shrank to a small pot on the windowsill.

Autumn rises from her chair on the deck. The power in her legs still seems odd. She'll never adjust to it, but that no longer matters. She goes inside and wonders about the progress of Zed's treatment as she pours herself a glass of water. As soon as there was any change, they would send a shuttle for her.

He didn't understand the futility of his quest. How could he?

She looks back out through open doors to the tomato vine. Zed had strongly opposed her leaving her life on Mount Tabor but in the end he yielded. It was the only chance he had of preserving their relationship. Her confinement had grown stifling, and she demanded a chance to redefine herself in the world at large. He insisted on Pinecrest for security reasons, and she conceded it was a workable compromise.

For the first few days after moving in, she stayed close to home, acclimating herself in welcome solitude. She realized how utterly Zed had dominated the rhythm of her days. Soon she was ready to venture out and took the air hop to the Trade Ring, with its glittering array of shops, restaurants, clubs and galleries. Wandering the streets and corridors, she could feel the invisible presence of Zed's security people quietly monitoring her. It didn't matter. She had no alternative agenda.

She basked in the acknowledgment and attention wherever she went. The smiles, the nods, the pleasant exchanges. In her previous life, such amenities had slowly evaporated as she aged. A pretty young woman was a beacon of promise, an older woman was not. Over time, enthusiasm and flirtation gave way to compassion and sympathy.

But no longer. When she ate dinner alone at a fashionable French restaurant, she felt the peripheral presence of several men. They gave her furtive glances, and one was bold enough to engage her with an amused smile – much to the annoyance of his female companion. But it wasn't her renewed sexuality that enthralled her as much as the range of options it presented, the unlimited choice of potential partners and experiences.

She was paying the bill when it happened, and it changed everything. She looked up at the waiter, a handsome man in his mid-thirties, probably an actor when he wasn't waiting tables. Something flipped within her, and in a heartbeat he was transformed from a possible lover into a child, an impossibly distant little boy. The gulf of nearly seventy years loomed between them without warning, like a rogue wave born of some momentous yet invisible event far beyond the horizon.

As she got up to leave, she looked out over the diners, who sipped their wine, laughed their laughs, and spoke their pieces. Children, all of them children.

She took the air hop back home and never bothered to return.

"I'm sorry, Ms. Wentworth, but you're going to have to refresh me about how you got this number," Arjun says politely.

The matronly woman on his screen takes immediate offense. She wears cat's-eye glasses and severely trimmed hair in a tight curl. "I was told there would be compensation if I reported a certain transaction."

"And you're calling from where?"

"Elkton," the woman declares impatiently. "Elkton, Nebraska. I work at the county courthouse."

"Ah yes, of course. Do you still have the ID number you were given?"

Eleanor Wentworth recites the number slowly, as if addressing a child or an idiot. The woman now has Arjun's full attention. After the extraction operation in Elkton, they set up a small security net, and apparently this frumpy clerk was part of it. Sure enough, her number checks out.

"If you open another window, you'll see the agreed-upon sum being credited to your bank account."

Eleanor looks way from Arjun as she watches the transaction. "We don't get any retirement," she laments. "Nothing. Not anymore." As if this justified her felonious intrusion into someone's privacy.

"Well, this should go a long way toward solving that problem. Now, what have you got for us?"

"A man showed up here this afternoon, and wanted a death certificate for an Autumn West."

"Did you get his name?"

"No. And he paid cash. But I have what you need. I have video."

"Good. I want you to send it to this number. Is there anything else?"

"Not that I remember."

"Well, thank you for your help."

He breaks the connection and opens the window where the video is loading. It's been shot from a high-res security camera overlooking a counter in a dreary old building. The plump figure of Eleanor stands facing away from the lens. She unconsciously tugs the back of her sweater down to cover the bulge of her generous bottom over her cheap slacks.

The man in question faces her and triggers an immediate alarm in Arjun. He zooms in to verify. The image remains sharp, even at 10-power enlargement.

Allen Durbin, the Pinecrest resident. The one that Linda Crampton tried to screw. The one that showed up on the security camera at the Institute. The one who casually asked her about Mount Tabor and the dead scientists.

Allen Durbin. He checked out all the way. So who would know how to create such a professionally crafted façade?

A cop. An experienced cop.

Arjun gives a voice command that connects him with Bellows, the deputy coroner in Washington County.

"Bellows," the voice offers in a flat, offhand tone. Audio, no video. Very arrogant, thoroughly bureaucratic.

"It's Arjun Khan." The video comes on. The attitude changes.

"Yes, Mr. Khan?"

"I'm putting up a video. I want to see if you can identify the man in it."

Bellows squints at his screen and nods. "Yeah, no problem. That's Lane Anslow. The cop, the one I met with about his brother and the crash. Remember?"

"Indeed I do. Thank you."

Arjun hurries out of his office and heads toward the conference room. He glances down the cavernous space to his left, where they are prepping one of the bays for the Phase Two test. All they need to do is decide which candidate it will be, but right now that may be the least of their problems.

He knocks on the door and steadies himself. He's still unsettled by what he's about to see.

"Come in." The voice is strong, forceful, driven by a generous volume of expelled air.

Arjun opens the door. Zed sits at the far end of a long table with his computer.

It works. It really works. Its value is nearly incalculable.

The wrinkles are gone, the palsy absent, the spine straight, the eyes clear and bright, the jawline firm, the movements sure, the musculature solid, the hands confident. Zed appears to be in his forties, which is as far back as they wanted to risk in a single treatment.

Arjun tries to conceal his shock as best he can. "Sorry to bother you, but we have an urgent issue. Remember Allen Durbin, the resident at Pinecrest that Crampton was messing around with? He's not Allen Durbin. He's Lane Anslow, the cop. Dr. Anslow's brother."

Zed puts it together before Arjun can speak again. "Autumn. He's on to Autumn." He pushes up out of his seat and begins to pace with his hands in his pockets.

"I'm afraid so. I just received video of him at the county courthouse in Elkton, requesting her death certificate."

"So how much does he know?" Zed asks. "Has he made contact with her?"

"We'd best assume that he has. Do you think she would tell him anything?"

Zed shakes his bald head, as he awaits the reawakening of the follicles. "Absolutely not."

"Even if she hasn't, he must be close to putting it all together."

"Which means he has to go, right now. Make it happen."

"Very well." Arjun turns to leave.

"And while you're at it, add Ms. Crampton to that list. We need to plug all our holes for once and for all."

Arjun nods. He approves. The inner circle is now Zed, Green, and himself. The fewer, the better, because people talk. They always talk.

18.

BETTY SCREWS UP

A great city glides by below in black and white. Wooden skyscrapers thrust up, topped by all manner of ornaments. An orchestra plays solemnly. At street level, a child's sled rests atop a lifetime of flotsam. A laborer's hands reach out and grasp its runners and carry it to the maw of a giant furnace. In it goes. The flames lick eagerly at its spruce topside. The varnish boils and bubbles across the signage, the timeless provenance.

Rosebud.

The blaze completely consumes the sled. It rises as black smoke up a stone chimney and forms a twisting column that dissipates into a dreary sky, marking the end of Xanadu.

Citizen Kane concludes. The recessed lights come up in the theater room in Zed's residence atop Mount Tabor. He and Autumn sit in adjustable chairs with a table between them holding wineglasses and hors d'oeuvres. Both bask in the glow of reclaimed youth. Skin clear and smooth. Eyes bright and alert. Spines straight. Musculature toned and supple. Hair lustrous. Lips full and sensuous.

Zed turns from the screen to face Autumn. "Did you like it?" he asks.

"It's sad."

"Yet beautiful."

"Yes, I suppose it is," she sighs.

"Have you seen it before?"

"Maybe I did. I'm not sure. I saw so many things."

Zed looks over to the far wall, which is covered by a mural of cinematic history, from Muybridge on. "But some things endure. They're memorable. And this is one of them."

"If you say so."

"I'm not asking you to defer to me. I've never asked that."

"No, you haven't."

"Then why are you keeping so much distance between us? I don't understand."

"It's like you want me to be grateful for what you've done." Her eyes are perfect, clear and cool, as she says it. "Am I supposed to be obligated to you?"

Zed flashes just a hint of exasperation before he collects himself. "No, I don't expect gratitude. After all, you never asked. You only received."

"Then what do you expect?"

"Right now, all I ask is a little patience. Look at me. I've already closed most of the gap between us. I need just one more pass and we'll be completely aligned"

Autumn stares at the new Zed, the renovated Zed. His skin glows in the recessed lighting that lines the ceiling. He's become a novelty, and novelties have little intrinsic value.

"Think of it," Zed continues. "Our experience is unique. No one else can share what we'll have together."

"I don't think you know at all what we'll share. You only think you do."

"Then tell me the truth of it. I want to know."

Autumn stares out to where the green foothills gather beneath the rock and snow. "I'm sorry. I'm not strong enough. Not anymore."

Zed looks at the blank video screen. "We all have our Rosebud. What's yours?"

"I was a little girl, maybe seven or eight. There was a pond nearby, one I could walk to. It was a warm day, probably early spring, and I saw a pair of Canada geese floating within a few feet of the shore. They looked huge in that tiny pond, and they scared me a little, but I moved to the edge of the water and stared at them. They couldn't have been more than a few feet way. They floated almost motionless and stared back at me. I was close enough to take in every detail: their long black necks, dark brown eyes, and a band of white that wrapped under their throats. And they could see all of me. The difference was, they weren't impressed, while I was in awe. I don't know how long it went on. Just me and them and the buzz from all the bugs. And then they turned like two tugboats and paddled off around a bend in the rushes. And that was that. The beauty and innocence of it has never left me."

"I appreciate that you shared that with me." Zed grasps his wineglass. "It helps me understand you a little better." He waves his hand over a sensing device and the windows go from opaque to clear, revealing the city below.

"Were there others before me?" She trains her eyes on his.

"What do you mean?"

"What happened to them?"

"I'm not sure I understand what you mean."

"I think you do."

"Yes, there were others. The outcomes were less than positive."

"Did they suffer, did they die?"

"There was no suffering. We made sure of that."

"Did they die?"

"In a sense, they were already dead. You know that. And for a moment, they stood on the precipice of a salvation they could never have imagined."

"But then they fell."

"As I said, they had already fallen. We put out a net to try to catch them, but unfortunately we failed."

Autumn closes her eyes. "How long are we going to go on like this? What's the point of it?"

"It's time. I'm nearly ready to be with you."

"And then what?"

"You won't be alone. We can rebuild. Together. Only this time, we can draw upon all that we've learned over so many years."

"So many years," Autumn repeats. "Can you feel the weight of them?"

"Yes, I can, and that's the point of all this. To shed the weight, to fly once again."

"And what if something goes wrong?"

"I don't see failure as an option. But if somehow something does go wrong during my treatment, I've made provisions that you'll be taken care of for the rest of your life."

"Which life?"

"You need to develop a more positive attitude. The potential here is tremendous. All you have to do is accept the possibility of a life without end."

Autumn rises. "I have to go."

Zed stands, but keeps his distance. "Just hang on a little longer. That's all I ask. You need to give us a chance." His voice assumes a soft urgency. "You have so much to gain and so little to lose."

Autumn turns and heads toward the door. "I'm going now."

From his living room window, Zed looks down on Autumn, who has just boarded the chartered air hop, which rests in the abandoned reservoir below.

It would be easier to build his case if he knew more about her. But in fact, no one knows much about her. That's one of the reasons she was chosen.

He's sent investigators back to learn more, but they've uncovered little. She's slipped almost completely out of living memory. Only matters of public record remain.

Autumn West. Born in Elkton, Nebraska, in 1922 to a Gerard and Trudy West. Another child of the timeless plains.

Zed watches the helicopter's rotors come up to speed and the navigation lights wink on the fuselage. He reaches back and recalls 1922. The Roaring Twenties were revving up, and he roamed the globe, assembling an anonymous empire.

Outside, the chopper rises out of the reservoir. A furious little storm of stray leaves spins in the wake of its rotors.

Autumn West. Attended Jefferson Grade School in Elkton and graduated from Midland High School in 1941. Her yearbook picture showed a pretty young woman with hair done in the soft curls of the time.

The helicopter clears the lip of the reservoir and rotates about its axis. It nods forward in ascent to the late afternoon sun. Zed watches it gain altitude for its trip back to Pinecrest.

She was married in 1943 to a John Miller. The announcement in the *Elkton Gazette* showed the archetypal radiant bride, staring out into a great beyond filled with domestic bliss.

She worked for the local school district, but a fire destroyed her personnel records in 1952. Her husband died in 1965. There was no record of any children.

Zed lingers at the window as the helicopter becomes a speck in the sky above the hills. After 1965, Autumn West fell away into a great void. No documents, either public or private, tracked her journey through the decades to come. No witnesses survived to give illuminating accounts of her character.

The aircraft disappears from view, but Zed remains stationary in the window. He recalls that day he walked through the snow on the edge of Central Park. Behind him, his wife and young son slept the perfect sleep of the innocent. Could Autumn understand this shameful act of desertion? Had she done something similar during those long decades of anonymity? Could they exchange forgiveness and move on to mutual redemption?

Right now, he can only speculate, and it causes a great fatigue to invade the very center of his bones.

Lane stands on the balcony of his house and looks out toward the front of his property in Pinecrest. A hundred feet of expert landscaping flows out to the main road, which is hidden from view, even from his elevated position. He closes his eyes and returns to Elkton, Nebraska, and tries to visualize Autumn West walking those dusty streets so long ago. It doesn't work. It's time to get a firsthand account from Autumn herself, along with an explanation of how it all relates to Mount Tabor and his brother.

He pulls out his phone and punches up the interface.

The Surgeon holds no degree, no license, no sanction from any regulatory body anywhere. Rather, his legitimacy comes solely from the unfettered play of market forces across the global sphere of commerce. For the Surgeon, it's not about the money; it's about performance, process and flawless execution. He relishes his work and has achieved a level of proficiency envied by his peers, who know him only by his product. He can say with certainty that if he'd entered the medical mainstream, he would have rapidly ascended to the top tier of surgeons worldwide. His success rate is 100 percent, all the way from pre-op consulting to completed procedure.

Even the guard at the Pinecrest gate notices the fluid grace of the Surgeon's hands as the man signs the clearance form after having his lobe scanned. The pen flows in beautiful cursive strokes, as if guided by an angel.

"Will that do it, then?" the Surgeon asks the guard, with a tiny crust of arrogance coating the words.

"Not quite," the guard says. "We'll need to scan your crew and take a look in the back. It's standard procedure here."

"Very well, then," the Surgeon says impatiently. "Let's get it done."

The Surgeon and the guard walk toward the ambulance, a big, boxy vehicle parked in a holding area just outside the gate into Pinecrest. Ambulance traffic is a routine part of life at the gate. Although the community has a well-equipped medical center with two operating rooms, the aging population often requires highly specialized treatments at one of the big facilities up at the Medplex. As always, this ambulance and its crew have been precleared through the security database; but still, the procedures manual mandates a personal inspection.

"So who's this Allen Durbin?" the guard asks as they approach the ambulance. "He must be new here. I don't recognize the name."

"I believe he is," the Surgeon says. "Probably just moved in."

"Well, I guess it didn't do much for his health," the guard comments as he pulls out his lobe scanner.

"I guess not," the Surgeon responds as they stop at the driver's window, which is rolled down to reveal a wiry, middle-aged man dressed in paramedic coveralls. The man manages a faint smile as the guard reaches up, scans his lobe, and checks the reading.

"This is a pretty big rig you've got here," the guard says as they move to the rear to open the double doors.

"We need to be prepared for every possible contingency," the Surgeon explains as he opens the doors.

"Jesus!" the guard exclaims. "Looks like you could perform a whole operation in here." He's seen the interior of a lot of ambulances, but never one this richly appointed with technology and tools. A female paramedic comes forward. She seems pleasant enough, and cooperates with the scanning process.

"Okay, you're cleared," the guard announces to the Surgeon while the paramedic climbs back in and shuts the doors. "Good luck."

"Thanks," the Surgeon says with a smile, and then watches the guard depart. They're done. There'll be no further inspection on the way out. The security people have learned through costly litigation that it's not a good idea to delay the departure of ambulances holding potential medical emergencies.

Once they're inside the gate, the Surgeon ignores the amenities of Pinecrest. The general population here is too old and presents very little product potential. The subject, Allen Durbin, is an exception. He's middle-aged and apparently in exceptionally good health. Better yet, the referring party is waiving the referral fee, which increases his profit on the job. The Surgeon goes to his computer, with its encrypted wireless link to the subnets. He travels quickly to a heavily protected location, a commodity exchange.

The global market for human organs.

He quickly scans the columns, checking the bid and ask prices on a variety of items. Any given organ is listed several times to represent different levels of quality determined by sophisticated factoring systems that assess age, disease history, etcetera. The Surgeon is pleased with what he sees. Livers are continuing an upward trend, as are kidneys. The Whole Body Index, which is the composite price of an entire body of A-grade organs, is just below its all-time high.

Mr. Durbin should fetch a nice price.

Betty and Anita are on a roll.

As Betty's big sedan cruises out of the air terminal at Pinecrest, Anita regales her with a long-ago college story. Seems there was this guy with a little tiny brain and a great big dick, and one thing led to another and another. At each inflection point in the tale, they laugh uproariously and Betty slaps the steering wheel so hard that the heads-up navigation display jiggles and bounces. Anita pounds her knees and spills cigarette ashes on the carpet, leaving telltale evidence of smoking that will probably put Betty's husband, Bill, in a great big snit, but that's okay. At least for now.

Sometime way back, Anita was assistant HR director at FiberBlaze before it was acquired and her options went platinum. That was the same year her third husband got cashed out in a technology swap that had something to do with communications satellites, although Anita never quite understood the significance of it. Betty, on the other hand, was a marketing wiz and had kept putting together these promotion packages that always left the target audience salivating for more. Her husband, a third-tier accountant, was simply along for the ride because he made such a pretty trophy boy. Both couples moved to Pinecrest about the same time, and it didn't take long for the two women to form an ad hoc affinity group.

Today, after shopping, they had lunch downtown but never got any further than the three gin and tonics they ingested on empty stomachs. No problem. They'd stop in the village, get a sandwich, and straighten halfway up before they went home.

And what if they didn't? So what? At twenty-six/sixty, and forty-one/seventy-two, it's great fun to be bad girls now and then. They deserve it. Screw the world.

"It's coming right up," the Surgeon announces as he glances down at the navigational display. He's switched to driving, and the other man is in the back of the vehicle putting on his working gear. He's contract military and prefers to be called Colonel although it's unlikely he was ever an officer in anyone's army. He presents himself as a combat specialist, an individual who has frequently dwelled near the tip of the national spear. His credentials in this regard are impeccable. Kazakhstan, North Korea, Venezuela, Nigeria, Yemen.

The Colonel pokes his head out of the back and surveys the scene out the windshield. "Stop for a minute," he commands the Surgeon, who complies. "Okay, I want you to pull forward and back into the driveway about thirty feet. I'll take it from there. Give me ten minutes and you've got your product."

Ah yes, the product. Always a cut above what the market expected. A grade-B liver extraction done by the Surgeon sold as grade A. A grade-C pancreas removal moved up to Phase Two. Some on his team thought that it was the cumulative effect of a finely honed process and superb execution, but the Surgeon himself thought otherwise. He firmly believed it was the EEG, the brainwave pattern, which made the difference.

In traditional organ harvesting, the procedure was done when the patient was technically dead, that is, when the EEG showed an absence of brain activity, the classic flat line. Of course, that didn't mean the subject was dead in the fullest sense. The more primitive parts of the nervous system often carried on quite nicely. Heart muscles still contracted, lungs admitted air, and so on. Which also meant the organs were suffused with oxygen and nutrients right up until the time they were yanked out. An ideal situation.

But not ideal for the Surgeon. He had a deep suspicion that brain death at the higher levels had a negative impact on robustness of the organs. Although he had no empirical proof, he was convinced that an ideal brain state for organ extraction lay not far below the normal sleep state. He made a careful study of the anesthetic procedures required to achieve this state and learned how to apply them. It was a delicate balancing act. If you went too low, the subject might slip into a more suppressed state and even flat line on you. Too high, and the patient might be pulled back to full consciousness while being disassembled, which profoundly disturbed bodily harmony.

The Surgeon was skillful enough that he'd never experienced this, but occasionally the level of sedation had wandered enough that he noticed a fluttering beneath the subject's eyelids. The REM state of sleep, the dream state. For the briefest moment, he tried to imagine what these dreams might be like, but then thought better of it and went on with his work.

"Ten minutes," the Surgeon confirms and reaches to put the vehicle back in gear.

"What's Bill gonna think?" Anita asks Betty as they float down the tree-lined road past an occasional gate. She's referring to Anita's fussy husband, who won't be happy with his spouse's inebriated condition.

"Fuck Bill," Betty proclaims woozily. She peers down her nose over the top of the steering wheel.

Anita guffaws, reaches into her purse and lights another cigarette. Fuck Bill. Then she remembers that she's already done exactly that, at that party at the Stevensons' last year.

And in a great burst of drunken candor, she spits it out. As a joke, of course. After all, they're on a roll, so why slow down and ruin it?

"Boy, lady, your husband's one lousy lay," she says and waits for the reciprocal burst of laughter from Betty.

Betty whirls toward her in disbelief. "What'd you say?"

Anita quickly backtracks under Betty's withering gaze, and struggles to rebound. "I simply said… that… "

"You simply said you fucked Bill, you bitch."

The collision alarm bellows and brakes automatically activate. Still, by the time Betty turns her attention back to the road, it's too late to take any action. All she sees are the two glowing brake lights on an ambulance as they collide squarely with its rear bumper and the airbags inflate.

The Surgeon and the driver have been concentrating on the driveway and are completely surprised by the force of the collision. The Surgeon bounces in his seat belt and the Colonel is thrown back into the interior. The female paramedic shrieks.

"Son of a bitch!" the Surgeon yells as he unbuckles himself and throws the door open. Due to the bulk of the ambulance, he can't see what hit them. The Colonel comes forward and thrusts the other door open. "I'm going in. Gotta go before he comes down here to see what's going on."

"And just what am I supposed to do?" the Surgeon asks.

"Security will be here pronto. You handle it while I take care of business. I'll hold the product until you're clear." He adjusts his armored vest and chambers a round in the compact combat weapon he carries.

Lane is just about to give the voice command to call Autumn when the explosive thud of the collision rumbles across his deck. It comes from out on the street in front of the house, but he can't see that far through the foliage. He hurries through the house and starts down the driveway, which curves downhill. He rounds the bend, and the accident scene comes into view. An ambulance with a sedan piled into the back of it, steam and smoke pouring from under the crumpled hood.

Then, the problem. A man with a combat vest stands next to another man beside the ambulance, both oblivious to the accident. The man with the vest reaches into the vehicle and pulls out a weapon. Lane retreats around the bend and watches from concealment. The man starts up the driveway, weapon at the ready. It's obviously a combat rifle, with a hefty clip.

Lane runs back toward the house. The rifleman will hear his footsteps, but that's the least of his problems. He sprints in past the open door and retrieves his pistol from his coat hanging in the anteroom. It possesses considerable stopping power but will be no match for the assault rifle.

He'll get one shot, if he's lucky. He extends his pistol and steadies against the door frame. The man comes around the bend in the driveway and spots him instantly. Lane aims for the center of the chest as the other man swings the rifle in his direction. A head shot at this distance is too risky. If he misses, he's dead.

He squeezes the trigger and the muzzle blast roars down the driveway. The man flies backward and out of sight around the curve.

Lane doesn't stop to investigate. He grabs his coat, runs through the house and out the back door. At best, the incident is over. At worst, he's bought himself some time before they regroup and come after him.

The Surgeon hears the shots as he starts around the ambulance to investigate. He didn't expect such rapid action. Maybe they can wrap this up quickly enough to avoid local security. So far, no one has seen them. He reaches the wrecked sedan and hears feminine wailing and moaning from within, where the air bags are wilting from their state of electronically triggered tumescence.

It's two well-dressed, well-coiffed women, blubbering and terrified. When the Surgeon opens the driver's door, he smells the booze. Some things never change. The driver's a rejuve, an expensive one. His expert eye calculates her at about thirty-five/sixty. Not a lot of value there, but better than nothing. They'll take her just in case they miss the primary target. He looks past her to the other woman, who appears to be about a forty-five/seventy. No value at all. They'll just put her to sleep right where she sits.

"It's all right now," he purrs to the sniffling Betty. "I'm a physician. We'll have you out of there in no time. Just relax."

He strides to the front of the ambulance, where the paramedic is climbing out of the driver's side. "We're going to need to pull forward so we can get the back doors open," he informs her. Just then, the Colonel appears, coming down the driveway on shaky legs. A big hole in the outer fabric of his vest exposes the point of impact.

"Jesus! What happened?"

The Colonel ignores the question. "Pull forward. I need to get in," he orders.

The Surgeon nods to the paramedic, who moves the vehicle forward, disengaging it from the sedan. The ambulance has a big industrial-strength bumper and has sustained almost no damage. The Surgeon follows the Colonel to the rear and watches as he enters and then exits with a large backpack.

"We're moving to the contingency plan," he informs the Surgeon. "Go ahead and leave. Once I've secured the product, I'll contact you."

"How long do you think it'll take?" the Surgeon asks.

"Don't know," the departing Colonel says. "It all depends on how good he is."

19.

THE BALLAD OF BOBBY OTA

Lane stands on the slope of a hill covered with low-slung forest and islands of dry yellow grass. Overhead, the clouds have blotted out the last traces of blue and carry the gray promise of rain. About thirty feet in front of him is the security fence that defines the outer perimeter of Pinecrest. Barbed curls of razor wire top its thick steel mesh as it snakes along the slope.

But the most formidable barrier of all is the hole scooped underneath the fence, a curved cavity maybe a yard deep and just as wide. The product of digging by a dog, a special kind of dog.

Sure enough, Lane spots three large mastiff-like canines loping along the outer edge of the fence. Enhanced. A few extra genes make them unusually bright and extremely dangerous. Even from sixty feet away, he can see it in their eyes. He removes the pistol from his jacket, clicks off the safety, and backs into the bush before they spot him. Fortunately, he's upwind from them and they haven't caught his scent.

While he waits for them to leave, he speculates on the origin of the shooter outside his house. Crampton comes to mind. Maybe the Institute did a little probing of its own and he was exposed. And what about Autumn? She was connected to Mount Tabor, and so was Johnny, who tried to make a deal with the Green people to blow the lid off. Lane sighs. It's all just speculation.

The dogs have disappeared, so he bolts up and runs to the hole in the fence. A brief bout of crawling puts him through. The dogs will eventually detect the scent of his escape and report it to Pinecrest's security apparatus. But by then he'll be long gone. Besides, the security people aren't the real problem.

The real problem is the man who came up the driveway, weapon in hand. If he's hard-core military, Lane's bullet into his armored vest is nothing more than a setback. The final assault is yet to come.

The Colonel hears the ambulance depart as he clears the last room of Lane's house. The open back door suggests that the product has fled on foot into the woods. So be it. The assault will now become the hunt. At the dining room table he deposits the backpack and extracts the components of a portable .50-caliber sniper rifle. With practiced hands, he assembles the bolt-action weapon, screwing on the barrel and flash suppressor.

He reaches back into the pack and pulls out a 3 x 9 scope with its big 60-mm objective that gathers maximum illumination. After fitting it to the rifle, he puts the weapon down and extracts a plastic box with a single switch and a power indicator light. The light winks on as he activates the device. He plugs in a slender wire that leads to what appear to be two thimbles as thick as pencil erasers. He puts the box in the backpack with the wire trailing out and then shoulders the pack, pulling the straps taut.

The Colonel grasps the protruding wire and carefully inspects the two thimble-like devices, which are held in a flexible plastic frame. At close range, he can see that most of their surface is actually a screen of fine mesh. He braces himself for what comes next. It will take all his discipline to withstand the initial shock. He inserts the thimbles into his nostrils while slipping a retaining band over his head to keep them in place.

The twin nasal amps pour an almost unbearable cascade of odors into his brain. He has entered a dog's world, where smell jumps forward in the priority of the senses and takes its place right alongside eyesight. He closes his eyes and grips the edge of the table while he struggles to become acclimated. The micromechanical structures embedded in the mesh of the nasal devices are sampling airborne molecules, then increasing their impact by several orders of magnitude inside his nose.

He can now smell Lane Anslow. After several minutes, he releases his grip on the table and walks to the bathroom, where he finds a clothes hamper. In fact, he could smell him even in the middle of the living room. Now, as he opens the hamper lid, the product's signature scent leaps out, shoots up his nostrils.

Time to go hunting.

Once the ambulance has cleared the gate at Pinecrest, the Surgeon drives to a preselected site that ensures privacy. He pulls into the parking lot of the withered remains of an old strip mall. Faded signs advertise pizza, new nails, video rentals, submarine sandwiches, pet supplies, and much more. Boarded windows and drifting refuse suggest otherwise.

First things first. He establishes a heavily encrypted and compressed link with the contracting party. A grainy video shows the man's face, which appears Indian.

"Are we done?" Khan asks.

"Not quite," the Surgeon says. "We're moving to a contingency operation, but I don't expect any further delays."

"It will be more than just an economic calamity for you if you fail to deliver. I hope you understand that."

"I do, and I can assure you that we will deliver, even though it's now a Phase Two project. I'll stake my reputation on it."

"You'll be staking a lot more than that," the man calmly tells him. "If I don't get what was promised, you'll become product instead of producer. Is that clear?"

"Completely," the Surgeon says. In spite of himself, he thinks of the organ donors with the fluttering eyelids, the subjects who dreamed as they were excavated. But more than fear, he feels resentment. His professional competence is being questioned. He remembers one time when the contracting party was a militia leader from a rural area in Alabama. The man had taken one look at the Surgeon's gleaming ambulance and started laughing. Seems it reminded him of the mobile butchering operations that used to cruise through the countryside to carve up deer and cattle. The Surgeon was instantly steeped in profound anger. It took five years, but he eventually arranged to have the man designated as product and personally performed the procedure.

"I'll expect a report later this evening," Khan says, and then the image fractures into random pixels.

The Surgeon sighs. Oh well, at least he can console himself with the accidental acquisition in the back. He looks at his watch. They'd better get started.

When Betty awakens, she is staring at the ceiling of what must be the ambulance they hit. A grid of big lights looms overhead, all extinguished as they await their call to action. Through a fog of alcohol and sedation, she gradually becomes aware of the restraints on her arms and legs, and feels a surge of panic. But then a young female paramedic comes into view and advises her that the buckles are just to keep her from tossing about when the vehicle goes around turns. Betty is reassured by the woman's impeccable bedside manner, and by the glittering array of medical technology that lines the walls. She wants to know where Anita is, but the paramedic explains that the most important thing right now is to get Betty's medical history. Betty cooperates as best she can under the circumstances.

There are a great many questions regarding previous transplants, of which Betty has had many.

Lane pauses on a wooded slope and looks out at the rolling woodland and fields. He's lost his bearings. By now, he should be hearing traffic noise from the freeway. His short-term strategy is simple. He needs to contact Rachel Heinz, and to do that, he needs to make an anonymous call. His cellphone is out of the question. The GPS data will instantly locate him. His best bet is to get to a commercial area off the freeway, steal someone's phone and then make the call.

All he has to do is survive long enough to pull it off. He takes out his pistol and stares at it. After the encounter in the driveway, the clip holds six rounds. His only option is to follow the eastward vector of the gathering clouds and hope for the best.

The Colonel stops on a hillcrest and crouches to rest. He smells rain. It won't be long before it precipitates from the huddle of clouds that scuds over the hills. He wants to smoke but knows it's a horrifying experience when you're wearing nasal amps. The product's smell is increasing in magnitude as he follows the scent. He's gaining on Anslow.

He unslings the sniper weapon, rests it carefully against a tree, and then removes his pack and extracts a box of shells. He pulls out a single round, kisses it for good luck – a habit he picked up in Africa – and chambers it. This species of bullet dates back nearly to the invention of smokeless powder. Over the years, its performance has been improved to where a 600-grain slug can achieve a velocity of nearly 3,000 feet per second, and impact its target with devastating energy. Powdered bone. Jellied flesh. Vaporized blood.

The Colonel chuckles to himself as he puts his gear back on. The Surgeon's loss is his gain. In Phase Two, all that's required is a single organ as proof of the target's identity. It doesn't even have to be in serviceable condition. All you have to do is kill the target, bag up a testicle, and it's all good. A much simpler proposition from a medical standpoint, and a far more interesting one from a hunting perspective.

As he starts down the slope, he puts a little extra spring in his step. It's good to be working again.

With maybe a half hour of light left, Lane spots the column of smoke rising from the far side of a wooded hill opposite. He can just make out the occasional trace of a small footpath, which winds along the base of a hill beside a small streambed that has yet to carry the new rain. The trail draws a ragged line of beige through the dry grass as it conforms to the gentle meandering of the stream. His arms and shoulders are thoroughly soaked through the thin material of his light jacket. Fortunately, the air remains warm. Still, he feels that instinctive longing for shelter.

He silently follows the path until he reaches a tiny valley where a tributary stream joins the one he's following. And there, among the stunted oaks, he spots the lean-to. A large sheet of green corrugated plastic roofing is propped up by wooden posts secured to ropes and pegs. Sheets of plastic tarp droop from the sides, held in place by big stones. The front is left open to the elements and reveals a floor of plywood sheets, warped and curled by the damp.

"Get your hands up! Right now!"

The command comes from his left. A male voice with a rich vein of fear. Lane complies. A man of medium height emerges from the bushes lining the trail ahead. He aims an old .22-caliber rifle at Lane and stares out from beneath a heavy brow that hides the color of his eyes. A thick mat of wet hair merges into a patchy beard marked by pale areas of exfoliation.

"What the hell ya doin' here?" the bearded man demands.

"A good question," Lane responds, racing to assess the situation. He grasps at the one straw he has. During his hurried exit, he instinctively grabbed his old jacket, which still holds the key to a civilized outcome. "I'm a policeman."

"You don't look like no cop to me."

"I'm a detective, not a uniformed patrolman. I'm out here looking for somebody."

"Lookin' for who?"

"For a fugitive," Lane improvises. "He's armed and dangerous. My name's Anslow. Lieutenant Detective Lane Anslow, Portland Police Department, and I've got a badge and ID to prove it."

"Where?"

"It's in my jacket pocket."

The man brings the barrel to bear directly on Lane's face and steadies his aim. "Take it out and throw it over here."

"No problem." Lane slowly reaches in his pocket, pulls out his ID with the attached badge, and gently tosses it near the man's feet.

The man keeps the rifle trained on Lane while he scoops up the ID and scans it. He visibly relaxes and relief floods his face. He lowers his weapon. "I guess you're okay."

"I don't blame you for being vigilant," Lane offers diplomatically. "It's not safe out here, is it?"

"It ain't never been safe out here." The man tosses Lane's ID back at his feet. A good sign.

"It's getting pretty wet," Lane says as he picks it up. "You mind if I get a little shelter with you for a while?"

The man shrugs. "Yeah, I guess that's okay."

Lane moves slowly forward on the trail toward the camp ahead. No sudden moves. "Well, you got my name, but I don't think I got yours."

"Name's Bobby Ota."

Standing on the wooded slope above the little valley, the Colonel tries to stem his growing irritation. First, there was the rain, which he'd hoped would hold off until after the hunt was over. His coat is waterproof, but unfortunately his rifle is not. The big Winchester has a waterproof stock of carbon fiber but the barrel is fabricated from matte stainless steel, and therefore vulnerable to rust. Normally, he would've carefully wrapped the barrel in a neat spiral of electrician's tape, but there simply wasn't time. Bad juju. He has an animistic view of weapons and believes they will be faithful and loyal if you treat them well but will fail you at a critical moment if you abuse them through lax maintenance.

Then there was the timing. He'd planned on finding a natural blind and then waiting for the target to approach, so he could track it until he had the best shot. But now he can see a column of wood smoke from an encampment hidden on the valley floor. The nasal amps tell him that the product has headed that way and will probably seek the security of a larger group.

A difficult situation, but not impossible.

As Lane and Bobby approach the camp, a woman watches them warily. She is squatting beside a woodstove whose chimney pierces the roof near the front of the big lean-to. The fire inside casts a peachy glow on her face as a premature darkness sets in, driven by the gathering clouds.

"That's my wife, Crystal," Bobby explains.

Two children pop out of the dimness at the rear of the windowless structure, a young boy and girl.

"And that's Kenny and Sasha."

Crystal stands, and the children cluster cautiously at her feet. Sasha instinctively grasps her mother's pants leg. All are rail thin, and Crystal looks out through hollow eyes and unkempt bangs. "Who's he?" she asks her husband.

Bobby erupts into a yellow grin of big, neglected teeth. "He's a cop! Can you believe it? He's a cop. Way out here."

They all move into the shelter of the lean-to. A folding table sits in the center of the plywood floor, and is littered with basic kitchen items. Underneath, a row of five-gallon water tanks stands at attention. Farther back are cots and sleeping bags. A ring of weathered aluminum lawn chairs surrounds the stove, and Lane sits down under the watchful eye of Sasha, a diminutive soul with pigtails falling over the collar of an old military field jacket.

"I'm Lane Anslow," Lane says to the woman, who manages a cautious but worried smile.

"Sheena's back there sleepin'," Bobby says and points to a lump in a sleeping bag on one of the cots. "She's not feelin' too good."

Lane feels the edge in Bobby's voice. "And how old is she?"

"She's four," Crystal volunteers. "She'll be five in December. We were still in Texas when she came."

"In Texas?"

"Yeah, in Corpus Christi," Bobby says. "I was workin' in shipping at Almatax. They had that big plant for those net immersion things. Know what I mean?" Bobby asks.

"I think so."

"Well, we'd just take 'em off the end of the line," Bobby continues, "put the foam around 'em, and slip a big box over 'em. Then we'd seal it on up and cart it to the truck. No paperwork, no nothin'. Real slick. Those camera brains did all the rest." He stops, and stares into the fire in the stove, whose door has been left open to provide illumination. "Know what really bugged me the most?"

"What was that?"

"Ya block one of them cameras, and the damn thing would say, 'I am sorry but you are impeding the shipping and packaging process by your current action. Please move to one side.'"

Lane notes how Bobby's accent shifted into perfect media intonation when he mimicked the voice of the camera.

"Yeah, boy. That bugged the hell outta me," Bobby repeats.

"But not for long," Crystal adds. "'Cause then they up and moved the plant to Bolivia."

"Yeah, Bolivia." Bobby says. "Can you believe that crap? Not Mexico or one of those deals. Bolivia! Looked it up on the subnet. Saw pictures of these little guys with funny hats and blankets."

Bobby lapses into a sad silence and stares at the glowing window of firelight from the stove.

The rain grows heavier and hammers at the corrugated lean-to. Outside, the trees are nearly lost in the darkness. Lane feels his stomach twist in hunger but puts the feeling aside. Whatever food these people have, he doesn't want to impose. Obviously, they live on the cusp of malnutrition.

The Colonel knows he's losing daylight as he reaches the edge of the woods where it gives away to the valley. Looking out across the opening, he can make out only the dimmest outlines of the lean-to around the small orange sphere of what appears to be stove light. If he had his nightscope there wouldn't be any problem, but in the heat of pursuit he forgot to pack it.

He walks along the periphery of the woods until he spots the rotting remains of a fallen tree. He settles down behind it, rests the rifle across the trunk, and puts his eye to the scope. A woman is entering the anemic cloud of light, and she carries a small child. A bearded man talks to someone who is obscured from view by the high canvas back of an old lawn chair. The target? No way to be sure.

He sighs again. If only he'd gotten here before they all convened, he could have scored a classic kill. Just like on the plains of Africa with the leopard. Such a lovely beast. Its spots sang a song of perfect motion. They'd shot the bait early in the day, a mature female antelope, slit it open, and left the remains to decompose in the sun near a ginger tree. The heat quickly wormed its way into the dead beast's tissues and set the resident bacteria into a furious, stinking blaze of consumption. In time, the leopard caught the scent, found the antelope, and with amazing strength carried it into the fork of the tree, where the earthbound hyenas could not reach it. With its dinner safe, the leopard left to continue its murderous patrol. The Colonel took up his position in the blind, seventy-five yards from the tree. As the light faded, the leopard returned to consume its prize, walking into his expertly calibrated crosshairs.

But tonight, the light is gone. And so is the blind. Only the killing remains.

Crystal returns and settles carefully into a chair, forming a womb with her arms to embrace the daughter who curls up tightly and takes in the fire with fevered eyes. The child erupts in a spasm of coughing and her face winces with the pain of it.

"That's all right, baby," Crystal says as she reaches for a handkerchief in her jacket pocket and puts it to the child's lips to catch the sputum. "You just got a little chest cold, that's all. You'll be just fine by tomorrow."

Lane looks at the rust-colored stains on the handkerchief and knows otherwise. He's seen it all before. In the Middle East of Portland. Pneumococcal pneumonia. When you're healthy, the bug languishes in the respiratory tract under the vigilant thumb of the immune system. But when malnutrition sets in, the bug attacks the alveolar sacs, the little grapes in the lungs that process the exchange of oxygen for carbon dioxide. The battle produces hemorrhaging, which stains the sputum a rust color. Some strains you can nail with antibiotics, some not. And like Bobby said, they charge you either way.

Sasha reaches down and gently pats her sister's matted hair. Kenny looks troubled, like he senses the truth behind his mother's denial. Sheena has a hint of death in her eyes.

"How long has she been like this?" Lane asks.

Crystal looks suspicious, like she knows that this line of questioning might reveal the desperate truth of the matter. "Couple of days, that's all."

Crystal rises stiffly with Sheena still in her arms. "Think I'm gonna tuck her back in, Bobby. Then I'm going to tuck myself in."

"'Night, darlin'," Bobby answers wearily. He turns to Kenny and Sasha. "You kids go on, too."

"But it just got dark," Kenny protests.

"Yep, that's right," Bobby agrees, "and we're also fresh outta lantern fuel. So go see if you can find some friendly ghosts to play with, okay?"

"Okay." They trot off slowly to the rear.

"You said you're doing lawns now?" Lane asks.

"Yeah. Over in the gates by West Linn."

"How's business?"

"Crappy. Really crappy."

"How come?"

"There ain't no lawns no more. They just landscape the shit out of everything." He rises slowly to his feet, stretches and then digs his long hands into his front pockets. "Jesus, I'm beat. Guess I'm turnin' in, too. You can bag out here in the chair if you want. I'll show you the trail in the morning. You're 'bout two miles from the road. That's probably where your bad guy went."

As he shuffles off, Lane considers the grim truth about the sick girl and early bedtimes. They simply aren't getting enough nutritional energy.

The bill of the Colonel's cap forms a little curved roof over the place where his eye rests on his cheek, and he peers into the scope, seeing the crosshairs settle on the encampment in the glow of the stove. The bearded man facing him through the laminated layers of optics gets up and walks off into the darkness of the inner recesses. The man seated in the canvas chair with the high back remains in place but out of view. Occasionally, his arm and elbow appear as he shifts position.

It has to be the product. The Colonel takes his eye from the scope, pulls out his phone and sends a prearranged message to the contracting party and the Surgeon. It confirms he's sighted the product and gives his current geographical coordinates.

Back to the scope. Nothing has changed. The product remains seated and facing away. He could put a round through the chair back and it would most certainly tear through some part of the upper body, but he just can't accept that. He wants a clean kill, a single round through the chest cavity and the heart that crumples the victim into an instant lifeless heap. Sooner or later, the product will exit the chair, and when he does, he will briefly present the necessary silhouette to get the job done.

The rain beats on the plastic tarp, splattering into the mud behind the lean-to. Lane stares at the warm glow from the ventilation slits in the woodstove. He knows he must stay awake, but his body has other ideas. His eyelids began to droop. Not good. He starts to rise from the chair to fight off the soft, gray blanket of sleep.

The Colonel is a master of calculated response and refrains from action until time and motion align perfectly. As the man rises from the chair, his finger tightens on the fine-tuned trigger, but he controls his squeeze so the weapon won't discharge until the target's whole upper body is dead center in the crosshairs. Then he will apply a pull pressure of exactly three pounds.

The pressure has just passed the point of no return, two pounds, when lightning flashes from above.

For Lane, the flash from the sky and the report of the rifle are separated by only a fraction of a second. Without the lightning – a single brilliant fork stabbing through the clouds – he would have recognized the gunshot. But the union of the two events creates an instant of confusion, which is compounded by the damage from the rifle shot. Thap! A hole appears in the overhead tarp, and a narrow stream of water pours through onto the hot stove top, creating a dense, hissing steam cloud.

In the mist of the cloud, Lane leaps out of the chair and lunges into the night.

The Colonel curses silently as he chambers a second round. Thunder rolls through the valley. His discipline almost carried the day, but the flash triggered a reflexive muscle twitch just strong enough to skew his aim. By the time his night vision recovered, all he could see through the scope was a white fog of steam where the stove had been, and no people.

Cautiously he raises the rifle and returns the scope to the lean-to, and realizes how the steam cloud must have come about. His shot went high, punched a hole in the roof, which poured trapped rainwater onto hot metal. They don't even know they've been shot at. They think the gunshot was thunder. They're probably out in the dark looking for something to fix the roof.

The Colonel lifts his eye from the scope and surveys the dimness out in the valley. Then he gets an extraordinary break. Once again, the lightning lays a brilliant carpet over the open ground, and he sees the product walking, hands in pockets, head and shoulders hunched against the rain. As this instant of illumination fades, he puts his eye back to the scope and catches a momentary glimpse of the man, then all is black once more. He shifts his aim a tiny fraction of a degree, to the spot where the target will take his next step into the night, and fires.

Lane starts his dive into the wet grass just as the lightning flash passes its peak and begins to fade. The bullet travels so close that he can hear its angry fizz through the sodden air. He lies still, waiting for his eyes to adapt, and fervently hopes that the shooter won't probe the night with some exploratory rounds.

The Colonel mentally marks the spot he last fired at and moves his scope back to the encampment, where the steam is clearing. The woman has come out and stares at the hissing stove. He grunts and gets to his feet. He can't wait until daylight to go out there and get the organ to complete the Phase Two procedure. The people in the camp may have a cell, and by morning the whole operation could be in jeopardy. He chambers another round and advances to where he put his last shot.

Lane slowly rolls onto his side, brings out his pistol and comes up on one elbow. His clothes are soaked, and he fights to keep from shuddering as the cold rain pelts him. The only sound is the patter of drops on the hard ground. He faces the direction of the shot, and his pupils expand to their full capacity. The hills and valley are almost completely black, but the sky is faintly illuminated by the urban glow from the north. By now, the shooter is probably advancing and, when he gets close enough, he will be dimly visible against the sky.

It happens sooner than he expects. The outline of a head pokes above the dark skyline. Lane comes up onto one knee so he can steady his aim and take his shot with two hands. In the process, his kneecap comes down onto an old fragment of tree branch, which launches a little burst of snaps and pops as it comes apart under his weight.

In response, the outlined head instantly disappears, but Lane knows he's committed. He lowers his aim slightly below where the head vanished and takes his shot. The muzzle flash strobes a figure holding a big rifle with a mounted scope.

Lane immediately knows from the figure's position that he's missed, and rolls to one side. An instant later, the shooter fires, painting Lane with a thunderous flash, but the round goes wide.

Fortunately, Lane has played this game before. In alleys, in rotting buildings. Rather than panic and scramble for a new position of safety, he recovers from his roll, comes to his feet in a low crouch, and silently circles to the right, his pistol searching for the slightest hint of sound.

None comes. The shooter is smart, perhaps just as smart as he. Two armed men, probing the blackness in search of sudden death, the odds now dead even.

Then the lightning flashes once more, a brilliant spread of forked fractals stabbing at the nearby hills.

Lane and the Colonel spot each other almost simultaneously, both with weapons held ready, both with the same distance to turn and shoot. But the Colonel has a fatal handicap: the inertia of his massive rifle. Lane whirls his pistol through a quick quarter-turn and fires four shots in rapid succession. The muzzle flash from the third reveals the Colonel's arms flying open and the rifle sailing through the air. The fourth shows him toppling backward toward the ground.

"Do you like my tiger kitty?"

Lane opens his eyes to the early morning light. It's the little girl, Sasha, the one with the sick sister. She sits upright in the lawn chair, holding a little stuffed tiger.

"Yeah, I like your tiger kitty," Lane mumbles. Pieces of the previous night come flying back at him. The rain, the lightning, the gun battle, the dead killer. He wishes he could close his eyes and sleep it all away.

"Hot damn! It's a beautiful day, ain't it?"

Lane looks up to see Bobby come shuffling out from the recesses of the lean-to. "Hey, ya hear that thunder last night? Pretty wild, huh?" Bobby says as he stretches his long, bony arms.

"Pretty wild," Lane agrees. He has to leave. Right away. If he stays any longer, he'll put the family in danger again. "Bobby, there was some trouble last night."

"What kinda trouble?" Bobby asks suspiciously as he sits down.

"Remember I told you I was searching for a bad guy?"

"Yeah."

"Well, he found us before I could find him. After you bagged out, he took a shot at me. You never heard it because of the storm."

"So what happened then?" Bobby asks as his eyes narrow.

"I went out to check. I ran into the guy and we fired at each other. I hit, he missed. That's pretty much it." Lane points out into the grass. "He's out there dead. Now, to tell you the truth, I think there's going to be big trouble over this. Really big trouble."

"But you're a cop, right? So how can there be trouble?"

"The dead guy's got powerful friends, even more powerful than the cops. They're going to come looking for him."

"And then what?"

"I don't think you want to wait around and find out, Bobby. You've got to pull up stakes and get out of here."

"And just how in the name of fuckin' Jesus I am 'sposed to do that?" Bobby asks as his fear turns into a desperate anger. "I got no money! I got no job! I got nowhere to go! Nowhere!"

"I know," Lane sympathizes. "And I feel responsible, so I'd like to help out."

Lane reaches in his pocket and pulls out one of several money cards that reside there. "Know what this is?"

"Yeah. It's one of them heavy-duty money cards. Five thousand bucks, I think."

"That's right. It's fully loaded. Here, check it out."

Bobby takes the card, presses the interactive space, and sees a tiny green LED come on. Then he looks up at Lane, waiting for a trap of some kind. "So how much of it do I get?"

"All of it."

Bobby's jaw comes completely unglued and his bargaining posture collapses. "You're shittin' me!"

"Nope. There's only one thing. You have to take Sheena to a doctor right away. She's in really bad shape. You got that?"

"Got it."

"Okay, now tell me how to get over to the freeway."

Walking over the I-5 overpass, Lane watches a truck convoy speed by below. A dozen highway rigs, with armored vehicles front and rear and several motorcycles on the side. It was said the security companies hired former bikers as riders, but that was beside the point. The farther you went from the relative safety of the city, the greater the danger of ambush. A lone rig was pretty much a ticket to the grave. They used to hold the drivers for ransom, but not anymore.

Lane crosses the overpass and heads toward the commercial compound, which has a fast food outlet, a convenience store and two service stations. All sit behind a periphery of security fencing and rolls of barbed wire, with a sandbagged entrance manned by armed guards. He draws strong suspicion from the guards, who unsling their weapons at his approach. They almost never see foot traffic.

He pulls out his badge and holds it up. "Lieutenant Lane Anslow, Portland Police Department."

One of the guards takes his ID and examines it. "How come you're not driving?" he asks.

Lane pokes his thumb over his shoulder. "We had some car trouble down the road. I need to get to a service station." His expert eye sweeps over the gate area. He's in luck. There's no lobe scanner out here. If there was, it would instantly flag the discrepancy between his Allen Durbin lobe and his Lane Anslow police badge.

He starts toward the nearest service station under a dull sky. Fast food wrappers blow by on the pavement and snag in the barbed wire. Paper ornaments on a bristled hedge of stainless steel. The warm air hovers near rain.

He contemplates his next move. Somehow, he has to steal a phone and hope it's unsecured. Cars parked at the plug-in islands present a possible opportunity. People normally don't lock their vehicles when charging. He needs it just long enough to call Rachel Heinz and have her people pull him out of here.

The vehicles suddenly appear from all four points on the compass. They converge quicker than he can run. Armed men leap out wearing bulletproof vests over their uniforms, which identify them as federal marshals.

"Hands in the air!"

Lane complies. "There must be a mistake. I'm a police officer."

"There's no mistake, Mr. Anslow," one of them says as he slams Lane down on the hood. "You're under arrest."

On come the cuffs. Off goes the lobe. "So what's the charge?"

"Well, sir, normally I wouldn't volunteer that kind of information. But since we know you're a police officer, I'm going to make an exception."

"And?"

"You're charged with the murder of Linda Crampton in the community of Pinecrest."

The Feed loves it. Killing in Pinecrest, the headline screams from the display on Rachel's phone. The copy is terse. Female CEO brutally slain behind gate. Another resident taken into custody and charged. A businessman, Allen Durbin.

Rachel stares out her office window. Whatever happened out there all rolled down off Mount Tabor. She's almost sure of it. So how did they get to him? Whatever it was, they most certainly knew that he's Lane Anslow, the cop, the brother of Johnny, and not Allen Durbin. It will eventually come out and the Feed will feast on it. Fired cop offs CEO.

She considers her own situation. No one seems to know about her connection with Lane. She's covered but she has to act carefully. There's no way to reach out to him directly. Whatever she does will have to be very circumspect, because Green's in on it. He has to be. Whatever they did to Autumn West, he's probably next in line. In the end, he may give new meaning to the old tin-pot title of "president for life."

She returns to her desk and absently slides into her chair. It's not hard to extrapolate Lane's future. They'll put him in Pima. But there's an odd twist to her concern for him, which runs deeper than she'd like. It's not his personal safety that gnaws at her; it's the fact that he'll be alone, without her, without anyone. In one sense, he seems so secure in his intent and actions, but in another, he seems utterly lost and on his own. All Lane has left is this search for his brother. He needs more, and she's not sure what will fill the vacuum.

There has to be something she can do.

Habeas corpus.

All experienced criminals and attorneys understand its significance. As do a few informed individuals in the general population. But there it ends, because the concept seldom impacts the life of the ordinary citizen.

Now that it's gone, fewer still grasp its meaning.

As a cop, Lane knows all about the phrase. It demands that there be a lawful reason why a person is being held in custody. In other words, you can't just randomly throw people in jail on a whim. If you try, a writ of habeas corpus can spring them, at least until they are formally charged and stand trial.

And so it was for the longest time in many countries, including the United States. But then came the Midland Mall Massacre, a massive act of terrorism involving multiple bomb blasts coupled with withering automatic weapons fire. It infected the electorate with a novel strain of revulsion. The World Trade Center tragedy had involved an atypical setting in an atypical city. Not so with the Midland Mall. It was full of average people in an average setting in average city. Moms, kids, babies, teenagers, fathers and grandparents. National paranoia ascended to a new level, and the government responded in kind. The long-dreaded strike on the heartland was now a horrific reality. There would be a "temporary revocation" of habeas corpus to ensure the safety of the public in these supremely troubled times.

Of course, the state of emergency never ended, and now Lane sits in the visiting room of the downtown detention center staring through the glass at the public defender who's been assigned to his case. The young lawyer is well intentioned, but she can't explain why he's being charged with a federal offense for a local homicide. It's all very complicated. And not surprisingly, there are delays in setting an arraignment date, so it seems that he will be detained indefinitely.

"Let me help," Lane offers the lawyer through the glass. "I was a cop for twenty years. I can boil all this down into one word."

"What's that?"

"Pima."

PIMA

—

20.

ENHANCED BEST FRIENDS

The truck jerks to a rude stop, and Lane sways violently on the wooden bench. He catches his balance against his duffel bag, which is stuffed to bursting with the standard prison issue. Denim shirts and dungarees. Socks, underwear and basic toilet items. A field jacket with wool lining for winter. A sleeping bag, liner and inflatable mattress. A single pair of work shoes. A mess kit with utensils.

Outside, Lane can hear voices. Male voices engaged in the universal banter of the workplace as they go about the dull comfort of their daily business. The truck is empty, except for him. A dim overhead light shines through a tarnished plastic cover to illuminate the vacant benches and metal-lined walls. Someone has scratched the word freedom into the metal on the opposite wall.

The back door jerks open and the desert light blasts in, full of heat and sky. Lane squints out at the searing expanse and sees a line of aircraft tails stretching to the horizon, like a great swarm of shark fins swimming the waters of a dead sea. The bodies of the permanently grounded planes are hidden behind a shiny steel thicket of razor wire and fencing across a no-man's-land of barren ground studded with sensors on small poles. The truck that brought him is parked at an outer gate at a secondary perimeter of fencing and guard towers. A gravel road runs to an open gate in the inner fence, where various crates and containers are stacked along the road's shoulder.

Lane knows that the gate swings shut one hour before sunset and that no one has ever succeeded in breaching the no-man's-land, because on the far side are towers with machine guns, floodlights and infrared scopes. But the guns are mostly symbolic, because the terrain is patrolled by packs of enhanced dogs, a novel and deadly layer of security.

Lane knows all these things about the Pima Detention Facility. Every cop did. Pima is all about money or, more specifically, the lack of it. With soaring incarceration rates and budgets cannibalized by dubious political agendas, the justice system needed a radical solution to the problems presented by its swollen penal system.

Then someone in the private sector stumbled across the Aerospace Maintenance and Regeneration Center at Davis-Monthan Air Force Base. Five thousand planes parked in the desert just south of Tucson. Seven square miles of aircraft in various stages of interment. Row upon row of dead, dying or embalmed metal birds, all plucked of their guns, ejection charges, and classified avionics; their canopies and observation domes sprayed white with vinyl plastic to ward off the heated blast of sun and the scouring of wind-driven sand. They sprawl over two and a half square miles of compacted alkaline soil and now house a prison population of more than two thousand men.

As Lane stands outside Pima and stares down the road at the great herd of metal tails cutting into the blue horizon, he hears the sound of footsteps, and a guard moves into view.

"All right, up and out," the guard orders.

Lane grabs his duffel bag, moves to the lip of the truck bed, and jumps out. He now sees three additional guards dressed in military combat gear and carrying assault rifles. Behind them, he sees the outer security perimeter stretching into the distance, the fence with razor wire and the squat towers topped with tinted glass and gun ports. Out in the no-man's-land, he can make out a cluster of slinking figures, a pack of enhanced dogs weaving among the sensors.

"Okay, duffel bag down and hands behind your head," the guard barks as he removes the scanner from his belt of many things, all anodized and black. As Lane complies, the guard scans his lobe and then retreats to a small building, where he checks the scan against a database.

"Hands down," the guard orders as he returns. Then he shoves his hands into his fatigue pants pockets and his face curves into a nasty grin behind big aviator sunglasses. "Welcome to Pima, Mr. Anslow," he says as he points down the road. "We hope you have a pleasant stay."

"Isn't there some kind of orientation?" Lane asks.

The guard shares a smirk with his peers. "Pima has a way of explaining itself," he replies. "Now hit the road, buddy. And don't go off it. The doggies don't like that. Know what I mean?"

Lane lifts his duffel bag onto his shoulder and starts down the road. Soon, the silence of the desert prevails as he travels across the barren stretch between these outer and inner worlds. A weak but persistent wind blows across him and churns small clouds of white dust in the afternoon heat. In the far distance, out on the open desert, a twisted funnel of dirt rises hundreds of yards until it dissolves into the blue emptiness. He checks to his right and notes the movement of the enhanced dogs, which appear to be loping away from him.

Waste containers cast short, intense shadows across the road, and as Lane passes them he looks ahead to the snarling cascade of razor wire, now very near. It seems weird to see the big gap where the double frames of the gate are wide open, giving a clear view down an open corridor lined by the great tails and fuselages of old C-130 transport planes. The corridor cuts to the center of the prison, where a large water tower sits on a high frame of four stout legs. Lane thinks he spots human figures there, but the detail is lost in the shimmers of radiated heat from all the baked ground and abandoned metal.

He picks up the sound of panting over the whisper of the wind. He stops. The dogs are here. He slows, until he can see around the corner of the last waste container, and then pauses.

Five bodies line the shoulder of the road, each laid out on a black plastic tarp. Three older men and two younger, all dressed in prison denims, stripped of their shoes, white toes pointed heavenward as the wind stirs a murmur of life into their dead hair.

Three dogs stand over the corpses and carefully sniff, then face each other and pant, their tongues flapping gently like pink flags between a wicked set of carnivorous teeth. They wear radio collars around their huge necks, which taper up into the skull and jaws of a breed descended from the bull mastiff. The nearest one spots him and shoots Lane a look of cognition he will never forget. The beast issues a sharp, abbreviated bark, and the other two also turn toward him. The first dog pants briefly and keeps his eyes locked on Lane as the other two return to sniffing the corpses. Lane understands: The quick pant is a code, an order. It's how they communicate, a code embedded in a stream of staccato breathing, a way around the lack of vocal cords. Their vocabulary is only roughly known but estimated to run into the hundreds of words.

Lane heeds the guard's advice and keeps to the center of the road as he moves slowly forward, eyes fixed on those of the dog. He now understands the dogs' current mission. There has to be some way to remove the dead from the prison, both for ID processing and burial, so they are brought out along with the waste material. But what about the escape possibilities? What if you injected a drug that nearly killed you and you got a free ride out? Not with the dogs. They could clearly smell the difference. He guessed there were standing orders that, if you were still alive, you became fresh dog food.

The alpha dog drifts out of his peripheral vision. Lane moves on, listening for the pounding of paws on the hard ground that would indicate a rear attack. But as he walks up to the open gate, he hears only the wind, which sings a strange little tune as it caresses the razor wire and tickles its harmonic resonance. As he passes through, he sets foot onto a bridge of corrugated and perforated metal that spans a pit full of even more coiled and barbed wire. Halfway across, he realizes he is on a drawbridge that would probably be raised at the same time the gates are closed in the evening.

The first planes are now only a few yards away, and Lane can see how the fat fuselages taper up to the big tail sections. He stops for a moment and looks back. The guards, the truck, even the dogs are gone. The outer perimeter looks seamless except for the road running up to it.

"Welcome to Pima, friend."

The deep voice shatters the desert solitude and Lane whirls around to locate the source. A man emerges from out of the shadow of the first plane's tail, a large man clad only in shorts, sandals, and a cotton vest draped over thickly muscled shoulders. A deep tan crowns his bald dome, and bright eyes beam out from below a jutting brow line. From the center of a black goatee, his broad smile reveals big teeth that take on an almost predatory cast. He walks slowly forward with a confident, athletic ease.

Lane unshoulders his duffel bag and counts his assets. The man is not armed, which gives him at least a fighting chance. Also, Lane has heavy shoes against his opponent's sandals. The man stops a few yards away and folds his massive arms, their sinews amplified by the angular afternoon sun. A small cross is branded in the flesh high on his forehead, above where the hairline would naturally fall.

"Are you a reasonable man?" the stranger asks.

"I suppose you could say that," Lane answers. He looks down the long line of fuselages. No one else in sight. He is on his own.

"Good," the man says. "Then you'll understand that there's a price of admission here."

"Says who?" Lane asks.

"Says me," the man snaps back without hesitation. "You might say that I have the box office concession."

"And how did you get that?"

"It's a long story and I wouldn't want to bore you with it."

"Then don't," Lane replies. He has a plan. If the man attacks, he'll counter with a powerful swing of the bag, which ought to be enough to knock the man off his feet, where he will be an easy target for Lane's shoes.

"Look," the man says as he unfolds his arms and shows his palms in a conciliatory gesture, "I'm just trying to earn my keep as best I can. Can you blame me for that?"

"No," Lane replies tartly, shouldering the duffel bag.

"Then let's be reasonable. All I want is the field jacket, and the wool socks. Yeah, the wool socks."

Lane goes to full internal alert. He's seen this trick before on the street. The man's passive bargaining stance is a ruse, meant to lull Lane into a false sense of control over the situation. The attack is probably already on its way. But from where? He takes his eyes off the man for an instant, scans the full periphery of his vision and sees nothing. The assault must be coming from behind.

He pivots to his rear and sees the same man who is standing in front of him.

His eyes dart back to the first man to make sure there are really two of them. They're twins. The second one, still a couple of yards away, has stopped now that he's spotted. Lane realizes that the shock and confusion of this routine probably gives them the edge they usually need. But not this time. He backs up out of the line between them so he can clearly see both.

The second twin clutches a thick metal bar about two feet long.

"Not a weapon," he says. "The code doesn't allow weapons. But that don't help you any. Now step away from the fuckin' bag before I bash your brains in."

"Don't think so," Lane says evenly. Besides the attitude difference, he notices that the brand on the upper forehead of this twin is a small rectangular bar instead of a cross.

"Then let me explain what I'm gonna do," the second twin growls. "First, I'm gonna break your arm with this," he says as he brings up the metal bar. "Then I'm gonna smack you alongside the skull. But not enough to kill you, no sir. Just enough to make you all gimpy, so you won't bother me while I shove it up your ass."

"Now hold on a minute," the first twin interrupts. "I've made the man a very attractive offer. Just the field jacket and the socks. Everything else he keeps. Who knows? He might even live. Let him settle up and be done with it." The first twin turns to Lane. "What do you say, friend?"

"Fuck him. I don't care what he says," the second twin shoots back. "We take it all."

The first twin sighs as if to apologize for the rude behavior of his brother. "He's probably right. We should probably take it all. I was just trying to get creative, that's all."

"If you take the bag," Lane says, "I walk in empty-handed. Everyone will know. Then I'm dead meat."

"Now there's some truth in that," the first twin says. "But we all die when we come here. In one way or another. Know what I mean?"

"We're though talkin'." The second twin smirks. "Now let's get it on, fuckhead." He comes slowly forward in a crouch.

Lane takes a quick look at the first twin, who gives a passive shrug while taking a step backward. Somehow, it's become clear he won't join in. Lane is about to bet his life on it. He places himself behind his upright bag, denying his attacker the advantage of a frontal assault. If the man lunges in to strike a blow, he'll have to take a side step, and become vulnerable to a counterattack.

The twin anticipates this problem. He lashes out with his foot and kicks the bag onto its side, knowing that Lane will be hopelessly exposed if he stoops to right it. He takes a step back and charges, leaping over the bag and swinging the deadly weight of the bar toward Lane's head. Lane nimbly sidesteps the charge and the man twists sideways from the torque of the missed swing. Before he can recover, Lane knocks the bar out of his grip. As the man crashes to the ground, Lane secures him with a choke hold. His left forearm locks the throat while his right pushes on the nape of the neck. Basic cop stuff. His opponent's air supply is now severely compromised.

The twin's arms flail widely but find no purchase. The man's great bulk and strength let him drag the two of them into a sitting position, but it does him little good.

The first twin comes over and squats in front of them. "Maybe we can work something out," he says calmly. "How about if I leave you the bag itself, with a pair of socks and the sleeping bag liner? How does that sound?"

Lane feels the second twin start to sag from the effect of the choke hold. "Not too good." He nods at his adversary's bulging eyes and purple face. "His brain is running on empty. You better get creative."

The twin purses his lips in resignation. "Okay, you keep it all and I guarantee your passage to the Inner Section."

"The Inner Section?"

"Right now, you're in the Outer Section. There's no code, here. The Inner Section's different. You just might be okay there."

"Throw in some water and we've got a deal."

"Third plane on the right," the twin responds. "There's a five-gallon can and a tin cup."

The second twin has gone completely limp, and Lane relaxes his grip, but doesn't let go. "Here's how we do it. You turn around and walk back to the main gate, and don't stop until you get there. You get far enough away, I'll let your brother loose."

"Agreed." The twin turns and starts off.

When he's some distance away, Lane lets go of the inert brother, who collapses onto the hard ground. Lane hoists his bag onto his shoulder and heads down the corridor between the planes.

He finds the water can and cup right where the twin promised. Standing in the shadow of the plane's tail, he fills the cup, and the gurgle of the water creates a whirlpool of liquid on metal in the great silence. Before drinking, he looks back and sees the first twin reaching the gate and the other rolling over on the ground, clutching at his throat. He drinks two cups of water and wipes his mouth with the back of his hand. Above him, the rudder on the plane's tail begins to swing and creak in the wind like a weather vane.

Jesus, how did it all come down to a place like this?

21.

ADVENTURE AND OPPORTUNITY

Lane stares though the rippled air down the long corridor between the gutted aircraft. Sweat beads over his brow. The road into Pima spans a distance in some unit of measurement he can't begin to understand.

He wants to rest but knows he can't, so the bag goes back onto his shoulder as he moves to the center of the corridor. Great streaks of shadow spill over the bone-hard ground, and the wind fades to a whimper. Ahead, Lane can see where the road ends in some great square, and he can make out an occasional figure in the wobble of ground heat: the Inner Section.

Closer to the central square the distant figures become men in prison denims, walking alone or in small groups. A different kind of plane lines the square: old B-52 bombers, the great drooping giants of the Cold War, their wings severed from their bodies in accordance with treaties at the end of the last century. Twelve dismembered bombers now face in nose first from each side of the square, and their former wings lie across the top of the fuselages, like planks across the rafters in an attic. In the shade of these wings, the prisoners swarm about haggling, bartering goods and services. Several hundred men, at least.

Wisps of smoke issue from the top of certain nearby planes, and the smell of frying meat hits his nostrils. The path around the sides of the square in front of the planes is well worn and filled with prisoners. Even though his duffel bag is clearly the signature of a new arrival, most ignore him. There must be law here, the code the twin spoke of, or he would already be in another battle over his bag.

"Lane!" comes a voice from behind him.

Lane turns to see a wiry man with a handlebar mustache and a prominent nose.

"Whoops, sorry," the man apologizes as he holds up his hands. "Thought you were someone else."

Lane ignores the man and quickly scans the immediate area. Sure enough, a second man is watching them, and quickly breaks off eye contact when Lane spots him. By now, the first man is already walking away.

He's been made. But why?

He considers following the pair, but thinks better of it. The big water tower in the center of the square catches his interest. No pipes lead from its base, so there must an underground system that distributes water. He continues down a row of kitchens projecting from the bomber fuselages, with open-air seating between them.

By the time he reaches the third kitchen, he has a plan of action, and goes right up to one of the cooks.

"What's a guy do to earn a meal?" he asks.

The cook, a sour man with brunched brows and mutton chops, glances up, sees the bag on Lane's shoulder, and goes back to his cooking. Lane waits patiently. It's a game.

"You slop garbage, you clean, you wash," he eventually answers without looking up. "Two coins a day, and one meal."

Lane manages a wry smile. In other words, you work all day and get just enough food to survive. "All right," he agrees. He's an immigrant, and like immigrants everywhere, you start at the bottom of the food chain. Literally.

The cook points toward the nose of the plane, where a short metal ladder runs up into the belly. Lane walks along the metal flank of the great winged beast, which still retains its green-and-rust camouflage. He climbs the ladder and pokes his head into the interior, which is significantly hotter than outside.

A diminutive man stands with his back to Lane. Wearing only shorts, sandals and a dirty tank top, he shoves a frying pan into a big tub of sudsy water. The man is quite elderly, with a feeble fringe of gray hair surrounding a pink, speckled dome.

Lane continues up and in and throws his duffel bag in a corner. The old man apparently doesn't hear him, and continues to scrub away at the pan. Lane moves closer.

"Hello?"

This time the old man turns. His face is a junkyard, except for the eyes, which are perfect: pale blue irises set in flawless white. Not even a single thread of bloodshot.

"Ah yes," he says as he reaches for a towel to dry his hands. "I'm Samuel Winston. Just call me Sam."

"Anslow," Lane responds as he shakes Sam's water-withered hand. "Lane Anslow."

Sam gestures toward the washtubs and cooking implements. "It's very simple. We scrape, we wash, we dry. Then we haul the garbage out back for the morning pickup."

"When do we eat?" Lane asks.

"Normal mealtimes. We take turns. That way, we don't get behind. How about I keep washing and you scrape and dry?"

"Fine by me." As Lane picks up a pot to scrape, Sam goes back to washing the pan.

"What did you do on the outside?" Lane asks.

"I don't remember," Sam answers. "My memory's going. Piece by piece. Or scene by scene, if you will."

"Do you remember how long you've been here?"

"No."

"Do you know what you're in here for?"

"To be honest, I can't recall."

They scrape and wash. The light of late afternoon finds a way in through the windshield behind them and plays across the murky water in the tubs.

"Couldn't they come in and check your lobe and tell you?" Lane asks.

"I suppose they could."

"Then why not?"

"It would only perpetuate the illusion that the past is still with us. It's not. There's more to it than that."

"There is?"

"Yes. There's the matter of poetic wisdom."

"Of what?"

Sam smiles. He points to a beam of light poking through the fuselage and terminating near the rim of the tub. "When the light leaves the tub, it's time to haul the garbage."

The tables under the wing of the kitchen plane are empty as Lane wolfs down his meal of fried pork and vegetables and looks out across the square. The great tails of the hobbled bombers slash through the deepening dusk, and the water tower looms like a black colossus. Then the lights come on and throw fuzzy pools onto the pale ground. At the same time, strings of small bulbs come on under the wings and in the fuselages.

"They go off at ten-thirty."

Lane looks up and Sam has appeared. He wears a denim shirt over his dirty tank top to protect against the mild chill.

"We got an extra spot in our squadron," he tells Lane. "Quite nice, really. Old B-12s from the Navy. Twin-engine radar planes. Big cabins with lots of room to stretch out. You'll have to talk to the boss but I'm pretty sure it'll be okay."

As they cross the square toward the bombers on the other side, Lane slows his pace to accommodate Sam's slow shuffle.

"A couple of guys got an ID on me today," Lane says. "That a normal thing for newcomers?"

"Not really. Most people would be more interested in your bag than who you are."

Soon they are weaving through smaller aircraft, some still up on wheels, most with wings and engines still intact. Occasionally they see a single light of modest wattage mounted on a slender wooden pole. Prisoners lounge in its circle, many sitting in makeshift chairs. "They're a squadron," Sam explains. "It's like a small neighborhood of people who've signed a mutual defense pact. One stays and guards the squadron's gear while the others work. Everybody contributes to pay the guard."

"Are we still in the Inner Section?" Lane asks as they pass by a decaying 727 jet transport, the flicker of lantern light coming through its windows.

"Oh yes. The Outer Section is mostly deserted. Forage parties sometimes go into it after salvage, but only a few live out there. It's extremely dangerous. There's no code."

Lane is tired by the time they reach Sam's squadron, which is marked by a light pole between two of the old twin-engine reconnaissance planes. Three men tilt back in chairs under the light, and one waves at Sam as they approach.

"Well, we're home," he says. "Let's have you talk to the boss." He addresses one of the men in the chairs. "Norman? I've brought a newcomer. Seems a decent-enough fellow. Worked in the kitchen with me today. Needs a place to stay."

"Have a seat," Norman offers Lane as he points to a vacant chair. "You're brand new, huh?"

"Yeah, I'm brand new," answers Lane as he sits down and watches Sam shuffle off between the planes. A dark brown beard covers Norman's face, but the advancing squalls of middle age drift out from his eyes and flood down his spare cheeks.

"So what brings you here?" Norman asks, his eyes playing out the humorous irony in the question.

"A midlife crisis," Lane replies. "I was looking for a second career. Something exciting and far from home."

Norman smiles softly. "And have you found it?"

"What more could I ask?" Lane answers dryly. "Adventure and opportunity in a truly exotic location."

"And what was your former occupation?"

"According to the prosecution, it was homicide, but you know how that goes."

Norman doesn't press the issue. "What's your name?" he asks.

"Anslow. Lane Anslow. It would seem I'm currently without accommodations. Can I bunk here tonight?"

"Don't see why not," Norman says as he points backward with his thumb. "Fifth plane down is empty. It's yours. You pay one coin a week to the squadron."

Given his present wage, he'll miss a meal each week to make the payment, but Lane decides it's better to suffer in silence at this point. "Thanks. Just one question."

"Shoot."

"What gives you hope in here? How do you go on?"

For the first time, Norman breaks into a full-fledged smile. "You know that gate you came in through?"

"Yeah."

"Every morning, very early, people wheel the carts out there. They drop off the garbage. They pick up the day's supplies. But someday, maybe not too long, they'll find the gate open but no supplies there. Then they'll tiptoe out into the security zone and notice the genius dogs are gone. Then they'll go a little further and find they don't draw any fire from towers. Then they'll reach the outer gate at the far side of the zone, and they'll find there isn't anybody there. Then they'll come back, get tools and more men, and they'll rip the gate down. Then it'll be over. Just like that."

"You really believe that?" Lane asks.

"I do."

"Why?"

"Civilization runs on big ideas, and this one is fresh out. The world outside those gates is like a giant car coasting with a dead engine. Soon or later, it'll come to a halt. Good night, Mr. Anslow."

22.

OFF TO SEE THE WIZARD

The streetlights still shine here. The sidewalks show no sign of buckling. The parking strips remain green and newly mown. Fresh paint covers the older, but well-maintained, houses. Their porch lights beckon.

The Bird looks out a second-story bedroom window from one such house. He knows the entire neighborhood is a façade, a heavily secured fortress to protect the residence of Harlan Green, directly across the street. As leader of the populist Street Party, Harlan has no choice but to live here on the East Side. After all his raving about commercially secured communities, it would be utter hypocrisy for him to live in one. As an alternative, the party has created a contradiction, a gate that isn't a gate. All the houses are occupied by heavily armed members of the palace guard. Even though they report to Green, they all come from The Bird's rank and file and are still on his payroll.

But the two armored SUVs now parked in front of Green's house have nothing to do with the Bird's payroll. Even more annoying, they arrived here on short notice. An hour ago his people received a brief message from Green himself to let them through. The Bird got this message while watching yet another remake of *Scarface* in his penthouse condo in the Pearl. He came all the way across town to assess the situation.

Green appears, flanked by two men. The trio heads down the porch steps for the second armored SUV. The Bird doesn't like that these two men are not his men, that these two SUVs are not his SUVs. He watches suspiciously as Green climbs into the backseat of the rear vehicle.

Two similar vehicles recently showed up to transport that comatose prisoner of Green's to a "permanent facility." Just like now, no other information or advance notice was given. That time the Bird let it slide.

The captive was a nuisance and he was glad to be rid of him. But not this time. He's already arranged to have the vehicles shadowed when they exit.

"They're here," Arjun informs Zed on the video link to his hilltop residence. The large door on the front of the Other Application has opened to admit the two SUVs. They drive through and roll to a halt on the vast cement floor. Green exits alone, and the two vehicles circle around and drive out.

"I'll be there presently," Zed informs Arjun over the video. "Go ahead."

Arjun leaves his office and walks across the floor to Green, who is taking in the scale of the place. "Good news," he announces as he reaches the grinning politician. "We've had a positive outcome on the Phase Two test."

"Glad to hear that," Harlan says. "And where is Mr. Zed?"

They reach Bay 3 and Arjun opens the door. "This is where treatment takes place, mostly under computer control."

They walk into a maze of instrumentation, tubing and wiring. The bed in the center seems almost like an afterthought.

"So this it," Green says. For the first time, he is confronting the enormity of the process.

Arjun nods. "This is it."

"So, what do you think?" Green and Arjun turn to the voice of Thomas Zed, who has just walked in behind them. "You ready?"

Green doesn't take the bait. "Tell me this, how tightly can you control the extent of the rejuvenation?"

Arjun supplies an answer. "It's yet to be precisely determined, but we estimate a minimum treatment would remove about five to seven years of aging. Of course, you can do more with subsequent treatments."

"Of course," Green repeats. "For now, five to seven years sounds just about right. How soon can we start?"

Arjun opens his mouth to protest, but Zed cuts him off.

"How soon do you want to do it?" Zed asks.

"The sooner, the better."

"We're going to need some samples first." Arjun says.

"What kind of samples?"

"DNA, blood, urine. The usual."

Green shrugs. "All right, have away."

"Excellent," Zed declares. "Just stay right where you are. We'll send in a technician."

"I'm not sure you should've agreed so quickly," Arjun tells Zed as they walk back over the cement to his office.

"The sooner Mr. Green participates, the sooner he's committed to our course of action," Zed says.

Arjun nods. "Which leaves him no option but to continue indefinitely."

"Quite right," Zed agrees.

Harlan Green shuts the door behind him as he enters Rachel's office. The room goes silent as the bustle of the Street Party office staff is shut out. He likes the dramatic flair associated with this move. It always presages something of exceptional import – at least to him.

"Can you keep a secret?" he asks Rachel as he slides into the chair on the far side of her desk.

For an instant she thinks he's about to disclose whatever he's doing with the people up on Mount Tabor. She recovers. "Of course I can keep a secret. If I couldn't, I don't think I'd be here."

Green smiles agreeably. "No, you wouldn't."

"So what's up?" she asks.

Green assumes an expression of faux embarrassment. "Now, don't laugh, but I've decided to have a little plastic surgery. Nothing serious, just a little touch-up work. Goes with the job, I guess. The public has expectations, and you need to meet them if you're going to stay on top of your game."

"Yeah, I guess so. How long are you going to be out? "

"Just a few days. Nothing that will hurt the schedule."

"When are you going in?"

Green gets up to leave. "Right away. They had an opening," he explains. "Anybody asks, I'm in conference off-site and unavailable. Got it?"

"Got it." The son of a bitch. He's done it. Beyond a doubt, he's made a deal.

"When you get back, will you have swelling or anything? Maybe we should control your media exposure for a while."

"Don't think so. Like I said, this is just a touch-up. We don't want to call attention to it. Let's just make this business as normal."

Normal, she thinks as Harlan leaves. Maybe for him, but not for her. His absence will give her a brief window of freedom, and she'd better make the most of it.

The armadillo resembles a perverse assemblage of pig, turtle and raccoon in a single animal. The size of a large cat, it curls quietly in The Bird's lap as he absently strokes its armored shell.

No one dares to mock his pet. Least of all, the wheelman, who is torn between the novelty of the animal and the spectacular view out the condo's window atop the Pearl.

"You know what makes this a really smart animal?" the Bird asks the wheelman.

"No, I don't," the wheelman cautiously admits.

The Bird taps the armadillo's shell with his index finger. "It starts making its own protection before it's even born. Now were you that smart?"

"No, I wasn't."

"Well, neither was I. But I caught on pretty fast." The Bird points to some video footage on the Ultrares display hanging on the wall. It shows two SUVs stopping at Mount Tabor's elaborate security gate. "You're sure this is them?"

"We never lost contact," the wheelman responds. "They were in eyesight during the whole trip. The camera caught it all."

The video shows a Mount Tabor guard in full body armor coming out of a blast-proof bunker to talk to someone in the lead SUV carrying Green. The gates open and the vehicles disappear into the dark interior beyond the brilliant floodlights.

The wheelman uses a remote to open a second video. The vehicles exit the same gate at a high rate of speed and rapidly leave the frame. "The elapsed time was just over two hours. They came straight back to Mr. Green's compound."

"Did he spot you?" the Bird asks, stroking the armadillo.

"Not likely. What we see is telephoto from seventy-five yards."

"Good," the Bird mutters as he lifts the armadillo upright. Its slender snout twitches as it sniffs the air. "Rocky's hungry. You want to feed him?"

"Sure. What's he eat?"

"Ants."

The wheelman appears stricken. "I don't have any ants."

The Bird explodes into sadistic laughter. The armadillo partially retreats into its shell. "You know what? Neither do I."

In a flash, he turns from tormentor to benevolent patriarch. "How long you been with us, son?"

"Seven years."

"Excellent. And let's hope you're here for a very long time. You know the best way to make that happen?"

"What's that?"

"Forget that any of this ever happened."

"I've already done that, sir."

The Bird pastes on his best paternal smile. "Smart guy. Talk to you later."

The wheelman leaves. The Bird scratches the armadillo behind its ears and gazes out the window. Mount Tabor pushes up out of the sloping urban plain in the distance.

"Okay, I've got it from here," Harlan Green tells the two bodyguards. He knows they report directly to the Bird, and the sooner he's out of their sight, the better. "Thanks." He joins the screening line at Portland International Airport. The security men wait and watch him pass through the body scanner and baggage imaging. He wonders if they're suspicious about him taking a commercial flight. Probably not. But their boss is another matter. The Bird lives in a sustained state of suspicion and will note Harlan's sudden travel arrangements with great interest. No matter. Green's already constructed a plausible story about the need for an occasional trip using public transport to avoid charges of hypocrisy and elitism, especially given the nature of this journey.

When he clears the screening area, he carefully surveys the spot where he parted ways with the bodyguards. They're gone.

He walks back out into the main airport lobby and hurries down the main corridor to exit the building.

After a brisk ten-minute stroll, he is cleared through a small, unmarked building and out onto the tarmac, where a sleek helicopter awaits him.

Transportation, courtesy of Thomas Zed.

23.

THEY COME IN THREES

"Five coins," the merchant says as he lounges in his canvas chair in the shade of the great wing. "An excellent bargain. A very fine product."

The main blade of the handcrafted multi-tool gleams in the noonday sun as Lane inspects it. The design is ingenious, especially when you consider that all the materials were scavenged from dead airplanes and then fabricated and assembled with handmade machines.

"Could I put it on layaway?" Lane asks.

The merchant gives him an incredulous look that collapses into a brief burst of laughter. "Of course. You give me five coins and I lay it down and you pick it up. How about that?"

Lane looks over to the big fuselage that holds the kitchen. "Back to work. See you later."

"Always a pleasure," the merchant replies with a jovial wave. Lane walks through the milling customers toward the kitchen plane and inhales the odor of fried pork floating on the dry breeze. He steps through the fuselage door and into the kitchen, where Sam is bent over a kettle full of dishwater. He's about to address Sam, when he sees a pair of shadows falling across the metal floor and whips around to look up at the flight deck. Two men gaze down on him from the pilot and co-pilot seats, the same two men he encountered yesterday in the crowd.

Sam turns and smiles. "Lane, we have visitors."

"I can see that." Lane holds his position near the door. If they jump at him, he can be out and running before they even hit the floor. But the men stay comfortably seated and show no signs of hostility.

"You know them?" Lane asks Sam.

"I don't, but Norman does," Sam answers as he dries his hands and rests on a short wooden stool by the kettle. "Ah, that's better," he says in relief. "It's nice to sit a spell."

"So what's the deal?" Lane asks the men. "Why'd you pick me out of the crowd yesterday?"

"We needed to make sure you were the right guy," one of the men answers.

"Right guy for what?"

"Can't tell you that?" the other man replies. Both are relatively young, strongly built and hyper-alert. Definitely not part of the mainstream prison population.

"So what can you tell me?"

The first man looks out the old windshield into the square. "There's a lot of people out there. A lot of Street people."

Of course. The Street Party is heavily represented in here. But why would they seek him out? "Street people," Lane says. "I wouldn't know much about that. I'm not very political."

"Then maybe you should talk to someone who is," the second man says. "Like Rachel Heinz."

"And given my present circumstances, how would I do that?"

"We'll be in touch."

When the two men leave, Sam turns to Lane. "I'm not sure I followed all that."

Lane puts his hand on the old man's shoulder. "You weren't supposed to."

The morning desert dawns on the trio, an unholy trinity born of darkness incarnate. An alliance forged in the sewers of desperation flowing through the world's hotspots. Military contractors, Alpha, Beta and Gamma. Ruthless almost beyond reckoning, yet pure in purpose. Their work defines their path.

"You've got twenty-four hours," the guard explains as he scratches the crotch of his fatigues and shifts his weapons belt. "After that, you guys are no longer visitors. You're prisoners. Understand?"

"Understand," answers Alpha. The guard has a flat, ruddy face made into mush by too much booze and too little exercise. The man is an annoyance, but a necessary step in carrying out the mission. The trio stares out from the truck bed down the gravel road at the opening in the razor wire that defines the main gate into Pima.

"And remember," the guard continues, "no gunfire. If there's any shooting, it's not only my ass, it's your ass, too. Got that?"

"Got it," Alpha says. He turns to his men, all clad in fatigues with rolled-up sleeves and jungle hats. "All right, let's go." Each grabs a transport case and hops down. None acknowledges the guard. In the warrior world the man is a rodent, at best.

The trio moves briskly down the road, with Alpha in the middle and slightly ahead. The synchronous crunch of their combat boots on the gravel spills across no-man's-land and reaches the ears of the enhanced dogs, who turn and sniff the air.

They don't like what they smell.

Lane steps into the kitchen plane just as Sam is firing up the propane burner to heat the day's dishwater.

"Morning," Sam says. "You sleep all right?"

"I'm not sure," Lane says as he eyes the cooks plying their trade up front.

"Usually takes a while," says Sam. "You'll get used to things, then you'll be okay."

A shadow fills the door. One of the men from the Street Party steps in. "You're in trouble," he informs Lane. "You've got to get out of here. Now."

"And go where? The downtown Marriott?"

"We just got word that three men entered through the main gate. A military pursuit team."

"And what might they want with me?"

"I don't think you want to find out," the first man says. "You've got to go out into the Outer Section. If you stay here, they'll track you down through informants."

"I'll put together a little food and water," Sam says as he reaches around behind the stool and pulls out a primitive canvas rucksack.

"Wait a few days, then check back at night with Norman's squadron," the man says.

"And then what?"

"We're working on it. Good luck." The man disappears.

"I have to say, you lead an interesting life," Sam says as he fills a plastic water bottle. "Even by the standards of this place."

Alpha peers down the long, open corridor between the towering tails of the big old planes and trains his binoculars into the rippled heat. At the base of the water tower there seems to be some kind of activity, at least a quarter mile away in what their brief called the Inner Section. The hot breeze kicks up miniature eddies of dust around his boots as he considers his next move.

Alpha turns to Beta and Gamma. "Okay, let's get set up."

They follow him off to the right of the main corridor, into the space between two planes, and open their transport cases. Each holds a gas-powered rifle with a single-action bolt for loading tranquilizer darts tipped with hollow, barbed needles.

Alpha's barrel-shaped transport case holds something quite different. It represents the best work coming out of the new weapons labs in Asia, who have moved beyond electronics into biologics. He carefully unsnaps the safety clasps and opens the two halves. The left half contains a glistening, folded shape that stirs like an insect emerging from a cocoon. Alpha steps back from the case and turns to his team. "Give it some room," he orders, and the men gladly take several steps back.

The thing begins to wiggle violently, flinging off its coating of moisture in a bright spray and tumbling out of the case onto the ground, where its wings unfold into a delicate network of small bones, cartilage and transparent membrane tissue. Each a foot long, the wings beat randomly and sporadically as it struggles toward a synchronous state. Then, in a sudden explosion of motion, the thing takes to the air, its wings beating as fast as a hummingbird's.

As the creature hovers motionless in front of them, Alpha can now make out the details of the body: a brown, scaly tube about ten inches long and thick as a toilet-paper roll. The rear tapers into a membrane-covered tail that provides control and stabilization, and the madly beating wings attach at the midpoint of the tube. Two inches from the front, a pair of bulbous eyes are embedded on each side, and now they dart about, taking in the planes, the desert, the men. But the thing's real sensory power begins just ahead of the eyes, where the tube shrinks slightly in size, like lipstick in a holder, and changes color to a tender pink. This large, fleshy projection is covered with dozens of small orifices, like holes in a salt shaker, and collectively they form a very powerful snout. A nasal probe that has been pre-tuned to the scent of Lane Anslow.

As Alpha and the men watch, the snout slowly rotates, rises to a height of six feet, and begins to leisurely drift down the space between the planes. Its wings emit a snarly hum, like a mob of tiny engines let loose at full throttle.

Alpha motions the men forward. They fall in single file behind the lead of the snout. The final phase of the pursuit has begun.

The heat is seriously affecting Lane by the time he spots the plane. A sneaky, dry desert heat, the breath of an oven set to bake. It instantly evaporates the sweat oozing from his pores and turns it to a salty powder long before he feels the damp. But now he needs shelter from the midday heat and rest.

He has reached a clearing in the tangle of junked aircraft, an elongated meadow of hard dirt in the forest of wings, engines and metal bodies. At the far end of the meadow, an old jet transport reposes. The body appears fully preserved, except that the entire front section has been neatly sheared off a few yards behind the cockpit. This proud old decapitated bird rests with its tail down, its front twenty feet above the ground facing the clearing.

As Lane approaches the plane, he looks up at the vacant cavity where the forward fuselage has been severed. It will give him a good view of anyone approaching and also provide a well-ventilated place to rest. Sam has warned him that temperatures inside the planes soar over two hundred degrees without shade.

After walking under the wing to the rear, he spots an open service door by the rear galley and enters. All the paneling is gone, and he sees up a long, inclined tunnel to the brilliant opening at the front, where a few seats still remain.

After climbing through the hot stink of overcooked metal and plastic, he reaches the front, where he removes seat covers to form a makeshift mattress. He positions himself to comfortably survey the clearing and wearily settles down. His path through the Outer Section was completely random, and the ground was too hard to leave footprints. He reaches into the rucksack and takes a carefully restrained swallow from the plastic water bottle. It's imperative he conserve energy so water and food last as long as possible.

He rolls onto his stomach, rests his head on crossed hands and listens. Nothing but the wind. A minute later he is sound asleep.

His eyes are still shut when the burning snarl of the hum awakens him, like a band saw struggling through hardwood. It bites gradually into his sleep and slowly pulls his eyes open. Lane raises his head to look forward out the front of the plane. Nothing. Just a great oval of blue sky and high cirrus at the truncated end of the fuselage.

He's only a few feet from the lip of the cavity, and about to peek over the edge to the clearing when the thing suddenly rises into view and hovers not a yard in front of him. The pink nasal probe, with its sea of small holes, points at him, and the brown eyes are firmly locked on his. Fascinating. Disgusting. And probably highly dangerous. Over the lip he sees three men in fatigues advancing at a brisk trot. They've spotted him. One stops to guard the front of the plane, while the other two continue out of sight down the flanks.

Lane bounds down the aisle. Behind him, the burning hum persists. Looking back over his shoulder, he sees the thing tracking him, maintaining a steady distance of about six feet. No time to deal with that now. As he approaches mid-fuselage, he sees a pursuer enter the rear galley and raise his rifle.

As the man t fires, Lane darts out an open emergency exit that puts him on the wing. Behind him, he hears a spang of metal on metal after an explosive pop. While he sprints down the wing's tapered and curved surface, a voice shouts, "Port side!" The wing tip bends perilously under his weight. Lane sits down so he can slide off the end without losing his balance. His slide dumps him atop a small aircraft snuggled under the wing of the jet. He slides down the curve of its fuselage and hits the ground running. A small break. His pursuers will have to run around the plane and by that time he will be deep in the maze of aeronautical flotsam.

Except for the goddam snout. It tracks him relentlessly and taunts him with the burn of its hum.

Lane sprints onward, past giant wheels, cast-off engines, sheared tails, fuel pods, stacks of rotors, and desiccated hydraulics. Deeper and deeper into the chaos of spent technology. He winds past radar domes, veers around black rubber hose, leaps over scattered ailerons. Soon the sun shouts at him to stop, and the nasty heat slaps his face. Time is gone, and only the fright-fueled rush of flight remains.

His legs grow heavy and his vision is impaired by perspiration. He trips over a tangle of steel cable, hits the ground in a grating skid that tears at his forearm and elbow. He rolls on his side, wrapped in the thunder of his pounding heart and heaving lungs.

The thing hovers at six feet and mocks him with its graceful tenacity. Behind it he expects to see armed men bounding out of the wreckage, hunters at the heels of the tracking beast. But no one appears. As he struggles to his feet, the thing backs up a few feet, then holds its ground.

Just as Lane considers hurling something at it, the thing rotates and flits off at high speed, disappearing in the wreckage, its mission apparently complete. The hum is gone. Only the heat, the breeze and the junk remain.

He moves forward with the sting of his scraped arm growing stronger, his pace slowed to a walk. He's lost his food and, most critically, his water.

His deliberations are broken by the same explosive pop he heard in the fuselage of the jet and a sharp stab of pain in his thigh. By the time he looks down at the dart embedded in his quadriceps, his vision is already dimming.

"Let me start with what we know," says Alpha. "That'll make it easier for both of us. Less confusion. Then we'll go on to what we don't know and what you can tell us."

"And what if I can't?" Lane's arms are stretched over his head and duct-taped to the top blade of a big propeller, while his legs are taped to the two remaining blades. His head throbs and all his limbs and joints ache mightily. Behind Alpha the other two members of his pursuit team sit cross-legged and stare at Lane with idle curiosity.

Alpha sighs and reaches into his shirt pocket. He pulls out a small case and opens it to reveal a row of hypodermic needles. "Potassium chloride. Very fast. No pain." He puts the case back and pulls a knife from its sheath on his belt. "Survival knife. Very slow. Big hurt." He returns the knife to its sheath. "Got the idea?"

"Sort of," Lane answers.

"We know you're looking for your brother. We know you moved into Pinecrest with forged ID and took up with a woman named Autumn West. We know a few other things as well, so lying wouldn't be a good idea."

"Never crossed my mind," Lane replies. He's beyond fear, in the realm of the absurd, where only humor makes sense.

"There's no way you could have done all that on a cheap-shit cop's salary," Alpha observes. "So who's footing the bill?"

"You know, I was going ask you the same thing," Lane fires back. "You work for the good people up on Mount Tabor?"

Alpha pulls out the knife and tests its blade with his thumb. "I always start with the testicles and work upward. It seems to get the best results."

"What have you done with my brother?" Lane says in an even voice. "Where is he?"

"You're missing the point," Alpha says. "So let's give you a little help." He brings the knife forward and cuts the belt off Lane's pants.

But just as the belt pops loose, both men behind Alpha suddenly topple forward. As Alpha turns to the sound of their heads hitting the dirt, Lane see the steel shafts protruding from their backs, each with three plastic fins attached. In a silent flash, Alpha leaves his range of vision.

"Mr. Anslow!"

Lane looks up from the bodies to see the short, stooped figure of Sam emerging from the wreckage along with three men wearing armored vests and carrying crossbows. Two of them are the Street Party members he met in the kitchen before he fled out here.

"Sorry to intrude like this," Sam apologizes as the group approaches. "But it looked like you could use a little assistance."

One of the men pulls out a knife and saws through the duct tape to free Lane, who is thirsty and very tired. Sam points in the direction where Alpha disappeared. "It looks like the big fish got away."

"Yeah. The big fish got away," Lane echoes wearily. "You wouldn't have a little water, would you?"

"Yes, I would," Sam says cheerfully and unslings a canteen from over his shoulder. Behind him, the three men drag the bodies into the shade. Lane now understands the power of a well-designed crossbow as a medium-range weapon. He reaches for the canteen and takes a long series of large gulps.

"Too bad about the belt," Sam observes, looking at Lane's waistline. "It would've fetched a nice price at market."

"I think I can live without it." Lane sits down and leans against the base of the propeller as the three men return from moving the bodies. The one that first spoke to Lane in the kitchen squats down beside him.

"I think it's pretty clear," he says. "You've got to go."

"You mean go back to the Inner Section?"

"No. I mean out of Pima."

24.

UP AND AWAY

"How often does this kind of thing happen?" Lane asks, walking through the darkness with the two Street Party men and Sam.

"Hardly ever," one of the men answers. "You must be pretty damn special."

"Yeah, I guess so," Lane says warily as they pass the last row of planes and enter the big square of the Inner Section, where the sky opens wide and pours out a great shower of starlight.

"We need to speak softly now," Sam whispers. "Voices carry a long way out here."

Soon they are approaching the central water tower, a great black hulk set against the silky haze of the Milky Way. Its four big legs are criss-crossed by metal bracing, mostly lost in the dark beneath the structure. When they reach the nearest leg, one of the Street Party men goes behind it and reappears with a rope that ends in a grappling hook. He twirls it and throws it up to the first set of braces, where it clinks in the stillness of the square.

"I must say I envy you," Sam says. They watch the man scale the side of the leg and scramble up into the bracing. "It'll be a grand adventure."

"To say the least," adds Lane. The remaining man on the ground is motioning to him, so he gently pats Sam's small shoulder and shakes his hand. "I won't forget your help."

"Good." Sam beams. "Because I will." He pats Lane on the back. "Good luck to you."

Lane walks to where the man is standing and takes the rope. "When you get to the first brace, crawl to your left," the man instructs. "Then you'll come to the ladder, and it's straight up from there."

The climb is tough and taxing, but Lane scrambles onto the metal brace and carefully inches to the ladder. Once on it, he turns and sees Sam, a tiny figure on the big stretch of open ground. Lane marvels at his courage in the face of his affliction. Then he starts the long climb up the supporting structure.

He turns to look at the view and is startled by the sprawl of lights from Tucson. Only a mile away, people are strolling the sidewalks, laughing in restaurants, or happily copulating in pale baths of flickering TV light. He turns and continues climbing. Toward the top, the rungs become less vertical and follow the tower's curve as it flattens out at the peak.

The rungs terminate in a circular maintenance platform bordered by a small railing. As Lane climbs over the top, he sees one of the men who guided him, and a second man.

"You're lucky," the guide from the Street Party says. "The wind's holding steady. Should be pretty easy." He points to the southwest, a big patch of empty desert nearly devoid of lights. "See where I'm pointing? That's your bearing."

Lane moves to get in a line of sight with the man's arm. In the blackness, he sees a single light blinking at one-second intervals.

The wind picks up slightly, and the dull crackle of plastic turns Lane's attention to his escape vehicle. Moored to the railing is a parachute with a standard wing-like canopy, the kind used in skydiving; only, this one is dedicated to going up instead of down. The canopy's underside is filled with a bulbous cluster of black plastic garbage bags, all inflated with gas and tightly shut. Each has a length of clothesline that joins to one of two termination points at the end of the harness.

"How much you weigh?" asks the second man, who is filling yet another bag from a tube that extends down into a covered metal washtub.

"One eighty-five," Lane tells him. "So how do you make the gas?"

"It's hydrogen. We get the metal off the planes and the chemicals from kitchen supplies, and brew it up right here on the spot. Don't touch the side of the tub. It's hot." The man ties off the bag, adds a line to it, and floats it up into the canopy. "There. Given your weight, that should be just about right."

"Well, let's get you rigged up," the guide says as he opens the harness buckles.

"How many times have you guys done this?" Lane asks as he slides in and adjusts the straps.

"Twice."

"How many times did it work?"

"We don't know. For security reasons. Same reason we can't tell you why you're going out."

"In case the wrong people get a hold of me. Right?"

"I suppose," the guide says casually as he hands Lane a flashlight and a paring knife from a kitchen. "Now remember, you get about halfway from here to the light, and you start cutting one balloon loose every five minutes. Every time you do it, you flash your light three times, so your contact on the ground knows where you are. Got it?"

"Got it."

"Okay then, let's go. Put one foot up on the rail so you can give yourself a boost when I cut you loose."

As Lane complies, the guide moves into position and prepares to cut a single line that tethers the whole apparatus to the railing. "Ready?"

"Ready." Lane quells an abrupt urge to call off the whole thing, to return to his sleeping bag in the belly of the plane and count the years rolling by in relative security.

"Good luck." The guide cuts the rope and ducks back out of the way.

Lane feels a sharp, upward tug on the harness as he shoves off. A shudder of fear and exhilaration runs through him as he surges toward the sky. A glance down past his dangling legs tells him the wind has already carried him out from over the tower and the square. By the time he reaches the first row of bombers, he has gained considerable altitude. Overhead, the plastic bags rustle gently as they adjust to the stress of his weight.

Ahead, he sees the security perimeter, with the big lights searing into the no-man's-land, and the towers and fencing beyond. In the foreground, the prison hides in semidarkness, the vague shapes of the dead planes littering the ground.

Passing over the no-man's-land, he feels vulnerable in the sky glow. Below, the dogs sense his presence. They stream like tiny germs toward a point directly under his path, but he is already too high to be seen from the towers. A few moments later, the perimeter is past, and he glides over a road flanked by streetlights. He is out.

Lane twists in the harness to check his position. Sure enough, time to start down. He gets out his flashlight and signals toward the blinking light up ahead in the dark of the open desert. Next, he pulls down the line on one of the lower balloons, and cuts it loose.

With almost no lights below, it's become more difficult to judge his drift and altitude. He frees more balloons at the prescribed intervals. A lone building with a small parking lot appears and gives him a sense of scale. He judges his altitude at about five hundred feet.

But his goal, the blinking light out on the desert, doesn't seem to be any nearer. Something is wrong.

A few minutes later, he spots the same small building and parking lot off to his left. The wind shifted. He's drifting in the wrong direction, back toward Tucson. What's more, the air is warmer, and he seems to be rising slightly. He also seems to be picking up speed.

Fortunately, there is a contingency plan if he fails to make the rendezvous in the desert. The guide mentioned an intersection in the middle of the city, Elm and Tucson, where he should appear at one-hour intervals until contacted.

By now, he is coming over the lights of South Tucson, where streetlights cut long strings of glowing beads into the night. He passes a shopping center and he sees an island of floodlights surrounding a pale green rectangle, a stadium of some kind.

Lane realizes that his landing problem may be solved. His present course is taking him toward the highlands rising up beyond the city. The ground will gradually rise beneath him to the point where he can make a soft landing.

But then he realizes his drift will take him right over the stadium – and right into its brilliant dome of illumination shining down on a football game. On the thirty-yard line nearest him, a play unfolds, a screen pass. The collective cheer of the crowd pushes through the night air.

Moments later he is floating directly over the field and realizes he has lost not only altitude, but also the cover of night. While there is no play on the field, a great cheer erupts. A cheer for Lane on his balloon-borne journey.

Soon, the red-and-blue flash of police cars moves along several nearby arterials, all converging on his general position. The synthesized babble of electronic sirens drifts up from below. Lane looks ahead. It'll be close, but he's going to make it. He is nearing the highlands, with their meandering roads and numerous canyons, where the police can't easily follow.

When he's down to about fifty feet, he sees he will land in a relatively large vacant area next to a low-slung building and several smaller structures.

The thick black shape of a tree canopy takes him by surprise. He lifts his feet so they won't drag through the upper branches, but eventually his toes are scraping through the foliage.

The trees end, and he faces a long, black pit. This is it. He cuts loose another balloon. His feet and legs ache with anticipation, and his toes probe for the ground. They hit. Grass. A level carpet of newly mown grass. With his feet on the ground, the remaining balloons try to pull him over, but he quickly wiggles out of the strapping. His shoulders and legs burn where the harness cut into them, but otherwise he is unscathed.

Then it hits him. He's landed on a fairway in a golf course. He must be near the tee, and through the trunks of nearby trees, he makes out a cluster of lights. Probably the clubhouse. He picks up the pace. Time is precious. If he's not at the appointed intersection by daylight, he's in trouble. With prison denims, no money, and the police alerted to a rogue balloonist, the odds of evasion are against him. And right now, he has only the vaguest idea where he is and how to reach the designated street. He can't walk the roads, and overland travel in the city is impossible. He has to get a vehicle and a map.

When he walks off the first hole and sees the sleek look of the clubhouse, it's obvious he's stumbled into a country club. Keeping to the shadows to avoid security cameras and sensors, he circles the main building and finds a cyclone fence and an unlocked gate leading to the maintenance area.

Once inside, he looks across a stretch of packed dirt that ends in a big metal shed. Beside it is an old van parked in a pool of halogen light. There's no way to approach it without being seen. He'll just have to hope there are no cameras covering the area. He takes off at a rapid trot across the hundred feet of ground between him and the vehicle.

As he slides into the driver's seat, he smiles. The key is in the ignition. Someone decided that the truck was too old to be worth stealing, and they were almost right. He twists the ignition key, and the old starter motor emits a deep mutter as it turns over the engine, which reluctantly sputters to life.

With the engine idling roughly, he hops out to check the plates, something only a cop or a crook would think of. Amazingly, they haven't expired. He jumps back in, drives cautiously through the gate, and heads for the exit. On the main road he cruises through the uplands toward the glittering matrix of downtown. He lets himself relax slightly, rolls down the window, and sucks the clean desert air into his lungs. But when he exhales, what comes out is the strange exhaust of Pima.

A two-seater electric sedan pulls over to the curb at Tucson and Elm, and Lane quickly checks to see if it's being followed. At this hour traffic is light, and no other cars are in sight. After he stashed the van in an alley a few blocks away, he circled the intersection on foot, looking for a trap, but found none.

"Good evening, Mr. Anslow," the driver says as Lane gets in. "You're quite the sensation. You even made the late news. The mad balloonist, they're calling you." The driver chuckles. "What do you think?"

"It's hilarious," Lane replies as they pull away and head down Elm. "Now, what's this all about? Who sprung me?"

"Wish I could tell you, but I really don't know." The driver is a plump man in his fifties, wearing a summer sport shirt and slacks. From a small speaker on the dash comes the bark of police dispatches. "Truth is," he continues, "I don't want to know. You're Street People, and that's good enough for me."

"This a rental?" Lane asks.

"Sure is."

The speaker box barks a license number and asks for a confirmation. The man chuckles. "Where did you stash the van?"

"How'd you know about the van?"

The man points to the box. "Everybody knows about the van. You tripped a neural camera going through the gate of that swanky golf club."

The driver pulls onto a freeway heading northwest.

"What do people around here think of the prison?" Lane asks.

"They don't," the driver replies as he gazes out the windshield at the luminous geometry lining the freeway. "Why should they? Would it change anything?"

"It might," Lane responds. Outside, the city lights taper off, and a line of hills looms against the sky glow. "Do I get to know where we're going?"

"No, but it's close by." The hills are soon behind them, and they exit and head east into the darkness. The road bores flat and straight through the desert. Distant lights appear. A pair of red and white specks descends through the sky at a shallow angle toward the source. An airport.

The driver pulls into the parking lot of a building that serves as the small airport's flight center. He stops at the front entrance and turns to Lane. "Bon voyage."

"Thanks." Lane opens the door to the low whine of turboprop engines. "See you around."

A man in his thirties comes out as the car drives off. He points over his shoulder with his thumb. "This way."

"Do I get to see my itinerary?" he asks as they walk through the lobby.

"Not yet." The man hands Lane a cowboy hat and a casual sports coat. "Put these on and face toward the plane when we get outside. You need to stay out of camera range."

He opens the door to a restricted area, and they come out onto the tarmac. The overhead floodlights shine on the plane, the old Piaggio 180. Lane keeps his head low as they cross to it and board.

"Lieutenant Anslow," Rachel Heinz says through the open cockpit door. "Welcome aboard."

She is already taxiing toward the runway as he slides into the co-pilot's seat. "So I understand you did a bit of flying all on your own," she remarks. "You know, it's best to take lessons first."

"You're right about that." Lane buckles his seat belt. "You've gone to a lot of trouble to extricate me. I hope I'm worth it. What's up?"

"It would appear that my boss has made a deal with the devil, the same devil that knows what's happened to your brother. It's going to take the best of both of us to resolve these issues in a satisfactory manner."

"So where do we start?"

"With your theory that those atop Mount Tabor used Johnny's research to perfect some kind of super-rejuvenation process. It looks like you were right on the money."

"How so?"

"Harlan told me he was taking some time off for plastic surgery. A little touch-up work, he said."

"Maybe it's true," Lane says. "Maybe that's all there is to it."

"Don't think so. Harlan's never taken time off for anything."

Lane settles back as the plane accelerates down the runway. "Well, there you go."

"Did you get hold of Autumn West before they nabbed you? I mean, it looks like she's the gold standard for whatever they're doing up there."

"Unfortunately, I was interrupted by a heavily armed contract goon," Lane says. "He made the feds look like a good deal."

"So whoever's up on the hill is onto us," Rachel says as she pulls back on the yoke. The twin turbines scream their way up into the darkened sprawl of desert sky. The lights of Tucson and Pima fall away beneath them.

"They're onto me, but I don't think they're onto you," Lane says. "If they were, we wouldn't be having this conversation."

"And where does that leave us?"

"Alive, for one thing. For another, we need to keep you clean. I assume you can cover your tracks about this flight and whatever you know about balloon trips"

"For a while. That's where the race comes in. I need to be back on the job before Harlan's done with his treatment"

"For now, you'll have to stay way clear of me," Lane says. "I'm highly toxic. If Harlan gets onto you, you may meet up with Mr. Nasal Tracker, courtesy of Mount Tabor. If the feds get onto you, you'll go down for aiding and abetting a fugitive."

"And what do you intend to do on your lonesome?"

Lane unbuckles his seat belt. A thick blanket of fatigue is settling over him. "Well, right now, I intend to search the cabin for a cold beer. After that, I'll need some cash, some clothes, and a really good lobe."

"Already done."

"What can I say? You're amazing."

25.

SMELL THE ROSES

They have the perp secured in plastic cuffs with his face up against the storefront of a boutique for stylish women's shoes. A female shopper inside the store briefly looks up at the offender through the glass front, then goes back to fondling quality boots. One cop pushes the suspect flat against the glass with the tip of his baton. A dozen others stand around the assemblage of patrol cars and just chew the fat. A classic tableau of urban law enforcement at street level.

Lane turns from the scene playing out several stories below his hotel room. A nice room, the best that his new lobe could buy. The Feed does its endless video dance on a giant screen on the opposite wall. A silver tray from room service holds a crumpled cloth napkin and the remains of a club sandwich. A thick comforter of soft cotton drapes across the king-size bed.

Sooner or later an electronic census inside Pima will reveal that he's missing, and his digitized face will be fed to every neural camera in the country. The massive processing complexes at Homeland will grind through a trillion images from anywhere and everywhere. And there he'll be, checking into this hotel. Right face, wrong lobe. Up go the flags.

And while the new lobe and the money will buy him some time, they won't get him any closer to Mount Tabor and Johnny. There's a way out. He's known it all along but didn't want to face it. But now it's time. He reaches for his cell phone.

Harlan Green plays it on the cool side.

When Rachel enters his office, he waits a beat to look up from his desk. She sees not even a trace of expectation in his expression. Business as usual.

"So what have you got for me?" he asks.

She reciprocates his nonchalance. "We need to go over the schedule additions."

"Can it wait? I've got a few things that I need to get to."

"Sure."

"Tomorrow morning okay?"

"That's fine."

"Good." He goes back to his reading as she leaves.

As if she didn't notice the ten years sheared off his face. The slack gone from the jaw. The crow's feet absent around the eyes. The texture of the cheeks turned soft. The creases missing at the corners of his mouth. No scarring, no swelling, no surgery. Just a short visit to Mount Tabor.

She puts her handheld in text mode and sends a prearranged message to Lane.

"At ten, boys will be boys."

The rosebushes form a dense tangle of prickly stems broken by an occasional blossom of dense color. They cover a two-acre plot below where Lane sits on a weathered wooden bench in Washington Park. He's old enough to remember when this place was called the Portland Rose Garden, with its cultivated flower beds set in a manicured lawn. Each rosebush was carefully pruned and labeled. But runaway growth has since buried the beds and lawn. Now the blossoms form in unlabeled anonymity. Only the fir trees in the distance bear witness to the process.

Lane hears the hiss of the tires and purr of engines as the vehicles pass the ruins of the tennis courts and roll to a stop in the parking lot behind him. He doesn't bother to look. Officially, the park is private property, owned by a consortium from Southeast Asia and the Persian Gulf. All entrances are sealed and guarded by a contract security firm while they decide the property's fate. But for certain individuals, exceptions could be made and access arranged. And so it was for Lane and for the vehicles now shutting down their engines.

Their armored doors open and close in the silence. A mild breeze flows down from the forest above, carrying the scent of decaying pine needles. The Bird takes a seat on the far end of Lane's bench, leaving two spaces between them. Without acknowledging Lane, he stares out at the wild knot of vegetation and the hint of downtown beyond.

"Welcome home," the Bird says with a smile, turning toward Lane. He wears a light summer suit, a white shirt, and a tie the color of dried moss. "Good to have you back. So what are we doing here?"

"I think that maybe we can reach an understanding."

"We tried that once before and didn't get very far, as I recall."

"Things have changed."

The Bird guffaws. "You think so? For starters, you're a fugitive from a federal detention facility. And as soon as the feds and their friends figure that out, you're going to have a short stay here and an equally short lifespan after they throw you back in."

"So what do you suggest?"

"You seek shelter, the safety of an organization that could guarantee your permanent security. I mean, in the end, that's what we all want, right? A place to call home."

"Maybe, but if we were to make a deal, there might be certain terms involved."

The Bird looks out at the billowing green of the tree line beyond the hopeless tangle of roses. He breaks into a patronizing smile. "And what makes you think you're in any position to bargain?"

"Mount Tabor."

The smile fades. "Now why would I have any interest in Mount Tabor?"

"My brother's up there, isn't he?"

"Come on now: How would I know that?"

"The same way you know everything. Or should I say, almost everything."

"And what don't I know?"

"Certain things about your boss, Harlan Green."

The Bird darkens considerably. "Boss? Did you say boss?"

A flock of crows flaps overhead and unloads a series of grating caws. Lane takes a moment to reconsider. "So let's call Mr. Green your strategic partner. Mind if I ask you a personal question?"

The Bird relaxes and grins. He shifts his weight to face toward Lane. "You got some balls, Anslow. I'll give you that. Maybe that's what I like about you. Okay, shoot."

"You ever had any rejuve work done?"

The Bird shrugs. "Yeah, so what? So would you if you could afford it, which we both know you can't. At least not yet."

"Well, Harlan Green can definitely afford it. And he's just had some very special work done."

"What do you mean, special?"

"He just had about ten years shaved off. No surgery, no drugs, no tricks. Ten years. Just like that."

"Sounds great. Where do I sign up?"

"Mount Tabor."

The Bird looks away and stares over the unkempt roses. Lane can almost feel him assembling bits of information.

Lane pushes his luck. "Let's talk about why you weren't invited to the party up there. Whoever's in charge put a low valuation on you, and Harlan went along with it. Think ahead. Every ten years or so, Harlan gets a new reset and you get squat. Pretty soon, you're dead, and Harlan's just getting started."

"Okay, so just what should I do about that?"

"I don't think you should ask Harlan for an invitation. I think you should crash the party."

The Bird goes silent again and looks out at the view. Finally, he turns back to Lane. "We'll see about that. And just what do you want to get out of all this?"

"I want to find out what's happened to my brother."

"And what if he's dead?"

"Then I'll know."

"What if he's not up there?"

"Then they can tell me where to find him."

"Anything else?"

"Yeah. If we start working together, I'll be giving counsel now and then. Right now, I'll give you a freebie. Don't tell Harlan you know what's going on. If you tip your hand, the man on the mountain, whoever he is, might suddenly fade into the distance."

The Bird stands. "I'll take that under consideration. Now tell me: How do I know you got all this right?"

"When was the last time you saw Harlan?"

"I dunno. Maybe a week ago."

"Take a good look next time you see him."

Harlan Green feels the youthful spring in his step as he strolls down the sidewalk to his house. It's a beautiful day on the cusp of fall, full of blue sky and green bursts of vegetation. He feels a sense of synchronicity with it, a great biological surge. He left headquarters early to walk through this gated place with no gate and inhale the crisp air. With every step, at least a half dozen eyes track him to provide security, all tucked neatly out of sight.

As he walks, he sorts through the details of the next presidential election, still two years off. By then he will have enough momentum to carry the vote of the impoverished, the disaffected, the sick and the rage-struck. He will be swept into office and will need to assemble a cabinet and make the proper appointments. On the last block to his house, he considers the problem of the Bird. He tentatively promised the Bird leadership of the Office of Homeland Security, the most sprawling security apparatus the world has ever seen. But of course, that's out of the question. The Bird has neither the background nor the sophistication to run it. Between now and the election, he needs to prep his rough-hewn associate for this eventuality, but he hasn't quite figured out the right approach.

He sprints up the steps and opens his front door. Two security men acknowledge him with nods of solemn vigilance. He nods in return and heads for the kitchen, where he fetches a beer from the refrigerator, then opens the sliding door to the patio with an energetic swing.

And there is the Bird, sitting on one of the chairs around the big iron table with its frosted glass top. He wears a tailored sport shirt, creased wool slacks and wicker loafers.

"Harlan!" he says as rises to shake Green's hand. "Sorry to intrude, but there's… " He stops and looks Harlan up and down. "Jesus! Do you look good! You taking vitamins or something?"

Harlan senses it going terribly wrong. "No, nothing like that. To tell you the truth, I had a little work done. Goes with the trade, you know."

The Bird vigorously nods in agreement. "Sure. Goes with the trade. Absolutely." He pauses and savors Harlan's mounting anxiety. "So what kind of work was it?"

"Oh, you know. Skin treatments. A little nip here and there. Some laser zaps. The usual rejuve stuff."

"Boy, if you ask me, it's a lot more than usual. It's absolutely terrific. Who did it? I want to sign up."

"Uh, that might be a little difficult."

The Bird feigns disappointment. "Oh yeah? How come?"

"It's an offshore clinic. It has a waiting list a mile long. I don't think they'll be taking new customers anytime soon. I had to sign a confidentiality agreement just to get into the queue."

"Understood." The Bird brings his powerful hand down on Harlan's shoulder. "Hey, why don't you put in a good word for me? See what you can do, okay?"

"Sure. Let me give it a try."

The Bird removes his hand and backs away to leave. "You know what? All that other stuff I had for you can wait. It's a beautiful day and you're a beautiful guy, so enjoy. See you later."

"I'll save some time for tomorrow. Thanks for coming by."

"Don't mention it."

Green watches the Bird's back as he walks through the sliding door. Alarm signals ricochet wildly around the inside of his skull.

"Point taken, Lane Anslow," the Bird declares as he climbs into the front of the SUV a block down from Green's. "He fucked me. He cut me out of the deck." A riptide of anger floods his face.

"So what did he tell you?" Lane asks from behind the wheel.

"He said it was done at some upscale joint offshore that wouldn't even consider the common man. Bullshit. All bullshit."

"That's all?"

The Bird locks eyes with Lane in a murderous stare. "That's plenty. You fuck with me, I fuck with you. Very simple."

Lane starts the engine and pulls out from the curb. "We need to get you a new lobe," he declares flatly. "Right away."

"How come?"

"Just a precaution. You may have fucked with someone a lot more dangerous than Harlan Green. We don't know yet."

Outside, the neatly trimmed neighborhood rolls by, a façade for the phalanx of security within.

"Well, bring 'em on," the Bird says. "There's something that I want to know, and I want to know it now."

"What's that?"

"You never told me your source. You didn't figure all this out on your lonesome. You had inside help."

"You're right," Lane proclaims. "And I think the time has come for you two to meet."

26.

LET'S MAKE A DEAL

Zed stares out his office window at the neatly tended islands of shrubs and flowers on the slopes beneath his residence. He drums his fingers on the armrests of his swivel chair with a savage force that unsettles Arjun. His boss no longer lives in a state of physical retreat. Without warning, Zed swivels his chair at alarming speed to face Arjun, who sits across a spacious desk topped with premium marble.

"Play it one more time," Zed orders.

Both men turn toward a video display on the wall as the audio interface responds to Zed's command. Harlan Green appears with his patio in the background, just as he did to Arjun only a few minutes before. Zed listens intently as the politician spills out his frantic tale of an offshore rejuve facility. It would seem from the Bird's behavior that he knows precisely why Harlan looks ten years younger.

Zed springs out of his chair and moves to the window. Arjun still finds the wobbly yet explosive kinetics of the renovated Zed somewhere between annoying and disturbing. They seem all wrong for someone who looks to be hovering around forty. Are they a spontaneous expression of resurgent youth, or blatant exhibitionism? Arjun can't be sure.

"You know what Richard Nixon said when everything started to go to hell during Watergate?" he asks Arjun.

"No."

"'We've got to cut the loss fast.' Problem was he didn't follow his own advice. He made the big mistake of letting it drag out, and it's not going to be ours. We need to act quickly and decisively. Get the best contract people and make it happen."

Arjun looks worried. "I'll do it, but we have to understand that it may not be enough. The longer the Bird's loose with what he knows, the bigger the potential for more leakage. I think we need the fallback plan."

Zed returns to his desk. The fallback plan happens in stages. First, demolition charges are placed to destroy the core facility. Second, Zed is evacuated from his residence. Third, Arjun initiates demolition and joins Zed at a remote location. All contract personnel are left to fend for themselves. Their loyalty lasts only as long their paycheck, and they'll cave at the first sign of serious aggression. "All right," Zed says. "Let's get on it.

Zed plops back into his chair after Arjun leaves. He finds one consolation in the current crisis. Autumn. Circumstances will soon demand that his life on Mount Tabor come to an end. He'll be free to move on and start over with her.

"Well, now," The Bird says with a tepid grin as Rachel steps out of the car. "Why am I not surprised?"

The Bird, Lane, Rachel and two vehicles form an oasis in the center of a paved desert of nearly two square miles. Long ago, virgin automobiles and weathered shipping containers covered its dark asphalt surface. Now only the huge gantry cranes remain, standing watch over the barren expanse and all that it represents in terms of lost trade, lost commerce and lost souls. No cameras here. No microphones. Only a cloudy breeze off the Columbia River, its waters hopelessly poisoned by the disaster upstream at Hanford a few years back.

"We so seldom see each other," Rachel answers The Bird. "I wonder why."

"I take it that Harlan believes in the separation of church and state," Lane observes as the pair warily assess each other. "I think this might a great time for a meaningful dialogue. Let's start with what you have in common."

"Simple," the Bird says to Rachel. "Your boss seems to be preaching one thing to your adoring followers and doing quite another. Looks like he's found a higher power. Tough to compete with life everlasting, isn't it?"

"Yes, it is."

"So how did all this go down?" the Bird asks, turning to Lane. "How do you know what you know? And why do think your brother's up there?"

"He was the key scientist in developing the super-rejuve technology," Lane says.

"He thought they were going to kill him to keep the project secret," Rachel adds. "So he came to me and wanted to make a deal with Green for protection, but Green sold him out."

"Yeah, Harlan seems to have a real knack for that," the Bird observes. He recalls the special job they did for Green, the guy they kidnapped from the bar in the War Front, the really smart guy, the guy they had to keep drugged. It has to be Lane's brother, but he keeps his silence. "I know for a fact that our Mr. Green recently made a little unscheduled nighttime visit up to Mount Tabor," the Bird adds.

"I also would like to make an unscheduled visit and ask about the current whereabouts of my brother," Lane says.

"Why think small?" the Bird replies. "We go in and hold the place for ransom. All that technology has to be worth a fortune. I mean, how much will people pay to have teenage balls forever?"

"I think we need to think this thing through a little more thoroughly," Lane cautions.

"Maybe we should simply confront Harlan," Rachel suggests. "That could give us some bargaining power and bring Mount Tabor down without a fight."

"I don't know who's in charge up there," Lane says. "But when they tracked me to Pima, they weren't interested in negotiating."

"Suppose we all go away and give it some thought," Rachel says, "and then meet back here tomorrow. Same time, same place."

"Twenty-four hours," The Bird says. "That's it. If nobody's got a better idea, we're going in."

"I don't like the lobe."

The Bird points toward his right ear as he takes a sip of custom-ground Peruvian coffee brewed in the little shop on Twelfth Avenue in the Pearl. A half-eaten cantaloupe rests on his plate. Behind, a half dozen customers sip coffee and munch on pastries. All large, male and part of the Bird's security team. They are a bad fit amid the tasteful décor and cheerful lighting, but The Bird couldn't care less, and staff here cares very much about what The Bird thinks.

"We'll get you a better one when we get a chance," Lane tells him. "But right now, just think of it as cheap insurance."

"Did you get a good look at my old lobe? Gold plate. Microcarving of an eagle. Scrimshaw deluxe. Little diamonds in each corner."

"What did you do with it?" For an instant, Lane thinks The Bird might have put it in his pocket, leaving a dangerous trail of digital crumbs. Lane has to marvel at the strange mixture of shrewdness and recklessness that simmers inside this man.

"I left it back at my place." The Bird points his thumb over his shoulder. "A safe in the wall. You can't trust the help any more."

Lane has to wonder why someone like The Bird is concerned about theft by the domestic staff. He lets it remain a mystery.

The Bird stands. "Let's get back. I need to feed Rocky before we take off."

They walk out into the morning air and start down Twelfth. That's when Lane first hears the sound, a kind of fizzing like uncorked champagne or the froth atop soapy dishwater.

The Heliraptor, a suicide machine born of global industry: avionics from Tel Aviv, airframe from Korea, firmware from Palo Alto, engine from Hanoi. A one-way expression of explosive mayhem. It claims its ancestry from the predators, the drones of old that circled lazily then dived for the kill with missile fire, before returning to base, hardware intact, investment preserved. Not so with the Heliraptor, an unmanned helicopter designed for the most sensitive of missions, where traceability was not an option. After launching its two missiles, it briefly confirmed the results and self-destructed.

On this clear morning, one such machine skims over the rusted framework of the Broadway Bridge on its way to the Pearl.

"If we have to force our way up into Mount Tabor, it could get pretty ugly," Lane tells The Bird as they walk the first of two blocks back to his penthouse. The security trails them from a discreet distance down the block.

"We don't how well the place is defended," Lane continues. "If the gate is any indication, it could be tough. And if my brother's up there, he could get in the line of fire."

The Bird shrugs. "Not likely. He's high-priced merchandise. They're not going to put him where he's going to go down."

"And what if they do?"

The Bird stops and glares at Lane. "Tell you what, I'm going make you a very special deal just to get you off my back. If we go in, you go in first. I'll give you a chance to fish him out before things get heavy. Satisfied?"

"Yeah, I guess." Lane turns his head east toward the river, where the fizzing has suddenly gotten louder.

The Heliraptor skims between two buildings on Tenth Avenue. Its powerful electric engine makes hardly a sound. The only noise is the effervescent beat of the rotor blades slicing the air. It measures about thirteen feet in length, and consists of nothing but a bare frame of carbon fiber with a small crossbar holding the missiles. Two high-res cameras peer forward, and a container the size of a shoebox holds the electronics, which chatter with a satellite overhead in the tranquil blue. And within this container a specialized, proprietary circuit performs its function with superb accuracy. Out of all the lobes hung on all the humanity below, it isolates The Bird's.

The Heliraptor pilot sits in a darkened room in Bangkok and watches the video feed off the satellite link. Raised on Xbox and Playstation, he views the image in distant and abstract terms. As the target building comes into view, the display puts up a semitransparent circle indicating the location of The Bird's lobe in the penthouse.

Rocky performs an atavistic calculation that equates the rotor's buzz with a swarm of highly edible insects. The armadillo scampers through an open door and out onto the deck, where it hops up on a piece of lawn furniture. It spots a giant black bug, something like a dragonfly, quivering motionless in the air not thirty feet away.

"What the fuck is that?" The Bird's jaw drops slightly after he asks the question. He and Lane halt on the sidewalk to behold the strange craft hovering a block and a half away and a dozen stories up. A helicopter, too big to be a model, too small to be the real thing. Everybody on the street has stopped to stare.

"Hey, it's up by my place," The Bird observes.

"Oh, Jesus," Lane says. "It's found your lobe."

The last thing the armadillo ever sees is the flash and twin streaks screaming toward the penthouse. Each missile carries a warhead designed to spread a horrible fan of shrapnel across an arc of nearly 180 degrees. The fan's vertical spread is highly constrained and focuses the damage into a narrow plane that concentrates on the penthouse floor. When the warheads explode, a million metal shards perforate, puncture, and shred every square foot. Sheared wiring creates electrical arcs near punctured gas lines that feed the Bird's industrial-class stove. A great ball of flame and smoke belches out of the kitchen and onto the deck.

At the same instant, the Heliraptor explodes in a brilliant flash, creating a sphere of debris that slams into the street and surrounding buildings. Windows shatter. Vehicles crumple. Spectators collapse under a spray of shrapnel.

"Jesus fucking Christ!" Lane looks over to see the Bird's jaw fully slack and his eyes bulging, a rare snapshot of shock and fear. But only for an instant. The Bird turns to Lane with a red rage already spreading across his face. "They fucked with me, Anslow. They fucked with me big time."

"We've got to get you off the street. There may be follow-up."

The security detail rushes up and forms a phalanx around the Bird and Lane. Together, they start wading through a crowd of stunned onlookers. Sirens fire up in the background.

"Green," the Bird declares as they move away from the calamity. "He told 'em I wanted in, and they tried to take me out."

"Could be," Lane says.

"He knew they'd try to take me out."

"Maybe so," says Lane.

The Bird takes out his handheld and says "Green" into it.

"You might want to wait on this," Lane suggests. "You're tipping your hand."

"Yeah? Well the other guy's got nothing left to bet," the Bird says. "So who gives a fuck?"

The Bird extends his free hand palm up. His call went through. "Hey, Green." He stares at the handheld, which is sending video of his face to Harlan. "Wanna see something?" He turns the handheld camera toward his building, where the entire upper story is now engulfed in flames, then back to himself. "That's where I live, Harlan. And you know what that means, asshole? It means you're dead meat." He shoves the phone in his pocket and starts down the street at a furious pace. Lane lengthens his stride to follow.

"He can run but he can't hide," the Bird declares. "Not on my turf." He gets back on his cell. "I want Street Party headquarters and the neighborhood sealed tight. Right now."

"We just got a break, Rachel. A really big break."

Harlan appears genuinely excited as he ducks his head into her office. "Grab your coat and keys. We've got to move on this."

"Move on what exactly?" Rachel asks as they hustle down the hall. Harlan had surprised her. He seldom talked to her this early.

"Can't tell you. Not yet. We have to do this on the QT or it won't work. We need to agree to the terms before it goes public."

Rachel sorts through this precipitous development as they leave the Street Party headquarters and head to the parking lot, where they keep an SUV for private use. Its tinted windshield and smoked windows provide an anonymous ride. What's he up to?

"Sorry I didn't let you in on this earlier," Green apologizes. "I've been negotiating with the corporation that owns Mount Tabor. They've agreed in principle to move out and let the land be returned to the public domain. It's a huge victory. All the demonstrating, all the speeches have finally paid off."

"Very impressive," a slightly dazed Rachel responds. Could it be true?

Green might have talked them into moving their rejuve facility some-where more secure. Everybody would win. The corporation would look public spirited for donating the land. Green would reinforce his image as a populist hero. And they would all grow forever young with nobody the wiser.

"So where to?" Rachel asks as she turns onto a main street.

"The gate at Mount Tabor."

"We've got Street Party people up there demonstrating right now," says Rachel.

"That's why we're in a vehicle with no-peek windows. Don't worry. They know we're coming and we'll be waved through."

Harlan spends the balance of the fifteen-minute ride discussing how to present this momentous development to the media. It's too big for the Feed to ignore and will probably run on dozens of news channels. The more he talks, the more Rachel hopes it's all true. Such is the primal force field of Harlan Green.

At the heavily fortified gate, they arrive unrecognized by the protes-tors and a simple lobe scan is all they need to drive on through. Just inside is a small military base of some kind. As they start up the hill, Rachel spots what appear to be bunkers among the trees, but the higher they climb, the less fortified and more parklike the place becomes.

"Now that we're straight on the media strategy, all you have to do is drop me off," Harlan informs her. "We need to work in parallel to pull this thing off. You go on back to the office and start putting a detailed plan together. I'll phone you when I've got the deal done and signed. It might take quite a while, so don't worry, and keep a lid on it. At least for now, okay?"

Rachel nods. She keeps looking at their shifting position in the heads-up display. Depending on what happens, it might be useful information.

"How do we know where we're going?" Rachel asks.

"They said it's near the top. Someone's coming to meet us."

They come over a crest and round a gentle curve. A massive concrete structure juts from the hillside, broken only by a large loading gate and a nearby door. Both entrances are constructed of heavy steel. As Rachel pulls into the parking area, the door lifts vertically and a man emerges with dark skin and a small frame. If Rachel had to guess, she'd say he was Indian.

Green opens his door the moment the vehicle stops. "I'll take it from here. Just wait for my call."

Rachel gives a wry grin as she watches Harlan walk off toward the slight man standing by the door. He didn't even bother to bring a computer or a briefcase. Not like him. Whatever just happened must have happened really fast.

27.

THE END IS QUEER

"Good evening," Zed greets Autumn as he enters the grand dining hall atop Mount Tabor. The fading light from the west casts a soft light over her. "How are you?" he continues. It sounds mechanical and formal, but it's the best he can do.

"I'm just fine," she answers with a polite coolness.

Zed masks his disappointment and steals a glance at his reflection in the large mirror on the far wall, which is paneled with Tasmanian blackwood. He appears to be about forty, and constantly confirms it in every mirror he passes. His head is still shaved, waiting for his hair to catch up with the rest of the process, but it gives him a look of rugged masculinity. He is still struggling to adjust to his shifting musculature, so his movements are somewhat awkward.

"I know I'm a little clumsy, but that'll pass," he explains.

"I know."

Of course she does. She went through the same readjustment. So what can he say to draw her out? The entrance of two waiters interrupts his rumination. Wine is poured. An appetizer of smoked salmon arrives.

They finish the appetizer in silence. The table seats fourteen, and they sit opposite each other in the middle. Two place settings amid a barren plain of polished rosewood.

"How was your flight over?" he asks.

"Pleasant."

After a long silence, his patience is spent. "Don't you have anything to say?"

"And just what would you like to hear?" she asks him in the most patient of tones.

"Maybe we could start with the obvious: That I've changed considerably since the last time you saw me."

"Should I be surprised?"

"No, but you might be a little more excited about it." Zed pauses and closes his eyes to compose himself. "Nobody else shares what we do. Nobody has lived so long and been given a second chance. All the wisdom we've accumulated can now be applied while we're young and healthy. You can have the children you never had. You can travel to where you never went. You can learn everything you never had time for. You can savor those experiences in a way you never could before. Think of it."

"I have thought about it quite a lot, Mr. Thomas Zed."

"Please, just call me Thomas."

Autumn rises and moves to the nearest window. Smoldering remnants of sunlight struggle through a dark band of clouds. "We all have a time, Mr. Zed; and for you and me that time has come and gone."

"You can't be serious. Look at yourself in the mirror."

She turns to him and smiles with a conviction he finds unnerving. "You think you've beaten the clock because you can bring your body back around. But nothing goes on forever. Everything has a beginning and an end."

"So what do you say to all those who believe you have a soul?" Zed counters. "Because along with a soul comes life everlasting. No time limit. No expiration date."

"Not really," Autumn says. "You're assuming that your mind and your soul are the same thing. They're not. Your mind has to die for your soul to move on, which means your body has to die, too. We all come with an expiration date. It's built into the rhythm of life, and there's nothing we can do to change it."

"You sound pretty sure of yourself," Zed says. "And just how would you prove such a thing?"

"An experiment. And that's precisely what you and I are. We're that experiment. And when it's complete, it'll show that we all have a time and that, once that time has come and gone, we go with it."

Zed rises and circles to Autumn's side. "All right then, we both believe in an experiment. Mine offers hope. Yours offers oblivion. I suggest we try mine first."

"As you wish," Autumn says. "It won't change the outcome."

"We'll see about that. In the meantime, I want you to go home and pack up and be ready to leave. You won't need much. Everything will be taken care of."

Autumn turns to face the last remnant of dusk out the window. "I'm sure it will."

Zed finds Green waiting for him at rigid attention in an anodized aluminum chair in a guest room at the north end of Zed's residential complex. The politician watches a big video display where the Feed replays the attack on the Bird's penthouse from a wide variety of angles and perspectives. Any event in the Trade Ring and its periphery now falls under the paranoid gaze of at least a dozen cameras, and the Feed is expert at ferreting them out and flinging them over the broadband in record time.

Green turns toward Zed's entrance. "You missed."

"Mistakes do happen," Zed admits.

"The Bird will come after you, you know that? He'll take us both out if he gets the chance."

"Then we won't give him the chance," Zed explains as he sits down on the couch. "We have options."

"Such as?"

"In case you hadn't noticed, it would take a major military action to get in here. I doubt that your friend has the means."

"You're underestimating him. He has thousands of fighters at his disposal, and he's very resourceful."

"I'm sure he is. And if it looks like he's going to pose a serious threat, we can always evacuate by air."

"And what about my career? How do we keep that from going up in smoke?"

"You're a man of peace," Zed declares calmly. "You're a man on a diplomatic mission who just made a big breakthrough. For the first time, real progress has been made to heal the differences between business in the towers and people on the street. On the other hand, the Bird would seem a madman who's hell-bent on extreme violence that threatens to undo all that you've worked so hard for. In the end, justice will prevail. And somehow, I doubt that your avian friend will survive the experience."

"And how might we expedite all this?" Green asks.

"At the first sign of real trouble, we'll evacuate you to one of your offices in another city, where you can make a heartfelt plea for peace and reason. It'll be a good move. Your campaign has been pretty much rage-based. Now you'll be seen as far more balanced and nuanced."

"Balanced and nuanced," Green repeats. "That just might work."

"Of course it'll work," Zed reassures him.

But it won't, as Zed well knows. Not with the Bird out there on the rampage. Green has betrayed him and Green will pay. The Bird will pursue him relentlessly and do whatever it takes to get revenge. And that includes telling the whole world about the miracle technology hiding up on the mountain under the stewardship of Thomas Zed.

On the other hand, if Green were no longer in the picture, the Bird might quickly become a very reasonable man, especially if he were to take Green's place on the short list.

28.

GO TELL IT ON THE MOUNTAIN

Rachel points to the big green rectangle of Mount Tabor, which domi-nates the video display in her office. She shows Lane the road that comes in off Sixtieth Avenue and winds up the former park's western slope past the drained reservoir. "This is the road Harlan and I took after going through the gate. We looped around the reservoir and went up to a little parking area in front of what looks like a huge bunker set in the hillside. If they're hiding something, it definitely has to be here... If your Johnny's up there, that's where you'll find him."

Lane nods at the image. "Sounds like it."

"I still don't know how in the hell the Bird thinks he's going get in there," Rachel says. "The gate on Sixtieth looks like Fort Knox, and they've got bunkers all the way up past the reservoir."

"Plus they've cleared the trees back around the entire perimeter," Lane adds. "Anybody up above has a clear field of fire on anybody com-ing up from below. It would be a suicide charge. Even if you got though the clearing, you'd have to fight uphill on foot to get to the buildings."

Rachel studies the map. "The only way that makes sense is to break in through the main gate so you can use the roads. But then they'd really have you in their crosshairs."

Lane's phone buzzes. He reads a text message and looks up to Rachel. "The Bird has just put out an order for his forces to assemble along seventy-second avenue on the far side of the mountain away from the gate. Now why would he do that?"

The Bird carefully steps around an oil spot on the hanger's cement floor. It might soil the leather soles of his chapel-buckled loafers of hand-chosen calfskin. The big structure's front door is rolled up to reveal the single runway of Troutdale Airport, several miles east of the city. A crop duster points its propeller-driven nose toward the door. Its single-seat cockpit pokes up from a fuselage painted bright yellow with blue trim. Underneath each wing hangs a linear array of spray nozzles.

Gary Jacobs, who serves as the plane's pilot and mechanic, pulls his head from the open engine cowling to greet the Bird. "So you're the guy, huh?" Jacobs is short and stocky under his greasy coveralls and sports an unruly shock of grizzled gray hair.

"Yeah, I'm the guy."

Jacobs looks over the Bird's shoulder at his two henchmen standing behind him. "And who are they?"

"They're nobody, and they like it that way."

Jacobs knows better than to press the point. "Well, each to his own, I guess."

"So can you do it?"

Jacobs scratches his head and looks at the plane. "Yeah, I can do it, but it's going to be real tricky. I've got to rig some kind of ventilation and wear an oxygen mask, just to make sure. Most likely, it's going to ruin the aircraft."

The Bird snorts. "Come on now, is that going to be a problem?"

"I suppose not. Especially with what you're payin' me."

"You have to be ready by later this afternoon. You'll go on my command. Is that understood?"

Jacobs grins. "It's gonna be a helluva show."

"It better be." The Bird turns and heads for the hangar door. On the way out he passes a relic of the distant past tacked up to an exposed stud of aging fir. A centerfold spills down, an image whose colors have faded almost to sepia. A woman with blond hair and enormous breasts smiles out upon the hangar and all who dwell there.

The Bird finds it vaguely erotic, but not nearly as stimulating as his plan to take down Mount Tabor.

The sky is heading toward a tarnished dusk by the time Lane walks south down Sixtieth Avenue. The wooded slopes of Mount Tabor loom to his left as he approaches the security gate on Salmon Street. Johnny's up there somewhere, his brilliant and hopelessly compromised brother. Lane wants to shout up the hill and tell him to hang on, that he's on his way just like always. They're all that's left, just the two of them. Without each other, they are lost in some inner space both dark and boundless.

There were once numerous entrances to Mount Tabor, but now there is only one gate. Brilliant floodlights bathe the streets and sidewalks. Twin bunkers of concrete and blast barriers flank the big hinged gate. Big guns in turrets atop the bunkers have the power to turn the street into an instant butcher shop.

The guards at the gate eye Lane as he walks on by but don't appear overly curious. All seems peaceful. A lawn sprinkler spits its wet rhythm down the block. A puppy yips in the distance. Automated porch lights wink on. Whatever the Bird is planning apparently doesn't involve this side of the mountain. In a phone call earlier, Lane had asked the Bird about his plan of attack. The big boss smiled into the video and simply said, "Surprise!"

In this fleeting moment of calm, Lane thinks of Johnny, of the perfect day on Miller Bay, the green water, the kelp, the old docks, and the skiff manned by two little boys. Before he knows it, he's reached Division Street, where the streetcar is just pulling up. He hops on.

The Bad Boys that sit all around him don't even bother to conceal their weapons. They sit in pairs, with vacant eyes and heads that bob slightly to the streetcar's motion along the tracks. Their combat rifles sprout as phallic totems from their laps. Bandoliers of ammunition drape from their shoulders. In all his years, Lane has never seen a display of civil anarchy this brazen. Until now the Bird operated like urban gangs worldwide, strategically applying violence in limited engagements at opportune moments.

The streetcar squeaks to a halt at Seventy-second and Division. The Bad Boys head out the doors at either end. Lane follows at a distance as they start up the sidewalks to the north. All sport the forearm tattoo of the Hoodoos, a north end gang with biker lineage. They strut along at a leisurely pace, laughing and punching each other on their deltoids. To their left, the sylvan slope of Mount Tabor rises just a few blocks away.

Modest homes line both sides of the street, some boarded up, some still occupied. The growing glut of Bad Boys doesn't distinguish between the two. They camp on parched lawns, they sit on porch steps with upright rifles; they emerge through front doors, eating pilfered food. A woman's scream spills out of a back room somewhere up ahead. Lane has to stifle his professional instinct to intervene. Cops are no longer cops here.

The Bad Boys spot a pair of yards filled with their own and peel off. The streetlights cast them in long shadows. Lane continues, block after block. More of the same, maybe a thousand men in all. Above them, the lower slope of the mountain reaches down to the street, all cleared of trees and brush. It forms a no-man's-land heavily favoring whatever firepower dwells in the darkened tree line above.

Lane reaches the house the Bird has commandeered as a command post. A long line of pickup trucks and SUVs stretches for blocks. The guards on the porch grudgingly part to let him enter. He recognizes several from his days on the street.

The Bird sits at the kitchen table next to Rachel, holding a steaming mug of coffee in the tradition of military commanders everywhere. He looks up from a laptop. "So, you have a nice little evening stroll? What's happening on the far side of the mountain?"

"Absolutely nothing."

The Bird nods agreeably. "And that's as it should be."

"I don't how you're going to pull this off, but remember I go in with the first wave and pull my brother out before it gets ugly. That was the deal, right?"

"Right. See those vehicles outside? You get the one at the head of the line."

"Is that a good thing?" Rachel asks suspiciously. "To be at the business end?"

"It's a very good thing." The Bird pulls out his phone. "So let's do it." He taps the interface and puts the device to his ear. "You ready? Good. Let's go."

Zed and Arjun walk across the cement surface of the empty reservoir near the bottom of the western slope. Up ahead, a matched pair of choppers awaits in silence with drooping rotors and doused lights. An idling engine would attract attention, giving outsiders time to arm antiaircraft missiles. After watching video of the sudden congregation on Seventy-Second Avenue, they initiated the second phase of the evacuation plan, which calls for Zed to depart in one machine, followed by Arjun in the second after he confirms that the demolition is successful.

They reach the choppers as the twilight thickens. Zed shakes Arjun's hand. "See you later."

"Yes," Arjun replies absently. "Later." He feels the strength of Zed's grip compared to the frailty of his own. He sees the clarity and intent in Zed's eyes contrasting with the apprehension and doubt in his own. The power of youth regained, or so it seemed.

Zed climbs into the seat next to the pilot in the nearest chopper as Arjun walks back toward his parked vehicle. Zed twists around to the passenger compartment, which holds Harlan Green flanked by two security people, men of great strength and little compassion. An emergency light bathes the trio in a pale red, which mercifully softens their features.

"I don't get it," Green says. Growing anxiety drives his voice into a higher register. "I need to contact my people and let them know I'm on my way."

"What we need to do right now is get out of here," Zed says. "Then you can pick your destination at your leisure. We'll drop you at the airport with some cash and you can take it from there."

A mechanical cough issues from behind them, and the chopper's turbine engine comes to life. The rotors come out of their torpor and start a lazy spin. The pilot looks at the multiple displays on the instrument panel and scans the numbers, vectors, symbols and graphs. He turns to Zed. "Ready."

"Go," he orders.

The turbine winds up and the rotors beat savagely against the evening air. The aircraft rises, the nose dips slightly, and they head southwest. A dull orange sliver of light over the West Hills marks the end of day. Safety lights on the broadcast towers call out to the night with their abrupt winks of red and white. Zed feels a tap on his shoulder.

"We're not headed toward the airport," Green shouts over the roar of the engine.

"Patience," Zed responds.

Gary Jacobs reaches the end of the taxiway and rotates the AT-400 Air Tractor onto the main runway of Troutdale Airport. He faces west into the last glow of dusk over the distant hills. The plane's 680-horsepower turboprop engine mutters and growls, waiting to be set loose into flight. He speaks into the microphone in the oxygen mask to get clearance for takeoff. An affirmative reply comes through the earphones in his crash helmet. The mask feels odd and restrictive. It clings to his cheeks. He acquired it and the helmet only this afternoon and hurriedly installed them in the dilapidated cockpit.

For this mission oxygen is a must to avoid being poisoned by the fumes. The aircraft's 400-gallon hopper, which sits between the engine firewall and the cockpit, no longer holds pesticide. Instead, it's filled to the brim with ethylene oxide. If he inhaled or touched it, the compound would twist his chromosomes into a mutagenic nightmare.

Jacobs pushes the throttle all the way forward. The engine roars and the plane hurtles down the runway under full power and lifts off. The pilot can feel the vibration of the tires, which continue to spin freely on their fixed struts. Ahead, the dark void of Blue Lake interrupts the sprinkle of residential lighting. Off to his left, the freeway cuts a luminous path through the cityscape.

Navigation will be simple enough. Just follow this freeway to where it intersects with the north-south route. Take a left and follow this second freeway for about two miles to a big black bump rising out of the glittering matrix below: Mount Tabor.

You can't miss it.

In the chopper, Green taps Zed's shoulder, this time insistently.

"Where in the hell are we going?" he asks over the noise. "That's Lake Oswego down there."

Zed looks out the window at the long finger of water embedded in the luxurious landscaping. He turns back to Harlan, who is leaning forward to hear his answer. "You're right."

The security man to Green's right sees the opportunity. He brings out the hypodermic and stabs Green's neck from behind. Green tries to twist and face his attacker, but the other security man grabs him around the chest and holds him fast until he collapses into terminal relaxation.

Gary Jacobs pushes the throttle all the way forward and banks tightly to his left. He is flying five hundred feet above Sixtieth Avenue along the western base of Mount Tabor. He pulls back on the stick. The turboprop engine ascends in a banshee scream. The propellers bite into the cool air and pull the plane skyward.

Jacobs glances at the speckles of light through the trees below. The plane is locked in a tight spiral, an upward corkscrew above the mountain. He reaches over to the spray valve on the instrument panel and twists it all the way to the right.

Liquid flows out of the tank behind the engine. It floods down to a pump that forces it under pressure to an array of nozzles under the wings and fuselage. Long, parallel trails of mist spew from the nozzles and merge into an elongated fog, a spiral vapor trail heading toward the promise of heaven.

As the plane soars, the nebulous spiral fuses into a single giant cloud. Over a ton of ethylene oxide floats in a volatile mist above the western base of the park, where the gate is located.

Zed's chopper touches down lightly in the bottom of a deserted gravel pit on the far side of the city of Tigard. The two security men drag Green's corpse out and leave it spread-eagled and staring at the urban glow overhead. Then they head for an SUV positioned for their exit.

"Go," Zed orders the pilot. He feels his spirits lift as the chopper surges skyward. God, it's good to be young again. The arc of his life is once more ascendant and traces a curve to heights beyond imagination.

The dead sprawl of Harlan Green shrinks into oblivion as the aircraft gains altitude.

Suddenly, a brilliant flash of light fills the night sky and rakes across the ground below. "Jesus!" the pilot exclaims. "What the hell was that?"

The final phase of the operation called for the pilot to open his door a crack, toss out a flare attached to a parachute and timer, then fly as fast and as far away as possible.

But a faulty seal in the liquid delivery system saves him the effort. A corroded rubber ring allows gas fumes to escape from the piping and accumulate in the vicinity of the pump, with its electric motor. A small spark ignites the fumes and triggers an explosion that rips through the firewall and flings the instrument panel into Gary Jacobs's face. He dies well in advance of burning to death.

The engine, the wings, and the fuselage all part ways in a brilliant fireball of crumpled orange, yellow and black.

And then the fog fires up, a fog from Hell itself.

In a millisecond, a chain reaction leverages the oxygen in the air to incinerate the entire cloud, creating an explosion of staggering extent.

The outward expansion of the fireball is so rapid that it generates a great wall of air compressed to the hardness of stone. A blast wave of proportions seldom visited upon an urban landscape of any kind. Hundreds of houses disintegrate on the far side of Sixtieth Avenue.

On the mountain's west side, trees fracture, pavement buckles, building disintegrate, vehicles flip. Humans turn to boneless jelly. The gate and its bunkers are pulverized into acrid dust.

Mount Tabor holds its breath in a vacuum of displaced air.

Lane and Rachel are out on the front porch of the command post when the bomb ignites. The sky over the tree line above them becomes a violent dawn. The house rocks on its foundation. The concussion slams their eardrums and surges through their innards.

"My God! What has he done?" Rachel asks as she recovers her balance.

Lane doesn't know the details but gets the general idea. The Bird just blew up the gate in a horrific explosion, using the mountain as a shield for his troops here on the far side.

Before he can voice his theory, the Bird comes bounding out on to the porch and yells to the men assembled in the yard. "Let's go!" He turns to Lane. "Okay, General. Lead the way."

"You better stay here," Lane tells Rachel.

"I think you're right," she says. "I'm a facilitator, not a fighter."

Pale clouds of swirling, agitated smoke blow across Division Street as Lane and company approach Sixtieth Avenue. Their SUV's headlights push twin tunnels of illumination through the haze, and Lane wonders if they'll be able to reach their objective, the gate up on Salmon Street.

Three Bad Boys along for the ride say nothing, but Lane sees the fear creep across their faces. They've lived lives of petty violence but never faced slaughter and destruction on a truly epic scale. The Bird gave them strict orders to stick with Lane and provide security if he found his Johnny, so they are committed. Nobody crosses the Bird.

"Turn right," Lane instructs as they reach Sixtieth.

The thick smoke comes and goes as the SUV slowly navigates downed power lines and splintered debris from demolished houses. Only the foundations remain. Great pillars of fire from blazing trees cast a golden light over the scorched remnants. Lane feels the heat blister the exterior of the vehicle.

So it goes, block after block. Nothing moves. Nothing lives.

"Shit!" one of the Bad Boys mutters as his stoic persona wobbles. They continue until they reach the heart of the blast area, where the gate into Mount Tabor once stood, with its massive bunkers and gun turrets. Now only pulverized concrete rubble marks the spot. They can barely find a clearing big enough to drive through. Beyond, all the structures in the military facility are sheared off at ground level. Several pools of phosphorus from demolished armaments burn a brilliant white and create wildly flickering shadows.

Up the hillside they enter a cathedral of flaming fir trees, crowns all ablaze. Showers of embers float down and twist in little currents on the pavement.

"Step on it," Lane says.

The driver accelerates. Their vehicle creates eddies of dancing sparks

as they speed through. They reach a clear space, and Lane recognizes the
empty reservoir with its old building of crenelated stone hanging on the
side, the only structure he's seen that survived the blast.

"Hang a hard left and head up," he orders the driver. Around the
curve the road follows a graded rise that affords a view of the city below. Hundreds of fires form bright beacons in the smoky haze stretching
west twenty blocks or more. The city teeters on the edge of a firestorm,
where little fires merge into an insatiable monster that creates howling
winds of fresh oxygen to perpetuate itself.

Has the Bird's rage trumped his political sensibilities? Did he have
any idea of the awful catastrophe that his vanity and pursuit of ven-
geance would visit upon the people of this city?

They climb up the grade and curve into an area with a thick mix of
deciduous and fir trees. The fires have yet to reach this high, but they're
surely on their way. Thin wisps of smoke already drift across the road.
The security lights from darkened buildings come and go, but Lane ignores them. He knows from Rachel's trip precisely where he's going.

There it is, a hulking mass of buttressed concrete protruding from
the hillside. Next to its massive service door, a smaller entrance stands
open and spills fluorescent light into the parking lot. "Pull in here."

As he does so, a man appears in the door, a smallish man slightly bent
with age. He smokes a cigarette with one hand and pockets the other in
his loose slacks. One of the Bad Boys cocks his weapon. "Stow it," Lane
orders. "No trouble." He opens the door and climbs out. "Wait here."

"Good evening, Mr. Anslow," the man says as Lane approaches.

The limo is late, and Thomas Zed knows why. It's the gunfire.

He stands in the deserted turnaround at the Pinecrest air hop terminal and looks out over the pond to the house lights beyond. Large,
comfortable houses economically gestating in a costly womb of carefully engineered security. Until now, anyway.

Behind him, the thin whine of the chopper's idling engine. To his
right, the random pop of small weapons fire. Pinecrest's main gate is
under attack.

They know, Zed thinks. The street has already told them, even this far out on the urban fringe. Mount Tabor is going down, the biggest, strongest gate of all. So what about all the other gates? Some outlier gang has already been inspired to mount a ragtag attack on Pinecrest. It's probably happening all over the city. Amateur hour. Most of the insurrection will be cut to pieces by contract military people. Still, the survivors will tell the tale over and over again for the rest of their miserable lives.

Zed gives up on the limo, which the security people were supposed to provide. He walks over to the access panel on the side of the building and orders a shuttle. He returns to the curb and waits. Crickets chirp. Frogs croak. Their nocturnal musing weaves its way into the chatter of discharging weapons out on the community's secured perimeter. He's always marveled at how, during great civil upheavals, tranquility and mayhem can coexist in such close proximity.

Autumn should be ready by now. All they have to do is get back here with her stuff and take off. The rest will take care of itself. He's certain of that.

The momentary solitude of the empty street starts to eat at him. Something is wrong, something deep inside. He has a vision of life redeemed, of life relived, but his soul suddenly refuses to follow. A sinkhole of fatigue is pulling him down. He's felt it before, many times as he's aged. But now, it should be a distant artifact, a biological relic from a time past, a time of decrepitude, dissolution and disrepair.

We all have a time, Autumn had said. And our time has come and gone.

What if she's right?

Zed climbs out of the shuttle from the air hop. Autumn's house is dark, the front door open. No light shines within.

His heart quickens as he strides up the steps. Has she fled and deserted him?

"Autumn?" He tastes the fear in his voice and moves from room to room, finding nothing. His master plan, so carefully engineered and constructed, spools out into the dim solitude.

He finds her in the garden, lit by the glow of a nearby streetlight. A small wrought-iron table stands next to the rocking chair where she reposes.

Eyes closed, lips at peace, skin cool, life gone.

A framed photo rests on the table, the picture taken in front of the theater in Nebraska so many years before. She smiles out at him full of life, ready for the promise of the future, a time that has come and gone.

Tears stream down his renovated cheeks. He can't bear to touch her. Was she dead from her own hand, or the hand of time itself? It no longer matters. She'd told him that they were an experiment, and here is its sad conclusion.

If Zed ever cried like this before, it resides somewhere in a past no longer remembers, in the smoke from the embers of fires long forgotten.

"You know me, which means you also know Johnny," Lane says to Arjun as they cross the floor to the older man's office. "So where is he?"

"Johnny's gone," Arjun says, sinking wearily into the chair behind his desk.

"How do I know you're telling the truth?"

Arjun smiles with a curious mix of irony and bitterness. "Let me show you the truth." He brings up a CT scan on a display. "See all those little white spots? They're cancerous tumors. And they've reached a point where nothing will stop them."

"You're saying Johnny has cancer?"

"No. Just that I'm dying. I'm almost gone."

"Sorry, but where does that leave Johnny?"

"It leaves him on a big yacht called the Eternal Heart. It's owned by the man that owns all that you see here. His name is Thomas Zed."

"And why are you telling me all this?"

"Because if you kill Thomas Zed, I can leave this world knowing justice has been done." Arjun looks away sadly. "I was next in line for the treatment, but that's not how it worked out. It looked like he would sail on forever while I wasted away."

"We can't always get what we want," the Bird interrupts. Lane turns to see him standing in the doorway wearing a lambskin leather jacket and tweed slacks.

"Well, I got what I want," Lane says and starts for the door.

"Stay in touch," the Bird says, "or I'll start to worry about you."

"I'm sure you will," Lane says.

The first flicks of fire creep though the crowns of the fir trees opposite the parking lot, where a noisy parade of vehicles filled with Bad Boys streams past. Lane hears a shout from up the hill. "Hey, there's a fuckin' mansion up here!" Weapons pop. Glass shatters.

He starts off on foot toward the far side of the mountain, the side spared the explosion and fire. He can walk down these leeward slopes with impunity. Zed's surviving security people were busy melting into the surrounding neighborhoods below. Lane leaves the chaos of the road, the shouting, the shooting and the vehicles and begins his descent His route through the forest is well defined, as the holocaust over the mountain has created a brilliant glow.

"So you're sick, huh?" the Bird inquires, sliding into a chair across the desk from Arjun.

"Yes, I am."

The Bird gives a nod of faux compassion. "After everything you've done, that's pretty ironic." He looks out the window down the row of bays. "It would be an even bigger tragedy if you let it all go to waste. I mean, it's your legacy. Right?"

"Correct." Arjun looks at his watch while answering.

The Bird assumes a thoughtful pose. "You know, even at this late date, you have choices. You could help me repackage all this so others could share. And then, when you really hit the skids, we could do all that was medically possible to keep you comfortable."

"Or?"

"You could keep all this to yourself and deny the world the benefit of what you've accomplished. And then we could do everything possible to make sure you spent your final days in maximum pain and agony."

"I see." Arjun checks his watch again. "Let's consider a third choice."

Lane feels the detonation as a muffled monstrous thud. He has no doubt of its origin, and continues down the hill.

The blast serves as a punctuation mark of sorts. All the shouting and gunfire abruptly stop. In its place, an ugly cloud of rumination settles in. Lane had vastly underestimated what the Bird was willing to do to reclaim his teenage balls – a horrible mistake on his part. All in the service of Johnny, all in Lane's quest to prove who was really the biggest brother of all. On the other side of the equation, Lane knows that a mistake and an act of deliberate malice are two distinctly different things. But his heart claims otherwise.

He looks up and sees that he's reached the bottom of the mountain, and walks out onto Seventy-second Avenue, now completely devoid of power. The sky's glow has surpassed the wattage of a full moon, and casts the street, the sidewalks and the houses in a spectral frost of delicate peach.

He passes a yard where three kids dart among the shadows and giggle in delight at the novelty of no lights. Up ahead, Rachel sits on the porch steps of the commandeered home. "You're all right. Thank God."

"Yeah, I'm okay." They meet in a spontaneous embrace and both realize that they've crossed some threshold, as yet undefined but bright in its possibilities.

"What about Johnny?" Rachel asks.

"I know where he is. I got what I wanted."

"Harlan?"

Lane shrugs. "You know, his name never came up. Like maybe he isn't around anymore. Want to guess why?"

"Don't have to."

Behind them, a great conflagration rages and shakes its fiery fist at the black void.

A pyre to life everlasting.

29.

BANTU SLIPSTREAM

Lane parks his rental car where the street ends near the shore of Puget Sound in the one-block village of Suquamish, just south of Miller Bay. He trains his binoculars on the distant vessel moored outside the bay. He can't make out the name but doesn't need to. A ship as big as the Eternal Heart requires substantial support and wasn't hard to trace.

Two weeks have passed since Mount Tabor went up in smoke. Thousands died in the nearby neighborhoods. Hundreds of homes and businesses yielded to fire. The Feed buzzed with speculation. Pundits flapped their jaws. Consultants opined. Commentators commented. No one got even close to the truth.

He stows his binoculars, gets out and smells his childhood drifting by on the breeze. A timeless composite of life and death churning beneath the cold green waters and washing up on the graveled beaches.

He looks over at the single row of old wooden buildings that house a tavern, a café and the ghost of some enterprise long expired. Two young men clad in khaki shorts and T-shirts emerge from the tavern, one tall, the other shorter and muscular. They stop on the steps to smoke. Loud music spills out, a recent genre called bantu slipstream. Lane knows it by name only. Its origins and nuances escape him entirely. But the name stenciled in white block letters on the men's black T-shirts does not. The Eternal Heart. They must be crew members. Through the open door, he can make out maybe two dozen more wearing the same garb at the bar and in the booths. Lane casually approaches the young men and engages them smoothly in classic street cop style.

"Hey, guys. You havin' a party here?"

The taller of the two grins. "Yeah, I guess you could call it that."

"So what's the occasion?" Experience tells Lane they're about three beers in, and loose enough to push a little.

"Sunday afternoon," his muscular friend says. "We get Sunday afternoons off."

"Oh yeah? Then who watches the boat?"

"For a couple of hours, the boat can watch itself just fine," the tall one says.

"Yeah, and besides, the new owner's sort of a moody guy," the muscular companion adds. "He likes to be left alone."

"The new owner? Who was the previous owner?"

"An old guy. Like un-fucking-believably old. The new guy's supposed to be his grandson, or something like that."

"Weird," Lane growls. "Hey, mind if I join the party?" He looks toward the open door.

"Only if you're buyin," the tall one says with a good natured grin.

"Yeah, I'm buyin," Lane says and turns to go in.

He steps across the threshold onto an old floor of worn wooden planking. A crude painting of a moored tugboat hangs over the bar. Its black hull floats in water turned turquoise with age. A narrow aisle runs the length of the place between the bar and half a dozen booths of varnished plywood. Energized chatter sprinkled with eruptions of spontaneous laughter floats through the thick air. All the barstools and booths are filled with crew people, young and animated. Lane senses a certain sameness to them, each unfinished and still on an assembly line beyond their understanding.

He thinks he spots Johnny at the end of the bar. The hair seems right, as does the agitated motion of the hands directed toward a girl seated next to him. But he's facing away, so Lane can't be sure.

A troubled stream of query flows through Lane as he closes the distance between them. If Johnny's free, why didn't he get in touch?

"Johnny?"

His brother turns, and Lane feels the shock, the terrible shock.

Miller Bay. Johnny looks only slightly older than he did then as a teenager.

Lane knows he should have considered the possibility but didn't because of denial. Facing the consequences in real time, he fights to maintain his composure.

"Hey, bro." Johnny grins across a fissure twenty years wide. "Man, it's good to see you. How's it goin'?"

"What are you doing?" Lane demands. It's all he can come up with as the room starts a slow wobble.

"I'm doing great. What about you? You okay?"

"Could we step outside?" Lane manages to ask.

"Yeah, sure."

The smokers are gone and the parking area empty, save for Lane's rental. A flock of seagulls screeches and flutters its way toward the open water. Lane and Johnny walk down the gentle grade to a concrete embankment above the shoreline. They stroll in silence. Johnny offers no explanation for his disappearance or current state.

"What happened? What did they do to you?" Lane finally asks his brother.

Johnny gives an amiable shrug. "Isn't it obvious?"

"Why didn't you get a hold of me?"

Johnny smiles at the ground. "It's hard to explain. I'm in an entirely new space. I still need to get my bearings."

They stop at the barrier and look out on the water. Lane glances over at Johnny, at his reborn face, and feels a great sorrow. They will never close the distance.

"Well, that's just fucking great. So how long were you going to wait?"

"I don't know," Johnny answers. "I really don't."

Johnny lights up a smoke and puts his hand on Lane's shoulder. "Let's go back in. Have a beer. We chase the babes and see where it goes."

But Lane already knows it goes nowhere. Looking back, Johnny never made it past eighteen in the first place. In a perverse kind of way, he's now perfectly synchronized.

"What's done is done," Johnny says. "We go on from here. End of story."

Lane turns away from the water. They start back up the grade toward the tavern.

"I think you should come with me," he tells Johnny.

Johnny shakes his head. "You don't get it, bro. It's too late." He sighs and stares down at the ground. Lane says nothing.

"Okay, I know you were worried, I know you tried to find me. So maybe I owe you." He reaches into his pocket and pulls out a featureless metal cube about the size of half a stick of butter. "Know what this is?"

"Yeah, it's an Exacube."

Johnny stares at the device. "It's all on here: the science, the technology, the documentation. It's the only copy." He looks up. "You're set, bro. You're set for life."

Lane takes the cube, which feels angular and cool in his hand. "Good luck," Johnny says. He pats Lane on the shoulder and heads back to the tavern.

Lane watches his brother disappear into the world of his newfound peers, a world Lane can never enter. He's lost him, and in a particularly awful way. If he were dead, eventually there would be closure. Instead, an aching void will be with Lane always, even if they sporadically see each other.

Lane starts the rental car and drives out to the main road while thinking of Rachel back in Portland. Her address to the Street Party faithful at the memorial for Harlan Green was both profound and forceful. It gave her the leverage she needed to assume leadership and begin to chart a new political course that offered a positive outcome based on reason, not resentment.

Lane's car reaches a clearing where Miller Bay spreads out with green sparkles dancing in the afternoon sun. He takes a coarsely paved road down to a boat ramp, where a narrow inlet links the little bay with the sound. A few hundred feet away, the tip of the sand spit, a childhood landmark, forms the far side of the opening. Large contemporary homes rise where great tangles of driftwood once dwelled. A guarded gate most certainly blocks the entrance at the far end.

The Eternal Heart sits at anchor out in the open waters of the sound.

Lane raises his binoculars and verifies the ship's name on the stern, which faces shoreward. A lone figure clad in shorts and sports shirt sits in a canvas chair on the deck.

Lane looks to the nearby marina. He can't rent a boat here. They'll trace it off his lobe. He heads back to the main road. He'll have to take the long way around, the old way.

He leaves the boat ramp, drives another mile and spots an opening in the dense forest. The barest trace of an old road runs down the slope, twin grooves in a tangle of ferns and nettles.

He leaves the car and follows the path by fallen rotting logs swathed in pouting lips of clinging fungi. Overhead, the great firs form a permanent overcast against intrusion by the sun.

He remembers the way. He remembers rolling down the window of the family car and sticking his arm out to catch the tree branches that licked at the glass. He remembers his mother yelling at him not to do it. He remembers looking at Johnny and snickering. He remembers the silence of his father.

The forest thins. The alders take over and admit the sky once more. Lush ferns yield to tall grass, damp at the base, lapping at his shoes and soaking the cuffs of his pants.

Abruptly, the cabin comes into view, a sagging ruin sunk in knee-high grass and locked in a death struggle with the rot of rain and wandering seed. Its roof has collapsed, leaving the chimney to stand alone against the eternal sky.

The past has closed in behind him, like the wake of a vessel traversing a chronological sea.

He pushes through a tangle of brush down to the beach. The grass sprouts waist-high, and a dense stand of alders and cottonwoods hides the bay. Still, he can smell the ooze of marine life welling up from the beneath the water.

The stairs. He's found the stairs. The railings have collapsed, but the big chunks of wooden steps remain intact. Two steps down, and the bay unfolds before him, and just beyond it, the Eternal Heart, its hull painted a magnificent white by the afternoon sun.

The dock here has gone to ruin. Great colonies of barnacles cover the remnants of the pilings, dead fingers of timber that point skyward.

Lane looks out across the sand spit two hundred yards. At this elevation, only the mast of the Eternal Heart is visible above the houses. He needs a boat to get there. Any boat will do.

He finds it on the far side of the first dock he comes to. A skiff, its oars shipped and protruding like alien ears. He walks down a gangplank to the float where the boat is moored.

Of course. It had to be a skiff. Only this one is painted with a gray exterior instead of blue. Lane climbs in, and the little craft rolls under his weight as he unties the mooring. He dips the oars and pulls away with a powerful stroke. The air is mild, the water emerald, and the sun splashes little sparks across its surface.

As he leans into each stroke, he fixes on the little wake that trails off the stern. It stirs the water into a modest roil of foam and ripples. Now he's farther from shore, the bay becomes like it always was. Sun, water, sky and the quiet boil of marine life.

He ships the oars and twists around to get his bearing. A quick strobe of Johnny the child flashes in the stern, his small hand gripping the line holding a fish he'd caught that now trails in the boat's wake.

"I won't lose it, Lane," he says. "I promise."

"It's okay," Lane mutters softly as he turns back and dips the oars. "Don't worry about it."

He falls once more into the rhythm of rowing, scanning the shoreline to identify the spot where an old navy plane, a fabulous metal carcass, was once beached. Gone. Instead, an elaborate docking structure houses a gleaming new seaplane.

He cuts across the mouth of the bay at its midpoint, and the drift of the tide aligns him with its outer shore. Soon he is sailing directly toward the stern of the Eternal Heart.

The scale of the big boat now looms. It's more than a hundred feet long, with at least ten feet from the waterline to its main deck. A ladder hangs over the starboard side of the stern, its aluminum frame blazing in the sun, and leads to an open gate in the deck railing. The deck surface remains hidden above, except for a large blue canvas awning for shade.

Lane slows, boats the oars and moves to the bow as he approaches the stern. Extending his arm to buffer the skiff's docking with the ladder frame, he brings the boat to a silent stop and moors. Then he grabs the tubular framing and plants his foot on the first rung.

Just before his head comes even with deck, he pauses and removes the small automatic from his pocket. Now he extends himself and cautiously peeks over the top of the deck.

Across the big spread of oak planking, the solitary figure sits in an aluminum folding chair and stares out at the sound.

Lane quickly scans for other people or surveillance cameras but sees none. He grabs a post on the deck rail and hoists himself aboard. He's sure that the man can see him out the corner of his eye, but there's no reaction, no shifting of the body, no tensing for action. Only the solemn stare over the water, with legs drawn up and hands curled over the edges of the armrest.

Walking slowly, Lane keeps watching for other people. They're apparently alone, with only the smell of sun-soaked canvas drifting down from above. Lane stops a couple of steps from the man.

"Lane Anslow," the man announces without turning to look. "Brother of Dr. John Anslow."

"Thomas Zed," Lane counters.

"Sort of," Zed says wearily. He appears not much older than Johnny, at least in body.

"I've seen what you did to my brother. I've lost him for good."

Lane brings out his pistol and aligns it with Zed's head. "You're facing at least one kidnapping charge and several for conspiracy to commit homicide."

"And?"

"I'm going to give you a choice. You can either come with me into custody, or I can start shooting off pieces of your cute new face."

"Ah, the cop," Zed says with mocking smile. He gets up slowly and Lane takes a cautionary step backwards. "Always the cop. So where are we going?"

Lane motions behind him. "Into the boat."

Zed rows in long, shallow strokes. His arms are firm and taut in the slanted and unforgiving afternoon light. He keeps his eyes cast down as Lane watches him from the backseat, the automatic trained on his chest.

"Head to the marina."

By the time they reach the mouth of the bay, the tide has reversed itself, and the current drifts seaward. Zed is forced to put more heft behind the oars. He rows against the current until they are clear of the mouth and the pull of its current, then returns to his slow, shallow strokes. Lane keeps the automatic carefully trained on him.

"I assume you spent some time with Autumn," Zed says, abruptly. "She was right, you know."

"About what?"

"We have a beginning, a middle, and an end."

"After all the money and research, you didn't know that?"

"No, I didn't." Zed stops rowing, arms slack against the oars. "I saw only the promise of life everlasting. It has a powerful pull to it." He smiles knowingly at Lane. "And don't tell me it doesn't."

Lane doesn't answer, so Zed goes back to rowing. After a few strokes, he speaks without looking up. "Every time I bend to dip the oars, I come at you with my arms extended. On one of these strokes, I'm going to drop the oars, keep moving forward, grab your weapon, and kill you. Your reflexes won't be fast enough to save you. I've got twenty years on you. Think about it."

Zed starts rowing again.

Lane does not deliberate. It's all the prompting he needs. He fires.

Lane beaches the little skiff on the shore beside the waterfront parking lot in Suquamish. He climbs some wooden stairs to look across to the tavern. Its front door is open, the music silent, the party people gone, and Johnny with them.

He walks a narrow pier that juts out and ends in a floating dock. At the end, he has a clear view of the mouth of the bay. Zed's lifeless form floats just above the water level as it drifts out into the open sound.

When the body is finally discovered, Lane is sure that there will be no record of its origin. Zed will be as anonymous and remote in death as he was in life.

Lane peers down into the greenish depths at his feet. He reaches into his coat pocket and pulls out the Exacube that Johnny gave him. He idly rolls the device in his fingers. A quadrillion bytes in the palm of his hand. He holds it out over the water. After it sinks, the current, the sand and the muck would conspire to bury it forever.

He puts the thought on hold and looks over to the western shoreline of Miller Bay, where the happy babble of children at play skips lightly over the water. Big houses perch on neat rectangles of trimmed lawn that descend to the narrow beach. They look out serenely on the bay and the big waters beyond, as if immune to the ravages of time.

Amid all this proud and posturing symmetry sits the old lot with the fallen cabin, where an overgrown glut of alders spills down to the rotting remnants of the dock.

Lane returns the Exacube to his pocket and heads back to the car.

CPSIA information can be obtained
at www.ICGtesting.com
Printed in the USA
BVHW090620181022
649626BV00007B/139

9 781733 100762